Get In
and
Get Out

The Battle for the Streets of Baltimore

~A Novel By~

Dante Hammond

Published by DHammond Publishing
P.O. Box 18669
Baltimore, MD 21216
www.dhammondpublishing@live.com

Author: Dante Hammond

Library of Congress Catalog Card Number:
ISBN-13: 978-1460942185
ISBN-10: 1460942183

DEDICATION

I would like to dedicate this book to my falling soldiers, Lunch (Cherry Hill), Lil Smalls (Pennsylvania Avenue), and Gerald (Winchester Apartments). You all will truly be missed.

Rest In Peace

ACKNOWLEDGMENTS

First and foremost, all praise is due to Allah, without him I am nothing. This book would not have been possible without the help of many people. I would like to give thanks to everyone who supported me, one way or another. I would like to especially acknowledge Tra and Meka for sticking with me and seeing this project through, I appreciate it.

I would also like to acknowledge Kareem, Lil Kiari, and Shirt (Thanks for being the men that you both are). Lano, Lil Chucky, Fleet, and Snook (Four of the Realest people you'll meet). Pooda, Fat Tedo, Uncle Lee, Big Ly, Eli, D-boi, Pookie, Fat Twan, Moo Moo, and Swole (The ones who keep it real). Head, Cool, Big Face Rome, Dirty, and Kenny Bean (You all are still family). Scoop, Aches Man, Kenny Mack, James Rogers, Disco, Weedy, Rick Mcdonald, and Cat Eye Tony (You all are not forgotten).

A special thanks to my family. Hoop Dreams Keron, stay in the gym, Weldon, and James, you all mean the world to me. Every man in this world has made a mistake, but it is what he does after that, which determines whether he has learned from it.

Last but certainly not least, I want to thank all of my haters. Keep doing what you all do best, keep hating and stay broke.

Already!!!

1 THE DRAWING BOARD

Damn it's hot as a bitch out here! Where the hell is the bus? Tremaine thought to himself while wiping the sweat off his forehead. The public transportation bus he was waiting on was ten minutes late on a day when the humidity had pushed Baltimore's temperature beyond the one hundred degree mark. It was the middle of July and the heat was enough to give anybody, that was crazy enough to be outside, a stroke. There Tremaine stood at the bus stop waiting on the bus to take him to the fast food spot that he quickly came to despise. His mother pulled a few strings to get him the job at Burger King.

His mother was riding the hell out of him always preaching the same speech, *your ass is fifteen years old now, and it's time for you to get a job. You're not going to spend the summer running the streets with them damn friends of yours. Y'all think y'all slick; I know y'all up to no good. Every time I see your ass, you're either sitting on somebody's front steps or hanging out with that damn Benny and them pit bulls of his. I done heard stories about Benny selling drugs and I know if you're hanging with him then your ass is too. So let me tell you one thing, the first time I hear about you selling drugs you getting out of my damn house! Son or no son you hear me? I'm telling you right now I'm not having that shit and I mean it!*

1

DHammond Publishing presents...

Tremaine's mother made sure she gave him that same speech at least once a week. Tremaine would always tell her that Benny was a grown ass man and he couldn't help what his friends did in their own personal lives. Tremaine wasn't too sure of Benny's age but knew that he was in his late twenties just by his wisdom at times.

Tremaine hated that everybody thought that he did not have a mind of his own. Tremaine knew the word on the streets was bullshit and he was his own boss.

It had been six months since Tremaine was introduced to the crack game. He initially started out selling purple but wasn't making too much of a profit due to the fact that he would always smoke half of his product. He would make just enough to buy a pair of shoes or a shirt and the rest would go to his re-up money.

He was doing a little better with the crack game. He didn't smoke crack so that made a huge difference. Crack sold so quick that Tremaine was able to get off at least a half an ounce in one week, with a one hundred dollar profit from each eight ball. He was pocketing at least four hundred dollars a week for a few hours of work. According to him, that was pretty good for a young nigga who was only fifteen. The frustrations still remained since he wasn't profiting what he should have been. He could've made a lot more but he was held back by the bullshit ass job his mother had gotten him two months prior. There were times Tremaine would only be able to sell two and a half maybe three eight balls a week since he was away from the hood so much. It was always at the worst times too, he worked from four in the afternoon to ten at night, which was when shit was jumping the most around the way. He was thankful for the crack heads on his job, Marie and Jelissa, who purchased a lot of his crack while at work.

"Man where the fuck is the bus at? It's too muthafuckin' hot out here." Tremaine grumbled to himself as he wiped more sweat from his forehead. "Fuck all this!" he said while throwing the book bag, which contained work clothes, over his shoulder.

Tremaine decided that he wasn't going into work that day as he walked down the sidewalk of Myrtle and Lanvale that led him through his neighborhood. Passing the many rows of brown buildings, he made his way to Benny's front steps. He figured he would be able to get in a few crack sales with the rest of his niggas who were always out on Benny's front steps. It was payday for many of his customers and it seemed that crack heads always kept a stash to cop at any given day or time of the year.

As Tremaine headed down the block, his attention was caught by one of the girls in his neighborhood that lived across the street name Quianna. She was phat as shit in her black leggings and her tiny gray tank top. At first glance, it looked as if she didn't have on any underwear since her ass was jiggling uncontrollably. "Damn Quianna when you gonna let me suck that pussy?" Tremaine yelled out to her. "When you let me suck those pockets?" she responded. "I got something else you can suck," he said while grabbing his dick.

"It's all good but like I said, when are you going to let me suck them pockets?" Quianna replied with a serious look on her face.

Bullshit ass bitch! Were the words that came to Tremaine's mind. He and Quianna was the same age but the only dudes she paid any attention to were Fats, Benny, Black Ty and the rest of the older niggas. They were damn near old enough to be her father but since their pockets were a little bit swole, that was all she cared about.

That was how all of the females were in their 'hood. Tremaine knew it was all good though. He would just wait until he or one of his niggas catch her late night and pull up on her with some purple and a pint of Grey Goose. It didn't take much more to get her or any of the other females in their 'hood, in his basement. Plugging them with dick was what would soon follow.

Tremaine wondered what excuse he was going to give his job for not coming into work that day. "Fuck it I'll think of something," he mumbled to himself. As he approached Benny's porch, he noticed his right hand man, Dirty, sitting on the steps alone. He knew Dirty was catching and figured he came out at the right time.

"What's up, my nigga?" Tremaine said, greeting Dirty. "Aint shit!" Dirty responded, "What's in the book bag? You on your way to summer school or something?" Dirty joked.

"Nah Nigga, these my work clothes."

"Oh what you about to go flip them burgers?"

"Nah, I ain't going in today fuck that shit!" Tremaine replied as he sat down on the step next to dirty.

"I can dig it," Dirty responded.

"Where that nigga Benny at?" Tremaine asked. "He just ran around back, Bonita and Quinine were barking and he went to see if they were fighting again," Dirty said referring to Benny's two pit bulls.

Dirty and Tremaine had been friends since the age of four. Ms. Wanda, Dirty's mother, used to smoke crack real heavy back when the buildings were up and never had too much time for the boy, leaving him to come outside looking grimy and dingy, which resulted in the nickname, Dirty. That was then and times have definitely changed. Ms. Wanda eventually stopped smoking crack when he was eight years old and met herself a sugar daddy. The man was damn near sixty years old and loved him some Ms. Wanda, who was thirty-five. Ms. Wanda's sugar daddy had a little bit of money since he had contracted lead paint poisoning as a child. The results weren't exactly evident to Tremaine since the older man looked to be normal. But there had to be something wrong with him since he received a big ass check every month and was always hitting Dirty off with a couple of dollars when he got it. That, combined with the hustling that he was doing, turned Dirty into a pretty boy. Dirty had a nappy ass bush on his head and a few black heads on his face. However, he was still a pretty boy because he stayed fresh.

"Well if it ain't Calvin, the burger boy. What's up Shorty?" Benny said as he stepped out onto the front step of his house. Niggas in the neighborhood called Tremaine by the name of *Tre* but Benny always referred to him as Calvin, the burger boy from the McDonald's commercial. Tremaine never knew why he chose to call him that.

"What up nigga?! You can kill all that Calvin, the burger boy shit," Tremaine said angrily.

Benny laughed before responding. "What you coming back from summer school or something?" He asked the exact question as Dirty while bending down to pick up Tremaine's bookbag.

"Nah they my work clothes in there."

"You getting off or you're about to go in?" Benny spoke with a grin on his face while tossing the bag down next to Tremaine. Tremaine looked at Benny with his shiny bald head. Benny was a little on the swole side after years of going in and out of prison. Tremaine knew that Benny was trying to be funny with that crooked ass grin on his face, "hell no I ain't going in today. Man, that job blowing the shit out of me."

"Shit, I feel you," Benny Replied.

"I need you to do me a favor though," Tremaine said to Benny. He knew he could use Benny's older, deeper voice to take care of the task of calling on his job for him, pretending to be his father.

"What's up?" Benny asked.

"Call my job for me and tell them I'm not coming in today."

"What's the number?" Benny asked.

Tremaine gave him the number and said jokingly, "Pretend like your old ass is my father or something."

Dirty began to laugh since he knew that Benny didn't like it when Niggas in the 'hood called him an old man.

"Nigga let me run in the house for a minute," he said as he got up to make the call.

"Damn my nigga you gonna get fired like shit, watch," Dirty said.

"Man fuck that shit. I'm only working there because my Mother always geekin. She's the one who got me that bullshit ass job. I don't see Ms. Wanda pushing up you about no muthafuckin' job."

"Shit, she do. It's just her old ass boyfriend be keeping her off of my back telling her I got plenty of time to get a job when I get out of high school," Dirty replied.

"That job is bullshit anyway, guess how much my last check was?"

"What?"

"Fifty-two dollars and forty six cent," Tremaine said shaking his head.

"What da' fuck are you suppose to do with that? A nigga spend more than that on haze. How much do you make over there an hour?" Dirty asked.

"five dollars and fifty cents an hour". With taxes, leaving early all the time, plus calling in sick, my check I get at the end of the week be bullshit."

"I can dig it," Dirty responded shaking his head.

"Tre, if you ask me, your ass is fired," Benny stated as he stepped back out onto the front step.

"What did you tell them when they asked you why I wasn't coming in?"

"I told them that you were locked up," Benny responded.

"Locked up!" Dirty and Tremaine both asked at the same time, wondering if Benny was actually serious or not.

"Locked up for what?" Tremaine pressed on.

"Nigga I ain't tell them all that, I just told them that you might be in for a while."

"And what did they say?" Dirty asked while laughing.

"That bitch ass manager of yours just said, 'oh yeah?' and hung up on me. I started to call his bitch ass back to see what was on his mind," Benny said with an angry expression on his face.

"This nigga told them that I was locked up," Tremaine said to Dirty still not believing what he just heard.

"Damn my nigga, you know you shouldn't have told that nigga to call your job," Dirty said.

"Nigga shut up! He ain't got to go to work today or for the rest of the damn month if he don't want to. Shit, Nigga I just did you a favor'." Benny had his chest poked out as if he had just come up with a genius idea.

Fuck it, Tremaine thought that Benny might be right. He had a few bags of crack in his sock so he decided to go ahead and get his grind on until he sold the seventeen rocks and then he would be done for the day. He knew it wouldn't take him no time to sell the drugs while he was sitting on Myrtle Avenue.

Even though Benny only sold purple, the crackheads would still come and see if he had some crack. His answer was always the same: *Bitch get the fuck out of my face, you know I ain't got no coke but if you want some purple then this is where it's at.* Benny would then pull out a ziplock bag filled with twenty dollar jars of haze. Once he would put the jars back into his pants the large jars of marijuana became unnoticeable.

Tremaine figured that must have stemmed from years of hustling and learning how to conceal large amounts of narcotics on himself without it showing. Tremaine decided when he was done pushing the rest of his stones he would call his cousin Juice, to see what he had planned for the night. Juice was the only boy their age that Tremaine knew who had his own car, at least a legit car. Dirty, Tremaine and Tremaine's younger cousin Dollar, would occasionally rent cars from addicts, for a few stones of crack. Most of the time, they would drive the cars that Dollar would steal. Dollar was the smallest and youngest in their crew. He was only twelve years old but was off the hook, as people would often say. That, and the fact that he was Tremaine's little Cousin, was the only reason they allowed him to hang with them.

Dollar always had a scheme on getting cars, he always found somebody slipping. He didn't carjack anybody but what he did was get up early in the morning and just ride a bike around and catch someone on their way to work leaving their car outside warming up. Dollar would watch the cars with the engine running carefully and then would act as if he was the owner of the vehicle and drive away, taking his bike with him. Muthafuckas' would come back out and see their car gone and begin flipping out. The females usually started crying on the spot while the males would walk up and down the street or parking lot as if they had parked their cars somewhere else, not wanting to accept the fact that their car just got stolen.

"Hey Benny, we're about to take Bonita and Quinine for a walk, alright?" Tremaine said to Benny as they stood on his front step.

"Alright but you and Dirty betta' not have my pits on The Avenue fighting and shit. I know how your ass is." Benny shot Tremaine a serious look.

"Shit, I ain't walking down that hill it's too muthafuckin' hot out here," Tremaine responded while pulling on his T-shirt, which was sticking to him.

The whole area was like little Vietnam for real. Tremaine could walk for three and a half minutes from his house on Lanvale Street and would be on Fremont Avenue. A lot of times if crack sales were coming too slow on Fremont and Lanvale, where Tremaine lived, he would walk over on Pennsylvania and Mosher to hustle and a lot of his niggas would do the same. But don't get it fucked up; it wasn't one big happy family because both sides stayed in constant beef with one another.

The only reason Tremaine was given a green pass to go back and forth without too much drama was because he was from Murphy Homes but moved on Lanvale Street with his mother as a child once the buildings were knocked down.

Besides, his homeboys Lil' L and the rest of the niggas he fucked with was from Mosher Street already knew how Tremaine carried it. He wasn't on no geographical shit. He fucked with niggas—period. Tremaine could care less where you were from. Whether it was Cherry Hill or wherever, as long as you were a real nigga and stood firm, that was all that mattered in his eyes. His philosophy was, 'it's not about where you were from its where you were at,' and more importantly, where you were trying to go.

"You want what, two dimes for thirteen? Nigga what kind of shit is that? You know it's two for fifteen and I don't even like giving your ass that deal." Tremaine spoke to crackhead Craig, who lived in on Fremont Avenue, as he and Dirty walked around with Bonita and Quinine.

"Come on Dogg, do that for me this one time. You know my money good and I'm coming back to see you in half an hour anyway you know this," Craig pleaded.

"Man I ain't trying to hear that shit, Craig. I'm fed up with your ass anyway nigga. The last steaks you sold me was all fat and shit. There wasn't no fuckin' meat on them muthafuckas'."

Craig was an addict, who Tremaine had been serving coke to ever since he first started hustling. Craig drove a meat truck for some type of Food Company and would always pull up in the 'hood trying to trade all types of meat and seafood for crack. He and Dirty usually got a couple of steaks, hams, or whatever else Craig was selling that day and gave them to their mother's. Tremaine's mother knew about Craig and his meat truck. But what she didn't know was that the meat was being traded for crack rock. She actually thought that Tremaine was paying for the wholesale meat with cash. Shit, he could get fifty dollars worth of meat for ten dollars worth of coke.

"Look here nigga, I'ma give you two dimes for thirteen this one time but the next time you come back with that truck I want U.S.D.A. prime cut shit and not none of that corner store market ass meat you gave me last time alright?" Tremaine said to Craig as he watched the man stare at the crack bags he held in the palm of his hand.

"Come on, you know I got you baaaaaby! Good lookin' out," Craig sang out happily while accepting the small bags.

After selling out the rest of his stones, Tremaine, along with Dirty, walked to the liquor store to get some Goose and a pack of Cigarillos. On their way, they ran into one of the young 'hood rats from around Mosher Street by the name of Michelle, who was sitting on her front porch.

"What's up Michelle?" Tremaine asked.

"Tsk." She shucked her teeth while rolling her eyes. She kept her eyes closed so long it looked as if she had fallen asleep.

"What da' fuck is all that for?" Dirty asked.

"What you mean what's all that for?" Michelle responded raising her voice, "don't play dumb," she said.

"Shorty, I don't know what the fuck you're talking about," Tremaine spoke while trying to hold in his laugh.

He knew exactly what she was talking about, Michelle was still mad at him and Dirty for an incident that happened a few months ago, during the winter.

On That particular day, Tremaine and Dirty had peeped Michelle walking down Myrtle Avenue with some boy that neither of them had ever seen before. At the time, they had Bonita and Quinine with them and the boy she was with was wearing a brand new over sized Ralph Lauren Polo winter coat. Tremaine and Dirty walked up on Michelle and her boyfriend and made the scared dude come out of his coat. Michelle's boyfriend should have known that if he fucked with a hoodrat from around the way, he couldn't just take it upon himself to walk with her up and down the block as if everything was cool, especially not around here. If you committed such an act then you were out of order. Their best bet would be to pick the girl up and take her to their house or go in her house and chill, anything but walk up and down the strip in this neighborhood. That was a no-no.

It wasn't until later that Tremaine and Dirty found out that the boy with Michelle was actually her cousin and not her boyfriend. That didn't really matter to them because the same rules applied.

Michelle's mother ended up calling the police and had them come around Myrtle Avenue. Michelle played her position and told her mother and the police officers that she didn't know where

Tremaine or Dirty lived, even though she did. But she did give them a description of what the dogs looked like.

A few days after the incident, the police pulled up on Benny while he was walking Bonita and Quinine. They asked him if he knew anything about the robbery. They were close to confiscating the two pit bulls but the report said that two juveniles were in possession of the dogs at the time of the robbery.

Benny was mad as hell about the whole scenario as he explained to Dirty and Tremaine how the police tried to take his dogs. The entire time they played it off as if it were news to them. Benny still didn't know that they were the reason behind the police fucking with him.

"Nigga you do know what I'm talking about, I see ya'll got them same dogs with ya'll today. I should call the police on y'all ass right now," Michelle threatened while standing up and acting as if she were going into the house to make the call.

Initially, Michelle had Tremaine's attention because of how the bright orange color of her thigh-high summer dress laid against her bronze-colored skin. But all that quickly went out of the window, with her half ass threats she was starting to piss him off.

"Well you know there's always a good chance of that phone call being the last one you ever make," Tremaine said with a cold, serious look on his face.

"What? You threatening me or something?" she asked with her hands on her hips.

"Who me?" Tremaine responded with his palms on his chest playing the innocent role. "Nah I ain't threatening you. Let's just say… Damn what's the word I'm looking for…Premonition!" He said snapping his fingers. "Yeah that's it let's just say it's a strong premonition."

"Premonition?" Michelle said, while frowning her face. "What the fuck that mean?" She asked.

"Look it up shorty," Tremaine Responded while grinning as he and Dirty walked away.

"Hey Cuz, I swear if that bitch call the police I'm a bury her ass," Dirty spoke.

"Shit Nigga, her ass ain't stupid. If she was going to do that, she would've told the day we took her people's coat, you feel me? Fuck that shit." Tremaine explained.

"Yeah alright we'll see," Dirty said looking back one last time towards Michelle's porch.

When Tremaine and Dirty finally arrived at Casino liquor store, Tremaine pulled up on old man Doc. He was a drunk that was never more than twenty yards away from a liquor store. He sent Doc into the bar with instructions to get two pints of Grey Goose, a pack of Cigarillos, a pack of Newports, and a couple of bags of red hot chips. After receiving all the items and allowing Doc to keep the one dollar and twenty seven cents change, Tremaine and Dirty decided to chill with lil' Black, Head, and the rest of his homeboys. Lil' Black and his crew made the liquor store an open air drug market. The liquor store was no more than two blocks away from Tremaine's neighborhood but that little distance seemed like a world apart. On Lanvale Street, where Tremaine lived, it was always at least twenty hustlers out there at any given time, trying to eat off one plate. Compare that to Lil' Black and his strip, where there were never more than six hustlers out there and the profit differential was definitely more abundant. The old man who owned the store would let Black and his homeboys stash crack in his freezers behind the soda's and beer. The owner always said that he felt a lot safer with them around because he knew as long as they were out there; there wasn't a nigga in his right mind who would try to run up in his establishment and rob him. The owner would even let them put their coats and jackets behind the counter when he knew they had their burners in them. Truth be told, Black and his crew had that store running like clockwork. They even occupied a room on top of the store where they would have sex with females and hold dice games. It was also used as a place to cook and cut up the crack. There was always one nigga in the upper room as a watchman looking out of the window for the police task force jump-out unit.

After chilling out in front of Casino liquor store with Black and the rest of his homeboys, Tremaine had to resist the temptation of fighting Benny's dogs. Lil Black had a little raggedy ass pitbull tied up out back of the store that he had stolen out of someone's yard. He was trying to convince Tremaine and Dirty to let Bonita and Quinine go on the scrawny dog, while at the same time taking side bets on how long it would take for the malnourished dog to get killed. Dirty argued that it would take less than five minutes for the two pits to kill the dog, but Black felt that it would take ten minutes or better. Tremaine was definitely tempted to let them go, but decided against it. Tremaine did not want to hear Benny's mouth. Finally, he and Dirty handed out pounds to all of the niggas down there and headed back down the block towards Fremont Avenue.

"Tre your ass just missed it," Benny hollered out to Tremaine as he and Dirty were pulled back towards his block by the two pit bulls.

"Missed what? Whats up?" Tremaine asked.

"Margo nigga! You know she was just around here."

"Oh yeah?"

"Yeah. Her husband just brought her a mean ass S500 Benz and she was trying to rent it out."

"Damn Yo, where the fuck she go?" Tremaine asked. "I don't know but I do know I got me a number two special up off of her wit' the super size," Benny said grabbing the crotch of his pants while grinning from ear to ear, "and then she rolled out."

No matter who you asked, hands down, she had the best head in town. She was one of those females that made a nigga knees buckle as she slobbed on his knob with oral pleasure. It was impossible for a man to stand up while getting head from her, it was a must that you sat your ass down. Her secret weapon was the fact that most of her teeth were false. The entire front and side sections, on the top and bottom were fake. She only possessed a few real ones in the back of her mouth. "She ain't say when she was comin' back?" Dirty asked.

"Nah but you know she probably heading around the Avenue to see if Lil' Black or one of them niggas tryin' to rent that car," Benny said.

"Is that muthafucka brand new?" Dirty asked. "Yeah nigga that muthafucka is mean, it ain't no used shit. That shit was fresh off the showroom floor," Benny said while grabbing the back of the pitbull's hind leg and shaking it causing him to growl. Bonita repeatedly snapped back at Benny's hand. "The only thing about it is it's a stick shift."

"Oh Yeah?" Tremaine spoke with a little disappointment since he didn't know how to drive a stick shift. "Fuck that shit, it don't matter. I'll burn her muthafuckin clutch out learning how to drive that shit."

"No bullshit," Dirty added.

"Alright since y'all done had my dogs out in this heat all day, you got to take their asses upstairs and fill up their water and food bowls," Benny said looking at Tremaine and Dirty. They both shot looks at one another and then back at Benny." Nigga they your dogs! You betta' take them in there and feed them yourself," Tremaine spoke.

"What?" Come here Bonita." Benny grabbed the dog by the collar and turned him towards Tremaine. "SSSSSSSK! SSSSK! Get some Bo-Bo. Get some boy!" He said as Bonita growled and slowly began to inch toward Tremaine.

"Go 'head wit' that Bullshit!" Tremaine said while taking a step back trying to keep his face with an evil mug on it to hide the fear he was really feeling.

"Hold up what you reaching for? Benny asked while still holding Bonita and letting him go a few steps towards Tremaine before pulling him back again.

"Stop playin' all the muthafuckin' time!" Tremaine shouted angrily as he reached for his phone.

"Who that? Some female hittin' you?" Dirty asked.

Tremaine looked at the number and said, "nah this Dollar lil' ass." He placed his phone back on his hip and began to walk off in the directions of the steps towards Benny's house.

"Here Nigga, take them with you while you're going in there," Benny said as he calmed Bonita down and let the two dogs run up the steps behind Tremaine.

"You keep playin' games with these muthafuckin' dogs. I told your ass, the first time either one of them bite me I got something for their ass." Tremaine had a dead serious look in his eyes.

"Shit, nigga hurting my dogs is like hurting my son."

"Yeah well, my nigga or not, if one of them pits ever bite me you gonna be buying more than dog food from the pet store. You'll be asking the store if they sell doggy caskets." Tremaine spoke over his shoulder as he proceeded up the steps. He could hear Benny telling Dirty, who was laughing, that the shit wasn't funny.

"Hello?" Dollar answered.

"What's up?" Tremaine asked only to receive an answer from a hyper Dollar on the other end of the line.

"Yeah nigga, didn't I tell you I was going to get up in that Niggas shit?!"

"Huh? What the fuck is you talkin' about?" Tremaine asked baffled.

"Didn't I tell you, huh? Didn't I tell you?" Dollar repeated.

"Tell me what? What the hell are you talking 'bout?" Tremaine was beginning to get impatient.

"Where you at now?" Dollar asked nearly out of breath.

"I'm over at Benny's house. Why? What the fuck is up?" Questioned Tremaine. He still didn't have a clue as to what Dollar was talking about and who shit he supposedly had gotten up in.

"Come down here. I want to show you something."

"Show me what? Tell me now," Tremaine said not wanting to wait.

"Just come over here. I'll holler at you when you get here."

Tremaine could see that getting an answer out of Dollar right then and there was out of the question so he reluctantly agreed, "Alright, I'm on my way."

What the hell is this nigga Dollar talking about? Tremaine thought to himself as he walked back down the steps to the front of the building where Benny and Dirty were arguing about which one of the police officers that patrolled Fremont Avenue was the fastest.

Dirty was saying that it was Officer Atkins, who was a k-9 policeman. He talked about how he saw Atkins and his dog chasing one of their homeboys and how Atkins was out running the dog as they both ran behind the nigga.

Benny, knowing that he had to outdo Dirty's story, said that he witnessed another officer by the name of Perkins run somebody down. He took the story to another level when he said that Perkins' suspect was on a dirt bike. He claimed the officer ran the bike down on foot and snatched the dude off of it by the back of his collar.

Now that shit there Tremaine and Dirty both knew, was a straight up lie. But once Benny got started with the story there was no need in arguing with him. He would be fully aware that he was lying but just to hold onto his pride he would argue for hours on end to get a muthafucka to believe him. Tremaine had heard enough of that shit. He was ready to go see what the hell Dollar was ranting about on the phone. "I'll be back, Yo."

When Tremaine arrived at Dollars' apartment his aunt, Sheila, wasn't home. It was only Dollar and another nigga' from around their neighborhood named Shade. Tremaine didn't notice when he initially walked in, but once he went to sit down on the couch, his eyes caught hold of the two and a half pounds of weed on the coffee table. Next to it was two fifths of Remy Martin and a bottle of Grey Goose. "Yo, where the fuck you get this shit from?" Tremaine asked as he reached down to pick up one of the large size buds of haze that were scattered out on the table.

"I told you I was going to get up in that nigga shit, didn't I?" Dollar said while tearing the wrapping paper off of a cigarillo.

"Who the hell are you talking 'bout?" Tremaine asked for the umpteenth time.

" K.G.! "

"K.G.?" Tremaine was trying to remember where he knew that name from.

"Yeah Yo."

Tremaine thought for a split second and then remembered who his little cousin was talking about. "Oh alright you talking 'bout the nigga on Division Street?

"Yeah yeah," Dollar nodded his head.

"That's where y'all got this from?" Tremaine was still holding the haze in his fingers. The shit smelled crucial plus it was that fire, having a feel as if it was wet and moist. "What happened Yo?"

"The Nigga left his window open, and I got him," Dollar said.

"What? You broke up in his shit?"

Dollar and Shade both held devious grins on their faces as they nodded their heads.

"Slim sleep on the third floor. How the fuck did you climb through his window?"

"Shade gave me a boost up to the first balcony then once we got there he boosted me up to K.G.'s balcony." Dollar was demonstrating with his body movement showing how he did it as he talked.

"Oh y'all lil' niggas terrible, for real." Tremaine could do nothing but laugh to himself at the sight of their little ass giving each other boosts to climb up on someone's balcony.

"Fuck that nigga! I told you I was gonna catch his ass slippin', didn't I?" Dollar yelled over his shoulder as he headed towards the kitchen to empty out the cigarillo tobacco fillings. "I know for a fact that nigga got shit in there other than some haze and three bottles of alcohol. Y'all ain't find no paper?" Tremaine asked in disbelief.

"Nope!" Dollar shook his head as if he was mad about the fact also.

K.G. really wasn't his name. It was a name he and Dirty had made up for the boy since he strongly resembled the basketball player, Kevin Garnett. Tremanie wished he had been there for the burglary for the simple fact that the nigga K.G. had recently moved on Division Street and never said anything to anyone around there. He would always be either coming or going as he drove a white Acura RL. What had initially caught niggas attention about K.G. was the fact that often times some of his associates would come to visit him and all of them would be driving something nice. Either BMW's, Benz's, Range Rovers, as well as everyday 'hood shit. It wasn't hard to tell that K.G. was hustling somewhere outside of their neighborhood since he would come and go at all different hours of the day.

Tremaine finally had an idea and decided to put it out there to see if it would work. " Is the door still open?"

"Yeah why?" Dollar asked.

"Come on." Tremaine got up and headed towards the door. There was a sense of excitement in him as he loved when a plan came together. "We gonna go see if that nigga car parked out there cause if it ain't we're going back up in there."

"Shit, what's up, let's go," Dollar said while sticking the freshly rolled up cigarillo behind his ear, "I'm sayin' who's gonna be our lookout?" he asked as he fell in stride behind his big cousin.

"Shade," Tremaine said while opening the door and not even bothering to look back to see what Shade's response was. When they arrived at the front of K.G.'s building they all peeped out the front and didn't see K.G.'s car, or any of the cars that his homeboys drove.

"Shade look here, I want you to post up right here on the front and I know you know what the nigga car look like, right?" Tremaine asked.

"Yeah I know what his 'RL' look like," he responded while nodding his head.

"A'ight but don't just look for his Acura. If you see any car pull up out here that you don't recognize, holla alright?"

"Alright," Shade responded while still nodding his head to Tremaine's instructions.

Tremaine tapped Dollar on the shoulder as they began to walk. The entire time they were walking up the stairs, Tremaine was thinking to himself, if Shade's little dumb ass was competent enough to be a lookout; he knew the boy wasn't the brightest lil' nigga on the block. When they got to the door, Tremaine put his ear to it to see if he was able to hear any movement on the inside. There wasn't a sound from inside, he reached for the unlocked doorknob and opened the door slowly. After listening to the stillness of the room to make sure the apartment was empty, Tremaine and Dollar stepped inside and began to contemplate on where to begin their search.

The bedroom was the first spot that Tremaine decided to search. The both of them went through each and everything in that room with no luck on finding any paper. Tremaine even took the initiative and got a knife out of the kitchen and gutted out the mattress as well as the box spring, all to no benefit of stumbling across any paper. When he searched the bedroom closet Tremaine found two burners: a nickel plated .25 with an extended clip as well as a large .44 Magnum revolver. Dollar was too busy moving the dresser out of the way and tearing up the carpet in the room to notice Tremaine's discovery of the burners. He thought about bringing it to his little cousin's attention but decided against it because he knew Dollar would want one. Tremaine honestly believed that Dollar wasn't ready for a burner in his hand for the simple fact it wouldn't have been long before he ended up killing someone with it and getting himself caught up.

After going through all of the coat pockets, tennis shoes, and every other article of clothing in the closet, they still didn't find any paper. Tremaine's frustrations were at an all time high. After spending twenty minutes in the bedroom room; he and Dollar headed into the second room to repeat the same routine with no luck. They tore up every inch of the apartment, pulling all of the pillows out of the cases on the living room couch. They even went so far as to opening all of the food boxes in the kitchen.

Finally they said fuck it and left. If the nigga, K.G., did have any money in there he did a damn good job of hiding it. Leaving without any paper has pissed Tremaine off. They had spent over an hour inside of the apartment and came out with nothing. He couldn't actually say it was a total waste of time since he did have two fresh burners in his possession. If you asked any nigga in the 'hood, having a burner meant having unlimited access to cash since one would always bring the other.

The summer was beginning to wind down and Tremaine was getting stressed out more and more everyday for the simple fact that the nickel and dime hustling he was doing just wasn't adding up to nothing. Dirty, Dollar and he had even started robbing on the regular. Even the robbing shit wasn't adding up because they were basically robbing niggas in their hood that was fucked up like them. They never walked away from a caper with more than three thousand dollars at a time.

After counting the paper from their last six capers the total came to eleven thousand six hundred dollars in cash. They also had twelve hundred dollars worth of 20 dollar jars of haze as well as some crack. Divided four ways, we each received $3650 in cash as well as some jars of haze. Dollar told Dirty and Tremaine they could have the crack since he was more than content with the new 9mm that he now owned.

Tremaine ended up spending all of his robbery money within a week, after buying two used cars from the auction. The cars were quickly taken by the police when they noticed his two hoopties parked in the parking lot side by side. He hadn't gotten around to getting legit tags.

To make matters worse, the crack that they took from the robbery was straight garbage, leaving Tremaine to sell it strictly wholesale just to get rid of it. All that shit, on top of the partying and shopping he was doing landed him right back at square one, trying to find another victim.

2 NICKEL AND DIME HUSTLIN'

"Who's that, some bitches hittin' you?" Juice asked Tremaine who looked at the unfamiliar number on his phone.

"Hello?" Tremaine answered.

"What up nigga?" Dollar replied.

"Ain't shit!"

"Where ya'll at?"

"Me, Dirty, and Juice 'bout to go to Druid Hill Park pool, why, what's up?"

"I thought you had to work today," Dollar said joking.

"What? Oh you call yourself being funny or something?" Tremaine asked since he hadn't been to work in close to two months.

Dollar let out a slight chuckle and said, "Nah I'm just fuckin' wit' you but I am trying to meet ya'll out there."

"What you snatched somebody else's shit?" Tremaine asked rhetorically.

"Nigga you know how I do it," Dollar responded.

"I'd say we 'bout five minutes away now. We probably stay for an hour depending on how many females out there." They were all planning on there being plenty of females out there since pussy was always at the pool in the summertime.

"Alright, I'm on my way," Dollar said before hanging up.

"Hey yo this lil' nigga's terrible. He took another nigga off for their shit," Tremaine said as he placed the phone back on the dash board.

"He gon' get the wrong muthafucka and they gon' fuck around and shoot his lil' ass watch," Dirty said laughing from the back seat.

"But nah yo' the shit that kills me is this nigga stay stealing somebody shit but his ass can't even drive. The nigga crash every fucking car he gets his hands on," Tremaine said as they all shared a laugh.

"Hey yo, they ain't got no metal detectors at this pool do they?" Dirty asked as he shifted the 10mm handgun that he carried in his waistline.

When they arrived at the pool, just as they had expected, there was nothing but females up in there. Tremaine, Dirty, and Juice's teenage erections began to grow before any of them even had a chance to get out of the car. Hands down, Tremaine was the freakiest one out of their crew.

Tremaine would always say that he wasn't the best fuck in the world. But when he was thirteen, there was a twenty-five year old female named Roslyn that lived down on Dolphin Street who he was fuckin' on the regular. She was butt ugly but had definitely put it on his young ass and taught him a few tricks of the trade. It was enough to the point that females his age were rarely on his level when it came time to get between them sheets.

Tremaine, Dirty, and Juice began peeping out the place in search of next female for the day. They definitely had their picks since there was a surplus of phat females inside. Park Pool consisted of three separate swimming pools. There was the Olympic-sized pool, which most of the swimmers hung out at. Also, there was a baby pool and a medium-sized pool. The medium pool was used strictly for diving; it was also used for swim classes or private parties.

"Yo, look over there by the diving boards. Ain't that Teanna and Summer?" Dirty asked while tapping Tremaine on his arm.

Tremaine squinted his face at Dirty, not knowing who he was talking about. "Who?"

"Teanna and Summer, they went up Harlem Park wit' us."

Tremaine looked over into the direction that Dirty was pointing, he almost didn't recognize the two girls. "Hell yeah, now I remember. Got damn! Teanna got phat as shit, cuz." He still couldn't believe how much the girl changed.

Teanna was wearing a two-piece peach-colored bathing suit. Her young ripe breasts were propped up nice and juicy, not too big and not too small but just right. She also had a transparent silk scarf that was tied around her waist. You could see the bikini riding up her ass on the left side where part of her ass cheek was sticking out. The sun rays had given her light complexion a golden brown tone to it. The braids in her hair were similar to Brandy's on 'Moesha', skinny individual pleats pulled back into a pony tail.

"Damn where ya'll say y'all know them from?" Juice asked rhetorically as all three of them were gazing at the two females by the diving boards.

"Come on yo let's go see what's up wit' em," Tremaine said stepping off into the girls direction.

Teanna and Summer had definitely changed since middle school. Dirty and Tremaine could remember them as being on some quiet and reserved type of females back then. Now they were freaked out and were talking about going to the motel and how it was whatever with them. As they continued to converse with the girls, trying to set up the motel rendezvous for the night their conversation was abruptly interrupted.

Out of nowhere, someone grabbed Tremaine from behind. Immediately Tremaine began struggling to get out of the bear hug in order to turn around. He was able to break free and spin around. As he was getting ready to throw a hail of punches, he saw that the person who grabbed him was his older cousin Lisa's baby father, Los, who was playing around and shit.

"Yeah nigga I had your lil ass. Look at you slippin' and shit," Los said as he reached out to pull Tremaine in for a one arm hug.

"Shit, nigga you better guess again," Tremaine said looking over at Dirty who had his hand in his waist line gripping his burner. He tapped Dirty on the chest and without any words being spoken he lifted the front of his shirt slighty revealing the insurance he carried with him.

"Nigga ya'll ain't sayin' nothin'," Los responded and exposed the handle of the Glock 9 that he carried.

"I heard that , what's up though?" Tremaine asked.

"Ain't shit what's up wit' ya'll lil niggas?"

"Shit just tryin' to set up some pussy for tonight."

When Tremaine said that they all looked back at Teanna and Summer who were a few feet away. They hadn't heard Tremaine's comment but were still grinning from ear to ear. *Yeah we definitely gonna run a train on their ass tonight,* Tremaine thought to himself. He knew that it was every hoodrat's dream to get a 'hood nigga with paper and on some ol' ghetto fabulous type of shit. They craved for a nigga to turn them from hoodrats to hoodrich.

On some real shit, neither Dirty, Juice nor Tremaine had any real money but a muthafucka would never be able to tell just by looking at them. The little capers they were pulling definitely kept them fresh. All four of them were standing there in some top notch everyday shit.

Dirty had on a white polo shirt, with the navy blue horse, and a pair of navy blue polo cargo shorts; on his feet were a pair of fresh grey 993 new balance along with a white polo hat on his head and a white Polo hand towel thrown over his shoulder. Tremaine rocked a white wife beater, a pair of dark blue lacoste shorts, and a pair of 95 air max on his feet. He also had the all white lacoste beach towel embellished with the gator in navy blue across his shoulder. Now Los had taken it to another level, he stunted with a pair of black Rock and Republic swim trunks with a gray stripe down the side along with a gray and black matching T-shirt. On his feet were a pair of Black and grey Nike aqua shoes and his pretty boy Indian hair was done in long shiny cornrows. *These broads must think they done hit the lottery or something but they ain't getting nothing but hard dick,* Tremaine concluded in his thoughts.

After getting Teanna and Summer's phone numbers Tremaine and Dirty set up the fuck session that same night for eleven o'clock. The plan was to wait until the girls' parents fell asleep so that they could each sneak out of their homes. Once that was established Tremaine, Dirty, and Juice went to sit down with Los and his two homeboys. Los was twenty-three years old and to be frank with you, he was caked up. He no longer messed with Lisa but everyone knew he still kept her and their daughter, Brittany, in the hottest shit. Lisa was driving a brand new BMW X6 and hadn't worked in Lord knows how long. She also had her own apartment out Towson, which Los was paying for every month.

It had been almost a year since Tremaine had seen Los. He remembered when Los had found out he was selling haze, he called one of his homeboys and had him come around on Lanvale Street to drop off a half of pound of haze to him for nothing. Los didn't sell haze but was deep in the crack game and yet he still went out of his way to get one of his homeboys to look out for Tremaine. Now that he was selling crack Tremaine knew that he had to holler at Los because he knew for a fact he was doing numbers.

They all sat there for about forty-five minutes to an hour and hollered at a few females that walked by before deciding that they had enough of the sun and that it was time to go. Tremaine used this time to holler at Los about some real shit. He waited until they all got in the parking lot before pulling Los to the side. He told him straight up that he was hungry and that he was trying to get on by any means necessary.

"I feel that Yo but you know I don't sell haze. I mean I could holla at a few folks for you to see what's crackin' tho'," Los said remembering the last time they talked Tremaine was selling marijuana.

"I'm tryin' to get my hands on that butta," Tremaine responded.

"Oh, what you stepped your game up now?" Los asked.

"I mean if you want to call it that, but for real that Bob Marley just wasn't working for me." Tremaine didn't want to tell him the reason being was that he smoked too much.

"I mean for real, a nigga just need a better connect than the one I'm dealing wit' now you feel me? Cause I'm sayin' the niggaa I'm fuckin' wit' now is charging me nine hundred an once and the shit be some straight garbage half the time."

"Nine hun'ed huh? Yeah I say ummm…" Los stopped in mid sentence and held eye contact with Tremaine as if he was contemplating something."

He wrote his cell phone number down and gave it to Tremaine, they gave each other some love and Los then stepped off to walk up the hill to his car. Just then, Dollar pulled up in a Toyota Camry station wagon. 'The Diary' C.D. by Scarface was banging on the cars stereo system. He pulled up next to Tremaine and damn near ran him over.

"Muthafucka you almost ran me over…" *Beep! Beep! Beep!* Tremaine was cut off by a forest green Maserati Quattroporte Sport GT S with tinted windows. When it pulled up next to Dollar's car, the window slowly began to roll down and Tremaine could see that it was Los behind the wheel. He was laughing at Dollar lil ass.

"I see yo' lil' ass still stealing people shit, huh?" he said while leaning out of the car window.

"Los, what's up Yo?" Dollar yelled out the window.

"Ain't shit. Look here tho' ya'll niggas be safe out here alright. Tremaine, I'ma holla at you later."

"Alright big cuz I'll be at you," Tremaine said.

When Los rolled up the window and pulled off in his brand new Quattroporte that number of his became the most sacred thing that Tremaine possessed at that moment. He knew that if he played his cards right while fucking with that nigga Los, it would be well worth it.

3 LET'S GET IT

BOOM! BOOM! BOOM! "Tremaine Stephan Jenkins, wake your ass up!" *BOOM! BOOM! BOOM!*

Man what the fuck, she think she the police or something banging on a nigga's door at twelve o'clock in the morning or should I say afternoon, Tremaine thought as he looked over at the digital clock on his night stand. He slowly began to climb out of bed.

"I'm up ma! What's up?" He yelled out while sitting on the edge of his bed.

"Get your narrow ass up and open this door! That's what's up!"

"Man I swear she be blowin' me like shit sometime," Tremaine mumbled as he slowly got up off the bed and went to go unlock his door. He wondered what his mother could possibly want that she couldn't say thought the door.

"Tremaine Stephan Jenkins you better open this damn door!"

"I'm comin' Ma," he responded irritably.

She was calling him by his whole name, which he knew from experience wasn't good. She was obviously mad about something and he was definitely about to hear it. Just as Tremaine was getting ready to unlock the door he paused. He began searching for a pair of shorts to put on top of his boxers because his early morning erection was on overtime at that moment. Once he had chosen one of the few pairs of shorts that were scattered around his room he went to unlock the door. Click!

"What's up ma?" He said slowly opening the door.

"What's up shit, what time did your ass get in this house last night? Don't even think about lying because I got up two o'clock in the morning and your ass still wasn't home yet."

"I don't know, it was around two thirty or something like that." Tremaine was trying to hide his irritation at her early morning interrogation.

"Yeah right," she said rolling her eyes. "If I would have told your ass that I got up at three you probably would have said three-thirty or something like that." His mother said mocking Tremaine's voice. "Now I done told your ass before, you're not a grown man yet, thinking you can just come and go as you please."

Tremaine didn't feel like arguing with her so he just gave her an 'Is that it' look.

"Now get up out of that bed," she continued. "Because I want you to find something to do around here before you go taking your tail outside and run them streets. I want you to take the trash out and go clean that bathroom and while you at it clean up this damn room," His mother said as she frowned her face up at the sight of his junky room.

What the fuck do I look like Mr. Belvedere or Kunta Kente or something? Tremaine thought to himself. "Alright ma you got that," Tremaine responded while continuing to hide his irritation.

"I gotta go to work today for a couple of hours and I know your ass gonna be gone before I get back so make sure you lock the door before you leave. Close the window and make sure the A/C is on too, alright?"

"Alright." Sometimes his mother could drive him crazy. Tremaine loved her passionately but she had to realize that in his eyes he was his own man and her time of nurturing and providing for him were no longer needed. His mother always thought that coming down on him with an iron fist would keep him in line. There were certain things she would say to Tremaine that he didn't agree with, but would adhere to anyway out of respect. In the same token he had made up his mind long ago that he would live his life how he saw fit and not how someone else wanted him to.

In Tremaine's eyes his mother was the essence of a Black Queen. She worked as a dental assistant for some habib ass dentists. That was the name that he and his homeboys gave to the people who wore turbans on their heads and usually worked at any local 7-11. His mother had been working there for close to eighteen months ever since she graduated from that trade school. Since the graduation she had been doing alright for herself compared to ten previous years she spent on welfare and section 8. After experiencing all of that, Tremaine had a lot of respect for his mother for pulling herself up by the boot straps and getting her life in order.

RIIIIING! RIIIIING! "The fuck!" Tremaine screamed out loud. He was trying to go back to sleep when the phone rang. He started to let it ring but decided it might be important.

"Hello"

Dirty's voice spoke on the other line, "What's up, you up?"

"Yeah, I am now."

"Hey yo, Benny 'bout to fight Quinine against Big Dre's pit, from out Cherry Hill" Dirty said excitedly.

"Which one of Dre pits, the brindle or the red nose?" Tremaine asked.

"The brindle joint and you know that's the vicious one."

"Yeah how 'bout that? But you know Quinine was the runt of his litter and you know the runts be going hard," Tremaine responded.

"So what's up, you comin' out to see it or what?" Dirty asked.

"Nah I'm just getting up. I'll be out in 'bout an hour," Tremaine said while still trying to wipe his eyes.

"Nigga let me find out them bitches got with your ass last night," Dirty laughed.

"What!? Nigga did you forget your ass was the one snoring and shit the whole ride back home. You the one who got wore out," Tremaine reminded him.

"Yeah alright nigga that wasn't the pussy it was that haze."

"Yeah whatever, let you tell it," Tremaine said.

"Hey cuz, I'm tellin' you, a nigga was gone for real. I had to put two Red Bulls in me this morning to give me a lil' boost of energy. After that I fired up a cigarette, a nigga felt like he was high all over again cuz, no bullshit."

"I feel you," Tremaine yawned, "Man let me get my ass up, I'ma holla at you in a minute."

"Alright."

Tremaine was quick to check Dirty when he talked about how the broads had worn him out the night before. *That nigga got the story twisted,* Tremaine thought to himself. He knew one thing though, and that was Teanna might have been a dime piece in the looks department but Summer was an all around dime. Her pussy had gotten so wet it was ridiculous. Tremaine promised himself that he would go another round with her on the solo tip instead of the train they had taken the girls on.

In the face, Summer was only a seven but her phat ass pushed her to the eight spot and the fact that her pussy was so wet elevated her to the ninth floor. What really pushed her to the dime piece in Tremaine's book was the fact that she could take it in the ass from one homeboy and still be able to suck another one's dick at the same time. All the while never slipping up and scraping the dick with her teeth in the process. That shit there took skill which in turn made her an overall dime not just a pretty face.

Dirty, Juice and even Dollar's young ass were right there with Tremaine as they each tried to plug any and every hole that the girl's body possessed. The purple that they had along with the Remy did it for them every time. All of them knew that drinking Remy, they could fuck for at least two hours straight without busting a single nut. The females be loving that shit.

Just thinking about last night made Tremaine dig through his shorts to make sure that he still had Summer's number. Even though he was faded out of his mind the night before, Tremaine could vaguely remember pulling Summer into the bathroom with him. It was just before they were planning to leave the motel and he wanted to make sure that she was aware of his intentions of scooping her up at a later date so that they could pick up where the night left off, just the two of them. He began to empty out the contents of his pocket, which consisted of keys, money, chewing gum, condoms. *Damn I must have forgot to strap up last night,* he thought, *Fuck !* He pulled out one dime-bag of purple and there it was, Summer's phone number.

"823-2976." He read the numbers on the tiny piece of paper out loud. "It's definitely gonna be on again." He plucked the piece of paper he held in his fingers.

Feeling another piece of paper in his shorts pocket, Tremaine stuck his hand back inside. When he pulled it out, and opened the folded up piece of paper the whole visual scene immediately popped back into his head. He remembered when Los had written the number down with instructions to call him later on in the week. He contemplated on whether or not he should wait to call Los in a day or two or call right then and there.

"Fuck all that," Tremaine said to himself. He made up his mind that as soon as he got out of the shower he would dial the number. Forget all that waiting shit, he was trying to break bread as soon as possible and time was money. Tremaine then began to head towards the bathroom while thinking, *let me clean this bathroom up before I got to hear my mother's mouth tomorrow morning.*

After cleaning the bathroom, taking a shower and fixing two grilled ham and cheese sandwiches, Tremaine called Los who was all the way over East Baltimore. Los wasn't trying to discuss no business over the phone and told Tremaine to meet him over Lisa's house down Fells Point about five o'clock that evening.

Tremaine called Dollar and told him to let him get the Camry. He wasn't taking any chances on missing the nigga Los so he was over there by four o'clock. Lisa was there with little Brittany. When Tremaine got there he could see that once again Lisa had redecorated her apartment. It seemed as if every six months she was buying brand new living room and dining room sets.

Lisa always possessed expensive things in her apartment, but it seemed as if everything had been upgraded to another level. The 50-inch floor model television was now a 50-inch flat screen T.V. The black plush velvet living room set she had was now a black butter soft leather seat. Black and Cream seemed to be the theme colors in her apartment as everything from black ceiling fans to the cream colored drapes matched one of those two colors.

Tremaine tried to think back and remember if Lisa had anything left in there from seven months prior, because that was about how long it had been since he had been in her apartment. Even his baby cousin Brittany looked like her little ass had been upgraded. She was three years old with diamond earrings and tennis bracelets, not that cubic zirconia shit either, but real diamonds. Tremaine always told Lisa that little Brittany was going to be a heart breaker once she got older because of her long jet black wavy hair like Los, and her golden brown skin and hazel eyes, courtesy of her mother. Tremaine and Lisa stepped out on her balcony to smoke some purple for a second and to play catch up about what's going on in each other lives.

"So what time Los tell you to meet him over here?" Lisa asked as she began lighting the rolled up haze.

"He said 'bout five."

"His ass didn't tell me that he was comin' over here today," she said taking a long pull off of the cigarillo. "I told him 'bout just poppin' up over here unannounced." She said as she blew the smoke out and passed the cigarillo.

"Stop faking," Tremaine said jokingly as he took a pull. "You know you still love that nigga. He can stop by here unannounced any time he pleases." The smoke seeped out of Tremaine's mouth and nose as he spoke.

"Tsk. Pass that shit you hoover ass nigga, and ain't nobody thinking about Los ass."

"All that shit sound good," Tremaine said as he took one more pull off the haze before he passed it.

"Nigga how come your ass ain't been over here to see me in a while?" Lisa punched Tremaine in his arm.

"I just been a lil' busy lately that's all. Ain't nothing heavy."

"Yeah, I heard your ass been flipping burgers." Lisa began to choke off the smoke when she started laughing at her own comment.

"Oh that shit funny to you, huh?" Tremaine reached over to grab the cigarillo from her as she continued to cough. "All that burger shit is dead so you can kill that." He put the haze to his lips and quickly took it back out saying, "Damn, wet mouth, you wet this shit all up." He then put it back to his lips inhaling slowly and deeply.

Lisa was still trying to catch her breath from all of the coughing. "Shut up nigga, so what you quit or something?" She asked, breathing heavily while tapping on her chest.

"You muthafuckin' right," Tremaine responded as he began to double and triple up on his pulls of the weed trying to take advantage of Lisa's small cough break.

"Well let me guess, that's why you need to hollar at Los, huh?" Lisa's face had now taken on a serious look.

"Maybe," Tremaine responded while still puffing on the purple.

"So I guess you're not selling haze anymore, huh?"

"Nah, I do too much of this to sell it, you dig?" Tremaine kissed the cigarillo and held it up in the air.

"Trem." Lisa called Tremaine by the name his uncles and aunts called him since he was a baby. "I want you to promise me something alright?" That serious look on her face was growing in mintues.

"What's up?" Tremaine asked, after finally noticing the change in Lisa's demeanor.

"Promise me you'll set a goal out here while you're doing dirt on how much money you want to save up, and if you're lucky enough to reach that goal, that you'll step back and leave this shit alone." Lisa had taken her hand and placed it on top of Tremaine's.

This was a different side of Lisa that he rarely saw. Lisa was only twenty-two years old and in all of their years of growing up together she had always been more like a big sister to Tremaine instead of a cousin. The fact was she and he both were the black sheep of the family, which brought them even closer together. Since Lisa's mother, Tremaine's aunt Donna, used to be a straight up crackhead and his own mother being on welfare, it left them both at an early age learning to take care of themselves. Juice had a mother and a father to take care of him, where as Tremaine nor Lisa ever knew their fathers.

There were at least ten more cousins that was around the same age bracket as he and Lisa, but they rarely saw them and when they did, they could never see eye to eye because the majority of them were squares. None of them grew up in the type of environment that they had. Dollar was too young back then to relate to their situation even though he wasn't much better. When Tremaine was eight years old his aunt Donna was back and forth out of rehab for almost two years and during that time Lisa had come to stay with him and his mother. Shit was extra hard then with an extra mouth to feed, but they all managed to get through it.

Being as though Lisa had been sexy all of her life, bearing a strong resemblance to Lisa Raye with more junk in the truck, she used to fuck all of the boys she was going with. They were all either drug dealers or robbed drug dealers for a living and whenever they took Lisa shopping she was sure to get them to buy little Tremaine a pair of tennis shoes or an outfit. All in all she and Tremaine definitely had a bond that was a lot stronger than average cousins.

"I'm sayin', why you say that?" Tremaine asked.

"Cause Tre, I know you're going to do what you do but I want you to be smart enough to get in and out and not get greedy like a lot of these other stupid ass niggas out here.

"Oh nah, I ain't going out like a lot of these other muthafuckas."

The way Tremaine responded must not have been convincing enough for Lisa because she continued pushing the envelope. "I'm serious Tre. Out of all the niggas I've known out here that were doing dirt you're the only one I see who has potential and I don't mean by looks either." She smiled to ease the tension of the conversation. "You got the street smarts as well as the book smarts."

"Usually they'll be 20% book smart and 80% street smart and end up getting their dumb ass locked up or buried because they were too stupid to leave the streets alone after a certain period of time. Then you got the ones who are 70% book smart and 30% streets and end up being broke as shit from always being a victim out here with niggas taking their shit or just straight up not paying them. They're out here in these streets when they should be somewhere working a regular nine to five." Lisa explained with a felt sincerity. "But you...," she said pointing at Tremaine's chest. "You got it all balanced out up in there and that's a dangerous combination if you know how to use it."

Tremaine was stuck for a second because he never heard Lisa talk no real shit to him before. He then asked her, "Shit, what's up wit Los, that nigga got it balanced out."

Lisa rolled her eyes at him and said, "Los is one of them 20% book smart and 80% street type of niggas. Because if he wasn't he

42

would take some of that money he's stacking and do something legit with it. He's made more than enough to leave these streets alone."

The two of them sat and talked a little longer about ordinary shit, but the initial conversation that Lisa brought up was definitely on Tremaine's mind. Los didn't show up until six-thirty, but it didn't seem as if he was late to Tremaine, who was fucked up from the haze and the Remy Martin and ginger ale drink Lisa made for him. He sat there on the couch stuck while watching videos on the flat screen T.V. when Los showed up he pulled out a manila envelope and led Lisa into the bedroom.

A few minutes later he emerged back into the front room and simply said, "Dogg ride wit' me."

"Alright," Tremaine said as he kissed little Brittany goodbye and promised Lisa he would be back over to see her again in a few days.

When they got outside in the parking lot Tremaine was looking for Los' Maserati but instead Los walked over to a late model blue Nissan Altima. As if he could read Tremaine's thoughts Los said on cue, "This my lil' chill shit right here. I had to make a few runs uptown and you know a nigga can't be riding through no projects wit' something big because your ass will stick out like a sore thumb. Now when that happens that's when the Feds start sniffing around." Los pointed at a Baltimore City police cruiser that was driving pass the parking lot.

"I feel you," Tremaine responded as he got in and adjusted his seat.

"You ain't got nothin' important that you got to do today, do you?" Los asked.

"Nah, why what's up?"

"Ain't shit I just want you to chill wit' me for the rest of the day that's all. It's been a while since a nigga been able to holla at you," Los said.

"Shit, it's whatever," Tremaine said while pulling out the .40 Smith & Wesson that was in his waist line and sitting it on his lap so that he could really get comfortable.

Los reached inside of the glove compartment and pulled out a box of Cigarillos with a ziplock bag that contained a little less than two ounces of haze and handed it to Tremaine. He didn't have to say anything; Tremaine already knew what time it was. They drove through Cherry Hill and Westport for a couple of hours while Los hollered at a few niggas that were out there. Afterwards he drove them all the way down to St. Mary's County to an old country looking home on a back dirt road. As they approached the house, Tremaine noticed the Maserati that Los was driving up Druid Hill Park. He wondered to himself if Los had moved and if so, why had he chosen a home that seemed so decrepit and run down on the outside. When they pulled up the dirt driveway, Los instructed Tremaine to go ahead and get in the Maserati while he ran inside of the house for a second. When he ran through the front door he left it open and Tremaine could see that the outside of the home definitely didn't compliment the inside. From what he could see, the living room had a leather set that was similar to Lisa's along with the exact same flat screen T.V.

Los emerged from the house with the same two homeboys that were at the pool with him the day before. One of the boys headed to the garage that was separate from the house off to the side and lifted the garage door revealing two SUV's on the inside. There was a grey four door Chevy Tahoe along with an all black Range Rover. The Rover was sitting on some type of Chrome rims which were hard for Tremaine to see from the angle that the Maserati was parked.

Both of Los' homeboys jumped inside of the Tahoe while Los hopped into the Quattroporte and they all headed back up the highway with the SUV in tow behind the Maserati. As Tremaine nodded his head to the Notorious B.I.G 'Ready to Die' C.D. that was playing on the car's system, he thought to himself, there was only $162 in his pocket but he felt like a millionaire riding with these niggas. He didn't even bother to ask where they were headed and still hadn't talked any business wit Los as of yet. *Fuck it*, he thought to himself. He knew that before that night was over, he would take care of business. For the time being, he was enjoying himself and chilling in the leathers of the Quattroporte allowing it's butter soft seats to hug him tighter than any female could.

When they pulled up on Baltimore Street in front of the 2 o'clock strip club, Tremaine already knew what was up; Titties and ass, the best way to end an already laid back day. Before they exited the car, Los pulled out a stack of money and handed Tremaine five hundred dollars. He tried to decline but Los wasn't having it and said, "Nah nigga you wit' me tonight you ain't got to spend shit. You're my guest alright?"

"Already," Tremaine simply replied never being one to turn down paper.

When they arrived at the front entrance it was evident that Los knew the bouncers. He addressed the large dark skinned bouncer, who looked as if he should have been playing in the N.F.L instead of moonlighting at a strip club, by the name of Dee. He told Dee that Tremaine was his little brother from out of town. The bouncer simply nodded at Tremaine and let him pass without showing I.D. Once inside, the first thing Tremaine noticed was the smell, a combination of sweat, ass and smoke. Ciara, "Riding" was gliding out of the club's speakers while a short thick light complexioned female with Long black hair with strands of blonde gyrated her topless body against the pole as if one with the music.

Los directed Tremaine to the bar where he traded in his five hundred dollars for all fives and ones. Los, in turn, along with his two acquaintances, who he finally introduced to Tremaine as L.B. and Mike-Mike, did the same exact thing, except they each got one thousand dollars worth of tens. They all ordered Coconut Ciroc with the exception of Tremaine who was still buzzing from all the drinking and smoking he had already done and chose to settle for a cold Bud Ice.

While heading to their table, Tremaine nearly tripped up more than once as his attention was diverted to the topless dancers who were giving out lap dances. He was glad that he had worn his Adidas sweat suit since there was nothing worse than going to a strip club with a pair of damn jeans on and not being able to feel shit when it came to the lap dances.

After at least ten lap dances in addition to getting his dick sucked in the bathroom by a sexy chocolate dancer who went by the name of Mocha for forty dollars, Tremaine was dead tired. He had no intentions of letting it show and planned to ride the night out with Los and his homeboys. His phone had been going off all that night with everything from females, coke sales, and his homeboys. He didn't even bother to call Dirty back.

The time spent with Los was considered as an investment by Tremaine and when it paid off he knew that he and his homeboys would eat good. Therefore, his homeboys could wait one night while he took care of business for himself as well as for them.

Finally at a quarter to two in the morning, and after taking a few pictures with the strippers, it was time to call it a night. Los hollered at L.B. and Mike-Mike but they still had a stack a piece that they wanted to throw. L.B. went first, throwing the thousand dollars that he had in ten's and Mike-Mike went next while Los and Tremaine stood back and watched. After they were done, Los and Tremaine left. Tremaine knew that right then and there was the perfect time to get down to business. Once again it seemed as if Los could read his thoughts when he asked, "Dogg how much paper you got saved up?"

Tremaine was a little hesitant to answer him before finally stating, "About fifteen hundred."

Los just nodded before saying, "Look here, hold onto that 'cause this Wednesday I'ma take a lil' trip. You think you might wanna go wit' me?"

Tremaine had already made up his mind but paused for a second not wanting to seem too anxious. "Where you going?"

"Up to New York for a couple of hours that's all."

"Fuck it, I ain't got nothin' else to do that day. It's whatever."

Los became real quiet for a second as if he was deep in thought. He had the radio turned down low on 92.3 as Alicia Keys, "Unthinkable" softly played out of the cars' crystal clear Alpine system.

"Dogg, you know why I fuck wit' you lil' cuz?" Los broke his thought and reached to turn the radio completely off. He didn't give Tremaine a chance to respond before he continued. "Let me take you back to the date March 25, 2005. 'Bout five years ago when you were 'bout ten years old I think." Los paused for a second to gather his thoughts. "I had started fuckin' wit' Lisa about four months before then, you remember?" Still not giving Tremaine a chance to respond he continued on. "Me, you and Lisa were on our way to your grandmother's house for some type of birthday party one of your peoples was having."

Tremaine now remembered what Los was talking about. It was the time his aunts had thrown a surprise birthday party for his grandfather.

Los continued, "On the way over there we got pulled over by the Police remember?"

"Yeah I remember that day," Tremaine answered.

"Now I was dirty as shit that day," Los said shaking his head. "I had that baby 9 in my lap and when they pulled us over I stuck it between my seat and my arm rest. At least I thought I did but it ended up falling in the back seat by your foot and I never knew it. Then that bitch ass police made us get out the car so that he could search the vehicle, talking 'bout he smelled marijuana. That was some bullshit!" Los raised his voice with an angry look on his face as the hatred he held for police quickly arose with the memory of that night. "I didn't even smoke haze back then so I know that muthafucka was lying. But I just knew...," he paused and pointed at his chest. "That I was going down that day 'cause when theat police searched the car he was gonna find that burner but he never did find it, did he?" Los let out a slight grin as he looked over at Tremaine.

The night was crystal clear to Tremaine, at that point, as he laughed to himself while looking out of the car's tinted window.

"Hey cuz, while we're sitting on that curb you talk about a nigga being fucked up in the head. Yo, that wasn't even the word for it. But when he came back from the car and said that were free to go. I didn't know what the fuck to think, you remember?"

"Yeah I remember," Tremaine responded with a slight grin on his face.

"And you..." Los poked Tremaine in his shoulder with his finger. "Ten-mother fucking-years old at the time had picked up the burner that fell by your foot and put it in your dip without any hesitations. The muthafuckin' Police searched me and went through Lisa's pocketbook hard." With a more serious look, he said, "you know what?" He asked Tremaine.

48

"What's up?"

"That burner had just been used in a homicide one hour before we got pulled over. I still had the gun powder residue and all that shit on my hands, so I know for a fact that I wouldn't be sitting here right now if it wasn't for your quick thinking that day," he said grabbing Tremaine in a firm handshake.

"Hey yo that wasn't shit, I was just doing what I had seen so many other niggas do, pick up the burner and put it in their waist line," Tremaine said brushing the whole matter off. "Shit, to be honest wit' you I thought you were lettin' me have that muthafucka for real when you reached back and dropped it on my foot. Believe me, if you would have never asked me about it when we got back in the car, my lil' ass would have kept that shit with the quickness." They both shared a laugh and mellowed out to the music for the remainder of the ride to Tremaine's house.

When they pulled up in front of Tremaine's house, Los asked him to hold on for a second. He then began to flick his headlights and turn his A/C on and off. Tremaine was wondering just what in the hell he was doing when all of a sudden the entire dash board began to slowly raise up revealing a .357 desert Eagle handgun along with a few small brown paper bags inside of a velvet lined compartment. Tremaine's mouth dropped open at the sight of what he had witnessed, which resembled some James Bond 007 types of gadgets. Los picked up one of the balled up brown bags and looked inside of it. He then closed the bag back up and handed it to Tremaine. "Here's a lil' something to hold you over until Wednesday alright."

When Tremaine looked inside of the bag he saw what looked to be no less than thirty grams of a grayish blue colored crack along with a healthy amount of residue at the bottom. He asked Los what he wanted for the crack.

"Charge it to the game, don't even worry about it and I can guarantee you one thing, won't none of these niggas around here have anything as crucial as that shit right there," Los said.

"Oh this shit like that, huh?" Tremaine asked.

"You'll see, just make sure you call me on Tuesday around seven so we can make sure everything is set for the trip alright?"

"That's what's up. Good lookin' too, Tremaine replied."

"I'ma holla at you," Los said as he extended his arm to Tremaine.

They gave each other a five and Los pulled off. Tremaine no longer felt like going in the house at that time and thought about taking his crack down stairs in the laundry room of his basement to chop it up so that he could catch a few late night sales. He decided against it and told himself that it was about to be on because tomorrow was looking sweeter by the minute.

4 DA TRIP

Tremaine was up at eight o'clock the next morning. The coke that Los had given him was burning a hole in his pocket even as he slept. It was Sunday morning and he was up at eight cutting up crack. It took him close to an hour to cut the whole thing into individual pieces of tens, twenties, and fifties as well as bag them up separately. Tremaine called Dirty and urged him to get out the bed and hit the block with him because they both had some grinding to do. He bagged up a little over two thousand dollars worth of crack, he was able to take the large quantity of crumbs at the bottom of the brown bag and add a little to each crack bag to stretch the product out as much as possible.

Tremaine had already decided he was going to give Dirty five hundred dollars worth of coke. Dirty was his man and he wasn't about to start stacking while his right hand man was hungry. Even though Dirty was doing his own thing on the side, Tremaine knew it was time to get some real money out there and stop bullshitting. He looked at the thirty grams of crack as being the first official step to their come up. He was scheduled to make his first out of state trip and didn't plan on looking back after that.

The crack that Tremaine had gotten from Los was some good ass shit. The shit truly was that butter and the fiends couldn't get enough of it as they would come back, barely able to talk while trying to cop more. Never had Tremaine purchased any type of coke from Fat Bird that fucked up a smoker's whole speech process.

By the time five o'clock came around that evening he and Dirty were completely sold out and were chilling on Myrtle Avenue, in front of Benny's house. They were posted up with Benny, Dollar, and Black Ty smoking a couple of cigarillos and sipping on Berry Ciroc.

As the night wore in, Tremaine was giving serious thoughts as to whether or not he should call Los in an attempt to buy some more of that butter since fiends were steady coming at him looking for more. It was killing him and Dirty to keep having to turning away paper and telling their clientele that they were all sold out.

Tremaine started to go holler at Fat Bird, but changed his mind quickly when he told himself that he would never go back to that bullshit product when he had just had his hands on that crucial shit. In his mind there was no going back because from this point on he was only moving forward therefore he could wait until Wednesday's trip. One thing Tremaine was learning on a daily basis was patience. Because when a muthafucka rushed things they were susceptible to make mistakes and at this point, there wasn't any room for error. A muthafucka might not have been able to get a second chance depending on how major the mistake was.

That night Tremaine and Dirty thought about rolling out with Dollar in that wagon of his but they changed their minds. Earlier in the day they were picking on Dollar, who actually had to catch the bus all the way out Towson to Lisa's apartment to get the Camry back. He was beefing with Tremaine because he left it over there the night before when he left with Los.

When Dollar found out that Tremaine left the car in the parking lot of Lisa's complex he began arguing about it. "Why you leave my car over there?" He actually thought that the cars he stole were his very own.

Basically, all the boys did was chill for the night but they could always find something in the projects to keep them occupied. By it being the weekend and the summertime, shit was definitely live in the hood.

The first incident that had everyone damn near pissing in their pants was when a fiend took Foots off for his crack. There was a smoker who pulled up trying to cop on Mosher Street. Foots was eager to get the sale before anyone else that he failed to notice that the crackhead was a new nigga that no one had ever seen around before. He also failed to notice that the fiend never put his car in park when he stopped but kept his foot on the brake as the car idled throughout the whole transaction. Nobody could blame the crack head because Foots was definitely out of order with his next move.

With a hand full of stones, Foots stuck his arm through the fiend's car window, into his face. Before anyone could get the words "Look at this slippin' ass nigga" out of their mouths the fiend smacked Foots' hand upwards sending all of the crack flying in the inside of his car and pulled off. Foots immediately latched onto the driver's side door with his right arm hanging through the window all the way up to his arm pits. He was trying to punch the driver with his left hand in an attempt to get him to stop. After being dragged for nearly twenty-five yards, he finally let go of the door, and ended up falling and rolling in the street. The whole strip was out there laughing, especially when Foots came back limping down the block with the entire front of his crispy red, grey and white Air Max black and scuffed up along with tar marks down the back of his T-shirt.

The second incident was when the boy lil' Chris, had gotten his hands on a few left over Fourth of July fire crackers. All that day he had been out there lighting cherry bombs and M-80's, throwing them at the stray cats and dogs in the neighborhood. He had one half of a stick of dynamite left and was waiting for the perfect time to light it. Perfect timing was when one of those habibs came on Argyle Avenue driving a Good Humor ice cream truck. No one knew where the ice cream truck driver thought he was, or if he had come around at night by mistake.

Initially everyone thought it might have been the police, disguising themselves because there had never been a Good Humor truck around there before. The only ice cream truck that came in the hood was driven by a black man named Steve, along with his five year old daughter and even he knew that being out here after sunset was not a wise choice. After the driver parked and turned on his interior light while ringing an obnoxiously loud bell everyone could see he was by himself. After close to a half of an hour out there watching everyone and their mothers seeming to buy something off the truck, lil' Chris stepped off and said, "Watch this."

As he walked towards the truck and crept around the backside of it, you could see him fiddling with something in his hand that looked to be a lighter. It finally dawned on everyone what he was doing. When he lit the quarter stick it was easy to see the sparkling edge from a distance.

He suddenly tossed it under the truck and took off running back toward the corner of Mosher Street where Tremaine, Dirty, and Dollar was standing.

BOOOOOOM! The entire rear of the truck lifted at least three feet in the air leaving it rocking from side to side. The habib ran to the front of the truck and stuck his head out of the driver side window trying to see what the hell had just happened. The look on his face was if he had been shitting bricks. Once again, everyone fell out laughing. The driver got his truck started after about ten tries and it was extremely loud since the muffler was now hanging on by a thread. The explosion had damaged the axle as well caused the back left wheel to wobble as the truck slowly drove off. They knew that they would never see that Good Humor truck around there again.

After that incident Tremaine, Dirty, and Dollar began fucking with the girls on Mosher Street trying to see who they could persuade to come inside their man Lil Chris house that night. They didn't have too much luck with the broads so they ended up getting crack head Carol to suck all three of them off along with lil' Chris for forty dollars altogether. They wanted to fuck because Carol was phat as shit, but changed their minds when they noticed she had on the same blue tights for three days in a row. They were beginning to change to a yellowish color and one could only imagine what her pussy would smell like.

Tuesday took forever to arrive it seemed to Tremaine. He called Los at exactly seven o'clock to make sure everything was still a go for the next day. Los assured him that it was good and that he would be by to scoop him up at two in the afternoon. Tremaine could hardly sleep that Tuesday night in anticipation of the next day. He was in bed by ten o'clock, just laying there in the dark contemplating on a whole lot of shit and ready for whatever came his way on the trip. One could never tell what would happen when they were fucking with out of town niggas in the game, or any niggas for that matter. He had heard plenty of stories about dudes doing business with out of town connects and their ass ended up missing or being a John Doe in a state where no one knew shit about them. Tremaine was determined not to become another victim out here in these streets. It was already embedded in his mind that if anyone ever flinched wrong in the middle of a deal, he would let his .40 Smith & Wesson sing with its black talon bullets, fuck what you heard.

When he awoke the next the morning the first and only thing on Tremaine's mind was the trip. He refrained from smoking or drinking anything that afternoon while waiting on Los to call. He wanted to be sober and careful for the trip as he kept reminding himself that there was no room for mistakes. When Los finally called and told him that he was out in front of his building, Tremaine went out there looking for the Maserati. He saw a Quattroporte alright; the nigga Los had a mother fucking Cadillac hearse.

Tremaine looked at him as if he had bumped his damn head or something. Los even had a white female with him to drive the hearse. She was decked out in the black business suit as well as chauffeur's hat. *This nigga off the muthafuckin' chain for real,* Tremaine thought to himself. Still not believing what he was seeing he asked Los, "Hey yo, what the fuck is this?"

Los looked at him like, 'what? You don't know? "Nigga, this is our guarantee in and out. Come on and get yo' ass in," he said as he went to go pull the handle and open the back door exposing a large grey casket sitting in the back.

"Hey yo, tell me ain't nobody up in there," Tremaine said pointing at the casket while still not getting in.

"Hell nah nigga, now come on and get in," Los said grinning as Tremaine climbed in the back next to the casket.

The first thing that popped into Tremaine's head, as he slowly made his way into the back of the hearse, was the song by Bone Thugs and Harmony 'For the Love of Money', and the things a person would do for it.

The driver, who Los called Mary Jane, closed the door and locked them in the back. Tremaine was sitting next to the casket a little tensed up because there was no telling what Los had inside of it. When they got on the highway, Los finally lifted the top of the casket revealing lots of pillows and snacks along with a cooler filled with bottled water. It was obvious that he and Tremaine were thinking alike: No smoking or drinking when going to take care of business. There wasn't a cigarillo wrapping or a bottle of liquor anywhere in sight.

On the way up, Los explained why he used the hearse and how the police wouldn't be so quick to pull over a white lady who was driving one. He also said that he sometimes used a minivan that held a large flower delivery sign on the side of it with a legit number to the flower shop and everything. Los spoke about when push came to shove he had a white man that would carry everything back on the train himself. Los' motto was: Use the white man to beat the white man. He knew that the odds were definitely in his favor when it came down to the police suspecting a white man of a crime as oppose to a black man.

As they began to get closer to New York, Los began to pull Tremaine's coat as to how long he had been dealing with his connect up north and how they had actually grew up with one another in Northwest Baltimore. He and his connect had played boys and girls club football together, and through all of that Los said that he still didn't trust his childhood friend who moved to New York as a teenager.

His man lived out in Brooklyn somewhere but before they got there, Mary Jane pulled the hearse over into a crowded mall parking lot. They exited the hearse and Los led Tremaine to an empty taxi cab that he obviously had waiting for them in the lot. Mary Jane opened up the door and went up under the taxis' front seat coming back up with a set of keys in her hand. Tremaine was beginning to see that the white broad definitely wasn't new to the move. She, without a doubt, had everything down packed.

Some might consider Mary Jane to be quite attractive with her shoulder length brunette hair in a ponytail and her piercing green eyes. She possessed a little more than the average white women in the ass department. His feelings wasn't anything personal because he was quick to admit that he had indeed seen quite a few bad ass white girls in his time but he preferred his meat dark and well done. He even had a thing when it came to messing with light complexioned black girls; it was just something about dark skinned females that drove him crazy.

Once inside the taxicab, Mary Jane changed her business jacket to a cutoff jean shirt. She drove while Tremaine and Los sat in the back of the cab as if they were tourists. Arriving in New York wasn't any different than Baltimore, with the exception of it being bigger, brighter, and busier. Tremaine had witnessed people walking down the sidewalk with outfits that were yellow and orange or a bright green color. Some of the outfits were slick the way it was thrown together, but he wasn't use to it since in Baltimore the swag was different. Unless a nigga was a pimp or some shit like that, one never would be seen in Baltimore with a canary yellow outfit on.

One thing was for sure in Tremaine's eyes and that was the females might have dressed differently in the big Apple but it damn sure didn't make them any less sexy. They looked just as good if not better than the females he was used to seeing back home. Mary Jane pulled up to a row of brickstone townhouses. The first thing Tremaine did was take note of how many niggas were out on the block that looked to be up to no good. His quick assessment picked out five individuals who could be carrying burners. The ones who wore tank tops with sweat pants he knew that if they were strapped they had to have their guns stashed nearby because the gun definitely wasn't on them. Now the ones who were in T-shirt and jean shorts were the ones who made his five list. That was good enough for two black Talons in their ass a piece with an extra bullet just in case something was to transpire that led to gun play.

Mary Jane sat in the cab as Tremaine and Los walked up the steps of the home, which was blasting out the sounds of Jay-Z on the stereo inside. A little Spanish mommy, who was so phat she made J-Lo look like Olive Oil from the cartoon 'Popeye', answered the door. The sexy Rican had a slim waist with a pair of white tights on that were transparent as they revealed the black thong she wore underneath. After being mesmerized by her for a second, Tremaine quickly caught himself. The first thing that came to his mind was that Los' connect was trying to use the girl as a diversion. Some ole' rock them to sleep with her beauty type of shit. Tremaine knew that he was probably over- reacting but fuck it, he thought, it was better to be safe than sorry.

The female showed them to the living room and instructed Tremaine and Los that Manny, Los' connect, was just getting out of the shower and that he would be downstairs in a minute.

The décor of the living room was the basic style of a bachelor's pad not being too flashy or anything like that. There was the usual big screen television and Tremaine could tell that Manny had a thing for tropical fish because his cocktail table and two end tables held tropical tanks in the bottom of them. The fish inside were various colors including yellow, green, and light blue. Some of the fish were covered in spikes and had all types of stripes on their bodies. Where Tremaine was from, if one happened to have a fish tank they only had one of a few types of fish: Red Devils, Piranhas, Oscars, or Jack Dempsey's. There wasn't any type of tropical fish.

It was evident that Manny wasn't too caught up on flossing his riches since his home was based on simplicity in comparison to the weight in coke he was pushing. When he finally came downstairs, Tremaine sized up the average looking male of six feet even with a track runner's build. Dominican or Puerto Rican, Tremaine could never tell the difference between the two nationalities, was wearing a simple pair of grey sweat pants along with a crispy white wife beater. On his feet was a pair of black Nikes and the only piece of jewelry he

wore was a platinum Movado watch. Tremaine was digging the
nigga's style because he was so laid back. Never the less, he was still
on point and ready for whatever.

Los introduced Tremaine and Manny to one another and then
they all headed into the kitchen to get down to business. Manny's
girl, who he simply called boo, offered the fellas drinks and when
they declined she exited the room and headed upstairs. Los and
Manny then began to make small talk about a nigga named Garland
that they both knew and how he had just gotten killed. The entire
time they conversed, they did it with saran wrap and glass vials.

The Spanish female emerged from upstairs with a large Louis
Vuitton pocket book and sat it down on the table before turning to
leave without saying a word. Manny opened the bag and pulled out
eight large white blocks.

Now Tremaine had never seen a kilogram of cocaine before but
he quickly figured that was what the eight individual blocks consisted
of. He was stuck just thinking about the money he could make off of
all that powder. Manny then went and opened one of the kitchen
drawers and retrieved a small steak knife. He poked a hole in one of
the kilos of cocaine and dumped out two match head size scoops of
the powder into one of the glass vials. He then took another vial that
contained a clear liquid and dropped 7 or 8 drops of the liquid into
the vial containing the powder. After slightly shaking it up, the liquid
turned into a dark blue color. Manny held the vial up for Los to
observe and he responded with a nod of approval.

The entire time this process was going on, Los and Manny
continued to converse casually and acted as if everything was cool.
Tremaine knew that wasn't the case and he was well aware that in the
back of their minds they both were analyzing one another and
looking for anything unusual that would raise any uncertainty, which
was usually accompanied by the 'Game'.

After testing and weighing the total of eight bricks and Manny getting Los' approval on each one, it was now Tremaine's turn. Los explained to his homeboy that Tremaine was trying to cop something that would help him get on his feet and get him started. Tremaine felt a little inferior when Tremaine asked him how much he had and all he could say was a measly fifteen hundred dollars. Especially after seeing over one hundred and fifty thousand dollars exchanged between him and Los. Manny was cool about it and told Tremaine that he had something for him as he went to the refrigerator and pulled out a six pack of sodas, sitting it down in front of Tremaine at the table. Tremaine looked at him as if he was crazy and thought to himself, *here comes the drama.*

He began shifting his eyes from Manny to the stairwell expecting his girlfriend to come down the stairs blasting or some shit. Just like in the movie "King of New York," when Laurence Fishburne robbed the Dominicans. Before he shot at them he gave them a briefcase full of tampons, and that was exactly how Tremaine felt as Manny sat the six-pack of sodas in front of him instead of the crack he had just paid for. Manny sat next to Tremaine and began unscrewing the bottom part of the soda revealing a bag of small glass vials. Each vial contained four or five nickel-sized pieces of crack inside of them. Manny then told him that he would give him six hundred of those vials for his fifteen hundred.

After doing a quick assessment in his head of just how much he would make if he sold the vials for ten dollars a piece Tremaine came up with $6,000. That was a four hundred percent return. Manny had definitely extended his hand towards helping him get on his feet. After putting the final touches on the deal and accepting a few of the fake soda cans from Manny as a gift, Tremaine was ready to leave. He and Los headed back outside to their taxi where Mary Jane sat waiting.

About a minute after they arrived back at the hearse in the mall parking lot, Los pulled a finger wide sized blunt from out of nowhere. Tremaine had no complaints about that since his mind was running one hundred miles an hour about his first out-of-state trip. In his mind, he had already sold all of the coke and was thinking about the next trip. The weed would calm him down, and have him take a one step at a time approach.

It took close to three and a half hours to get back to the Baltimore area. On the way back Tremaine and Los conversed about when Los would be heading back to N.Y., which he said would be in two and a half weeks at the latest. They also talked about a strip up Whitelock that Los was supplying with crack. He told Tremaine that he was more than welcome to hustle in that area. Tremaine's response was thanks but no thanks, to be honest he didn't plan on standing on any corner for too much longer. Tremaine had made his mind up and was adamant about all that hand to hand, running to cars bullshit and had plans in the near future to be the one who supplied the strips with crack and not just a hustler on the block.

5 WELL CONNECTED

The morning after the New York trip, Tremaine hit the block and was more determined than ever to get rid of all his crack within two days. He planned to go straight back to Los to re-up the minute he was finished. He took all of the coke out of the glass vials and placed them into individual crack bags. He did that because it was impossible for him to stash the glass vials between his ass cheeks or next to his balls as he would do while on the block. One hundred, ten dollar crack bags were given to Dirty with Tremaine telling him to give him four hundred dollars back off of it.

When he put the bag in Dirty's hand the first thing he said was, "Why you give me all these fat ass dubs? What you didn't feel like cutting up no dimes?" Dirty looked at the sandwich bag full of tiny plastic bags he held in his hand and then looked back and fourth from Tremaine to the crack.

"Yo, we got plenty more where that shit came from just trust me on this alright?" Tremaine said with a sense of sincerity.

"With these fat ass boulders we're gonna be the first, second, and third muthafuckin' ones on their minds." Dirty said still not believing the size of the stones he held in his hand. Just as Tremaine predicted, the fiends couldn't get enough of the new shit once he and Dirty opened up shop. The first few crack heads looked as if they had seen a ghost when they came to cop and were given such a large quantity of crack for their money. A couple of them closed their hands rather quickly with the thought that Tremaine had placed a twenty in their hand instead of a dime and didn't want to give him a chance to realize his so-called mistake and correct it. A few had even asked him, "This shit ain't no wax is it?" Not believing the shit could be real. But on that particular day he just took it as a compliment because he knew they weren't use to getting that much quantity for their dollar.

That initial day Tremaine and Dirty sold close to seven hundred rocks on Lanvale Street and knew that they could do four hundred bags before six o'clock if it kept going the way that it was going. The next day was Friday, they knew that the remaining bags would not last them two hours on the block. Tremaine decided to call Los that night to see if he would be able to purchase at least an ounce in order to get through Friday's payday rush. Los told Tremaine that he would call him back in twenty minutes. Once Los called back, he informed Tremaine that he was in Towson, MD and instructed him to meet him at Towson Town Center. Tremaine agreed but had to think about whose car he could borrow in order to make the pick-up. Dollar had to get rid of the Camry when he caught a flat tire the day before.

The funny thing was while he was in the process of changing the tire, the police pulled up on him after seeing this little ass boy trying to jack up a car. Dollar was forced to break out and leave the

car behind, so that car was gone and he have'nt had a chance to steal another one at the moment. *Who the hell's car can I use*, Tremaine pondered to himself. He finally came up with Craig and that old raggedy ass Hyundai of his. Usually when he rented a crackhead's car, Tremaine would at least try to get something that was a late model or halfway decent. All that went out the window, he had to make a quick run and Craig's old ass hooptie would have to do.

Tremaine made the twenty minute drive to Towson Town Center in Craig's car and it cut off on him three times just on the ride up there. When he arrived at the mall's parking lot he noticed Los sitting in the same Tahoe SUV that L.B. and Mike-Mike were driving the night they all went out to the strip club. Tremaine pulled up next to him, got out of the Hyundai and climbed into the SUV. The mall was beginning to close, resulting in the parking lot thinning out so they had to make it quick.

"Whose raggedy ass shit is that?" Los asked grinning.

"Nah that's a fiend's car I had to get real quick."

"What's up though, you sold out already?"

"Shit, just about. That shit's going like flap jacks cuz, no bull shit. I was trying to cop some now, so that I can make it through tomorrow."

"Well all I got left on me is a six deuce," Los said referring to the sixty two grams of crack packages that was sold up Whitelock.

It was the same two ounces but instead of the regular 56 grams, a nigga would give you 62 of them instead. It was the same way with one ounce of crack. Baltimore hustlers would call them thirty-ones since that was the amount of grams you would get instead of the usual 28 in a standard ounce.

"You can get that right now if you want to," Los said.

Tremaine thought about it and realized that it would be the best if he got that instead of continuing to deal with the thirty-ones. It was time for him to step up and keep elevating his game. Next it would be an eighth of a ki followed by a quarter ki and then it wouldn't be long before he was in a position to buy his first whole brick. Tremaine paid Los the thirteen hundred that he wanted for the crack and hopped back inside of Craig's hooptie.

The following weekend Tremaine, Dirty, and Dollar went out to Elkridge, MD auto auction with Dirty's older cousin, Tone. They needed Tone to go for full access to the auction because he has his dealer's license. Tremaine had a little over five thousand dollars saved up with fifteen hundred dollars worth of crack left. He figured it was time to purchase his own car instead of having to ride around in rented or stolen vehicles. He purchased himself a 2000 Acura TL for fifteen hundred dollars, and in his mind he was the shit. Even though the car was five years old, it was still very clean and in mint condition with its pearl white paint job, along with a Bose Stereo system and tan leather seats. The manager at the auction said that the car used to belong to an elderly couple who rarely used it. When Tremaine initially saw it, he figured that the only thing that was missing was a set of dark tint on the windows and a set of rims.

Dirty purchased a 2001 Honda Accord Coupe for two thousand dollars. This was a different auction than the one Tremaine previously went to in Mannassas. The people at this auction presented him with a pair of ten day temporary tags to put on his TL so that he wouldn't have to worry about the police snatching his car because of stolen tags. Tremaine made it his business to put the car in his cousin's, Lisa, name and get a legit pair of tags before the temporary's expired.

After leaving the auction and racing each other's car back up the highway, they all went straight to U.S.A. Boutique in Mondawmin mall to get fresh. It was nothing heavy, just a few pairs of Polo shirts, a couple of pairs of Air Max, Nike Boots as well as some Rock and Republic and Seven jeans. Tremaine was learning to curb his spending habits to save his money in order to get to where he needs himself to be. He wanted Los' money and beyond, and knew that stunting was not going to get it.

Everything was beginning to go smooth for Tremaine. He had just brought a car; his pockets were slowly but surely getting bigger. His clients were steady growing and he was still taking trips up state with Los to cop. He and Los had even talked about them taking a vacation by going on a cruise to the Bahamas or some place of that sort. But things weren't always peaches and cream like the song said, "Mo Money Mo problems."

Tremaine was beginning to hear certain things about the hating that certain niggas were doing around Pennsylvania Avenue concerning him. Word on the street was that a lot of niggas were starting to notice how he and his homies were moving up and didn't like it. Mainly it was the older cats in the neighborhood that were starting to say slick shit. None of them would say it to him directly; they did that bitch shit behind his back. All that shit was like gas to Tremaine's fire because it was a sure sign that he was moving up. He was just starting to see the older niggas for what they were.

All his life Tremaine subscribed to the notion that if an older nigga who's been in the game since a young age, he would be considered an "O.G." in the hood. Now as an O.G., you are supposed to be above certain things, but sitting on the sidelines insulting the character of an up and coming lil nigga, who was only fifteen shouldn't have been in their character. For the simple fact that hating on a muthafucka was a sign of weakness, even worst when that man is ten years your junior.

Tremaine decided to not even give them niggas much thought because it was whatever with him and his homeboys. As far as he was concerned, them older niggas could suck his dick. What really pissed him off was the fact that some of the older dudes had been out on the same strip for over ten years and were still nickel and diming with that hand to hand bullshit. They were twenty-five and twenty-six years old and still fucking with fifteen and sixteen year old girls. If they had been out there all that time and still hadn't made it to the next level, then they were dick heads for sure.

Tremaine and Dirty decided to start putting their burners in potato chips bags and stashimg them in the grass. Either that or they would ride around on their mountain bikes catching coke sales with the burners on them, just waiting for one of the older niggas to crack slick with them. Other times they would give their burners to Dollar and let him ride up and down the strip with them on him while they got their hustled.

On one particular day, Tremaine and Dirty witnessed all of the hate and envy with their own two eyes; they saw just how the older niggas felt about them. The two of them, along with Dollar, and a few of their other homeboys: Forty, Smuggler and Lil' Chris were all sitting out in front of the 800 block of Fremont Avenue while Fats, Black Ty, Foots, Midnight, and Eric were two blocks up on Lafayette Avenue. They were all out in their separate clicks hustling. No more than twenty minutes before they were all in one big group, Tremaine, Dirty, and Forty left to walk to the ice cream truck. Instead of staying on Fremont Avenue, they decided to chill on the corner of Lanvale Street on Ms. Mary porch. Chris, Dollar, and Smuggler walked up afterwards.

As they sat out there waiting for their next sale, crackhead Bruce was seen walking briskly down the sidewalk past the older niggas, coming towards Tremaine and his homeboys. Foots hollered at Bruce but he shook his head and kept walking in the direction of where Tremaine and them were standing. They could all hear Foots say something and then they watched as he stepped down off of the front step. He punched Bruce, giving him a right hook to the side of his face. The punch didn't knock him out but it did daze the hell out of him, each time he attempted to get up on one knee he would fall face forward again. After watching Bruce stumble forward two or three times, Foots finally went into the fiend's pocket and took whatever money he had.

Now Smuggler, Chris, and Forty were all laughing at the scenario as well as a few other niggas out there, but Tremaine, Dirty, and Dollar held concrete looks on their faces. They already knew that those niggas were jealous of them and when Foots pulled that stunt, it had basically confirmed their thoughts. Foots had whooped Bruce's ass because he was coming to cop, not from them, but from Tremaine and his homeboys. Tremaine knew right then and there that it wouldn't be too long before he would eventually have to bury one of them muthafuckas.

Tremaine and Los continued their bi-weekly trips up top depending on how fast Los would sell out. Tremaine had stopped buying the vials. Manny was selling him four and a half ounces of powered cocaine for twenty-five hundred dollars. He would then take that four and a half to a Cuban woman by the name of Josanda that Craig had turned him on to. Josanda had been doing her thing in the coke game back in the mid 80's, pushing a little weight and ended up getting locked up. She began smoking crack during her incarceration and was now a full blown crackhead. Josanda worked at the meat company with Craig, but she could cook the shit out of powered cocaine.

Out of Tremaine's four and a half ounces she could whip it up to six and a half ounces. She told him that she could even take it up to eight if he wanted since the power was so potent. He told her that six and a half was good enough since he didn't want to dilute the coke too much, he didn't want his crack being average like the rest of the shit out on the block. Out of those six and a half ounces, one hundred and eighty-two grams, Tremaine would sell four thirty-ones for eight hundred a piece and the remaining 58 grams would be broken down into tens and twenties. All together he would make no less than sixty-five hundred dollars off of a twenty five hundred dollar purchase.

It has been four months; Tremaine and Dirty were killing the competition. Even lil' Dollar had stepped it up and was now sending his money with Tremaine up top to buy the same vials from Manny that Tremaine, himself had started out with. In his first two months, Tremaine had accumulated a savings of eighteen thousand dollars and knew that within a month or two he would be ready to purchase his first kilogram of powder. The more trips he made up north the less he was seen on the block. He began to hustle strickly off oh his phone, he had a number of fiends that brought no less than four hundred dollars worth of crack a piece each week. A couple of them were in the hood but a majority of them were in Baltimore County. Their money was like gold allowing Tremaine to trick them. He'd give them crack on credit, four to seven hundred dollars worth during the week and on Friday, they would pay him his money like clockwork. With clientele like that he was able to say fuck all that standing on the block shit all day.

But his lil' peoples, like Dollar, was still out there on hand to hand status with his shit, standing out on the corner serving any and every fiend that came along. Dirty was still out on the block as well, slowly wearing himself away from it. Tremaine would still go out there a couple of days out of the week. He thought he was playing it cool by being out there every once in a while, but shit was always happened unexpectedly in the hood.

One night on Argyle and Mosher Street things were a little slow in the hood so Tremaine, Dirty, Benny, Black Ty, Fats, Foots and the nigga Zeke, who had just came home from doing a six year bid in prison, were out behind one of the apartment buildings shooting dice. While Foots and Fats were on the dice everyone else was side betting. Fats was chasing his point, which was eight, while Foots had him faded. Tremaine and Zeke were betting on the side for twenty dollars a point.

"Eight bitches huh!" Fats would yell while down on one knee. "Six deuce baby! Five huh!" he would say as he rolled the dice and snapped his fingers.

He was chasing that eight as if his life depended on it and after at least ten tries he still hadn't hit his number nor crapped out. The entire time he was rolling the dice chasing his point, Tremaine was challenging Zeke to bet twenty more.

"Shit, bet that nigga, you ain't sayin' nothing slick," Zeke responded as they went back and forth like that at least six times. Before they knew it, they had accumulated close to three hundred dollars in their side pile alone.

Finally after rolling for what seemed like forever, Fats crapped out. "Bitch!" he yelled.

"That's right, that's right. "Get me paid nigga," Tremaine said as he bent down to pick up his winnings.

Before he could pick up his paper, Zeke reached out grabbing his hand. "The fuck is you doing nigga you bet wit' him," he said while squeezing Tremaine's hand.

"What?!" Tremaine responded snatching his hand away." Nigga, you bumped yoor muthafuckin' head." He then reached down in an attempt to pick up the pile once again.

Zeke reached down and grabbed the paper with two hands before Tremaine could grab it. "Ya bitch ass, you did bet wit' him!" Zeke said with a tight grip on the money.

I know this nigga don't think he gonna just bitch me like that, Tremaine thought. He then stepped up into Zeke's face and said, "Zeke I know one muthafuckin' thing, you better stop playin' and give me my mufuckin' paper!"

"Nigga I ain't givin' you shit!" he responded while looking down on Tremaine slightly.

Zeke was a full 6'2 in height and weighed 220lbs. He had just done a six year bid so he was definitely big as shit physically. Not caring that he was out matched by four inches in height and fifty pounds in weight, Tremaine wasn't backing down. He could see Foots and Black Ty eyeing the situation with pleasure as if they were glad to see someone get on him since their soft asses didn't have the heart to do it. Tremaine had his 40 S&W on him and wasn't about to hesitate for a minute to wet Zeke's ass up.

He put his finger in Zeke's face as he said, "I'ma tell you one more muthafuckin' time, give me…" Crack! Before Tremaine could finish his words, Zeke hauled off and punched him square in the jaw.

Tremaine stumbled back at least five steps and had to catch himself by putting his hand down because he nearly fell flat on his ass. Through his dizzy spell, he could hear Dirty pull his burner and cock back the chamber. Tremaine could hear Zeke saying something along the lines of how he was a little bitch ass nigga when he got locked up and how he was still a little kid to him amongst other things. After finally regaining his posture together and shaking off the punch Tremaine could see Dirty and Zeke in a heated argument, with Benny standing in front of the burner holding Dirty back.

"Hold this yo. I'm 'bout to punish this nigga," Tremaine said as he handed Dirty his burner.

Benny was now stepping in front of Tremaine talking about, "Fuck that shit, let that shit ride."

Tremaine and Zeke squared up, and Tremaine had already sized him up. Zeke was big, but he was slow, and Tremaine already knew that he would try to wrestle him and slam him since he himself was smaller. They instantly began fighting; Tremaine's first three punches caught nothing but flesh. Zeke stumbled back a few steps, you could instantly see a golf ball sized knot beginning to form under his eye. When Tremaine rushed him, in order to catch him while he was dazed, Zeke gave Tremaine a left hook. He then shoe stringed him, grabbing Tremaine around his legs and slamming him to the ground. Before he could pin Tremaine to the ground, Dirty stepped forward and began whipping Zeke in the back of the head with the handle on Tremaine's gun. The blows caused Zeke to raise his hands in an attempt to cover the back of his head, which awarded Tremaine the opportunity to slide up from under him.

To everyone's surprise Tremaine began to walk off. Dirty was calling out behind him saying something about holding up but Tremaine couldn't really tell since he was so focused on his next move.

Finally, Dirty came running up behind Tremaine. "Hold up yo, where you going?"

"Take my keys and go start my car for me. I'll be around there in a second," Tremaine said breathing heavily while handing Dirty his car keys.

He pulled out the black bandana that he kept folded up inside of his back pocket or in the glove compartment of his car. Either way it was always within his reach. Dirty would always ask him what was it was for, and his reponse would always be, he would see one day and today was that day. Tremaine kept the rag so that if he ever had to run down on some niggas on a spur of the moment type situation, he would always have something to cover his face with. When he pulled out the bandana and began tying it around his face, Dirty already knew what was up. Tremaine took off his grey T-shirt leaving his white tank top on. He already knew that when he went back around that corner all of them would know that it was him, but that was the whole point. Even if the incident did happen to make it to court and one of those niggas got loose lips, at least having a mask on with different clothing would give his lawyer some type of defense.

When he stepped back behind the apartments, Tremaine couldn't believe that they were actually back to shooting dice again as if nothing had happened. *Slipping ass niggas, they must think that I'm a bitch or something,* he thought to himself. When he walked back up on the dice game, Benny and Foots spotted him first and they immediately froze up. Black Ty spotted him next while saying, "Da fuck!" When he said that Zeke turned to look, but it was too late. The first shot caught him square in his temple and the impact of the .40 Teflon bullet sent a red mist out the side of his head. Zeke fell face forward with a rather unusual peaceful look on his face and gazed out into oblivion as Tremaine fired two more shots into the back of his skull.

By this time, Fats and Black Ty shook ass, they ran down the back of the apartments toward W. Lafayette Avenue. Benny and Foots were still standing in the same spot on the bricks as before, still stuck in a trance. Tremaine looked down at Zeke's lifeless body and the sticky purplish red puddle that his blood was forming on the concrete beneath his head, and turned away, runningnthrough the split that lead to the Dome. The whole time praying that Dollar peeped his move, Tremaine cut through the Dome parking lot that lead to Pitcher Street, he emerged out on to Pennsylvania Avenue.

After walking pass Shake and Bake Skating Rink for a minute or two he could see his TL heading up the Avenue towards him. He hopped in the passenger seat, he and Dirty turned left on Laurens Street. They drove around for a while smoking a few cigarillos all the while joking about how all them bitch ass niggas froze up when Tremaine came around the corner. They ended up going over to Dirty's uncle, Troop's, house out Lansdowne and spending the night over there.

Now Troop was a true "O.G.", Tremaine and Dirty always said he was nothing like them fake ass niggas in their hood. Troop had done three different bits in Hagerstown prison and was now "retired", as he would say, from the streets. He was now working a regular nine to five as a maintenance man at M&T stadium where all the football games for the Ravens were played. Even though he wasn't in the streets anymore, he would still get a kick out of other niggas doing dirt. Troop even got one of the dudes from around the way to melt down Tremaine's dirty gun for three hundred dollars before they spent the rest of the night smoking that haze and mixing Grey Goose with Moscato.

As the night wore on, Troop, Tremaine, and Dirty got high as shit. Tremaine found himself not giving what happened earlier that day with Zeke a second thought. It wasn't the first time that he had banged on a nigga. There were two prior incidents, but this was the first time that he had actually gotten up close and personal on someone. The two previous incidents resulted in a little blood shed but no one was killed.

The first time was when he was coming from The Paradox, a popular eighteen and over club in South Baltimore. The Bouncer at the door was from the hood, so showing I.D. was not an issue. After spending the night partying with Juice and a few other dudes from the hood they ended up following some niggas on 295 highway that were doing a whole lot of stunting in the club that night. The niggas were at least fifteen deep and clearly had Tremaine, Juice, and their three homeboys were out numbered. After the party, the main five that they wanted to catch slipping just so happened to pile up in the same car to leave. When Juice pulled up on the left side of them on the highway, Tremaine was the one who leaned out of the passenger window and open fired on the car, which ended up running off of the road, up on the curb, and into the field of grass at the Westport exit of the highway. When Tremaine watched the news the next morning, it said that two of the occupants were in critical condition and the other three were stable. Those niggas got wet, but didn't drown. The crazy thing about this story was that the news stated that after the car became immobilized, some lil niggas from Westport came like they was gonna help them and robbed them niggas for everything they had, cell phones and all.

The second incident came up when he opened fire on a crowd of niggas up Gilmor projects on a basketball court. A few of the niggas on the court had jumped lil' Chris a few days earlier when he went around there to visit his grandmother. That incident was nothing but a few shoulder wounds and a couple of head grazes. Once again niggas got wet, but didn't drown. Even though Zeke was Tremaine's first murder it wasn't on his mind how he thought it would be, he didn't really feel anything. It wasn't like in the movies when a muthafucka would kill somebody and the visual constantly plays back over and over in their heads from the moment the murder took place. Shit, that incident just seemed to have passed like any other ordinary incident that would have took place in their hood.

6 ALL IN DA GAME

Several months had gone by since the incident with Zeke and nothing ever came of it. Tremaine heard that word on the street was that Zeke had a few brothers from Greenmount that were supposedly looking for him. *Shit, if they were then they weren't doing a very good job of it*, he thought since he still came through the hood on a weekly basis. It was as if he made it his business to come through there more now than ever, for the simple fact that them bitch ass niggas showed him that they were whores when they froze up, they didn't even attempt to retaliate.

Tremaine already had it in his mind that he was about to lock that whole strip down. Dollar was Tremaine's ears on the street. After that incident with Zeke, Dollar started bitching the shit out of them older niggas. To be so young, Dollar was going dick hard. A few hoodrats had told Tremaine how Dollar leaned on all of them old heads one night, calling them all types of bitches in front of the whole hood. He told them that if anyone of them had anything on their chest toward him that it was whatever with them and that they could bring it how they wanted to. The girls were saying that the people out there were talking about the only reason why Dollar showed his ass like that was because Tremaine is his cousin.

That wasn't the case because everyone knew damn well that Dollar was a bona fide goon and that he could hold his own at the young age of thirteen. He was letting his little nuts hang and wasn't going for nothing. He had stopped stealing cars and purchased his own hooptie, an Oldsmobile Delta 88. He even improved on his driving skills. Since business was doing pretty good Tremaine, Dirty, and Dollar decided to get their own apartment up Greenspring. It was a nice three bedroom spot that Los had turned them on to. Tremaine got one of the older bitches he was dealing with to sign all of the paperwork in order for them to move in.

Tremaine and his mom's became cool, despite the fact that she now know that he is out there in the streets doing him. All she asked of him was that he graduate from high school. She didn't have to worry about that, Tremaine knew that the least he could for his mother was finish school, besides that's where all the females were. Some of the lames there were as green as grass; Tremaine would sell them eight balls and quarter ounces for $120 and $250 respectively. The same way Fat Bird was taxing him when he first started out, Tremaine was taxing his classmates.

The trips up N.Y. weren't as frequent as before because Manny had opened a car dealership in D.C. and his cousin Randy, who ran the dealership, would have some of the coke over there with him half of the time. Tremaine was now purchasing half of kilograms, 18 ounces, from Manny or Randy for eleven thousand. He would take that to Josanda and she would blow it up to twenty-seven ounces for him. He would sell all of that in weight, with the exception of the four ounces he would break down for his loyal customers, and make between twenty three and twenty four thousand back.

Tremaine no longer had his TL; he had given it to lil' Chris right before he went out and copped himself a 2003 745 BMW. The look on certain niggas faces when he pulled up on the block was enough to let him know he was sitting up for real. The car was charcoal grey with black leather seats. It had charcoal grey wood grain, and the tint

on it

throug...

Som...
the hood b...
taken them ...
birthday, he g...
before, then the...
in his face, espe...
knew all along they...

The grandmoth...
Tremaine. Ms. Pearl,
would sit on their balc...   ...d
drinking Hennessy and C...   ...nn near
an entire carton of cigarette...   ...o get Tremaine
up on one of those balconie...   ...with them. Sometimes
if he knew for sure that he w...   ...in the hood for a few hours,
Tremaine would go buy each of them a half gallon of whatever it was
they wanted for that day. Afterwards he would sit and chill with the
grandmothers and laugh at them while they told old stories and
cursed each other out over their card games. They would open up
their homes to him when the police would come through fucking
with niggas on the block. Those old ladies had a deep hatred for the
police just as everyone else in the hood.

A lot of the residents said that they felt a lot safer with the hood
niggas hanging out on the block than they did with the police's
presence. Tremaine was a little mesmerized by their thoughts, but he
could understand it because it was all 'hood around there and
everybody knew everybody. Ms. Pearl and the rest of the older
women knew that they didn't have to worry about anyone trying to
rob them or anything like that while all of the lil niggas were out
there. Even if one of the crackheads out there got to geeking for a
quick fix and decided to break up into someone's apartment to steal a
T.V., VCR or something of the sort, before the night was over, word

DHammond Publishing presents... The pe... would be out about who did it because once ... and everybody knew everybody. Even tho... most were the hood... living in they saw themselv... projects they type w... be the ones ... Their type ... kids. Th... littl...

gain it was all 'hood'

le who were harassed the

ugh they were too good to be

ugh they lived in the heart of the

s as being better than everybody else.

s easy to spot in the projects because they would

o didn't want their kids outside playing with the other

ey were the main ones who would call the police for every

thing that happened, making themselves to be targeted as victims. Whenever a crackhead started fiending and did pull a B&E job, the ol' too good for the 'hood' family would be their first choice since no one cared for them anyway. They didn't give any respect therefore they didn't receive any in return.

7 GRINDIN'

It has been almost two years now and things were beginning to get more hectic in the hood, more so than usual. Lil' Black, who used to hustle out in front of Casino liquor store, had shot Benny. Word on the street was that Benny kept spreading rumors about how the niggas around there were snitching.

"Them niggas tellin' I know it. Everytime O.C.D. run down on them they're always right back on the streets or not getting locked up at all," is what Benny has been saying.

Benny had basically been talking out of the side of his neck because he didn't know the full set up of their operation. He wasn't aware of how the old man would let them stash their drugs in his store, and that if they ever did get caught with anything it was never more than one or two stones, just enough to get them through their next sale. Their big stash was always inside of the store to prevent them from having to keep a lot of coke on them.

Word on the street was that lil' Black walked up to Benny's front door, no mask, no nothing, and just knocked on it. When Benny answered the door, Black opened fire; he wet him up with a .45, putting six shots into Benny's chest and stomach. What was unbelievable is the fact that Benny didn't die. He did, however, end up being on life support for two months before pulling though. If you asked anyone in the hood though, Benny would have been better off dead. The shots had caused him to be paralyzed on the whole left side, which had shriveled up to nothing but skin and bones.

That wasn't even the fucked up part about it. What really threw everyone for a loop was when Benny crawled his cripple ass up on the stand and testified against Black. He pointed Lil' Black out and basically paved the way for the life plus twenty year sentence that Black was handed by the judge. A lot of niggas were trying to get at Benny to finish his ass off when word got out that he was snitching. After he got shot, Benny seemed to have up and disappeared without a trace. No one ever saw him until the day of the trial, afterwards he vanished once again.

Another incident that played a part in getting rid of some of the useless, dead weight around the hood was when Dollar finally fed the demons he had brewing in his little body. He ended up killing Foots one night after Foots pulled the same stunt that he had before, when he whooped crackhead Bruce's ass for wanting to cop from us instead of him. This time was a little different though, the fiend was on his way to pay Dollar some money that he owed him when Foots jumped out there. The fiend tried to explain this to Foots but Foots wasn't trying to hear that. He went in the fiend's pockets anyway and took his money. When Foots took that money, Dollar took it as a sign of disrespect. He felt as if Foots had bitched him personally instead of the crackhead.

Later that night Dollar waited for Foots to leave the strip and followed him downtown to a 24 hour food spot called Upper Deck, where he stopped to get something to eat. Little did he know that the chicken box he ordered would be his last meal. As Foots stepped back out of the carry-out with a chicken wing in one hand and a bag of food in the other, he failed to see Dollar hiding on side of the store in the parking lot. While heading towards his car, Dollar ran down on him with his gun blazing. He left Foots' brains all on the side of his car as he damn near emptied the entire sixteen round clip into his head. Foots' family was forced to have his funeral with a closed casket.

As a result of Lil' Black and Dollar's trigger fingers, Tremaine and his homeboys had the block exactly where they wanted it. Black Ty and a few of the other oldheads began straying away from the strip slowly but surely. The ones who didn't leave chose to ride with them instead of colliding with them. Fremont Avenue began bringing in straight cash for Tremaine. He was the coke distributor for everyone on the block. Fiends knew that no matter who they went to and no matter what time of the day it was, they would get that good shit.

Dollar was holding it down on the home front while Dirty had begun to post up in Juice's neighborhood on Calhoun Street, making sure things were running smooth in that area since Tremaine had recently opened up shop around there. It wasn't hard for him to move in on certain areas and get niggas out there to cop from him especially since he have family from around there, not to mention he had the best crack for the same prices as the garbage they were used to buying. Tremaine had spent almost as much time on Calhoun Street as he did on Fremont Avenue while growing up and once other niggas that he knew up there caught wind that he had that good shit, it was on. It was a must that Dirty watched over Juice's shoulder since he couldn't be trusted enough to watch over an entire drug strip due to his pill popping habit.

Truth be told, Juice was in the streets slacking and not taking this shit serious, mainly because he had no real need to be out there in the first place. His mother and father were taking care of him more so than ever since he was in his last year of high school. They had plans for him to go to college and beyond, and knowing this, Tremaine would try to convince him that there was no need to indulge in the lifestyle they were in. He even took the initative to have Lisa try and talk some sense into Juice but it was all for nothing.

Things were definitely looking up for Tremaine and his homeboys especially after adding Calhoun Street to their resume. Dollar came up with an idea to extend their hands into an apartment complex in Lansdowne called Lakebrook Circle. Nadine, a girl that he was fucking, had put him on to the spot where she lived. The complex was a nice size and it was already an up and running drug strip but the dudes out there who were hustling had small stones and the coke was garbage, as usual, compared to what Tremaine had. After checking the spot out himself he confirmed what he had been told about the complex. Tremaine decided to orchestrate a plan that would really get the area jumping.

After hollering at Nadine, Tremaine was able to get a profile on all of the hustlers in that complex. There were six main hustlers around there and they ranged from the ages seventeen to twenty. Nadine told him the one who had the most paper out of the crew, who went the hardest, as well as who was supplying them with their crack. Nadine supplied them with all the information that a muthafucka could get on any neighborhood, if they took the chance to get in good with one of the hoodrats or fiends around there.

Initially, Tremaine thought about just forcing his way into the complex and setting up shop with the mentality that if any of the niggas around there said anything, or acted as if they wanted some drama then they would get buried. He then decided against it, not wanting to disrupt the opportunity to get more potential money by leaving bodies littered in the area. That would make things hot and bring the police in the area before any real money was even made. Taking a more subtle approach is what Tremaine decided to do.

The first thing Tremaine did was send Lil' Chris into Lansdowne complex and had him go to their recreational center everyday for two weeks. Chris was a monster in basketball and the boys in that area went to the rec center on a regular. Tremaine figured that after Chris burned their asses on the court a few times, they would slowly but surely warm up to him.

After those two weeks, Tremaine sent Forty to begin accompanying Chris to the rec. Now forty was pretty good in basketball but that wasn't the reason for his appearance. Forty was a young knockout artist. The fact that he was nice with his hands was useful in the next phase of Tremaine's plan.

It was explained to Forty that he was to start a fight with Boogie, the so called leader of the crew in the complex. Tremaine knew that after Forty whooped Boogie's ass none of the other niggas out there would try to jump out there with him. Forty was to make sure that before he got into it with Boogie that he pulled his burner out and hand it to Chris, making sure all the other boys out there saw it. That way the rest of them would know that Forty was willing to punish them with his hands or burners, it didn't matter.

Just as Tremaine thought, everything went smooth. Lil' Chris burned them up on the court, and afterwards Forty challenged Boogie to a one-on-one game for one hundred dollars. After losing the game on purpose, Forty flat out told him "I ain't payin' you shit!" One thing led to another and the two ended up exchanging blows. Forty did what he did best and split the entire bottom of Boogie's left eye, not to mention he that he stomped him while he was down. All this occurred while Boogie's homeboys sat looking from the sidelines not believing that they were witnessing their homeboy get his ass whooped.

After that incident, them boys in that complex didn't want any trouble at all, they were on Chris and Forty's dick. With the passing of five months and being out Lakebrook Circle a few nights out of the week, Forty and Chris got to know all of the fiends in the area so they decided to lease an apartment on the premises. There was definitely money to be made in the area especially since they replaced that garbage with that potent shit. Their new strip became capable of going through nearly a kilogram a week strictly with hand to hand sales.

Just when it seemed like everything was everything in the complex, one person had to come along and start some bullshit. One of the boys who lived in the newly acquired complex had an uncle named Pee, who was supplying the area before Tremaine and his homeboys took it over.

Pee was from Cherry Hill. He heard that Lakebrook was jamming more than ever. This news had him in a frenzy because it made him realize just how long its been since niggas up there bought weight from him. In turn, he called himself getting retribution the best way that he knew how. He began to bring a few of those wild ass niggas from Cherry Hill to rob different muthafuckas in the complex; they did other little dumb shit too. For example, they would ride through shooting their guns in the air, not at anyone in particular. They were just doing it to make it hot around there, forcing the police patrol the area, to slow up progress. Tremaine had his mind made up, if that nigga wanted to play these weak-ass games he definitely had something for him; it was no question about that.

Pee's nephew that lived in the complex was a young nigga by the name of Blue. He was a regular out there with Chris and Forty, so Tremaine already knew that his plan wouldn't be hard to follow through with. The plan was for Chris to pick up Blue on a late night with a few bitches to take to the motel. After fucking with the bitches, Chris was to tell Blue that he needed to buy a six-deuce of crack that night to take care of something but his regular connect didn't have anything at the time. He was instructed to tell Blue to call Pee in an attempt to buy the product from him.

Tremaine planned the set up for a weeknight. He preferred a late Tuesday night; Tremaine figured that a nigga who sold weight in the crack game would be in the house at least by 12 a.m. If they weren't at their own spot, they were definitely in somebody's house. There wasn't too much jumping off on a cold ass Tuesday night in February.

Tremaine thought this plan out thoroughly but it had one glitch that could fuck up the whole plan. He needed Pee to have the crack on deck to sell it to him right then and there. The bonus would be for him to allow Blue to come to his house in order to pick it up. Needless to say Tremaine went along with his plan, hoping that it would work out how he arranged that it would.

Chris executed the plan perfectly. He got the two biggest freaks he knew, he paid them to fuck and suck Blue every way imagineable. Afterwards, he brought up the six-deuce issue and convinced Blue to call his uncle.

I'll be damned if Pee dumb ass didn't fall straight into the trap. He said he was in the house for the night and that if Blue wanted the coke he would have to come pick it up. He broke one of the biggest codes of the street: NEVER SELL NO CRACK WHERE YOU REST AT! You don't make any exceptions for no one, not even your right hand man. You tell him to meet you at a gas station, a corner store, anywhere but your house. If a muthafucka didn't feel like coming out of the house, then a muthafucka wouldn't get served, simple as that. Blue had no clue that he had just signed his uncle's deathcertificate.

8 NOW IT'S PERSONAL

As Tremaine and Dirty sat in the crowded parking lot of what appears to be some expensive ass condominiums, Tremaine sat behind the wheel staring at a piece of paper with an address written on it. After double checking the address, he felt confident that they were at the right place. The condos consisted of the address that Chris had given to him; this is where Blue directed Chris to take him the night before. Tremaine noticed that the parking lot had two black Lexus GS400's, one of which belonged to Pee. Lil' Chris had already put him on the car that the man drove; he also gave full a description of him from all of the times he would come up Lakebrook Circle to holler at Blue.

Once Chris gave Tremaine the directions, him and Dirty went and posted up at five o' clock that next morning. They were sitting in the parking lot waiting for Pee ass to show his face in the early morning light. They had it in their heads that they would sit in that parking lot for as long as it took to complete their mission.

The two Lexus' were parked on opposite ends of the parking lot so Tremaine positioned their vehicle in the middle of the lot so that he could watch them both with ease. He and Dirty were in a Grey Caravan with tinted windows that was purchased at an auction

89

almost four months ago. They brought the Caravan along with a number of other cheap cars for miscellaneous purposes. Sometimes Tremaine would use them as stash spots or just have them parked in different areas of the city that he had work in, just in case he needed to get out of a jam. He never knew when he would need one of the cheap cars for something but on this particular morning it definitely came in handy.

The first Lexus was owned by a white man, who came out of the building a little after seven. That only meant one thing; the second Lexus was the one that they were looking for. Tremaine moved a little closer to it and waited for that nigga to show his face.

"Yo, where the fuck is this nigga at?" Dirty asked, letting out a yawn.

Tremaine couldn't help but to let out a yawn and stretch himself. "I dont know, but I know this nigga slippin' like shit for real."

"Why you say that?"

"Man, check this out alright? Since we been out here who's been comin' out of the front of this building?" Tremaine asked.

"What you mean by who?" Dirty asked, with a confused look on his face.

"Crackers nigga! That's who," Tremaine responded, "This nigga livin' in some condos out here in Elkridge, in this cracker part of town. He pushing a Lex, he a black man, and he don't work. Now it's only a matter of time before one of these white folks start getting a lil nosey, like they always do; they gon fuck around and have one of their redneck ass police friends check this nigga out. If his ass was on point he would be getting up early and leavin' out at least fakin' like he's going to work." *Niggas kill me for real,* Tremaine thought as he shook his head.

A lot of dudes that's in the streets seemed to amaze Tremaine, their whole train of thought be fucked up. Knowing the type of lifestyle that they have, they will move into neighborhoods like this with nothing but uptight ass white people. They actually think that they could come and go as they please without drawing any attention to themselves. Tremaine felt this strong about the situation because he always believed that in order to stay one step ahead of nosey folks, you had to get up and leave their home at six o'clock each morning in a suit and tie.

Los talked to Tremaine about a lot of the dos and dont's of the game during their many travels up and down the highway. That was one of the main subjects that stuck in Tremaine's head. He explained to him that you can not take ghetto ways and mentalities to an enriched neighborhood full of white folks. He stressed to Tremaine that the shit was a no-no, and that if he did, him and his illegal money would stick out like a sore thumb, better yet a black thumb.

"What difference do it make where dis nigga live?" Dirty asked.

"I'm just sayin' the way this nigga' out here slippin', it's only a matter of time before the feds snatch him up," Explained Tremaine.

Dirty shrugged his shoulders with a grin on his face, "we sending the nigga to paradise or hell or wherever the fuck he's going, either way is better than doing twenty-five years on lock you feel me? Shit, this nigga should pay us for helping his ass out."

Tremaine couldn't help but laugh, Dirty would say some of the craziest shit and the crazy part about it was that he would be dead serious about what he said. In a way Tremaine knew that Dirty was telling the truth, he knew that Dirty personally would rather for someone to put two in the back of his head as oppose to doing a quarter century behind bars.

"I know one thing, I wish this fool come the fuck on because this parking lot is starting to get a lil' empty and this raggedy ass caravan gonna stick out in a minute inside of this bourgeois ass neighborhood," Tremaine said.

"What if that Lex ain't even his? I'ma be mad as shi..."

"Hold up Yo, I think that's the nigga right there!" Tremaine said while tapping Dirty and nodding his head towards the front of the building.

It was ten thirty in the morning and Tremaine figured that it had to be their target since he was the first black man to come out of the building in jeans and Nike boots. The previous two black men that he saw exit the building were dressed in suits and ties. The man that he was looking at also matched the description that lil' Chris had given him.

When he began walking towards the Lexus, Tremaine and Dirty both knew that it had to be him and patiently waited for him to get inside of the car. Tremaine started up the caravan and drove slowly, with the twelve gauge pistol grip shotgun in his lap. He stopped behind the parked Lexus on Dirty's side of the van. Dirty calmly got out with the Tec-9 in his grips and approached the driver's side window from the rear.

Just as Tremaine turned his head to make sure there wasn't any witnesses in the parking lot, Dirty began to open fire through the glass window. The first shot caught the driver on the left side of his face, and through the Lexus' back window Tremaine could see his left hand raise in shock as he automatically latched his hand to the burning sensation on his face. Dirty then began to fire in a rapid series with the impact of the hollow points pushing the body clear into the passager seat. The last five or six shots connected with nothing but head and neck. Finally, Dirty leaned in through the shattered window and placed four more shots directly into the side of the victim's lifeless head.

Tremaine once again scanned the parking lot to make sure no one was watching. Most of the cars had long left with the drivers heading out to their destinations. Dirty jogged back to the caravan, after firing no less than fifteen shots close range.

Afterwards, he and Tremaine drove to Columbia and set the caravan on fire before getting back into Dirty's GMC Yukon and heading home to Baltimore. They no longer had any problems with the complex and that muthafucka was pumping so hard that there were fiends coming from as far as twenty miles away in order to get the quality crack that the complex provided.

A few days after the condo shooting, Tremaine decided to call Los. It had been almost two weeks since the last time they had spoken. He and Los no longer had to go and cop their coke together. Tremaine had basically built his own relationship with Randy and Manny and no longer needed Los to be the bridge between the two for him.

"Hello"

"Los, what's up cuz?"

"Shit, what's going on young gunner?"

"Ain't shit yo, what's going on, where you at?" Tremaine asked.

"I'm out Towson right, but I'm bout to head to another mall and shit. Why, where you at?"

"I'm in the house right now but what mall you 'bout to head to?"

"Probably down Pentagon City. What's up you tryin' to go wit' me?" Los asked.

"I don't know, I got some shit to take care of," Tremaine lied.

In all actuality he was making the day a laid back day as he and Dirty were in the process of getting high and were just starting to get fucked up.

"Come on yo, a nigga ain't seen your ass in a minute, got damn! What you got some bitches over there or somethin'?" Los asked.

"Nah, it's just me and Dirty."

"Alright, well look I'm 'bout to come to scoop ya'll niggas up then," Los persisted.

"Hold up let me holla at Dirty." Tremaine removed the phone from his ear and placed it on his chest. "Hey yo … Dirty!" He yelled out.

Dirty was inhaling the haze with his eyes closed, slowly letting the smoke trickle out of his mouth as he inhaled it through his nose. He finally opened his blood- shot eyes halfway and asked in a slow and low voice, "What's up?"

"You tryin' to go shoppin' wit' Los?" Tremaine asked.

"When?"

"He talkin' 'bout comin' to pick us up right now."

"I don't care, it's whatever," Dirty responded while blowing smoke out of his nose.

Tremaine placed the receiver back to his ear. "Alright. Come on cuz."

"I'll be over there in 'bout thirty minutes," Los responded.

"Alright we'll be here."

With that said, Tremaine hung up. By the time Los arrived to pick them up, he and Dirty both were feeling nice. Tremaine decided to take five stacks in spending money. He had just stunted out on a shopping spree a week before, so he didn't want to spend that much.

The majority of his money was in Linthicum, MD at a little one bedroom apartment that no one knew anything about. It was no more than fifteen minutes away from anywhere that he had business dealings, making it convenient and quick to get to yet, it was away from the 'hood. That was his little getaway spot, the place where he could go for peace and quiet without anyone knowing him. Tremaine was also in the process of getting his own brand new town home that he had to put twenty thousand down on; he was just waiting on his cousin Lisa friend, Tia, to finish all of the paperwork since the home would be in her name. The town house is in Laurel, MD. The neighborhood, from what he'd seen, was basically upper-middle class, and it mainly consisted of an even division of working black and white folks.

He still had his BMW, but he had recently hollered at Randy at the dealership about purchasing a Mercedes Benz Wagon or a Range Rover, either or, it didn't matter. Randy informed him that he would have one of the two for him within the next few weeks. With him currently purchasing two kilos at a time from Randy for the price of Forty thousand, Tremaine was able to whip up fifty-four ounces off of each kilo. Individually, those ounces would be sold for nine hundred dollars, depending on how much he fucked with the person. He would still put a few ounces to the side for his limited clientele of crackheads that he continued to deal with on a hand to hand basis. He had labeled them as 'The Gold Club' because their money was so good. They weren't your average dopefiend in 'The Gold Club', a number of them held job titles. The club consisted of two laywers, an engineer, an architect as well as an owner of a construction company. All in all, Tremaine was now close to pulling in a twenty-thousand dollar profit every week.

When Los came to pick up Tremaine and Dirty, he was driving a midnight black C500 Mercedes Benz with dark grey leather interior. *This mufucka' killing niggas softly for real,* Tremaine thought. Seeing that Benz had him thirsty for Randy to call him and let him know that his new whip had come in. When they arrived at the mall, just like Tremaine knew he would, Los was stunting his ass off. It was cool though because he and Dirty weren't too far behind him.

The whole time that they were in the mall they were tripping off a few females in particular who "just so happened" to pop up in each and every store they went into. They knew the broads were following them and trying to get their attention, but they didn't pay them any mind. They wanted to see just how far the girls would go. The females began getting a little loud in the stores while saying slick shit like, "Girl, I'll fuck his brains out!" And "There ain't too many niggas who can handle this pussy!" They would say it loud enough for Tremaine, Los, and Dirty to hear. Each time one of them looked over at the girls they would act as if they weren't directing their conversation towards them.

Now to be truthful, all three females were phat as shit but on that particular day, they were on some other shit. Any other day they would have had them three broads in a hotel, no less than an hour after meeting them. But that day they didn't feel like being bothered with any females.

Spring break became the main topic of discussion, which was coming up in a few weeks, and what they were planning to do for it. After going back and forth, the choices were narrowed down to South Beach, New Mexico or Florida. Either or, all three spots would be flooded with females. There will be so many college females trying to get wasted, get fucked and party for a week straight.

The decision was finally made to go to South Beach after Dirty brought up the fact that he had seen a program on television that did a special during Spring break. He said that the program talked about most of the people from the colleges down South chose South Beach and that was all niggas needed to know. Nothing sounds better than a little fun in the sun with the females from Georgia, North Carolina and Texas. The thought of all those nice and thick country females, it didn't take a rocket scientist to figure out where to go.

After leaving the mall Tremaine, Los, and Dirty saw no need in procrastinating, so they headed back to Baltimore to a travel agency office. They purchased a vacation package for six to South Beach, which was enough for Tremaine, Dirty, Dollar, Los and his two homies Mike-Mike and L.B. The package consisted of a six day five night stay that included hotel, air fare, meals and two rental cars all for a little under ten thousand dollars.

The last few weeks before the vacation were excellent for Tremaine. He made almost fifty-two thousand dollars in profit, plus Randy had gotten back at him with a sky blue Mercedes Benz Wagon with cream colored leather seats. It came fully loaded and already had a Bose system installed. Randy charged him forty thousand for it and in Tremaine's eyes; it was worth every penny as he put the cash in Randy's hand. Also, his townhouse papers were complete; once the carpet, hardwood, tile, and the final painting is finished, he would be ready to move in. Everything would be ready for sure by the time he returned from South Beach.

Initially, Tremaine was a little reluctant to go on the Miami trip. His main reason was that he would miss out on all of that potential money. He quickly retracted those thoughts and figured that it truly was time for his first vacation. The farthest he had been was N.Y., so it was definitely time to see a little bit more of the world. To make sure that his paper continued to flow, he gave all of his clientele double in quantity of what he normally would have, with firm instructions for them to make sure they had his money when he returned that following week.

9 SPRING BREAK

After much anticipation, the break finally came and it was time for the fellas to get their South Beach freak on. They were scheduled to catch their flight at two in the morning and Tremaine, Dirty, and Dollar were drowning shots of 1738 and blowing big chocolate ditches of purple haze that they copped from his man Lil Aches on McKean and Baker. Neither of them had ever flown anywhere before so this trip was big for them.

They all went down Chevy Chase, Maryland and stunted out for the South Beach trip. First stop was the Gucci shop, they already had the old green and red Gucci belts. So for the trip, they copped the new all white Gucci belts, two hats, and six Gucci shirts. A piece for every day that they were going to be down there. Tre copped two pair of Gucci tennis to match a few of his pieces, while Dirty and Dollar bought matching Gucci watches. Tre bought one of Los's Brightons, which was a good look for him. After that, they all hit the Burberry shop in bought some linen shorts so their nuts can breathe. To say the lease, they were all feeling themselves.

When they boarded the plane Tremaine, Dirty, and Dollar had each forgotten all about their fears of flying since the Remy was doing it's job. Tremaine found himself anxious for that plane to get it's ass in the air. Flying the friendly skies wasn't so bad after all, Tremaine soon discovered as he and his partners lounged in their first class seats nibbling on shrimp cocktails along with fruit patters. After almost two hours of being in the air, Los hollered over to Tremaine and asked him to come and switch seats with L.B. so that he could talk to him about something. As Tremaine sat down, he could see that Los was buzzing a little bit himself from the Vodka Martinis that were being served on the plane.

"Nigga, I see them weak ass Martinis creepin' up on yo' ass, ain't they?" Tremaine joked.

"Oh nah nah, I'm cool," Los spoke with a slight slur in his voice.

"Yeah whatever yo, I been watching you go hard on these glasses."

"Yeah, these mufuckas are starting to talk to a nigga," Los admitted with a grin.

"Oh, I already see that, you ain't got to tell me. Nigga don't be running to the hotel room trying to go to sleep when we get there, either." Tremaine began to laugh because he knew Los was feeling his liquor more than he was letting on.

"Shit, I got me a fresh box of NoDoze for that. If I wanted to sleep I could have stayed my ass at home, you feel me?"

"Yeah how 'bout that, but what's up tho'?" Tremaine asked.

"Nah I wanted to holla at you 'bout something," Los said as he sat his reclining seat up and leaned towards Tremaine.

"What's up?" Tremaine responded sitting his seat up as well.

"Yo, you wouldn't happen to know anything 'bout a nigga getting killed in his Lex' last month out in Elkridge would you?" Los was staring Tremaine in his eyes as if he was trying to detect some type of lie or hesitation on his part.

Tremaine was definitely caught off guard. He wondered if Los had seen his brain lock up as he became stuck for a millisecond. He quickly got his composure back.

"Nah yo, why what's up? Why you ask me that?"

"It ain't nothing heavy, it's just one of the niggas who used to cop from me from Cherry Hill that got killed and I thought you might have heard something," Los responded nonchalantly as he reclined his chair backwards once again.

Tremaine was trying to mask his frustrations because he knew Los didn't think he could ask him some shit like that and then act like he was going to drop it as if he had just asked for a piece of gum or something. Hell No!!!

"For real cuz, why you ask me that?" Tremaine pressed on.

"The only reason I asked is because a few weeks ago I was around the way and a couple of lil' niggas were out there talking about Paris." Tremaine knew from reading the newspaper the day after the murder, that was the niggaa's real name that Dirty had killed.

Los continued, "and nigga's was talkin' 'bout how Pee was taking them out Lansdowne to this lil' apartment complex to lay niggas down and shit. They were basically reminiscing and shit. They think that one of them niggas might have killed him. But I found out the spot they were talking about in Lansdowne was the niggas you be fuckin' wit' and I figured you might have heard something about it. For real, I don't think it was somebody he knew that killed him for the simple fact that Pee had seventeen thousand on him when he got killed and everybody he fucked with knew the nigga kept at least fifteen on him at all times in his car," Los paused,

"I used to always tell him to stop carrying that much money around wit' him but that was just how he was. But anyway, the person who smashed him didn't even bother to take the money so I figured it had to be somebody who didn't know him like that and didn't know that he had all that paper he would keep on him on a daily," Los said with expressions that showed he was harboring deep feelings about the topic.

"So what you think, I had something to do with that shit?" Tremaine asked feigning to be offended.

"Nah nah…" Los responded shaking his head. "I thought you might have heard one of them Lansdowne niggas talking 'bout that shit, that's all. On some real shit, if you did hear something then fuck it, he deserved that shit anyway wit' that bullshit he was doing out there wit' his bitch ass." Los shrugged his shoulders as if he didn't care but it was too late, Tremaine could see that he was holding back more than what he was telling.

Due to the fact that Tremaine was a little drunk himself from the drinks on the plane as well as the Remy he already had in him, he didn't really think too hard about what Los had just said to him. He did, however, make a mental note to meditate on their conversation a little later since he knew there was a lot more to it than what Los was exposing.

When the group arrived in South Beach, it was in the early morning hours and the weather was already a warm, eight-five degrees outside. The fellas had received their rental cars along with directions to their hotel. Once there, they decided to shower and change before heading out to the hotel's pool where there were a number of people already out and about. By three in the afternoon of that first day, the hotel festivities were in rare form and the females were out in abundance. There were ladies of all races walking around with bikinis on, looking phat as shit in the ass.

Their first night there, Tremaine and his crew ran into a group of girls that were from the University of Tennessee. There were nine of them and each female in the pack was at least a low eight, physically. They just so happened to be staying in the same hotel as them, and had rooms exactly two floors under them. With three rooms between the six of them, Dollar and Dirty's rooms were adjacent to Tremaine's and Los with L.B. and Mike-Mike's room being directly across the hall from the two.

On that first night, Los called the Tennessee bitches from the phone in his and Tremaine's room. After spitting some of that pretty boy game that he possessed to one of the girls, Los was able to persuade all nine of them to come up to their rooms.

Waiting for the females were a few bottles of already chilled Dom P., Alize', and Grey Goose. The girls brought some haze with them and after an hour of smoking, sipping, and flirting, the spot turned into an all out fuck party. L.B. took three of the girls across the hall to his and Mike-Mike's room leaving six behind with their four homeboys.

The entire scenario held a strong resemblance to a wild-ass freak movie that one might see on Cinemax, late night. Everyone was ass naked as they made sure to keep all of the lights on in the two rooms. Tremaine had one female riding on top of him reverse cow girl style while another girl was sitting on his face and leaning forward to lick the ass of the girl on his dick. Next, the girl on his face got up to go into Dirty and Dollar's room in turn passing another female coming out of their room who was ass naked. The girl from Dirty's room then headed straight to Los' bed which was already occupied by him and another girl. One of the ladies grabbed a sheet and wrapped it around her naked body before heading across the hall to L.B.'s room, only to have another one return from their room with a sheet wrapped around her.

The entire time, there were naked women coming and going. After three hours of the fuck fest, them niggas came at least twice and was still going strong. While Tremaine was in the middle of getting his dick sucked by a thick and juicy, dark-skinned female, he took an interest in her and wanted to know her name. He did know one thing though and that was that Grey Goose wasn't to be fucked with. That Goose had these bitches loose as a muthafucka.

None of the other nights could hold a candle to that first night in South Beach. The boys had been up in a few other females on some one on one shit, they even ran a train on these three girls that they met from Georgia Tech, but nothing could compare to that initial night. On their last night, they wanted another night like their first night so they decided to find those Tennessee bitches.

While downstairs in the hotel's outside bar, they decided to get a few drinks in the hopes of stumbling across the Tennessee pack while sitting there. In the meantime, they were all hollering at other females so they could have a back up.

As Tremaine, Los, Dollar, L.B, and Mike-Mike sat in the corner booth with a round table in front of them, Tremaine noticed L.B. was downing shots of Hennessey with his Moet and the nigga just wouldn't shut the fuck up. He we went on and on about any and everything that came to his mind and that's when Tremaine came up with an idea. When L.B got up to use the bathroom for what seemed like the umpteenth time, Tremaine went with him. He knew L.B was always out Cherry Hill with Los and figured that since he was in a talkative mood he would pick his brain to see what he knew about the whole Paris situation.

"Damn nigga you fucked up for real," Tremaine joked as he and L.B. stood side by side at the urinals taking a piss.

"Shit, I'm alright. I'm just getting a buzz, dat's all," he responded, drunk as a bitch.

"Man, a nigga needed this here vacation for real," Tremaine said.

"Shit, who you tellin'? This joint was definitely needed 'cause shit been hectic lately," L.B. said.

"Yeah, I feel you. My man just got killed last month and that shit still fuckin wit' a nigga." Tremaine threw out the bait just to see if L.B. would bite.

"Oh yeah? Where he get kilt' at?" L.B. asked.

Got him! Tremaine thought. "He got smashed out Elkridge but you might know him because he used to be out ya'll end. His name was Pee."

"Pee... Pee..." L.B. was trying to remember where he knew that name from.

"Los knew him," Tremaine added as he began to wash his hands.

"Oh yeah, now I know who you're talking 'bout. That was Los man, real talk!"

L.B. had now joined Tremaine at the bathroom sink.

"Yeah, he told me he used to fuck with yo."

"Hell yeah! Los don't like talkin'bout that shit but mufuckas tell me they were like this." L.B. held up his soapy hand and crossed two of his fingers to demonstrate how tight they were.

"Like that since they were about twelve," he continued.

"Yeah I heard." Tremaine deliberately talked less in order to coach L.B. onto talk more.

"Hell yeah, that nigga was fucked up about that shit and still is. He whipped out on some nigga's around the way and all that shit, because word was that one of them set Pee up."

They were both made their way over to the hand dryer before Tremaine decided to speak,

"I'll tell you one thing though whoever did it, that shit is bound to hit the fan sooner or later."

"No bullshit, and when it do I'm tellin' you, yo gonna crush whoever the fuck it is," L.B. said.

Talking about Los right then and there resulted in all of Tremaine's trust for him going out of the window. He knew his gut didn't lie to him when it told him that Los was holding back on his info. *Pee was Los' motherfucking homeboy and if he thought I had something to do with his death, better yet he had to know something for him to come at me like that. I definitely gotta keep my eye on that nigga*, he thought to himself.

Tremaine needed to change the subject with L.B.'s drunk ass before they got back to the table. "Hey yo I know one thing, we gotta find them Tennessee bitches before the nights out," he said.

"Hell yeah 'cause the broad wit' the blond ponytail can suck the shit out of a dick. I'm tellin' you yo, the broad..."

Tremaine stopped paying any attention to what L.B. was saying as they made their way back to the table because his mind was on Los and what that nigga was up to.

After having a few more drinks, they all decided to go to Wet Willies to find their plan B bitches because the Tennessee broads were nowhere to be found. As they were leaving their table, Tremaine and Dirty decided to stop at the bar to get one last drink to take with them. While they were waiting to be served Tremaine could have sworn that he heard someone call him by his real name.

He then heard it again. When he turned around, he stood face to face with one of the most beautiful dark-brown skinned females that he had ever seen. She wore a pair of tight jean capris with a sky blue bikini top. The top matched the blue Aldo sandals she wore on her feet with the straps that criss crossed around her ankle. Her long wavy black hair was combed back, reaching a few inches pass her shoulder. She resembled Maia Campbell, the girl who played on LL Cool J's show T.V. show, "In the House." There was something about her face, but Tremaine just couldn't put his finger on it.

"What's up boy?" she asked.

"Ain't shit, what's up?" Tremaine was staring at her awkwardly still trying to remember where he knew her from.

"You don't remember me do you?" she said sounding a little disappointed.

He looked at her one more time trying to figure out exactly where he knew her from. "I'm sayin' you do look familiar but I just can't remember your name."

"It's me, Khalilah."

"Khalilah?" The name did not ring a bell with Tremaine.

"Khalilah Turner." She said standing with her arms folded as to say "Nigga you better remember me."

It then hit Tremaine. Khalilah Turner was his childhood girlfriend from around his grandmother's neighborhood on Saratoga and Calhoun Street.

"Oh damn what's up girl," he said reaching out to give her a hug.

"I thought I was going to have to punch you dead in your chest if you didn't remember me boy," she said playfully.

"Oh nah nah, you don't have to do that. I mean, but you can't blame me? You look different as shit girl." Tremaine looked her up and down and realized that time definitely had done her well. Khalilah had filled out in all the right places.

"Hmmph, look at you. I wasn't even sure if it was you or not until you got up and I saw that scar on the back of your neck and then…" Khalilah ran her finger across the scar. "I knew it was you."

She was referring to the scar that Tremaine had gotten one summer when he spent the weekend over his grandmother's house. He was ten years old at the time, he and Juice were climbing under a metal fence. Juice went under first and was supposed to hold up the fence so Tremaine could go under too. Juice let go of the fence claiming it slipped and it scraped the back of Tremaine's neck. He ended up having to get four stitches on the back of his neck and when Khalilah saw him a couple of days later she changed the bandage and cleaned his stitches for him. A few weeks later when Juice came back to visit their grandmother, Khalilah cursed him out something terrible for letting the fence go on Tremaine like that.

"Oh you remember this scar huh?" Tremaine asked.

"Mmm hmm."

"So I take it you're out here for spring break, too?" Tremaine asked staring directly at the gloss on her lips.

"Yeah me and a couple of my girlfriends."

"Where you live now?"

"I stay on campus," she said, "I go to Penn State."

"Oh yeah?" Tremaine then thought about something. "Hold up I'm in the twelfth grade now and don't graduate for another couple of months so how are you in college already?"

He remembered that they were both in the same grade when they were younger.

"I got skipped after the ninth grade and went straight to the eleventh," Khalilah said smiling.

"Oh I heard that lil' Einstein," Tremaine teased, tapping her on her chin with his index finger.

Tremaine could remember that Khalilah had always been real smart, which was one of the main reasons he liked her so much when they were younger. She would fight a boy or girl at the drop of a dime after school but in school, she was all business. She never got in trouble and kept straight A's. After almost forgetting that Dirty was next to him, Tremaine introduced him to Khalilah.

"Yo, this is Khalilah… Khalilah this my man, Dirty."

"What's up? How you doing?" Dirty asked as he looked Khalilah up and down obviously liking what he was seeing.

"Fine," Khalilah responded.

"What's up nigga, you still with Wet Willies with us or what?" Dirty asked.

"Yeah I'll be out there in a minute, I just gotta take care of something," Tremaine responded while looking Khalilah in the eyes.

Dirty stepped off and headed out the door to the cars with the rest of his team.

Tremaine bought him and Khalilah two tropical Long Island ice teas and they went out on the beach alone under the night breeze to catch up on old times. Tremaine found out that Khalilah majored in accounting. They talked about her father getting a new job with higher pay and that being the reason why she moved away. Khalilah told him that she tried to call him from her new house but the operator recording said that his number was out of service. Tremaine could remember around the time that their phone was cut off for over a year when his mother couldn't afford to pay the bill. It had been around the same time that Khalilah had moved.

Their conversation then moved on how much her father hated Tremaine because he thought he was a little bad ass project kid that his daughter was too good for. Khalilah joked about how her father knew about Tremaine's bike stealing operation that he had going on around his grandmother's neighborhood. Back then Tremaine would go a few blocks from his grandmother's house to steal other kids' bike out of their yard or take it from them directly, depending on how nice the bike was. He'd take the bike in the woods and spray paint it. Afterwards, he would sell it to someone in another neighborhood for twenty or thirty dollars. They conversed about a number of things.

Dollar hit Tremaine's phone to him know that they had found the Tennessee bitches in Wet Willies and they were on their way up to their rooms. Tremaine told him that he was cool and for them to go ahead and knock themselves out.

Before Tremaine knew it, he and Khalilah had gone through three tropical Long Island iced teas a piece, they were feeling their drinks as well as eachother.

"Damn it's almost six-thirty in the morning," he said looking at his watch.

"For real? I guess it's true what they say about time flying when you're having fun." Khalilah said while picking up sand in one hand and letting it trickle down into the other.

"Is that right? So I take it you enjoyed the time that you spent with me?" Tremaine asked.

"It was alright," she said rolling her eyes and then cracked a smile. "Sike nah, I always enjoyed talking to you Tremaine, even though you were a little nasty ass boy back then."

"I wasn't hardly nasty, girl so I don't know what you're talking about."

Khalilah looked over at him as if he was crazy. "Boy please, you use to run around touching me, and every other girl around there, on the butt and trying to feel our breasts even though we didn't have any yet."

"Who? I was a good lil nigga back then, I wouldn't do anything like that," Tremaine said lying through his teeth.

"Yeah right, I still remember the time when I was going somewhere with my mother and father and we rode past you in the parking lot. When I looked back at you through the back window, you pulled your pants down and shook your little ass ding-a-ling at me." Khalilah began laughing.

Tremaine couldn't help but laugh with her since he could remember that day clearly. It was around the time he had begun growing his first pubic hairs and he would pull his penis out on any little girl that would look to show his hairs off.

"But did you notice that after I would catch the other girls and feel on them, I would roll out to the next one? But wit' you, I would stay there and rap to you afterwards. Everybody didn't get that type of treatment."

"Is that right?" Khalilah asked.

"For real, I knew that you were the one back then," Tremaine said.

There was a moment of silence between them as they both just sat and gazed at the sun which looked as if it was emerging out of the ocean's water. It wasn't an awkward moment of silence that they shared between them, because in the last few hours they had become very much comfortable with one another. Tremaine and Khalilah had rekindled the same comfort level with one another that they both shared as kids.

"What do you have planned for today?" Khalilah asked.

Tremaine remembered that they were scheduled to leave that day.

"Damn you just reminded me that we're leaving today."

"For real?" Khalilah asked with disappointment in her voice.

"Yeah, When are you and your girlfriends leaving?"

"We don't leave until tomorrow."

That same silence arose, except for that time it was very much awkward as they both contemplated on where or what they would do next.

"I'm sayin, the time that I spent with you tonight has definitely been different you know what I'm sayin'…"

Khalilah then put her finger over Tremaine's lip and leaned forward to kiss him. Memories of the first time they kissed when they were nine years old rushed through Tremaine's mind. He could remember that she had just finished eating a pack of cherry flavored Now & Laters; her tongue still held that sweet flavor. Back then Tremaine figured it was the candy that made her mouth so tasty. But to his surprise, that was the natural taste of her tongue and lips.

They didn't just shove their tongues down each other's throats; it was mainly just the tip of their tongues playing tag. Then after a few moments they stretched their tongues all the way out taking in the full taste of one anothers', then back to the tips again. Tremaine began to suck on her bottom lip gently as she began to caress the back of his head and neck with her finger nails. He could feel his erection begin to pulsate as it slowly rose. He reached out and gently began to caress Khalilah's nipples, which had begun to protrude through her bikini top. With that, she let out a soft moan from deep within the pit of her stomach where she could feel a fire begin to simmer. Tremaine's soft touch on her breast was a far cry from what he truly felt like doing, which was to lay her down on that sand and have deep passionate sex with her.

Hating to admit it, Tremaine knew he had to cut the moment short when he heard the foot steps and voices of a couple walking in their direction. They were holding hands, talking, and strolling the beach. Once the kiss was over, Tremaine and Khalilah both looked at each other for a few second. As much as they hated it, they knew that he had to go get ready for his departure to the airport in a couple of hours. They sat for a few more moments before finally exchanging phone numbers with promises to hook up when they returned home.

On the plane ride home, Dirty and Dollar rode Tremaine for not joining them with the grand finale with the Tennessee bitches, especially after they found out that he hadn't even fucked Khalilah. Tremaine wasn't tripping though because he and Khalilah was chilling, not to get it fucked up, he would have loved to have fucked her that night but their conversation took precedence and he was cool with that for the time being.

In the meantime, Tremaine was dead tired from lack of sleep throughout the entire vacation. All of them were tired to be honest. They ended up going to sleep for most of the plane ride back home. Tremaine thought about Khalilah a lot but mainly his thoughts were on Los' hidden agenda and how to carry it with him from now on.

10 FRIEND OR FOE

Tremaine was finally able to start moving things into his new townhouse and it felt great. In his eyes, there was nothing like owning your own place. He could have moved into his own apartment months ago but chose to wait until his townhouse was finished. Tremaine wanted to keep his apartment in Linthicum a secret. Dirty, Dollar, and he still had the Greenspring apartment that they shared, but eventually they planned to turn that into a stash spot or a spot where they chilled. Dirty was in the process of moving into his own place and Dollar wouldn't be too far behind him in finding a new place of his own as well.

Juice had turned Tremaine onto a homosexual boy who had a nice little credit card scheme going. Tremaine didn't know how the faggot did it, but all he had to do was pick the dude up and take him to any store. Whatever Tremaine pointed out the boy would buy it for him with one of the many credit cards he possessed. Menage', as the homosexual liked to be called, bought sixty-five thousand dollars worth of household items for Tremaine in return for fifteen thousand dollars in cash. Tremaine was able to get three bedroom sets, one king sized set for his room and two queen sized for the guest rooms. There were two living room sets, one egg shell colored, french collection for the living room and one Italian leather set for the family room in the basement.

Menage' also purchased four 64-inch flat screen T.V.'s, one for each bedroom as well as for the basement. Those credit cards purchased the hand carved mahogany dining room set, stainless steel refrigerator, matching microwave, lawn mower, and anything else one could imagine. Thanks to Menage' every single item in Tremaine's home was brand new and fresh off of a showroom floor. Tremaine was unable to get anything sent to his home directly for the simple fact when the paperwork came back on those credit cards it would have led the police straight to his house. Therefore, he had to rent a moving truck and get Dirty, Dollar, and Juice to help move his things into his townhouse. Tremaine still hadn't told Los about this new townhouse, he still didn't have an idea what Los was up to and didn't plan to let him put him to bed like that.

A week after he was completely moved in, Tremaine decided to give Khalilah a call. It had been over three weeks since they had been back from South Beach and Dirty informed him that she had called the Greenspring apartment a couple of times looking for him. He meant to call her back more than once, but always ended up forgetting to call, but when he would remember it would always be too late or something would come up that would prevent him from calling. That is until one night he was finally able to catch up with her.

"Hello." The sweet familiar voice answered the phone.

"Can I speak to Khalilah?" Tremaine asked.

"Speaking."

"What's up? How've you been?" he asked.

"Fine, I thought you forgot all about me or something," she said.

116

"Nah nah, it ain't nothin' like that I just been a lil' busy lately. You ain't get my messages?" Tremaine asked.

"What messages?"

"I gave my new phone number to your roommate about two days ago."

Khalilah sucked her teeth. "That girl acts like she's half retarded sometimes," she said. "She's always forgetting something."

"So what's up, what are you in there doing?"

"Nothing, just studying for my final exams."

"Oh my bad, you want me to call you back then?" Tremaine asked.

"Nah you alright," Khalilah said hoping she didn't sound too pressed, when in reality, Tremaine had been on her mind constanly since their night on the beach. "I need to wait for my roommate to come home so she can quiz me anyway."

Tremaine and Khalilah conversed for two more hours talking about Tremaine's up coming graduation from high school and exactly what he was planning to do with himself afterwards. He told her about how he was thinking of going to a trade school, or something of the sort to learn about computers. He even talked about his entrepreneurial itch and owning his own business someday. Khalilah was explaining how she was considering taking an internship at a big-name accounting firm in Chicago that summer and her plans of attending graduate school after her senior year.

Tremaine couldn't even fake, she definitely had him open all over again just like when they were kids. Khalilah possessed so much ambition, and that quality was a definite turn on for him. He could honestly say that he had been with all types of females while growing up, ranging from hoodrats to so called nerds, and with both types, there was always something missing. The hoodrats were cool for when Tremaine was trying to chill with a broad and get his brains fucked out and as far as holding a nigga down while in the streets, they would always have his back. It was just that when it was time to venture out into different avenues aside from the drug game, the hoodrats would end up responding like a fish out of water. They were lost and didn't know what the fuck to do.

Tremaine craved for a female that could hold him down in all aspects and situations. If he should decide to make a legitimate move like open a business or something along those lines, he wanted his woman to be able to handle things. He desired the ability to toss ideas back and forth with that special woman in his life and that was why he dated the nerdy type of females. They were capable of talking legal business with him and even able to offer little suggestions that might help him prosper. However, they couldn't relate to him when it came to the streets.

If shit happened to get thick and some drama kicked off or the feds came kicking down doors, their types would to crack under the pressure. With all that being said, that was one of the reasons Tremaine was so impressed with Khalilah. She was one of the few females who could hold him down in all situations; giving him the best of both worlds.

Ever since they were younger, Khalilah was able to put together boxing combinations as if she were a boy when it came to fighting. She was down to earth, pretty, street smart and book smart. To him she was the perfect example of being a lady in the light and by the way she moved her tongue around when they kissed in Miami, he knew she had to be a freak in the dark. Their conversation was brought to an end when Khalilah's roommate returned home to help her prepare for her finals.

Khalilah returned home from college on the weekends, so she and Tremaine made plans to see each other then. Her parents lived in Jessup, MD which was less than fifteen minutes from Tremaine's new town home.

Tremaine found himself expanding his territories a little more when he began the process of opening up shop on his man lil' L's block, Pennsylvania and Pitcher. Word was the supplier that lil' L and all of his homeboys, use to cop their crack from, had recently gotten locked up and the whole spot was open for the taking. Tremaine had already sold lil' L an eighth and he had been chasing him constantly ever since trying to purchase some more for himself and a few of his homeboys from around there. Tremaine made up his mind that he would just sell lil L the eighths of crack for three thousand and let him resell it to his homeboys for the thirty-four or thirty-five hundred that they were use to paying. Tremaine wanted to narrow down the number of people he was dealing with as much as possible in the future.

Whenever he was dealing with new clients in a different area, Tremaine was looking to find one main person in that area to deal with, and sell them the crack in weight, for dirt cheap. Afterwards, they could distribute it to their homeboys, instead of him having to serve five and six niggas on one block. Do business with one and try to keep all risks to a minimum was his mentality. There was no such thing as a sure bet in his way of living. Whatever route a nigga could take to slightly tip that scale into their favor, just might make the difference between life and death, or a five-year bid versus a life sentence.

It was obvious to anyone who had eyes that niggas weren't playing fair in the street. A lot of niggas may not have been on no 'gangsta' shit but they definitely were on some snitching shit; that seemed to be the new name of the game. Bitch ass niggas who didn't have enough heart to get a nigga out of the way themselves instead would get the police involved, letting the law do something that they couldn't. As soon as one was locked up they would have a telephone book sized stack of statements pushed in front of them from the so-called confidential informants. Unless there was solid proof, it was hard to distinguish who was telling the truth because there were so many cruddy ass niggas.

That was why Tremaine chose to limit his business transactions to just a few people. He tried to keep a low profile since a jealous nigga was a dangerous one. Tremaine currently possessed six different hoopties that he brought from the auction. There was his '89 Chevy Caprice, a '85 Cadillac Sedan Deville, a '91 Nissan Maxima, another caravan and a '88 300 ZX. All were old, cheap cars that were inconspicuous yet reliable transportation. Still to this day he has them scattered out in various neighborhoods and side streets throughout the city. The only difference now is that they are only driven when he made his rounds. The Benz wagon was parked at a fiend's house in Howard County, MD and would only be driven by Tremaine on the weekends when his day was clear. He still drove the BMW to school on the regular.

Tremaine was trying to do whatever it took for him to do in order to stay one step ahead of the streets. He had adapted the menatality of telling his clientele who were trying to cop something to meet him at a store or somewhere out in the open. Before they arrived he would already be at the meeting spot sitting in the background watching. His presence was never known as he observed them for unusual behavior. He was adamant about not being caught slipping, if he could prevent it.

Tremaine would wear a UPS uniform when he left his home in the mornings. He was well aware that people were watching him in his new neighborhood, blacks as well as whites. He quickly noticed how they were being nosy and trying to act as if they were washing their cars, or mowing their lawns, while his things were being moved in. They were snooping to see what type of things he possessed or if there was someone else moving in. Tremaine felt as though everything was cool because he was definitely playing his part and trying to blend in with the rest of his neighbors. He had even taken up the habit of beeping his horn and waving to his neighbors whenever he drove pass one of them, playing the role of a real life square nigga.

That Friday afternoon Khalilah called Tremaine to let him know that she had just left school and was on her way to the mall. After she left there, she would be ready to hook up with him. Tremaine had taken the initiative and made reservations for the two of them at a restaurant down on the waterfront of the Baltimore Harbor, called Canton Dockside. Manny's cousin Randy told him about the place and said that the food was expensive but that it was well worth it, leaving Tremaine curious to check it out.

At six o'clock that evening, Tremaine was making a call on his cell phone to Khalilah informing her that he was waiting out in front of her house. He was hesitant about going to knock on her door thinking that her father was home. Lord knows he and Mr. Turner never got along in the past, he doubted if they would that day. Khalilah asked him to come inside because her mother wanted to see how he was doing. Sensing his hesitance, Khalilah informed Tremaine that her father was not home. Tremaine thought about it and remembered he and Mrs. Turner never had any fall outs so decided to go in.

As he walked the pavement of the horse shoe driveway of the house, Tremaine noticed how big their house was. The house had to have at least four bedrooms along with a three car garage. Tremaine did a quick last minute assessment of himself before he knocked on the door. His entire outfit was Armani Exchange. Everything from his blue jeans to his black t-shirt, with a black short sleeved button up shirt that had the A/X symbol embroidered in thick black stitching on the back. The t-shirt was tucked in with the button up open, exposing his black leather "A/X" belt. On his feet was a pair of black Pradas. Not being too flashy on the Jewelry, Tremaine chose a simple platinum Cartier watch and a platinum Cartier necklace.

Satisfied with his looks, Tremaine reached out to knock on the door only to have Khalilah open it before he had a chance to. The sight of her left him a little stunned, her beautiful body was complimented by a pair of Rock and Republic skinny jeans and a short sleeved, fitted plaid button up. The high heeled Jimmy Choo Pumps that she wore matched the stitching in her jeans. Her wavy hair was pulled back into a long tight pony tail that left not one strand of hair out of place. There was also a blazer hanging over her arm that perfectly matched her outfit. Khalilah possessed that natural beauty that required no make up, nevertheless the light coat of Chanel lip gloss on her lips gave them a glistened and suckable look.

"Mmm you lookin' sexy as shit," Tremaine spoke while staring down at Khalilah's lips.

"Thank you. Come on, my mother's in the kitchen." She grabbed Tremaine by the hand and led him through the foyer into the kitchen.

Mrs. Turner was fixing some sort of smoothie in the blender. Tremaine could see that she must have just gotten finished working out because she wore a black sports bra with a towel tossed around her sweaty neck, along with a pair of grey yoga pants that exposed the print of her vaginal area. Tremaine could literally see the outline of her pussy lips. He wasn't trying to look, but got damn Mrs. Turner was making it hard for him not to, considering how she was putting the shit on display. He knew Mr. Turner had to have been hitting that every night, if he knew what was good for him.

Still looking the same as Tremaine could remember from when he was younger, Mrs. Turner had aged very little and her once long hair was now cut short into a Halle Berry style. To be honest, Khalilah and her mother could pass for sisters. Tremaine thought to himself, if Khalilah was going to look that good in twenty-five years then he just might have to hold on to her.

Mrs. Turner was all smiles when she saw Tremaine and said, "Ooh look at you boy you have grown, haven't you?" reaching out to give Tremaine a hug. "How've you been?" she asked.

"I'm doing pretty well, Mrs. Turner, how 'bout you?"

"Oh, I'm fine," she said.

You got that right, Tremaine thought.

"So how's your grandmother doing?" she asked.

"She's doing well, still living in the same place."

"What? Well next time you speak to her, tell her I said hi, alright?"

"Yes ma'am," Tremaine responded.

After talking a little longer with Mrs. Turner about himself, Tremaine told her he was living out in Laurel with his uncle. He also boasted about his upcoming graduation.

Tremaine and Khalilah got up to leave with Mrs. Turner walking them out to the door. When she saw his Benz wagon out front of her home she commented on how nice of a car it was and asked if it was his. Once again he used the uncle line, telling her that the car belonged to him. Tremaine could see that Khalilah wanted to ask him the same thing when she gave him a side glance upon seeing the car. He wasn't about to give neither one of them a reason to have their minds running a mile a minute, bombarding him with questions by telling them that it was his.

When they arrived at Canton Dockside, Tremaine informed the concierge that he had reservations for a Mr. and Mrs. Jenkins. As they were shown to their table Khalilah gave Tremaine a playful smile and said, "Oh I'm Mrs. Jenkins now, huh?"

Tremaine grinned at the comment as they were seated.

"You know I always drive pass this restaurant but I never bothered to stop in here. I didn't know it was this nice inside," Khalilah said as she looked around and admired the establishment.

"Yeah, it is tight. I never thought about it until my man put me on to it."

Anyone would say that "Canton Dockside" was a five star restaurant upon entering it. Each table had its own dim crystal chandelier hanging above it that gave the whole place a nice soft look. The waiters were prompt and serious about their services and changed the entire linen table cloth after each course of the meal was served. After observing food that was served to other patrons, a few of the dishes looked rather bizarre to Tremaine. Judging by the reactions of the patrons who were devouring the food, it had to be delicious.

The waiter, which was a young Italian male, wore a long sleeved crispy white dress shirt and a pair of hard pressed black slacks brought Tremaine and Khalilah their menus. He introduced himself as Tonio. It was obvious to see that his outfit was the dress code for all of the waiters. All of what seemed to be young Italian males who resembled one another, as if they were brothers or some sort of relation, indicating that it was a family run restaurant.

Tremaine studied their wine list and could see that the wines and champagnes on the list were well over twenty years old, and none of them were less than one hundred dollars. Not really familiar with the different types of wine, Tremaine went with what he knew best and ordered a two hundred and fifty dollar bottle of '88 Dom P. He and Khalilah sipped on that while they tried to decide what to eat.

Tremaine noticed a change in Khalilah's demeanor as she read the food selections. When he asked her if everything was cool, she came out and told him exactly what was on her mind. "Tremaine, I don't mean any harm but we could have gone somewhere else," she said.

Tremaine was a little caught off guard by her comment. "What you mean? Why you say that?" he asked.

"I'm just sayin', I'm looking at the prices on these dinners and these people must have bumped their heads," she said as she frowned up her face at the menu.

Tremaine let out a slight chuckle before responding, "I feel you but umm... don't even worry about it," he said brushing off her worries.

"I'm just saying, I can cook half of the stuff on here, I don't want you to feel as though you have to spend your money like this. There isn't a meal on here for less then eighty dollars and the highest is two hundred dollars."

"I feel you on that but don't worry about it. I'll tell you one thing though, I'ma definitely take you up on that offer and see if you can burn in the kitchen." Tremaine was trying to down play the situation but that girl had a nigga going for real. It was the first time that any female complained about him spending too much money on them.

All of the Canton Dockside's meals were five course dinners. Tremaine chose the lobster tail with a mushroom buttered sauce while Khalilah ordered the steamed scallops covered in a honey lemon dressing. Just as Randy had promised, the food was to die for. Over dinner Tremaine joked with Khalilah about her cooking skills, in which she was determined to prove him wrong. Tremaine had always prided himself on being able to handle his liquor but there was no denying that he was feeling the bottle of Dom Perignon '88.

He could see that Khalilah was feeling it as well as she began to get a little loud, which was cool because he was digging her and her drunkened sense of humor.

By the time dessert arrived, they were both too full to indulge. Tremaine ordered another bottle of champagne, a '91 bottle of Cristal. The bill was nine hundred and seventy six dollars plus a one hundred dollar tip for the waiter. He paid the bill with the credit card he received from one of his crackheads in the "Gold Club". The card was in their name but Tremaine paid the monthly bill, that way he'd never have to worry about the card ever being declined. He didn't want to be subject to pulling out large stacks of paper in public on occasions such as this. They decided to go back to his house for the rest of the night to chill out and see what else they could get into.

As they drove along and conversed, Tremaine realized halfway into the ride that he was driving the Mercedes instead of his BMW which was parked in Howard County. His nosey ass neighbors had never seen him in his Benz and he wasn't trying to spring that on them, instantly raising suspicions in the process. He thought about just saying fuck it and driving the wagon out there but quickly checked his self, it wasn't the time to start getting lazy and cutting corners. He had to think of a way to switch cars while Khalilah was with him without drawing too much suspicion in her mind. He picked up his cell phone and acted as if it was vibrating and someone was calling him. He turned the radio all the way down so that Khalilah could clearly hear him.

"Hello… yeah, what's up? Nah I was just on my way to the house… But I'll be at the house in two minutes! Yo, you taking me out of my way for real with that… Why can't you just drive that muthafucka?" Tremaine was sighing while sucking his teeth and throwing facial expressions. He was using whatever he thought it would take to sell his act. He could have won an Oscar for his performance.

"Hey yo, I'm like two minutes away from the house and you want me to drive all the way back out that way for real?... Yeah, I got somebody with me... You don't know her... Matter of fact you might know here, it's lil' Khalilah that lived on grandma's block... her father used to drive that brownish colored Cherokee 'bout eight or nine years ago."

Khalilah was starting to pay attention to Tremaine's fake ass conversation even more, now that she heard her name mentioned.

"Nah forget it because you a little slow in the head, anyway... Yeah whatever but look for me, I'll be out there in 'bout twenty minutes a'ight? Matter of fact; make it ten minutes 'cause I'm a floor this bitch... Yeah whatever, you want this shit, don't you? It don't matter how you get it as long as you get it... Yeah a'ight whatever!"

After the fake conversation, Tremaine acted as if he was hanging up his phone.

"This nigga blowin' me like shit!" he said while shaking his head.

"What's wrong, everything alright?" Khalilah asked.

"Nah that was just my uncle, getting on my damn nerves, as usual. You might remember him; he used to come over my grandmother's house driving that ummm... What was he pushing back then?" Tremaine was snapping his fingers as if he was trying to remember. "A grayish colored Maxima." He blurted out the first thing that came to mind. "You remember?"

"Nah, I don't think so," Khalilah said drawing a blank.

"Fuck it, anyway this nigga want me to bring him his car and pick up the other one all 'cause he tryin' to stunt for some broad he just met."

"Oh. Well where is he?" Khalilah asked.

"All the way in Howard County."

"You going out there?" she asked.

Tremaine frowned his face up and let out a loud sigh. "It looks like I ain't got no choice," he said.

When they arrived at the fiend's house, Tremaine immediately noticed the crackhead's car wasn't parked in the driveway, which meant his ass wasn't home. He had to improvise a little bit. He told Khalilah to sit in the car until he ran around the back of the house into the basement, where his uncle's friend had a room, to get the keys. When he got to the rear of the house, Tremaine stood there for five mintues and then returned back around front where Khalilah sat waiting. She got out of the Mercedes and they climbed into the BMW and left.

When they got to Tremaine's house, he took Khalilah into the basement. He put a movie on then laid his head in her lap. An hour later, they were playing around and wrestling, which led to kissing and heavy touching. Just when Tremaine was getting ready to go all the way, or thought that he was, Khalilah fucked up the whole mood when she spoke the words, "hold up Tremaine, I can't."

"You can't?" Tremaine asked a little confused as her words didn't seem to register in his horny mind.

"It's not that I don't want to, but I'm on my period."

And what the fuck is that suppose to mean? Tremaine thought. The only thing that meant to him was extra lubrication down there, that's all. "Oh yeah?" he asked trying to hold in his frustrations.

"You don't believe me do you?" Khalilah asked seeing the look of frustration upon his face.

"Oh nah, I believe you I mean..."

"Come here. Just to let you know I ain't bullshitting." Khalilah grabbed Tremaine's hand.

"What you doing?" he asked.

"I'ma show you," she said as she unbuttoned her pants. She then took Tremaine's hand and pushed it down into her panties. "See for yourself." She said as she stretching her legs out straight making it easier for him to reach down into her tight jeans.

Shit she wasn't saying nothing but a word because Tremaine damn sure went searching for that string and sure enough there it was. Now with any other broad he would have told her fuck that shit because a little blood didn't stop anything. He had fucked a number of females while they were on their periods because all that was required was a towel to be laid down on the bed and it was on from there. Either that or he would tell the girl that there wasn't anything wrong her mouth or asshole.

"Fuck it. It aint nothing heavy, everything cool," he told her.

"If I knew the touching and feeling were going to take us this far I would have told you earlier," Khalilah said.

"Shit, don't tell me tell it to my man down here staring at you with the one eye," Tremaine said as he leaned back on the couch and lifted his shirt exposing his erection that was pressed against his jeans.

"Did I do that? Oooo I'm so sorry," she said putting on her best innocent little girl face and poking her lip out. Tremaine couldn't help but grin at her little act.

They sipped a little bit of Rose' and eventually Khalilah fell asleep with her head on a pillow in Tremaine's lap. He carried her sleeping body upstairs to his room and laid her down on top of his bed as they both slept, unfortunately, with their clothes on. Tremaine wasn't tripping for the simple fact he knew that he would have sex with Khalilah in due time. He had already been given the green light and was just waiting on the right moment to come back and present itself.

11 CELEBRATION

The day before Tremaine's graduation; he, Dirty, Dollar, and Juice all went out to do a little celebrating. It was a Thursday in June, with the weather being nice and warm they all decided to go to "Six Flags" in Largo, MD. Before heading out, they were all together at the Greenspring apartment, which Dollar now lived in alone. Dirty moved into a condominium Downtown on St. Paul Street a few weeks ago. They were smoking haze while playing Playstation on the 50-inch. After getting fucked up, they decided to stop out Towson Town Center to go in Nordstrom's on the way to the park for new swimwear.

Immediately after arriving at Six Flags, they knew it was crouchy because there were females everywhere. After each of them paid the fourty dollars to get in, they headed straight for the water park and then agreed to hit the roller coasters afterwards. They hopped in the 'Wild Wave first, which was half of a football field sized swimming pool that had four feet tall waves, which were created by a machine at the back wall of the pool. The deepest part of the pool was the back and they headed straight there. They all knew how to swim so the waves weren't a factor. It was all basically on how they timed the waves. A lot of people had rafts that they were floating on, which could be rented from the park for five dollars. After no more than five minutes in the pool, and making sure to stay above the waves, Dollar came floating along towards the rest of his homeboys on the raft. They all gave him a crazy look wondering where he had gotten it from since none of them had rented one when they first arrived.

"Yo, where you get that from?" Dirty asked as they all wondered.

"Lil kid over there let me use it." Dollar pointed behind him with a crazy grin on his face.

When they all looked over his shoulder to see who he was referring to, all that could be seen was a drowning young white boy. The child was swinging his arms all around as if he were reaching for an invisible rope to keep himself from drowning. Just when the boy was starting to lose the battle and his head began to go under the water, the female life guard dove from her chair and pulled him from under the grips of the waves. She then placed a red floatation device under the boys arm pits. One more minute and he definitely would have been just a memory. Tremaine looked back at Dollar and tried to hold a serious face but he had to admit the shit was funny.

"Hey cuz you out of order like shit," he said out of breath as he continued to tread water.

"What?" Dollar asked with a blank expression on his face.

"Nigga you snatched shorty off his raft and left him for dead," Tremaine said as he grabbed hold of the side of Dollar's stolen raft since he was getting tired from treading the water wave

"Oh nah nah, that's my lil' man. He said I can use this muthafucka."

They all gave Dollar a look as if to ask, do we look stupid to you or something?

132

Dollar looked at all of their facial expressions and burst out laughing. "Ya'll niggas ugly as shit," he said.

They all then began to laugh along with him as they each held on to the side of the raft. They were still high as fat Charles ass, but still the sight of the drowning boy did not look funny to them. After getting a good forty-five minutes in the water, they all decided it was time to walk the rest of the park and link up with a few females. They rode two or three roller coasters but mainly hit the funnel cake stands, and a few other snack vendors, due to the munchies that were now coming down on them.

When they arrived at a basketball stand, Dirty bet Tremaine a hundred dollars that he could make at least one off the stand. Dirty swore up and down that he had a jump shot and Tremaine bet him because he knew that the rims that Dirty would be shooting at were slightly bent. That was how all of the amusement parks basketball rims were, which made it harder to make the shots.

The vendor, who was a tall light-skinned gentleman with a goofy look on his face, appeared to be a little too old to be working at an amusement park. All of the other employees there held the appearance of high school kids, most likely working a summer job. But Mr. Basketball vendor looked as if he was trying to make a career out of it. Dirty gave the man five dollars, in return he was handed three basketballs to shoot. His first one was a total air ball.

"Yeah that's money in the bank," Tremaine responded.

"Bullshit nigga, I'm just warming up," Dirty responded as he bounced the second ball three times and then spinned it in his hands while concentrating on the rim as if he were shooting free throws in the NBA finals. His second shot hit the front of the rim and bounced back.

"Yo, you a bum. Since you're in the mood to give away your paper let me get in on that bet," Dollar said while pulling out a stack of money.

Dirty was getting more frustrated since Dollar had now begun to talk trash. "Nigga you ain't sayin' nothin'. Bet that," Dirty responded.

"Bet two hundred you don't make this next shot," Dollar challenged while holding up two one-hundred dollar bills.

"Like I said nigga, bet that."

After missing his last and final shot, then three more after that on a double or nothing bet, Dirty was pissed. He had just lost a quick six hundred dollars. The vendor eyed the group as if they were crazy for betting one and two hundred dollars on basketball shots. That shit was more than he made in a week of working at the park. Dirty was extra pissed when Dollar took one of the hundred dollar bills that he won from him and handed it to an ugly ass fat broad that was walking by. The woman was no more than five foot three inches tall but weighed every bit of three hundred plus pounds. Her hair was screaming for a perm while in a pony tail, or more like a hamster tail, because that was about how much of her hair was sticking out in the back. The ice cream cone she was eating had melted all over her chin and mouth.

"Here you go Miss Lady, this from my man right here." Dollar nodded in Dirty's direction.

"He said he was trying to holla at you but he's a little shy, you feel me?"

The broad took the money and was gazing at Dirty, with that ice cream still on her chin and mouth, as if what Dollar said was true. Tremaine, Dollar and Juice burst out laughing and that's when she knew they were getting their kicks off at her expense. She sucked her teeth and rolled her eyes at them all before walking off with the hundred dollars still in hand. Dirty was the only one who wasn't laughing, even the basketball vendor was cracking a smile.

"The fuck you laughin' at nigga?!" Dirty asked the vendor with an evil glare in his eye. If looks could kill the vendor would have been flat lined. The vendor turned his head and tried to put on a straight face but they could see he was still grinning. "Matta of fact nigga, I won! Give me my shit!" Dirty jumped on the counter and snatched down a four foot Tasmanian Devil stuffed animal that was hanging on the side of the wall.

"Hold up man, what you…"

"Hold up what nigga?!" Dirty responded while jumping down off of the counter and into the vendor's face. The vendor had Dirty beat by at least six inches in height, but fear was still very much evident as he looked down into Dirty's eyes. "Huh? That's what I thought nigga, this my shit! I won!" Dirty jumped back over the counter with the stuffed animal in hand.

The fellas had all long stopped laughing as they watched to see if the vendor was going to respond to Dirty. They were all ready to give out a quick ass whooping in the middle of that park. Unfortunately, the vendor said nothing leaving them to walk off.

Afterwards, they continued their rounds in the park and conversed with a few females. They gave out their numbers in hopes of setting up future hotel dates. Finally, they decided it was time to leave and get home so they could shower and change clothes for the strip club they planned to attend that night.

As Tremaine, Dirty, Dollar, and Juice began to head out of the park, there was already a line formed at the entrance and exit, which was moving along at a snail's pace. Tremaine could see a few dudes sneaking into the park through the exit line in order to avoid having to pay. As they got closer he could see the group of niggas bumping into patrons with no disregard as they squeezed through the line going in the opposite direction. The one leading the pack of five was a blue-back complexioned nigga with long corn rows in his hair that reached down to his shoulders. He wore a black bandanna tied around his head, a wife beater tank top, along with a pair of jean shorts and a pair of black Nike boots on his feet.

The entire time the group was forcing past everyone and making their way closer, Tremaine was thinking, *Fuck that! If one of these niggas bump into me, it's whatever!*

Blue-black had an evil look on his face as he lead the pack which let Tremaine know that he was doing that bumping shit on purpose and he wasn't gonna stand for that. Dollar was the lead in their pack followed by Juice and then Tremaine with Dirty coming up the rear as they stood in a single file line.

Once the leader of their pack reached Dollar, Tremaine noticed that he turned his shoulder slightly to let him pass but it was when he got to Juice, blue-black bumped the shit out of him and then looked back as if to say "nigga what?" Just as Juice was about to say something, the nigga was already in the process of bumping Tremaine on his left shoulder. That was all she wrote because before he and Tremaine's shoulder separated all you heard was CRACK! CRACK! Tremaine quickly unleashed an over hand right followed by a left hook that slid blue-black's ass straight down the side of the small gate on both sides of the exit line. One swift kick from Dirty to the boy's head after already being dazed, there was no getting up for him.

One of blue-black's homeboys punched Tremaine from the blind side. The whore didn't hit him with his fist but with the balled up palm part of his hand. The hit landed directly on the side of Tremaine's head. The smack felt like it had busted Tremaine's ear drum. Before he could turn and react, Juice had already grabbed the boy by his collar with his left hand and was punching the shit out of him with his right. Behind Juice, Tremaine could see Dollar with his back against the rail, wrestling one of the boys while the last two damn near punched each other and their man while trying to throw a hail of punches at Dollar. Tremaine and Dirty slid pass Juice, who by that time had his opponent's shirt pulled over his head while hittng him with uppercuts.

Dirty grabbed one of the boys off of Dollar and put him in a choke hold and then slammed him to the ground. It was straight stomp time from there as Dirty grabbed hold of the rail and began jumping up and down on the nigga's head and back. After three of those niggas were already in an unconscious state, Dirty kept kicking them soccer-ball style on the side of their temples. Dollar had already crushed the nigga he was wrestling with, and now he and Tremaine were in the process of pulling the last boy from under the rail that he tried to get under in an attempt to make a run for it. By this time, the people involved in the fight were the only ones left in the narrow aisle since everyone else in the exit line backed up when the brawl started.

Tremaine noticed one of the park's fake ass rent-a-cops run up and grab the boy that Juice was still beating the shit out of, from behind. In the distance behind the security guard there were two P.G. County policemen running towards the commotion yelling into their hand held walkie talkies. Tremaine, Dirty, Juice and Dollar all scattered and blended in with the rather large crowd that had gathered at the edge of the exit walkway. Once past the crowd, they all split up and met up one by one in the parking lot. There was no mistaking the sound of sirens in the distance, which in turn caused them to rush even faster to get the hell out of the parking lot.

They headed home to get cleaned up for the strip club. Little did they know, the bitch everyone called "Lady Luck" had a few more tricks up her sleeve to fuck up their day.

12 CIRCUMSTANCES

After arriving back to the Greenspring apartment, showering and changing clothes, the fellas sparked a few more cigarillos and cracked on Juice about the fight and how he was having problems with the one dude he was wrestling with.

"Nah Yo, that bitch-ass nigga kept grabbing me. I couldn't put that muthafucka on his ass like I wanted to," Juice said shaking his right fist in the air.

Dirty tapped Tremaine on his arm and said, "now I know you saw me put these mufuckin' Gary Paytons on the side of the nigga head that snuck you Dogg."

"Oh yeah, I peeped that." Tremaine reached out to give Dirty a five.

"I tried to put my whole size ten in them nigga's temple," Dirty bragged.

"Yo, for real my mufuckin' ear still ringing from when that nigga hit me wit' that fake ass palm fist." Tremaine was digging his finger into his ear trying to stop the buzzing sound.

"Oh yeah I feel you, 'cause that joint was loud as shit. That's what put me on point that the nigga had hit you. I was on my way to help Dollar out, until I heard that loud as smacking sound," Dirty said.

"Nigga your lil' ass was bluffin' when them three whores were on you at first," Tremaine joked with Dollar.

"Shit nigga, them whores wasn't even hitting me. They were hitting each other trying to get at me," Dollar said.

"Yeah no bullshit; I peeped that," Tremaine responded.

Everyone was cleaned up and ready to roll out. They headed downtown with plans to go to Mo's to get a few drinks and something to eat, then around the corner to the 2 o'clock strip club to see what they can get into. Tremaine and Dirty hopped up in Dirty's brand new Lexus LS430 he had just brought from Randy while Juice rode with Dollar in his Chevy Impala SS. They had just drove through Druid Hill Park and had to stop at a red traffic light. Dollar's car was the first at the light while Tremaine and Dirty were two cars back in the next lane over to their right.

SKRRRRRRK! SKRRRRRRK! All of a sudden an oversized F-150 pick up truck pulled up out of nowhere in front of Dollar with an Expedition, and a Caravan following on its left side. Two large white men jumped out of the truck, followed by two more averaged sized white men and a black man out of the Expedition. Out of the caravan jumped a Spanish gentleman along with a white and black female. They were dressed in regular civilian clothes with bullet proof vests showing on the outside of their clothing. The badges that were either displayed on their hips or dangling from the chains around their necks quickly let everyone know that they were homicide detectives. All of the officers were running towards Dollar's car with their guns drawn, which consisted of nine millimeters, forty-five's and pistol grip shotguns.

"The fuck!?" Dirty sat all the way up in the seat with his chest pressed against the steering wheel.

"Aww shit.!" Tremaine immediately began to look around to see if there were any officers pulling up on their car but there weren't any.

"Don't Fucking Move! Police, let me see your hands. Now! Goddamit! Let me see them now!" The officers were yelling all types of orders to Juice and Dollar.

Tremaine could see Juice's hands raised up in the air through Dollar's back window but there was no sign of Dollar doing as instructed.

"Let me see your hands right now! Let me see them driver!" Dollar sat in that front seat looking back and forth at all of the police that had his car surrounded and then down into his lap.

"Come on cuzzo, be smart about this shit," Tremaine mumbled as if Dollars could hear. Tremaine already knew what Dollar had in his lap, because it was the same thing all four of them had at the time, Guns! Tremaine knew Dollar was seriously contemplating shooting it out with the police. After what seemed like an eternity, but was actually thirty seconds, Dollar finally lifted his hands up in the air. The entire time, Tremaine and Dirty were in the next lane over watching the scene unfold. Once Dollar submitted, the officers snatched him and Juice out of the car and laid them face down on the ground handcuffing them.

"Yo, fuck all this!" Dirty turned the steering wheel as if he was going to drive up on the green patch of grass to their right.

Tremaine grabbed hold of the steering wheel and said, "Hold up yo, what the fuck are you doing!?"

"I'm gettin' the fuck away from here, that's what!" Dirty was looking around to see what, if any, space he had to make a quick U-turn.

"Nigga if you bust this turn right now you're gonna draw them muthafuckas straight to us." Tremaine reasoned while still holding on to the steering wheel. "Now if they wanted to, they would have been run down on us, think Yo!"

Dirty looked at Tremaine and then at the police squad. "The fuck is all this shit Yo?!" he asked looking back at Tremaine for answers as if the police had just explained everything to him.

The only response Tremaine could give him was the shaking of his head while letting out a loud sigh. The light had finally changed and the cars ahead of them began moving along slowly. People were creeping by staring at the scene, being nosey as hell. Only Dirty still hadn't move yet.

"Come on Yo, put that shit up and drive!" Tremaine placed his brand new Desert eagle .357 up under his seat.

Dirty did the same with his firearm and began to slowly drive pass the officers who never even looked their way. They were forced to swerve just a little in order to avoid rolling over Juice, since the upper half of his body was lying across the white line of the street. Dirty and Tremaine headed straight out to Dirty's mother's house on Mount and Mosher, which was about ten minutes away. The entire drive there, they were throwing ideas back and forth about the reasons for Dollar and Juice getting jammed up. There were so many different reasons, since there was a number of things taking place in all of their lives, that they decided to give up and wait to see what the police told Tremaine's aunt.

When they arrived at Niecey's, Tremaine was hoping that his uncle Petey answered the door so that he could give him the news first, because he knew that his aunt would get all hysterical on him. A few seconds after ringing the bell Tremaine could hear Niecey yell out, "Coming!"

Shit! So much for Uncle Pete opening the door. Tremaine thought.

"Hey Tre what's up?" his aunt asked after opening the door.

Tremaine didn't know how to go about telling her the news so he came straight out with it. "Aunt Niecey, they just locked Juice up?"

His aunt gave him a confused look like, "nigga say what." "They locked him up for what?"

"I don't know what for." Tremaine said honestly.

"Petey!" Niecey yelled upstairs. "Tre what the hell you done did?" she asked with a serious face.

Ain't this about a bitch. Of course she would blame me for shit, since Juice seems to be some sort of saint that can't do no wrong in her damn eyes.

"What I do? I ain't do nothing," Tremaine answered with a hint of anger in his voice.

Uncle Petey was in the process of making his way down the stairs.

"Tre what brings you over here?"

"Kevin is locked up?" Niecey shot at her husband calling Juice by his real name and getting straight to the point.

"Huh? For what?" Petey asked looking back and forth from Tremaine to his wife.

"I don't know. Tre what happened?" Niecey asked. After Tremaine explained everything to her about how the police jumped out on Juice and Dollar, the only thing his aunt had to say was, "Where did they take Kevin?" She seemed to care less about her nephew, Dollar.

After answering the same questions from his aunt and uncle over and over, Tremaine went back outside where Dirty waited, and they left. They headed back out to Greenspring so Tremaine could get his car, they both agreed to call it a night. Their entire night had been re-routed to the point that they couldn't even think about a damn strip club. The mood for celebration was long gone. Halfway to his house, while riding on the highway, Tremaine received a phone call from his mother.

"Tremaine?"

"What's up ma?"

"Did Sheila call you yet?" She asked talking about Dollar's mother.

"Nah, I haven't heard from her."

"You know Dollar and Juice is locked up, right?" She asked.

"Yeah I heard." Tremaine wasn't about to tell her he was there, he wanted to avoid another thousand questions. "They locked Juice up for a gun but Sheila said Dollar was locked up for a murder."

"Murder?!" Tremaine said damn near swerving in another lane.

"Yep, that's what Sheila just told me."

"The fu-" Tremaine had to catch himself and get his thoughts back together.

"Ma I'm on my way home now, I'm a call you back when I get in the house, alright?"

"Alright. But who did Dollar supposed to have killed?" His mother asked.

His mother's guess was just as good as his. Besides, Tremaine wasn't about to go back and forth with her. "I don't know ma, but I'ma call you when I get in the house."

"Alright, I'll be here."

After hanging up with his mother, he began to contemplate.

Murder?! Murder who?! He began to think back to the Foots incident that had happened over two years, almost three years ago. If it was that, Tremaine had to wonder who in the hell had ran their mouths after all that time. But knowing Dollar the way he did, Tremaine knew that the charge could be a recent homicide. He forced himself to stop stressing until he found out the full details and would take it from there.

13 GRADUATION DAY

Tremaine awoke at eight o'clock that morning because he had to be at the First Mariner Arena, where his graduation was being held, by nine thirty. He was still a little thrown off by the events from the day before. After arriving home last night, he talked to his aunt Sheila and found out that Dollar was actually being charged with attempted murder and not murder. The incident occurred two months ago. The boy Dollar was accused of shooting had been on life support for four weeks. The minute he came off of it and was capable of speaking, he dropped Dollars' name like it was hot. He informed the police that Dollar had been the one who filled him with bullets.

Sheila talked about being with Dollar in the interrogation room during his questioning. At the moment he was under no bond status and was scheduled to have another bond hearing that upcoming Monday. Sheila also told Tremaine that they were charging Dollar as an adult, even though he was only a juvenile. The shooting occurred in the Walbrook Junction area, which was no more than fifteeen minutes from where he lived.

Tremaine recalled Dollar telling him about a few dudes he was doing business with in that area so he figured it had to be one of their assess. One of them had to have taken Dollar's age and size as a weakness but ended up learning the hard way. Whatever the situation, Tremaine knew something had to give because he wasn't about to sit back and let his little cousin go down at the hands of a rat ass nigga.

After getting dressed, Tremaine headed out the door to his graduation. When he arrived at the First Mariner Arena, the parking lot security guard directed him towards the rear of the Arena. They hadn't began to let the graduates in the Arena yet, leaving the entire twelfth grade class in the parking lot sitting in their cars or standing outside conversing. Tremaine wasn't in the mood for a whole lot of talking since Dollar was still very much on his mind. Juice had nothing but a simple gun charge, which was minor compared to Dollar's situation.

After parking, Tremaine chose to sit in his car, away from the rest of his class until it was time to go inside. He sat in his car looking around at all the other graduates and noticed how they looked so joyful and at peace, as if they didn't have a care in the world. For most of them, that day was the beginning of the rest of their lives, their journeys were just beginning. A lot of them were going off to college or straight into the work field. Tremaine had saved up enough to do either one. But looking at his classmates, he pondered on how their lives seemed a lot simpler than his own.

Here Tremaine was, already paying mortgages and insurances. He was thinking about opening his own business. He had to stay one step ahead of nigga's in the streets, as well as the authorities. But to top it all off, his lil' cousin had just caught a fresh attempted murder charge, which Tremaine knew would be the end for him if he was found guilty. The only things the other students had to worry about was where the graduation parties were being held that night and how much money or what gifts they would be getting for their graduation. They would have a couple of summer months to chill and get on top of things, whereas his life was busy all day, everyday. There wasn't any room for so-called chilling and relaxing.

TAP! TAP! TAP! Tremaine's thought were broken by a knock on his window. He looked over and saw one of his homegirls, Trina and her girl Moniqua, standing at the passenger side of his car.

"Let us in Nigga," Trina yelled through the rolled up windows.

Click! Tremaine hit the power lock for them to get in.

"Why are you sittin' in here by yourself, boy?" Moniqua asked as she slid her light skinned petite body into the BMW's back seat.

"No reason. What's up wit' y'all though?" Tremaine asked.

"Nothing. We was trying to see if you wanted to smoke this purple wit' us," Trina spoke from the passenger seat while going into her pocketbook and pulling out a twenty dollar bag of weed with a vanilla cigarillo.

"Y'all trying to get high before graduation? Oh ya'll be going too hard," Tremaine said jokingly.

"Shit nigga, you know how we do it," Moniqua said.

Yeah Tremaine definitely knew first hand how they carried it. Their all girl clique consisted of seven broads. Tremaine called them anything bitches, since he had fucked each of their crew members at least twice, and a couple of them he fucked three or four times. Looking at the two, Trina with her golden brown skin and almond shaped eyes and Moniqua who was a red bone with nice wide hips and thighs, a person would never be able to tell from their graduation dresses that they were straight freaks.

"What's up, I know you're comin' to my party tonight?" Trina asked while using her manicured finger nails to split the cigarillo down the middle.

"Come on shorty, you know that goes without saying," Tremaine was lying like shit. He already made plans with Khalilah for that night which included a stretch Benz as well as a hotel suite on the waterfront.

After Tremaine and the two girls were done smoking, the employees at the Arena finally opened the doors for the graduates to enter. Once inside, all the students were broken off into different groups according to the first letter in their last names. They were then subjected to stand around for an additional hour and a half for the arrival of the parents and the other graduate guests before the ceremony began.

Tremaine was glad that he was high, had he not been, he would have been mad as hell with all the standing and waiting around. When the coordinators informed the senior class that it was time, all of the graduates were instructed to walk through a tunnel, that led to the main floor of the Arena.

Immediately after the students began emerging through the tunnel, there were all sorts of cheers and hollering. Students, parents and families were holding up signs with graduate's names. A number of guests even had air horns along with a lot of other crazy devices, as if they were at a basketball game or some sports event. All of the graduates were seated in center stage, row by row, and Tremaine was looking to see if he could find his mother or anyone else he knew in the crowd. His attempts were useless due to the fact that there were so many people in the crowd. He doubted if his family could distinguish him either, since all of the graduates wore the same black cap and gown and gold tassel.

Numerous speakers spoke before the ceremony began. An hour and a half later, Tremaine's name was called to receive his diploma. Once he crossed the stage, Tremaine was able to spot his mother, Khalilah, Dirty and Lisa in the stands because they were jumping up and down while screaming out his name. After an additional hour of calling the rest of the graduates, more guest speakers and a surplus of other things, the ceremony came to a close.

When Tremaine headed back outside into the parking lot looking for his family, the first thing he noticed was a large, silver "Congratulations Tre!" Lisa smiled as she handed him the balloons with a little black velvet box. "Did you see us in the stands?" she asked.

"Yeah but I heard ya'll before anything," he said. "What's this?" he asked staring at the velvet box in his hand.

"Open it up and find out nigga." Lisa playfully punched him on his shoulder.

When he opened the box there was a platinum chain with a diamond hit letter "T," the chain alone weighed at least 50 grams. "I saw the picture Los had of y'all in South Beach and you were rockin' the shit out of that Gucci but you were missing one thing… this." Lisa was pointing at the box.

"Good lookin' out but you know you didn't have to get me nothin'."

Lisa reached out to give him a hug and said, "Boy, please shut up!"

"Congratulations son," Tremaine's mother said with tears in her eyes. She handed him an envelope and told him not to open it until he was alone.

"Ma this ain't no money is it?" Tremaine asked hesitant to accept the envelope.

"No, its not money. It's just something I want you to open when you're alone," she said while dabbing the tears in her eyes with a piece of tissue.

Khalilah then congratulated Tremaine with hugs and kisses while handing him a graduate teddy bear hugging on a bottle of Rose' wrapped up in clear plastic with the words congrats all over it.

After taking a number of pictures with his family and friends, Tremaine pulled Khalilah to the side to make sure they were still on for that night and then he left. It was Friday and as usual, he had a few matters of business he had to attend to before he could spend any time with Khalilah that night.

After making his rounds and taking care of a few things, Tremaine headed home to get ready for his night with Khalilah. After showering he threw on his tan Giorgio Armani slacks and matching short sleeved dress shirt. He then checked with the limousine company to make sure everything was cool with the ride. The limo was scheduled to pick them up over Khalilah's house because he damn sure didn't want it pulling up in front of his.

When he arrived at Khalilah's house, Tremaine noticed that the limo still hadn't arrived and decided to call the company once again from his cell phone. They informed him that the driver was less than ten minutes away and would be arriving shortly. He then called Khalilah to let her know that he was outside and once again she asked him to come inside, unlike the last time, her father was now home. Tremaine damn sure wasn't trying to go in there, but said fuck it because he refused to keep ducking the man.

"Hey Tremaine, how are you doing?" Mr. Turner said reaching out to shake Tremaine's hand when he answered the door.

"What's up Mr. Turner? I'm doing pretty well how about you?" Tremaine was giving the man a once over while noticing how much he had changed over the years. Mr. Turner was a slim man from what he could remember. He was still slim built but was slightly protruding in the stomach area, which stood out of place with the rest of his slim body. The short curly black hair, that he had as a result of his Cuban grandparents, was now graying around the sides and thinning noticeably on the crown of his head. Unlike Ms. Turner he had definitely aged.

"Just working hard that's all. Congratulations on your graduation."

"Thank you."

"Look at you, you've gotten tall too."

Tremaine just stood there with a fake grin on his face. He and Mr. Turner were almost the same height and in the back of Tremaine's mind he knew he could take the man if it ever came down to a physical confrontation.

"So what are your plans now that you're out of high school? College maybe?"

Here we go, Tremaine thought. He knew it was coming, Mr. Turner and his fake ass was interviewing him to see where his head was. "Nah not really, I was thinking about attending a trade school to learn about fixing computers."

"Trade school, huh?" Mr. Turner said that shit as if it was a disease or something. "That's okay, It's good to have that as a back-up to your college degree."

Man where the fuck is Khalilah at, this nigga is starting to get on my damn nerves already, Tremaine thought. It would have been cool had Mr. Turner just been throwing out ideas but the way he was saying things, combined with his body language, made Tremaine feel as if he was being talked down to.

"Did you take your SAT's?" Mr. Turner pressed on.

The fuck, is this fifty questions? Tremaine wanted to scream out.

"Nah I ain't take them," he said with his attitude beginning to surface.

"Really?" he responded with a slight frown on his face while staring at Tremaine. "Why is that?"

"What's up Tremaine?" Khalilah said cutting their conversation short as she emerged down the steps. She wore an all black Prada strapless calf length dress that left her back and shoulders exposed but hugged her in all the right places. She wore black a pair of strappy four inch stiletto Prada shoes. That wavy black hair of hers was neatly curled and pulled into a pin up that truly brought out her freshly waxed eyebrows, long eyelashes, and pretty brown eyes.

"What's up?" Tremaine stood staring at her taken by her appearance.

"My bad, I took so long." She said looking from Tremaine to her father and only imagining what their conversation consisted of.

"Nah it's cool 'cause you more than made up for the wait with your beautiful appearance." Tremaine said while staring at those glossed lips of hers.

BZZZZZZZZZZZZ! BZZZZ! Tremaine's cell phone began to vibrate and he answered it. It was the limo driver telling him that he was out front. "The driver just pulled up out front, are you ready?"

"Driver?" Khalilah walked towards the window and looked through the curtains. "You rented a stretch Benz Limousine?" she asked surprisingly.

"Benz huh?" Her punk ass daddy asked as if Tremaine was some little project child who wouldn't know anything about that.

"Yeah a Benz," Tremaine said with a hint of arrogance in his voice. Tremaine couldn't help but notice that she was looking phat in that dress. The stretch Benz limousine was dark blue and as long as a MTA Bus. When the driver opened the door for them to step in, Khalilah paused and said, "Hold up, I almost forgot something." She then headed over to her car, which was parked in the driveway, and opened the trunk.

"What's up? What's wrong?" Tremaine yelled out behind her.

"Nothing, I just forgot something," she yelled back to him as she closed her trunk. When she returned back to the limo, she was carrying a small white box with a red ribbon wrapped around it. She handed the box to Tremaine.

"What's this?' he asked accepting the box.

"It's your graduation present," Khalilah said before climbing into the limousine.

"I thought I received my gift earlier?" Tremaine asked with a smile.

"Your first gift was for tonight." Khalilah said while guiding his chin with her index finger, inviting him in to a kiss.

When they got inside of the vehicle the interior was more than exquisite. There was enough room to seat eighteen people along with three minibars, three televisions, a DVD player and two Playstation three's. The driver called them from the phone up front and asked them their destination. Tremaine told him just head towards downtown Baltimore and he would let him know once they hit the city. To be honest he had no plans of doing anything but riding around for a few hours and then it would be straight to the hotel suite.

"Open up your present," Khalilah said as she slid closer to him and placed her leg over Tremaine's lap. When he opened the 5x7' sized box and folded back the paper wrapping on the side he saw that it was a book. "Black Enterprise Titants: Black CEO's Who Redefined and Conquer American Business." Tremaine said reading the title aloud.

"I was at a bookstore on campus and I remembered a phone conversation when you said that you wanted to own your own business. So with that in mind, I figured maybe this book could give you a little insight on it."

Once again she had Tremaine speechless. A Book? Were the words that Tremaine said to himself since he could never recall anyone giving him a book as a gift. He was a bit mesmerized by the whole situation. "Yeah I did say that, you're right. Good lookin' out I appreciate it," he said as he sat staring at the book's cover.

"Who knows in a few more years you might be in the new edition of this book." Khalilah was staring him square in the eye as if she could see straight into his soul.

"Yeah anything's possible with a little hard work," Tremaine said reciprocating her gaze.

"I know that's right."

The two of them ended up becoming so comfortable inside of the Benz that they instructed the driver to stop at Nick's on Washington Boulevard. They both ordered themselves two rotisserie chicken breast dinners with a side of macaroni and cheese and greens and they were good. Something simple and easy like the big homie

Biggie Smalls said, *"I know you're use to slow C.D.'s and Dom P., but tonight it's six packs an eight tracks while I hit that."* The limo drove through all Baltimore City. The entire time, Tremaine and Khalilah were enjoying their rotiserrie chicken breast dinners and one another's company.

After completing their meals, Tremaine and Khalilah decided to tap one of the mini-bars and open up a bottle of Rose' to sip on. Khalilah had taken her shoes off and had her legs dangling across Tremaine's lap again. Eventually they began to kiss which led to Khalilah sucking on his bottom lip. Tremaine then placed his hand over her breast and began to caress her nipple slowly through her dress with his thumb. He then began to kiss on her neck, softly dragging his moist lips across her neck, while releasing soft breaths to increase her arousal. Every two or three kisses he would go back and rub his tongue across the spot he had just left, before moving on to the next.

Tremaine slowly began to slide his hand under Khalilah's dress. She slightly opened her legs on his lap, making his journey that much easier. When he guided his hand beyond her soft warm thighs, Tremaine could feel the smooth silk feel of her underwear. Finding what he was looking for, he began to caress Khalilah's clitoris through her underwear causing her to let out soft moans that seemed to come from within the pit of her stomach. There was no mistaking the wetness that could be felt trickling through her panties as Tremaine took his index finger to move them to the side. He then entered her with his middle finger.

"SSSSSSSS!" She inhaled deeply and let out a louder moan while Tremaine still kissed and sucked on her neck and ears. Khalilah's pussy had become so wet it felt as if her juices had formed a puddle of water in the palm of his hand. He began to use his middle finger and curl it back and forth, while simultaneously rubbing on her clitoris with his thumb. Tremaine wanted her so badly and his erection was so hard that it was beginning to pain him

as it pressed against the zipper of his pants. Khalilah quickly subsided all of that when she reached down for his zipper to free his member. She began to rub the pre cum all around the head of his dick before stroking it gently up and down.

Removing his finger from her pussy, Tremaine rubbed his fingers together, they were nearly dripping with Khalilah's sweet juice. He then licked her sweetness off of his fingers enjoying the taste of watermelon scent that she gave off. He then knelt down on his knees in front of her placing his hands under her thighs and pulling her towards him. When he did that Khalilah's dress arose up to her waist exposing the wet crotch of her underwear. Tremaine gripped the panties on both sides and pulled them down slowly. After removing them, he held the soft material to his face inhaling the true essence of her aroma.

As Khalilah lay back in the seat, Tremaine was able to see that not only did she have good hair up top but down low as well. It was smooth and possessed the feeling of a single rose petal. He leaned forward and grabbed her thighs, placing them one by one over his shoulders. Both of her feet were flat on his back as he spreaded her pussy lips and watched that golden brown clitoris smile back at him. SSSSSSS! Mmmmmmmmmm! Ohhhh! Tremaine!

As Tremaine sucked her clitoris in a downward stroke, allowing his full flat tongue to glide against it on the upward stroke, Khalilah began to graze her nails along the back of his head. She would dig a little deeper each time Tremaine hit that spot and sucked on the clitoris as a whole. Not being able to take it anymore, she grabbed him by his ears gently while pulling him up towards her face.

"Put it in Boo, please put it in." Khalilah begged as she began to suck her juice's off his lips.

Tremaine gripped her thighs and rested them on his forearms while Khalilah wrapped her left arm around his neck. She pulled him closer and used her right hand to guide his erection inside of her. As he slowly entered her, she wrapped both of her arms around his neck and began to lick the outer edges of his ear on to his earlobes. Tremaine felt goose bumps form on his skin as the feel of her tight, very wet, vagina engulfed his penis. The more he began to stroke her, the tighter she would hold on to him. Khalilah then leaned back and gave Tremaine a full view of her playing with her clitoris as he entered her.

Tremaine was beyond words as he watched the sight of his penis glide in and out of her pussy with a glistened shine on it from her abundance of wetness. Feeling herself beginning to climax, Khalilah pulled Tremaine back into her grasp, while digging her nails into his back as her body tensed up. Even after the shock waves subsided within her, Khalilah and Tremaine sat there in that same position holding one another. He hadn't reached his climax, but wasn't the least bit worried since he knew there would be plenty of time for that in the suite. The peaceful look on her face, as she rested her head on his shoulder with her eyes closed, was more than enough at that moment for Tremaine. For the rest of the ride to the hotel he and Khalilah whispered sweet nothings into each other's ears in anticipation of getting to the hotel.

Before arriving at the hotel, Tremaine's cell phone began to vibrate in his pocket breaking the mood.

"Hello"

"Tre?" His aunt Shelia spoke into the line.

"Yeah what's up?"

"I have Dollar on three way," she said.

"What's up Yo?" Dollar joined in.

159

"Shit what up nigga?"

"Tre watch your mouth," his aunt Sheila said.

"Oh my bad Aunt Sheila. What's up tho' yo?"

'Pssssh, just trying to maintain without complaining, you feel me?" Dollar said.

"I feel you cuz. What time is your bond hearing on Monday?" Tremaine asked.

"I don't even know, on some real, I ain't even gonna hold my breath for that shit 'cause these crackers don't be tryin' to give no bonds out on murders or attempts."

"Yeah I feel you," Tremaine said feeling his anger rise at the fact that his lil' cousin was even in that situation. "When are your visiting hours though?"

"For real Yo, you ain't gotta visit me, I just need you to holla at them peoples for me and make sure everything's everything…you know?"

Tremaine already knew that Dollar was talking about the nigga that he shot and told on him. "Hey cuz come on, that goes without sayin'. Just let me know where the store at that you want me to get the shoes from and I'ma get them off the top first thing smokin' alright?

Tremaine coded it knowing that Dollar would catch the meaning of his words.

"Alright but look here I ain't got that much time left on this phone but I'ma get at you Monday after I come from court?"

"Already, I'ma holla at you my nigga."

"Later."

Tremaine could hear stress in his little cousin's voice, but he also knew that Dollar was a soldier and could maintain. He was also sure that as long as he was out in the streets with this bitch nigga who put him in there, Dollar's chances of beating the case were very excellent. Tremaine wasn't really going to stress that to Dollar because actions always spoke louder than words. On that note, he planned to let his actions scream out as if he were holding a bull horn.

The stretched Benz pulled up at the hotel, as the conversation with dollar came to an end. The suite that Khalilah and Tremaine occupied was more like a penthouse than a hotel room. It had an eat-in the kitchen, living room, bedroom and a Jacuzzi with separate shower. Shit, for five hundred a night Tremaine wasn't expecting anything less than perfect. He and Khalilah had sweaty, passionate sex in each and every room in that suite. They were both so hungry for one another that they had sex in the living room, on the kitchen table, in the bed and beside the bed.

Khalilah kept Tremaine going with her sexual appetite as if she were the energizer bunny. He started to ask her when was the last time she had some dick, since it seemed as if she were making up for lost times. In spite of his thoughts, Tremaine knew better than to ask a female about her past because for real, he didn't want to know. He had learned long ago to never ask a question that he wasn't prepared to hear the answer to.

The next morning, about check out-time, Tremaine noticed that Khaliah's demeanor had changed. She had become real quiet and reserved, not saying too much. *The way I just put pipe in her ass, she was supposed to be walking around singing as if she were Patti Labelle,* Tremaine thought. "Come here, why you so quiet?" he said walking up behind her while placing his hands around her waist.

"I was just thinking about something that's all," Khalilah said placing her hands on top of his.

"What's up? What's on your mind?" Tremaine turned Khalilah around to face him.

"Nothing," she responded not looking him into his eyes.

"Nah, come here for a minute." He led her over to the couch and sat her down on his lap. "Now what's up? Talk to me."

Khalilah hesitated for a second trying to figure out how to word her feelings. "Tremaine let me ask you something," she said.

"I'm listening."

"Have you always been totally honest with me?" she asked staring deep into his eyes.

"Huh? Yeah I been..."

"Hold up." Khalilah put her finger over his lips. "You don't have to answer that. I'm just gonna come out and tell you why I asked you that." She took a deep breath before she began to speak. "Since we met back up over the spring break and started spending time with each other, I've been watching you very closely and not by choice but by force. The reason why I say that is because when I first saw you in Miami, all my feelings for you came rushing back to the forefront making me feel as if I were ten years old all over again. Now I've noticed every time that we go out you don't spend nothing less than a thousand dollars, and you're not working Tremaine. Now I know you say that you're staying with your uncle but I also noticed that the night I stayed over your house we slept in the master bedroom where all of your clothes and belongings were, and there was no sign of anyone else staying there."

Damn I guess she was more on point than I thought. "Hold up I'm saying right..."

"Tremaine you don't owe me any explanation, just hear me out for a minute." Khalilah grabbed both of his hands and held them to her chest. Tremaine nodded his head and she continued. "Now I don't really know your situation and I don't need to know, for now, but I just want you to be careful Tremaine, because whether I'm with you or not, I couldn't stand to see you hurt. You are too smart to allow yourself to get caught up out here."

Tremaine cut in, "I feel that but let me say this…" He kissed her twice on her lips and said, "I'ma be alright, don't even stress it." There was nothing else that he could say since she had already known that he was lying about the uncle. There was no denying the money

he threw around whenever they were together. Khalilah had gotten closer to him, in a shorter period of time than any other female he dealt with in the past. She was the first and only one who had been inside of his home, where the rest of the broads he dealt with, either found themselves in a hotel or at the Greenspring apartment. It was almost inevitable that she would catch on to certain things since they had become so close to one another.

The entire cab ride back to her house, Khalilah slept with her head on Tremaine's shoulder. She had him thinking about what she said, in addition to all the fucking they had done the night before. Tremaine watched her as she slept, and thought about how sexy she looked even with her mouth hanging open.

Thoughts he never pondered on began to cross his mind. He found himself wondering just how long he planned to do the things he was doing. He had close to two hundred and fifty thousand saved up at this point, thanks to his man Lil' L and them Pennsylvania Avenue niggas. They were going through a whole brick every five days, strictly hand to hand corner sales. Word had gotten around on their hood that 'L' had them six deuces of butter for a hundred dollars, cheaper than regular prices. When that happened, Tremaine estimated that he would be sitting on at least four hundred thousand dollars within the next four to five months. He made a mental note to start checking out the process that a person would have to go through in order to open their own business.

****

When they finally arrived at Khalilah's house, Tremaine got in his car and headed home. As he placed the book that Khalilah had given him inside of his glove compartment, he noticed the envelope his mother had given to him the day of his graduation. He recalled how she stressed to him the fact that he was to read the contents when he was alone. Tremaine decided that he would read the letter once he arrived at his house.

14 UNCONDITIONAL LOVE

Dear Son,

First and foremost I want to congratulate you on your achieving a remarkable task, that's graduating from high school. I know that I don't have to tell you, many have failed while trying to accomplish it, but you have shown perseverance and resourcefulness to complete that goal in your life. It seems like yesterday that I was waking up in the middle of the night to feed you your bottle while holding you in my arms. Son, I want you to know that I love you with all of my heart and even though I may not tell you as much as I should, I just wanted you to know that I do. You have your whole life ahead of you now and I want you to think long and hard on how you plan on spending it.

Tremaine, it's important that you take notice to a lot of your peers and how their lives have turned out, and ask yourself what you want for yourself. We both can vouch for the fact that a lot of the boys that you played kickball with and rode bikes with are either dead or incarcerated. Understand this Tremaine, I've always thought of you as being special from the other kids. I'm glad that you have Khalilah (My future daugther-in-law, Smile!) in your life. She's a smart girl and you are a smart young man. The two of you together in life can accomplish anything.

Even though I used to yell and scream at you about some of the things that you were doing that I didn't, and still don't, agree with out in these streets, I wanted to let you know on this day that I am proud of you. I also wanted to let you know that no matter what, I'll always be here for you. Now I'm not going to lecture you, but I ask that you take some time out for yourself, some Tremaine time, and make an assessment on what it is that you truly want out of life. I know that with careful consideration and the love and support that you have from your family and loved ones, your decision will reflect the true knowledge and wisdom that you've acquired over the years.

Sincerely & Respectfully,

Loving you always!

MOM

Over the years, Tremaine's mother had reluctantly come to accept her son for the person that he was. She could never agree with some of his choices but nonetheless, she still loved him. Mrs. Jenkins had witnessed the way her son was treated in the neighborhood and wondered if people respected or feared him. There had been a number of stories circulating about what her son had supposedly done and though a few of the things she could believe, there were some things she just would not allow herself to accept as the truth.

Tremaine's mother blamed herself for a lot of his ways, thinking back when she was on welfare and had developed a crack addiction. The entire addiction only lasted for a year; Tremaine was about five years old. He was too young to understand what was going on at the time. It took a horrific experience one night, while trying to cop some crack, to change Mrs. Jenkins entire life. Two local drug dealers, who couldn't have been more than sixteen years old, accused her of paying with counterfeit money on a crack purchase from earlier that day. Even though she strongly denied the accusations, being as though that night's purchase was her first of the day, the dealers still took it upon themselves to lash out on her.

That night Mrs. Jenkins was beat and raped viciously. In the midst of the beating, the young dealers got their hands on a broom stick and rammed it repeatedly inside of her vagina damaging the insides to the point where she couldn't have more children. After that experience, Tremaine's mother never smoked another narcotic a day in her life and placed all of her focus on getting off of welfare and pulling her life together. That was why, even though she knew her son was participating in illegal activities, she would never disown him because just like in her own life, she knew the call of the streets that was heard by young black men.

Mrs. Jenkins often prayed that her son would realize that the road he was taking was bound to end in destruction. She prayed that he would turn off that road before it was too late. She dreaded the thought of it taking a dramatic experience similar to hers for him to decide on another course in his life. She had come to the conclusion that her son was heavily involved in illegal activities. There was no denying the material things that Tremaine possessed. He would often shower his mother with expensive gifts and jewelry. Everything that Tremaine ever bestowed upon his mother was placed in a box inside of her bedroom closet and never worn. She was hoping that instead of telling him, she would show him that life was about more than materialistic things and that with or without them she was happy.

There was a time when Tremaine offered to put up the money for his mother's new house only to have her decline his offer. She happily used her own money to put the down payment on a small, yet comfortable, repossessed home that she bought from the government. To be honest Mrs. Jenkins hadn't planned on moving, but Tremaine was so adamant about her moving from on Lanvale Street. His reason to her was that she deserved better, but Mrs. Jenkins knew that in all actuality he no longer felt comfortable with her staying in the old neighborhood.

Through it all, his mother believed that Tremaine would wise up and turn out just fine. He showed her signs of that when he continued to not only attend school, but excel at it also, even after moving out on his own. Tremaine maintained a 3.20 GPA and even though it wasn't honor roll, she was still proud of him; especially since she could count on one hand how many young men his age attended school, let alone graduated. Mrs. Jenkins knew that Tremaine had a good head on his shoulders and in time it would prevail. She strongly believed in Proverbs 22:6, "Train up a child in the way he should go: and when he is old he would not depart from it."

****

Monday morning, Tremaine's Aunt Sheila called him to let him know that she was on her way to the court house for Dollar's bond hearing. She told Tremaine that she would call him that night with Dollar on the three-way to discuss the outcome. In the meantime, Tremaine had begun to read the classified section of the newspaper to see what a few storefronts and barber shops were going for. He decided that if he did choose to open his own business, he would start out with something of the sort, or maybe a strip club. Tremaine knew that if there was one thing that would always sell and never get old, it was sex.

Tremaine came to the conclusion that to start up his own establishment would cost him an average of sixty-five thousand dollars, give or take ten thousand. With the financial end taken care of, he doubted if it would be too hard to find a store for sale. The one road block he seemed to be facing was finding a front man to sign their names on the papers. The person would have to have a legitimate income that would have allowed them to have at least fifty thousand saved up, or good enough credit to qualify for that type of bank loan. Even though Tremaine intended to pay for the whole thing, the front man's financial records had to be able to back up the investment. He planned to sign on as a silent partner, putting up something under ten thousand which wouldn't draw any suspicions from the government.

A family member was Tremaine's first thought as a front man, but he had doubts. He then contemplated on one of his pipers in the "Gold Club" and decided that would be his most likely route. He estimated that it would take more than one year before he would be able to sign the papers on future establishments but first, he needed become solidified as a partner in his first establishment. Tremaine had read a few chapters of the book that Khalilah gave him and two things stood out from the few entrepreneurs he read about was that as long as one had financial backing and dedication anything was possible. He already had those two steps covered and it was now time to surround himself with people who know what it takes to run the type of business that he wanted to open.

Tremaine thought long and hard about who he could put on his team if he wanted to open a barbershop. He came up with Malik and Al, who worked at the shop where he got his hair cut. He didn't see it as a problem, getting them to work for him while bringing their regular customers along with them. With the simple offer of a nice signing bonus everything would be cool.

The storefront venture is where Tremaine drew a blank. He couldn't think of anyone who had a sufficient amount of experience in the food business. Even though all of the females in his family could cook their ass off, none of them had knowledge about what it took to hold a business together. On top of that, Tremaine reminded himself that family and business just didn't mix, at least not in a legitimate business, in his opinion. After meditating on all those things until he received a headache, Tremaine finally came up with an idea.

****

"Welcome to Burger King, my name is Latoya how may I help you?" The girl behind the counter asked.

"Yeah umm… is Marie here today?" Tremaine asked.

"Marie?" she asked with a confused look on her face.

Tremaine could see that she obviously didn't work there any longer.

"Well what about Jelissa?"

"Yeah, Jelissa's here hold up." She turned around to instruct the skinny kid on the fry machine, whom she called D.J., to go back and tell Jelissa that she had a visitor. She then turned her attention back to Tremaine. "You sure there ain't nothing I can help you with?" she said sucking in her bottom lip.

"Nah, I'm cool thanks anyway though." Tremaine noticed that while he talked, she continuously stared from his lips to his eyes, lustfully.

"You don't sound too sure of that," she responded with a little grin.

She was becoming very flirtatious and Tremaine couldn't help but to notice. He also noticed that she was definitely cute with her hair done in a bang wrap that stopped in the middle of her back. The girl was a typical little red bone, and Tremaine could see the print of her cleavage hanging over her bra through the tight uniform shirt she wore. She was definitely fuckable and he was close to hollering at her until Jelissa came walking in from the back.

"Tremaine? Boy what are you doing here?" Jelissa asked with a big smile on her face.

"What's up with you?" he returned the smile.

"Not too much. How's it been going on your end?"

"I can't complain. I see you done stepped it up and made manager, huh?" Tremaine noticed the manager tag that was pinned to her shirt.

"Yeah I've been manager for about a year now."

"I heard that. I'm saying I just stopped by because I wanted to holla at you about something."

"Oh okay. Latoya I'll be right back." Jelissa looked back at red-bone as she made her way around the counter. "Come on we can sit over here." She directed Tremaine over to the eat-in area.

When Tremaine looked back at the girl Latoya, she stuck her tongue out at him and began smiling. He knew he was definitely going to holla back at her before he left.

"So what's on your mind, Tremaine?" Jelissa asked as they both sat down. "Where's Marie? She doesn't work here anymore?"

"Nah, she hurt her back about two months ago, and right before she was scheduled to come back, her father died and left her a nice piece of change. Now you know that hussy, she decided to take some time off to splurge a little bit."

"Oh yeah? Shit she must be well off if she ain't coming back to work."

"I mean it ain't nothing for her to retire off of or nothing like that but it was close to like seventy thousand."

Bam!!! There it is right there, Tremaine thought. He had just found his front man, Marie. With a fresh seventy-thousand dollars inheritance, and her many years being in the restaurant business, he could definitely make that work. Tremaine wanted to put Jelissa down on the idea first because he knew with that Marie would follow.

"Seventy G's, huh?" he responded while trying to seem nonchalant about it.

"That's alright, but what I wanted to holler at you about a business proposition."

"A business proposition?" Jelissa said with a curious look on her face. "Like what? What did you have in mind?"

"Well, right now I'm in the process of opening my own restaurant and I was looking for a few good men."

"For real?" she asked Tremaine, who just nodded his head in response without saying a word. "What kind of restaurant are you thinking about opening?"

"I was thinking of maybe a soul food spot, you know, a place that would allow a person to get a meal that's as close to home cooking as they're going to get without being home."

"You're serious aren't you?" Jelissa asked.

"Am I serious?" Tremaine was this close to asking her ass what the fuck she thought.

"Come on Jelissa, have you ever known me not to be serious?"

"I guess you're right about that. Well I mean, I have been looking for a part time job."

"Nah Jelissa, I don't think you understand. See this place I'm opening up is being paid for out of my own pocket, every single dime of it. Now I wanted to get you and Marie on the team since you both know so much about this field of work. I wanted you to run the spot and we divide the profits 40, 30, 30." Tremaine leaned back in his chair and crossed his legs, waiting to see how she responded.

"Forty-thirty huh?" she asked. Tremaine continued to nod his head. "Where is the restaurant?"

"I want the three of us to put our heads together and come up with the perfect spot. Like I said this will be a partnership and I wanted input from the both of you."

Jelissa smiled, "I've always wanted to run my own spot."

"And here's your chance. Now I know the restaurants gonna take about three or four months before it can stand on its own two feet and turn a profit. So in between time, if need be, I'll help you with your rent and shit so you won't be assed out on your bills and plus..." Tremaine leaned forward close to Jelissa and whispered, "and if you still get down, I got some new shit that's always straight butta'."

Jelissa smiled which let Tremaine know that she still fucked around.

"Yeah it's that good shit for real. Real talk," Tremaine said.

"I know that's right," she said with an even wider grin on her face.

Tremaine "So if you're in, let me know so we can holla at Marie and get this ball rollin'."

"Yeah, I guess it's worth a try."

"Shit, worth a try? We aint gonna try shit, we're gonna do it!" Tremaine was dead serious about that statement.

"Well we can holla at Marie tonight after I get off of work," Jelissa said.

173

"Cool. Here take my cell phone number and call me an hour before you get off so I can be on point alright?" He wrote his number down on a napkin.

As Tremaine got up to leave, Jelissa asked him if he happened to have some of that good shit on him right then and there. It was a new day but nothing had changed, Jelissa was still chasing like she was when they had worked together more than three years ago. Tremaine told her that he would have that for her later that night; she continued to smile as if she was a male locked up inside of an all female prison.

Before he left, Tremaine was sure to tell Jelissa to pass his number on to Latoya. While driving home he was becoming a little skeptical about having Marie and Jelissa running his business with their crack habits. Tremaine then remembered that they both had over twenty-five years experience working in the food business and besides, he was going to be on their ass like flies on shit.

15 STATE OF AFFAIRS

BZZZZZZZZZZZ! Tremaine reached for his vibrating cell phone. "Hello."

"Tre?"

He recognized the voice as his Aunt Shelia. "Yeah, what's up?"

"I got Dollar on the line."

"What's up Yo?" Dollar chimed in.

"Ain't too much what's going down? What happened in court today?" Tremaine asked.

"Just like I thought, these people ain't tryin' to give a nigga no bond," Dollar said.

"Oh yeah?" Tremaine's disappointment was evident in his voice since he was hoping that the state would make an exception for Dollar, given his age.

"They got me on James No-Bond status for real?" Dollar joked in an attempt to lighten the mood.

"So, what's next?"

"I'm waiting on my indictment to come back from the grand jury so this whole process can start."

"So who do you want me to get you for your lawyer?" Tremaine asked.

"I'm sayin' I've been hearing about this dude named George Derusso. He's supposed to be vicious when it comes to beating murder charges and shit."

"I'm sayin' did you holla at the nigga yet to see what he was talkin' about?"

"Yeah we rapped for a minute before I called you."

"What he talking 'bout?"

"He supposed to be coming to see me tomorrow or Wednesday and then I'ma see what's up."

"I'm sayin' Yo, when are your visiting days cause a nigga tryin' to holla at you about them clothes and shit," Tremaine said knowing Dollar caught his drift.

"Nah don't worry about that, just holla at my mother cause she got something for you," Dollar said.

"Oh yeah?" Tremaine asked confusingly, wondering what it could be.

"Yeah, holla at her and check that out and I'ma be getting back at you some time later on in the week alright?"

"Alright cuz. Shelia?!... Shelia?!..." Tremaine called out into the phone.

"She must have put the phone down," Dollar said.

"I'll just call her back in 'bout ten minutes then," Tremaine said before he and Dollar said their goodbyes.

When Tremaine hung up the phone he wondered why Dollar didn't want him to come and visit him. When he caught back up with his aunt, she told him that the public defender from Dollar's bond hearing had given her a letter from Dollar for him.

When she went to go and retrieve the letter, the sight of his aunt, who usually kept herself up in appearance, was disturbing to Tremaine's sight. Even when Shelia was a crack addict and heavy into alcohol a few years ago, she was still always presentable. What stood in front of Tremaine at the front door was a worn down woman in a bathrobe with bags under her eyes. She still possessed her smooth mocha-colored skin, only now it was ashy along with her hair being a mess. It was clear to Tremaine that Dollar's whole situation was taking a toll on her.

Dollar was Shelia's oldest of two sons, his little brother Kelvin was six years old. It was Dollar who had been the one to stand beside his mother throughout her whole ordeal of trying to kick her habits. Up until a few months ago, when Shelia found a job, Dollar was the one who took care of all of the bills and meals inside of the home. He and his mother were more like close siblings than mother and son. Seeing his aunt's pain and understanding what she was going through, Tremaine decided to stay a while to make sure that she was alright. When he asked her if she was holding up she simply responded, "Yeah I'm okay," while running her fingers through her hair in an attempt to straighten it up a little bit. The finger combing was ineffective in helping to correct her appearance.

"You know everything's gonna be ok, right?" Tremaine spoke as he sat down on the couch next to her.

"Tre, they're treating my son like he's some type of damn animal or something. I mean he's only fifteen years old and I was told that if he's found guilty of this he could get life in prison," she said with tears starting to form in her eyes.

"Come on Shelia, don't even think about that right now." Tremaine grabbed hold of her hands and said, "We're gonna get him this lawyer and everything's gonna work out just fine."

Shelia firmly squeezed his hand. "I hope so Tre, I truly do. The umm... the letter Dollar sent you is over there on the table."

When Tremaine picked the letter up he acted as if he was going to the bathroom but cut over into his aunt's bedroom instead. He took all of the cash that he had in his pocket, which was close to fourteen hundred dollars and put it on her dresser. He knew that if he had tried to put it in his aunt's hand she wouldn't have taken it.

Shelia offered Tremaine something to eat while he sat with her for a little longer but he declined and eventually left, feeling anxious and curious to know what Dollar had put in his letter. If he was lucky, Tremaine figured it would be the nigga that he shot address. When he got outside to the car Tremaine began to read it.

Big cuz, what's up Yo? If you're reading this then you already know that they denied my shit, which was to be expected. The card inside of here is the number to the lawyer that I'm going to hire. I need you to get the money that he wants in order to take my case and take it to him. I got seventy-five G's stashed up in the spot. It's behind the head board of my bed. You might need a hammer to pull the cover off of the back of it in order to get the cash out.

When you call the lawyer, take him whatever he needs. As far as coming to see me, I don't want you to do that because they keep records on everybody that comes to visit us, and you know that's going to be one of the first spots they check out when the demonstration is done. As soon as you pay the lawyer for me it's going to take him a couple of weeks to get my discovery package. When he gets it, I'ma make sure that he gives you a copy of it so you'll know where that store is because that package will have everything you need to know. I'm about to let this kite fly, but I'll holla at you later this week cuz. One Love!

From a soldier (Lil' cuz)
to a
To a general (Big cuz)

P.S. you know they got me on the tier with Fat Leon. He said Lil' Black been trying to holler at you. Here's his name and info where he's locked up at: Brian Landers #280-292

Baltimore City Detention Center

401 E. Madison Street

Baltimore, Maryland 21202

Tremaine now saw why Dollar didn't want him to come and see him. He had totally forgotten all about the signing in and I.D. that a nigga had to go through when they went to visit an inmate. When he was able to catch up with the nigga Dollar was locked up for, Dollar and all of his associates would be the first people the police suspected. Dollar's visiting list was one of many ways the police could find out who his closest associates were. The last thing Tremaine needed was for the authorities to come snooping around for a murder and stumble upon the other activities he had going on in his life. He could definitely wait, he told himself, until the lawyer handed him a copy of the discovery package. It would have the name of the victim, his statements as well as his address so everything wouldfall into place.

Tremaine was fucked up at himself that he hadn't hollered at lil' Black since he put those hot balls up in Benny almost two years ago. He had intentions of getting at lil' Black but that shit had slipped his mind. If it wasn't for fat Leon, who hustled out of the same store as Black, he probably wouldn't have hollered at lil Black. Tremaine wasn't about to let his homeboy slip his mind again. The first chance he got that day, he went and purchased ten one fifty dollar money orders, dropped Black a few lines to go along with one of the money orders while mailing the rest separately. The letter consisted of his cell phone number and the address of a member of the "Gold Club" with instructions for Black to holler at him about whatever he needed.

****

A few weeks had gone by and Tremaine, Jelissa and Marie began to check out different store fronts in an attempt to find the perfect location for their new restaurant. When Tremaine and Jelissa threw the proposition at Marie she was more than happy to go along with it. Especially when she found out that she wouldn't have to spend any of her inheritance money. She had already spent close to twenty-five thousand dollars of the money on clothes, furniture, and crack. After much researching and debating, they all agreed on a spot that was no more than five minutes from Pennsylvania Avenue. The place was an old "McDonalds" restaurant that was located on W. North Avenue.

Since she was studying to be an accountant, Tremaine wanted to run the paperwork by Khalilah, but she had already left for her internship in Chicago. She had already been there for one month and wasn't due back for another two months. Tremaine couldn't even front with his game face, Khalilah was gone and he was missing her heavily. They would talk on the phone daily but it wasn't the same as being able to hold and touch her.

****

It had been a little over three weeks since Tremaine had spoken with Los. It was becoming a normal routine for them to go almost an entire month without speaking to one another. It was definitely obvious that shit had changed between them; the feeling was in the air. To be honest, since Tremaine knew that Los was aware of him having something to do with his man getting killed, he had to seriously fight back the urge to kill Los. He didn't like the feeling of sitting back and wondering what Los had up his sleeve. With all that aside, Tremaine was the first to admit that he would always be indebt to Los for putting him on in a major way. Had it not been for him he knew that he would not have made it as far as he had in such a short period of time, so there were some things he could never forget.

Tremaine's closest homeboys, at the time, were Dirty and Dollar, in spite of him being locked up. Juice had begun to tighten his game up a tad bit by slowing down on smoking so much haze and setting his sights on getting some real money. He went ahead and plead guilty to the gun charge in turn receiving two years unsupervised probation. Tremaine had also begun to fuck with lil' Chris more and more since he also was beginning to step his game up a notch. Chris took his business out to Anne Arundel County and set up shop out there. The entire county was jumping a lot more because of him. Tremaine was selling him whole bricks of powder and he was going through them like shit.

All in all, each member of their crew was getting money in impressive amounts. Each of them was sitting on something nice and they all had their own spots and individual clientele that they were dealing with. But not to get it fucked up, if anything went wrong or any problems arised, they would unite like Voltron on a nigga's ass. The most difficult task that they faced was to get where they all were without any real complications. They each were fairly known throughout Baltimore but it wasn't to the point that their names were ringing out of everyone's mouths. Tremaine had to admit that being inconspicuous was something he learned from Los, who would always quote Jay-Z's verse, *"You gotta let your shit bubble quietly and then you blow."* Regardless of where the phrase came from, it has basically become the motto of Tremaine's crew.

With Tremaine's suggestion, the crew, including Los and his boys would still all go to parties or strip clubs to hang out. But they were more content when they would rent out a banquet hall or hotel suite with seven or eight strippers. After inviting eight to ten of their closest homeboys, the fellas would have a private party with the best strippers the city had to offer. The night clubs were cool, but their way, everybody was guaranteed to fuck a phat ass female that night, which was the whole point of going out to party in the first place.

After seeing how things were coming along with Tremaine and his restaurant, Dirty had begun talking about opening his own Barbershop/Hair Salon. Everything was moving in the right direction but the main thing that was missing was that nigga Dollar, but all of that was soon about to change.

16 THRU DA WIRE

"Hello."

"Mr. Jenkins?"

"Who dis?" Tremaine asked not recognizing the voice.

"It's Mr. Derusso."

"Oh, Mr. Derusso what's up, how've you been doing?"

"I'm doing pretty good I was just calling to let you know that I've acquired Mr. Carter's discovery package and I'm in the process of having your copy made as we speak."

"Okay, okay umm…" Tremaine had to catch himself because a rush of excitement had overcome him, "When do you think you'll be ready for me?" he asked feigning calmness.

"Well my secretary's copying it right now, so I suppose she'll be ready within the hour."

"Well I guess I'll be seeing you in an hour then," Tremaine said.

"I have a prior engagement that I have to tend to so I won't be here, but I'll make sure to tell her you're coming by to pick it up. How's that?"

"Okay that's fine, I'd appreciate that."

"Okay and I'll be calling you sometime later this week to let you know my assessment of the case once I'm done dissecting the whole package. But I'll tell you since I've given it a look over; so far the victim's statement is the main thing that's incriminating us."

Yeah not for long, Tremaine thought. "I understand that. I guess I'll be talking to you later," he said.

"Okay I'll talk to you later," Mr. Derusso said hanging up.

When Tremaine got off of the phone the only thing he could say was, "About time!" He was beyond anxious to get the ball rolling and to be able to get on top of the situation for his little cousin, Dollar. He was disturbed that they were even holding Dollar for the bullshit case. Mr. Derusso wanted twenty thousand to take Dollar's case but Tremaine had only given him ten thousand with the promise to get the other ten to him before trial. He saw no need to pay the entire twenty since there wasn't much chance of the case making it to trial in his eyes. Tremaine decided against hitting Dollar's stash for the lawyer money and paid for it out his own pocket.

When Tremaine arrived at Mr. Derusso's office downtown, he was handed a manila envelope by his secretary that was at least an inch thick with papers. He immediately returned home and began reading the papers, which contained everything that he had expected. Police reports, hospital records, and a diagram of the victim's body, showing where he had been shot. The envelope also contained the victim's age, height, weight, eye color, social security number, address, phone number and an excessive amount of other information. Just as Mr. Derusso had said, the only thing against Dollar was the victim's statements.

That night Tremaine went down the street from his house to call Ernesto's home at a gas station's pay phone. After the second ring a female picked up the phone.

"Can I speak to Ernesto?" Tremaine asked.

"Hold on," she said, "Ernesto!... Ernesto!... Pick up the phone." Tremaine could hear the female yell into another room.

After a few seconds, a young male voice answered the phone. "Hello?"

Tremaine went into his best female impersonation voice that he could muster up, "Ernesto?"

"Yeah, who's this?" the male asked.

Click! Tremaine disconnected the call, which was all he needed to know. Ernesto was still staying in the same place as the package stated he was. It was now time to pay Ernesto a visit.

The next day, Tremaine drove up Park Heights in search of Ernesto's home. He initially had to ride around the area a few times since he wasn't too familiar with the street name. When he finally located the address, he saw that Ernesto lived in a complex called Loyola Southway complex that consisted of twenty-five buildings. Tremaine initially wanted to walk up to the door, hoping Ernesto would answer, and wet him up on the spot. He quickly dismissed that idea. He told himself that he had been watching too many movies, as that plan had a thousand and one loop holes in it. If by chance someone else were to answer the door then he would have to wait for them to go and get Ernesto, kill him and the person who answered the door, in addition to whoever else was in the home that could identify him. All of those unnecessary shots were bound to draw too much attention from nosey ass neighbors.

After coming up with a second plan Tremaine decided to drive to the carry-out down the street from Ernesto's home and use the pay phone to call the number. After three rings the same female voice from the day before answered the phone and informed Tremaine that Ernesto wasn't home and that he would be back within the hour. With that, Tremaine drove back out to the complex and decided to simply wait for the boy's arrival. It was already starting to get dark and the sun was in its middle stages of setting.

Tremaine parked the 300ZX he was driving in between two cars, one building down from Ernesto's. After three hours of anticipating Ernesto being inside of each passing car and getting more excited when a car stopped in front of his building, Tremaine was becoming irritated. Besides that, he had already made up his mind that he wouldn't be leaving until he got who he was looking for.

One man didn't realize how close he came to becoming a memory when Tremaine spotted him and thought he was the target, but quickly realized that the man was taller than what the police reported.

Two teenaged boys heading down the sidewalk caught Tremaine's attention. One of the boys walked with a limp on his right side and Tremaine was aware that the report said the victim had been shot twice in the chest, once in the neck as well as a single wound to his right hip. Tremaine readjusted his rearview mirror, because he was backed into the parking space, and slouched down in the front seat. The boy with the limp fit everything in the profile but the weight, which Tremaine couldn't tell because the boy had on baggy clothes. He was sure the second one wasn't Ernesto since he was a fat boy of the right height, but was at least eighty pounds over the profile weight.

When the two boys got close to Ernesto's building they hooked a right and headed up the walkway of the building. Tremaine pulled up the black bandanna he had tied around his neck in order to cover up his nose and mouth, hurried out of the car carrying his pistol grip shotgun close to his side. It was completely dark outside. Unless a person was close up on him, there was no way that they could tell that there was a shotgun clung to the side of his leg. He jogged slightly to catch up with the duo.

Just as they were entering the hallway and going up the steps, Tremaine called out, "Ernesto". The boy with the limp turned around first, followed by the heavy one.

"Ernesto, what's up homie?" Tremaine pressed on trying to be sure that he had the right person.

With his hands held out in front of him and fear written all over his face the smaller of the two boys said, "Hold up main man, do I know you? What's up?"

"Ain't shit I just got a lil' message for you that's all," Tremaine said noticing that the fat boy had his fist balled up and was grilling him with an evil look. Tremaine's initial intentions were to shoot the fat boy in the leg or some place, just to take him down, but let him live since Ernesto was the target. But since his fat ass wanted to play super thug in the eye of a shotgun toting killer, then he brought that on himself, Fuck Him!

BOOM! Chk-Chk BOOM! Chk-Chk The first blast caught big boy square in the chest, directly above his heart. The impact of the blast spun him around leaving him to fall face forward on the railing of the steps. The second shotgun landed on the back of his neck, leaving peeled off chunks of meat from the shoulder area to the back of his head. After the second shot, Ernesto's body shifted sideward as his eyes became as big as fifty cent coin pieces. He looked at Tremaine, literally shaking, and was too afraid to move. In one last act of desperation he let out a loud cry, "HEEEEEEELLLLL…." BOOM! Chk-Chk BOOM! Chk-Chk.

The first blast slammed the fat boy's body down on the steps behind him when the slugs met directly with his stomach area, opening it up and leaving it with the image of a busted watermelon. The follow-up shot found its way to his chest cavity leaving traces of flesh and cloth splattered on the brick wall that lined the stairwell. His eyes were stretched open as he gazed up towards the ceiling. His left leg and right arm shook uncontrollably from the interrupted nerves as a result of being shot.

Tremaine walked closer towards the two bodies and placed the barrel of the shotgun on Ernesto's forehead. BOOM! He left what used to be the boy's face looking as if it were a pile of mince meat with a chunky dark substance, that resembled a cherry and blueberry pie filling, leaking out of the back of his skull. Closed casket like a mother fucker!

Tremaine could hear the sound of a lock turning on one of the apartment doors in the building and quickly turned around to exit the hallway. He didn't bother to look back while he jogged across the grass and back towards his car. He tossed the smoking shotgun onto the passenger seat and drove out of the lot, making sure not to turn on his lights until he reached the exit of the parking lot.

That following morning, Tremaine was up early to find a newspaper stand that carried the Baltimore Sun in search of the Maryland section. He immediately found what he was looking for in an article with the headline that read *"Two Teens Shot and Killed in Loyola Southway complex."* The paper stated that Ernesto died on the scene, but the second teen, whose name was Lawrence, died while the paramedics attempted to work on him. The article also mentioned that the police didn't have any leads or suspects at the time. The first thing Tremaine did was call Mr. Derusso and asked him if he had read today's "Baltimore Sun?" He said he hadn't and when Tremaine informed him about what was in there he immediately sent his secretary to buy one.

After reading the article, Mr. Derusso informed Tremaine that on the date of trial, he would request that the judge to drop all charges against Mr. Carter, in light of the unforeseen occurrence.

When Tremaine called his Aunt Shelia, she began to get excited and was getting ready to call Mr. Derusso with a thousand and one questions. He informed her of everything that the lawyer said and she decided to go and visit Dollar to tell him the news in person. Tremaine simply told her to tell Dollar that he would see him when he got out.

Dirty was beefing with Tremaine because he hadn't put him down with the move ahead of time. He wanted desperately to be a part of taking out Ernesto. Once the fellas realized that Dollar was coming home soon, they began making plans for another vacation. Jamaica or either a cruise was at the top of their list.

A couple of days went by; Mr. Derusso called Tremaine to inform him of the arranged meeting that he had with the Judge, which was requested by the State's Attorney after acquiring the new information about their witness. The news wasn't exactly what he expected. Mr. Derusso said that, in spite of Ernesto's death, the state's attorney still wanted to proceed with the case on the grounds that they had the victim's statement and that was all that mattered. Tremaine asked him how the fuck could they try to give Dollar prison time for attempted murder when the victim was already dead. It wasn't as if the nigga was still able to press charges or anything.

Mr. Derusso explained to Tremaine that the judge had set a decision date for two months away. He told Tremaine not to worry because he was certain that Mr. Carter would be released on that date. He said the only reason the date was set so far ahead was because Mr. Carter was now a suspect in the murders of Ernesto and Lawrence. They didn't want to set him free before they had a chance

189

to investigate. Tremaine wasn't worried about that, since he left no loose ends. He took Mr. Derusso's word about dollar coming home and began to put his attention back on his restaurant, which was scheduled for grand opening in two weeks.

17 HOOD RICH

On the day of the grand opening everything was straight. In the weeks leading up to it Tremaine had hired a few more people, taking advantage of the opportunity to get Marie's mother on the team. She could make ten different flavors of hot wings and every last one of them was kicking. Tremaine, Jelissa, and Marie decided on the name, "Str8Soul" for the restaurant. At the grand opening, the spot was packed wall to wall with patrons licking the sauce off of their fingers. Tremaine had two for one flyers distributed for the grand opening and people were flocking for the deal.

With Khalilah returning from her summer internship, she was there by Tremaine's side to celebrate his vision coming to life. She was there encouraging him as he ran his spot like clock work on that first day. When she first returned home, she and Tremaine spent the entire weekend in his town house fucking and eating. They walked around his home that entire weekend butt ass naked as if they were out in Africa or some shit. They made up for being apart the entire summer, in just two days.

It was no secret that the two of them were definitely getting closer to one another, as Khalilah now had a drawer in his room with her underwear in it, and a few of her outfits hanging up in Tremaine's closet. That was so that she'd have a change of clothes when she spent the night over his house, which seemed to be every weekend that she came home from college. Khalilah was without a doubt playing her part and bringing shit to the table. Tremaine loved that she wasn't on no take, take, take shit.

For example, when she returned from her Chicago trip, she bought home a load of Gucci clothes for Tremaine, everything from pants and sweaters to hats and scarves. He told her that she didn't have to keep buying him things and her response was, "If I'm in the mall and I see something that would look good on you I'm buying it-period!" She stuck to her word each time. Whenever she went shopping she would always bring him something, even if it wasn't nothing but a belt, she always brought something for him.

Tremaine was caught off guard when Khalilah asked him to attend a Black Entrepreneur Conference with her in New York City. A number of black business owners and political leaders were scheduled to attend. Khalilah had been so supportive to him, especially with every idea he had ever had that the minute Tremaine noticed her Ford Taurus giving her problems, he went and hollered at Randy and bought her a new BMW X5. It cost him sixty thousand brand new which wasn't a problem since he figured that she was worth a lot more.

****

Knock! Knock! Knock!

"What's up Tre?" Shelia opened her door looking like her old jazzy self again.

"Where that nigga at?" Tremaine asked with a grin on his face. "He just got out of the bathtub. He's in the room getting dressed. What's up Dirty, Juice and I'm sorry I don't know your name but your face looks familiar." Shelia said referring to Chris as she let the four of them in her house.

"That's lil' Chris. He used to live on Argyle Avenue," Tremaine yelled over his shoulder as he headed towards the bedroom to see his little cousin. Dollar had just gotten out that morning after doing six and a half months over Supermax. All the charges were eventually dropped against him. "BABY BAAAAAABY!" Tremaine yelled out as he walked into the bedroom.

"BAAAAAAABY!" Dollar yelled back while standing in his boxers and socks. He and Tremaine slapped hands and then embraced one another with a firm hug. Dirty, Juice, and lil' Chris followed with the same routine.

"Nigga yo' lil' ass done got big," Tremaine said noticing Dollar had grown three inches and put on about twenty pounds in weight.

"All that muthafuckin' eating and working out Yo," Dollar responded while flexing one of his biceps and making a muscle.

"I heard that nigga. What's up tho?" Tremaine couldn't seem to wipe the smile off his face at the sight of seeing his little cousin again.

"Shit, ya'll niggas tell me. I'm home now, holla at a nigga. What's up? What's going down?" Dollar said.

"What's up you down for a lil' trip tonight?" Dirty asked.

"Trip? Trip to where?"

"This trip nigga. "Tremaine responded pulling out an envelope he had in his back pocket that contained all five of their tickets to the Bahamas?" They were scheduled to leave that night, giving them just enough time to do some shopping.

"The Bahamas?" Dollar asked looking at the tickets and cracking a smile "When we leave?" he asked.

"We leaving tonight Yo," Juice told him.

"Oh yeah? Shit it's whatever," Dollar responded.

"We got a lil something else for you too, cuz." Tremaine nodded at Juice, who pulled out an envelope that was five inches thick and had a rubber band wrapped around it.

"Oh yeah that's what's up," Dollar responded as he pulled off the rubber band and noticed the stack of hundreds, fifties and twenty dollar bills inside. "If it don't make dollars then it don't make sense," he said as he began attempting to count the whole stack right there.

"Yeah that's fifty thousand worth of sense right there cuz from all of us," Tremaine told him.

"Shit, good lookin' out." Dollar stuck his hand out and one by one pulled each of them in for a one arm hug.

Once Dollar was done getting dressed and was ready to go, they all headed out and hopped up inside of Juice's new 750 BMW. They headed straight to Chevy Chase to holler at their man Pierre who works in the Gucci store. After three hours of walking in and out of different stores, they had each bought enough clothes to last them for their entire four-day stay in the Bahamas. Afterwards the fellas went straight to the airport.

The trip to the Bahamas was much needed. None of them had realized just how much stress they had accumulated until they hit those beautiful shores of Nassau. Tremaine was more appreciative of their current trip for the simple fact all of them on the trip had started out together, some young and hungry lil' niggas who were strictly out chasing, going for theirs. They didn't have much, but were down for whatever. Over the last few years shit had definitely come together for them.

As he sat back in his beach chair with a large umbrella over top of him, Tremaine gazed out at the clear blue ocean water while rubbing his toes through the warm golden sand. The thoughts that flooded his mind were of the Black Entrepreneur Conference that he and Khalilah attended in New York. It was the first time that he had ever seen so many professional black people in one place. There were those who owned multi-million dollar companies all the way down to people such as himself who were just starting to get their foot in the door. The meeting provided Tremaine with a great quantity of networking as well as workshops on how to acquire capital and gain new ideas.

While at the Convention, Tremaine interacted with a gentleman from Minnesota, by the name of Anthony Johnson. The man owned a few strip malls down there and told him if he were ever interested in tapping into the market, to give him a call. Tremaine also had the pleasure of meeting a brother who owned a very lucrative vending machine company in Texas. The brother seemed to take an instant liking to Tremaine, saying that Tremaine reminded him of himself when he was younger, trying to break into the vending business. The gentleman sold everything in his machines from cold cuts to condoms. After he and Tremaine crunched a few numbers back and forth, Tremaine came to realize that there was money in vending sure enough.

The conference had an awards dinner for some of the big name brothers and sisters who were there. It also hosted a golf outing that weekend that all the attendees were invited to. Tremaine and Khalilah chose to pass it up and instead hit the hotel Jacuzzi, with later plans to fuck the rest of the afternoon. Tremaine was glad that he had been introduced to a different side of the game, one that dealt with stocks and bonds as well as mutual funds and things of that nature. He was also able to get a general idea of how CEO's were running those Fortune 500 companies.

The entire conference experience was running through Tremaine's mind as he sat there in the warm sun with a slight breeze blowing. He observed lil' Chris and Juice who were racing one another on the jet skis, while Dirty and Dollar were a little further down the beach talking to two very sexy females who looked to be of Hawaiian decent.

Tremaine imagined him and his homeboys running one of those fortune 500 companies with the sky scraper buildings and all. Those thoughts made him contemplate that much more on just how much longer he planned to live the street life.

At the tender age of nineteen, Tremaine was over the four hundred thousand mark with his savings, close to a half a million to be exact. He told himself that after his twentieth birthday he would stick to selling weight strictly to his closest homeboys, meaning the ones who were there with him in the Bahamas and no one else, no outsiders. By the time he hit his twenty-first birthday Tremaine was sure he would have his second business venture up and running and well on his way into starting his third. It was set, within the next eighteen months, Tremaine planned to move from the current phase of his life and progress to the next. His drug dealing days would soon be over.

18 THE TURNCOAT

Dogg,

"What's up cuz? Ain't shit here just still pushing on, struggling and striving you dig? I say good lookin' out on that 'Green Machine' book. I got that a few days ago. I got them pictures too. I see ya'll niggas out there funnin' like shit. I can definitely dig it though. Hopefully I'll be out there soon if it's Allah's will to let me get a lil' rhythm on the post conviction that my lawyer supposed to be filing for me next month. I'ma go ahead and get to the main reason I'm pushing you this kite right now, and the reason being is that I definitely got to holla at you about some serious shit. I wasn't trying to talk about that shit on the phone that's why I didn't call you and I didn't know about it until after you came to see me last week but on some real shit, you need to hear this shit here. I know you busy cuz, but try to find some time ASAP 'cause I definitely gotta pull your coat to this here. D.B.D.

Much Love soldier 'till my casket drops,

Black

The fuck is Black talking about he has to tell me some serious shit?
Tremaine thought. He had been making it his business now to go
see Lil' Black at least once a month in addition to hitting the C.O.
bitch, that Black was fucking, off with a pound of haze once every
two weeks. That was what Black meant about getting the 'Green
Machine' book in his letter. Until Black told him, Tremaine was
unaware that it jammed off the way that it did in the penitentiary.
Black explained to how he was making more money in jail than he
was on the streets. He explained how dudes in prison pay ten times
the price that they would pay on the street, for a smaller quantity in
jail.

After reading the letter three or four times and not having a clue
as to what he was talking about, Tremaine just said fuck it and
decided to visit him to see what was up. Black was Tremaine's
homeboy and all, but he hated the process he had to go through in
order to see him. He was always sure to go home and take a shower
first and change his clothes because there were times when those fake
ass, wanna-be police, ass C.O.'s would have a drug sniffing dog smell
the visitors before they were allowed in the facility. If by chance
those funky ass dogs sat down while sniffing a visitor, indicating
there was a detection of drugs on the person, the guards would call
the real police to have the visitor's ass laid out for a full body search,
in preparation to search the vehicle if they found something on the
person. In order to avoid that whole scenario, Tremaine made sure
he was fresh whenever he went to visit.

There were quite a few times when he'd witnessed people
getting pushed up on like that. They might not have had anything on
them but may have been smoking weed earlier that day or came in
contact with some type of narcotic and wind up getting caught on the
humble. Just the residue of drugs on a person's clothes was enough
to be detected by the dogs.

"Inmate name and number you're here to visit," the pudgy ass C.O. broad at the desk asked Tremaine as he signed in. Tremaine swore that before he began visiting Black, he had never seen so many ugly ass females in his life. It was as if there was a large sign up in front of the prison that read, "All Ugly and Out Of Shape Females Apply Within." He could count on one hand how many cute female officers he had seen in the jail and they weren't actually cute just alright, meaning they were fuckable. The other 98% of them resembled big ass silver-back gorillas. The girl that Black had picking up his purple was a skinny ass red bone whose teeth shared the same qualities of a jack o' lantern. When Tremaine asked him how he could fuck with the broad his answer was simple, "When I look in her face all I see are dollar signs."

"Brian Landers #280-292." Tremaine recited Black's name and number for the C.O. while trying to avoid staring directly into her face for too long. Looking directly at her was like looking straight into the sun, it would hurt your eyes.

"Here's a key to the lockers over there," she said pointing towards the far wall, which was occupied by fifty or more small lockers. "All watches, chains, rings, pagers, cell phones and cash must be placed inside of them." She was speaking as if she was bored with having to repeat the same line over and over again for each visitor that came in.

The prison's waiting room was full of a few younger women with kids as well as older women who looked as if they were someone's grandmother. The entire room smelled of one big potpourri basket with all of the different female's perfumes clashing. A majority of the younger girls in the room all seemed to go by one dress code, jeans and form fitting shirts with either high heels or tennis shoes. Half of them were either going to visit their boyfriends or baby's father but that never stopped any of them from trying to holler at another male that was up there for a visit.

The shit never failed for Tremaine since there was always one or two out of the bunch that would stare at him and smile. A few had even pulled up on him in the parking lot immediately after visiting their man. It was funny because they'd tell their man all types of lies about not fucking anyone and how they can't wait for them to come home, yet they weren't even off of the jail premises, trying to get some dick. Tremaine had even witnessed some of the male C.O.'s pulling up on inmate's girls and getting their phone numbers at the front desk, just before the girl went in for their visit.

"Brian Landers... Brian Landers..." the loud speaker called out in the waiting area informing Tremaine that Black was in the visiting room waiting. When Tremaine arrived inside, he had to look down the two aisles to locate where Black was sitting. The two aisles consisted of a small wall in between them with a divider on top of it, along with two wooden benches on both sides to separate the inmate and their visitor. Embracing between loved ones was permitted at the beginning and ending of a visit but any contact in between that time was unacceptable. Due to the suspicion that they could possibly receive contraband of some sort from their visitor, the visit would immediately be terminated.

Tremaine began to question Black about one of the tattoos on his arm that he had recently gotten while locked up. Tremaine had reached over the divider to lift up the sleeve on Black's T-shirt in order to see the tattoo clearer. Out of nowhere, the big doofus looking male C.O. stood up, pointed, and yelled out a final warning to Tremaine and Black about the contact. Tremaine shot the C.O. an evil look.

Throughout the rest of that visit, Tremaine occasionally looked at the guard sitting at the desk supervising the visiting room. Each time he would look their way, Tremaine would look back at him making direct eye contact with the guard, who would in turn quickly shift his eyes somewhere else or look towards the ground like the bitch ass nigga that he was. He reminded Tremaine of the type of person who had been picked on growing up and was now using his fake authority to get revenge on all of the inmates for all of his childhood stress. Tremaine did not have a problem with reassuring the guard that he wasn't a motherfucking inmate if he had to.

"What's up yo?" Tremaine said as he lifted the back end of his Dolce & Gabanna T-shirt before sitting down.

In the prison where Black was locked up, the inmates were still allowed to wear their street clothes. Actually, it was like that in the entire state of Maryland prison system. To be a prisoner, Black stayed fresh. One visit he wore a custom made dapper dan Gucci track suit that was so slick, Tremaine asked him where he'd gotten it so that he could cop one for himself.

"What was so important that you had to holla at me in person?" Tremaine said getting straight to the point.

"This shit about one of them niggas in those pictures you sent me when ya'll was on the beach."

"Which one you talking 'bout?" Tremaine had sent pictures from South Beach as well as the Bahamas trip.

"The nigga that had the linen shorts with the tank top."

Tremaine twisted his face as he tried to remember who was wearing what in the pictures.

"The light-skinned one," Black said.

"How many of us were in the picture?"

"It was you, Dirty, lil' Dollar, and three other dudes."

"Oh you must be talking 'bout the South Beach flicks then."

"I don't know but the nigga's name is umm…" Black began snapping his fingers as he tried to remember. "Carl or Charles."

There was only one homeboy in that picture whose name was close to the two. "Who you talking 'bout Los?"

"Los that's the nigga," Black said getting a little loud. "His real name Carlos ain't it?"

"Yeah yeah, why what's up wit' him?" Tremaine asked leaning closer to the divider since Black had his full attention at that point.

"If this is the same dude that I think he is, then, I gotta let you know that nigga ain't right Yo."

"He ain't right?" Tremaine was caught completely off guard with that one since "ain't right" meant that Los was talking to the police.

"Yeah, I was showing my cell buddy the pictures that you sent me and my man Delvon was at the door hollerin' at me about some other shit. He asked me if he could see the flicks and when I showed it to him he started zappin' out and gettin' all loud talking bout, "Fuck no which one of these niggas your man Black?!" So I'm like what, what's up Yo?" Black explained with a confused look on his face. "So my man was like, "I know this ain't the same nigga." He handed me the picture asking who slim was, talking 'bout the dude Carlos. I told him I didn't know slim and pointed out you, Dirty and Dollar as being the only ones I fucked wit' in the picture."

Tremaine continued to take everything in stride while he just nodded his head once or twice.

"So my man goes back to his cell and comes back wit' his photo album and some police statements and brings them to me. He showed me pictures of a rack of niggas mobbed up at the club called Redwood Trust and told me one of the dudes is the same one in your picture. Now the dude in his flick do resemble the one in your flick but I really couldn't tell because his picture was taken like seven years ago and it's about twenty heads bunched up in that one picture. Then he showed me the statements slim wrote against him."

"Yo stop playin'," was all that Tremaine managed to get out. He didn't want to believe that Los had actually done some shit like that.

"Yo I'm telling you this, no bullshit. I can't remember the nigga last name but do it start with a W? Something like Williams or Wilson?" Black asked.

"Wilcox," Tremaine said shaking his head because he was beginning to realize that they were indeed talking about the same Los.

"Yeah that's the same nigga. Straight up, slim ain't right, for real."

"This nigga testified on yo and all that shit?" Tremaine asked talking to himself as oppose to asking a question.

Black said nothing but gave a simple nod.

"Look here, tell your man I'm trying to get a copy of that statement and everything else," Tremaine said.

"You got that; I can have that in the mail to you by tomorrow."

"Cool! You do that because Yo, if this nigga did that bitch ass shit then I'ma…" Tremaine trailed off with his thoughts and let that hang in the air because he and Black both knew that shit went without saying.

After leaving from seeing Black, Tremaine still didn't want to believe the things he had just been told. Black was telling him that one of the police reports also listed Los as one of their confidential informants.

When he finally got the statements in the mail three days later, the shit hit Tremaine like a big ass boulder in his chest. There it was as big as day Los' name at the top of the statements and all of his other information. He had even testified on Black's homeboy who was actually Los' co-defendant in a murder case.

The double body homicide was in retaliation for another one of Los' homeboys who was killed two weeks prior. Tremaine read how Los explained to the police how he and his co-defendant were over a female's house off of Coldspring Lane and she was telling them about who had killed their man and where the person lived in her neighborhood. As Los and his co-defendant were leaving out of the apartment complex, they just so happened to run into the person that they were looking for. He was walking with one other person and Los' co-defendant just said fuck it, jumped out on the pair in broad day light with his guns blazing. When the smoke cleared, their target and the person walking with him was dead.

Initially, the police were clueless as to who committed the double homicide shooting but ended up hearing rumors of the culprit six months later. The name that came up was Los and the authorities caught up with him and took him in for questioning. There was no solid evidence against him and they were totally unaware of the second shooter in the case. The cops were basically foxing for information and Los bit the bait. He broke down and told everything that happened and even told that his homeboy stashed the gun over at his grandmother's house in Woodlawn. At the trial, Los crawled up on the stand like the rat he is and testified against his homeboy avoiding any charges in exchange for his testimony.

The more Tremaine read, the more furious he became. He couldn't believe the papers that he was holding. He knew that Los couldn't be trusted but he didn't think that he would do something of that caliber to a friend. In total, his co-defendant ended up receiving two life sentences plus sixty-five years.

After Tremaine showed the information to Dirty and Dollar they both were basically ready to load up and blast Los's ass. It wasn't about who he betrayed because personally, they could care less about his co-defendant. It was more about what he had done period. If he did it once, then he damn sure was capable of doing it again. The next time could be one of them on the other end of his pointing finger and that shit there was a no-no.

"Yo', why the fuck this nigga ain't call me back yet?!" Tremaine growled out as he picked up the phone and began to dial Los' pager number again for the eighth time.

"Call Lisa back and see if he got back at her yet," Dollar said as he, Tremaine, and Dirty sat in the living room of Dollar's new townhouse in Painter's Mills.

They had been posted there all day trying to catch up with Los. Lisa said that she hadn't talked to him in three days and each time she calls his phone the voice mail would pick up on the first ring.

"Fuck all this, let's ride up Parkheights and out Cherry Hill to see if his car is at one of the spots he be at," Dirty said as he sat on the couch wiping down the AK-47 that he just got his hands on a few weeks before. He was itching to put it to work.

"No bullshit, I been seriously contemplating that same muthafucking thought," Tremaine said getting very impatient with Los' not calling him back.

"Fuck that shit, he gotta be in the city somewhere. All we gotta do is ride around, find him and crush him. If any of them other niggas act like they want it, they can get it too," Dirty said while holding holding his assault rifle with a firm grip.

"Shit, I got one of the throw away whips parked right down on Dolphin Street," Dollar said.

He was referring to the collection of hoopties that they all built up for these kinds of situations. Between the three of them they had eleven throw away cars in all, which were all still spreaded throughout Baltimore.

"Which one?" Tremaine asked.

"The delta 88."

"The four door, right?" Tremaine asked making sure because he wasn't about to be jumping out on no niggas in a two door car.

"Yeah," Dollar answered.

Tremaine was ready to gas up the hooptie and not return home until Los' was found. He began to think about their plan but it seemed sloppy and uncalculated to him. He took a little time to think about other routes they could take. Dirty and Dollar began packing the AK in a gym bag along with the Tec-22 and mac-11 that they carried.

"What's up, you good?" Dollar asked Tremaine.

"Nah I was just thinking about another way we could do this cause this shit here is going to be too sloppy." Tremaine was shaking his head as he continued to brainstorm ideas.

"What other way is there? We don't know exactly where he live, all we know is where he got work at," Dirty spoke while zipping up the gym bag full of burners.

"We don't have to rush this for real because the nigga don't even know that we know what's up, so he's bound to call back before the day is out. Now if we go and shoot up the whole fucking strip for his ass, that's unnecessary work that we putting in, you feel me?"

"Dirty and Dollar sat there thinking about what Tremaine had just explained to them and it was starting to make sense. There really wasn't a need to go and shoot a whole block up like the Wild West for one nigga that didn't even know that they were looking to kill him. It wouldn't be hard for them to put their game face on around Los and act as if everything was cool before kidnapping his ass and taking him somewhere to kill him. As they all sat there in silence, deep in thought, Tremaine's cell phone began to vibrate.

"Yeah?" he answered.

"Tremaine?" It was a female voice that he really couldn't recognize because it sounded as if she were crying.

"Who is this?"

"Los' mother called me. Tre, she said that he was dead."

Tremaine immediately recognized the voice of his cousin Lisa, as she began to sob louder.

"Dead!? What do you mean dead? What happened?"

"I don't know. She said he was in a car accident and he died. What's Brittany going to do Tre?" Lisa cries were getting louder.

"Lisa come on, look check this out, I'm on my way over there alright? Just hold on, I'm on my way." He hung up the phone.

Dirty and Dollar were staring at him. "What's up my nigga?" Dollar asked.

"That nigga Los' ass already dead!" Tremaine said with a tad bit of anger in his voice, *dying in a car accident was too easy of a death for a rat bastard to die,* Tremaine thought.

"What happened?" Dirty asked, still clutching the gym bag of burners in his hand.

"Lisa just said he died in a car accident."

"Bitch ass nigga, that ain't no way for his snitching ass to go out," Dolla said speaking out loud, exactly what Tremaine was thinking.

When they arrived at Lisa's apartment, the trio was confronted with a red and puffy-eyed Lisa, who had been crying uncontrollably. Little Brittany was asleep on the couch. Tremaine could tell she had cried herself to sleep because he could see the dried up tears on her face. She began to resemble Los more and more over the years and as Tremaine sat there watching her sleep he couldn't help but to feel a bit guilty because either way his baby cousin and Lisa would be going through the same thing even if Los hadn't died in that car accident.

Lisa finally got herself together and explained that Los was on Patapsco Avenue, at a stop light, when a truck ran full speed in the back left side of his car hitting the gas tank and causing the car to burst into flames immediately. By the time the fire trucks arrived, he had been burned beyond recognition. It took the authorities two days to locate his dental records in order to identify him so that his family could be notified. Tremaine felt an eerie feeling of satisfaction when he found out that Los had burned to death, a hot death for a hot nigga.

19 SNAKES IN DA GRASS

On the day of Los' funeral, Tremaine, Dollar and Juice did not want to attend the service but felt the need to, out of the respect and love for their cousin Lisa. It was a closed casket funeral that consisted of various pictures of Los in different stages of his life, decorated on top of the coffin. There were so many attendants at the service, that people were forced to stand in the back of the church along the wall, in an overflow room with a big flat screen T.V., or outside due to lack of room.

Tremaine wondered if everyone there knew Los as the honorable little saint that the preacher made him out to be or as the snake ass nigga that Tremaine knew he was. After Los' mother, a few of his aunts and friends stepped up to the podium and told various stories about him and a few songs, including "It's so hard to say goodbye," everyone headed out to the cemetery.

Once they all gathered in the parking lot, Tremaine noticed L.B. and Mike-Mike, Los' homeboys, walking to their cars which were parked side by side. Mike-Mike was getting into a brand new charcoal gray S600 Mercedes Benz, while L.B slid into a late model 740i BMW. As he watched them get into their cars, he noticed that they were joking and laughing with one another as they opened their car doors. Tremaine thought to himself that for them niggas to have just lost one of their closest homeboys, not to mention their main connect, they sure were taking the shit rather well.

Hold the fuck up, Tremaine thought, *I know for a fact that those two niggas were Los' flunkies. They were all getting a lil money, but I know mufucking well, Los was keeping his foot on those niggas necks, just giving them enough to keep them happy.*

With that, Tremaine began to wonder just where they got the money to buy a brand new big body Benz and BMW. Anyone could tell that they were new because both of them were riding around with temporary tags on the cars. Suddenly it hit Tremaine and he kicked himself for not thinking about the situation earlier. Where was all of the paper that Los saved up over the years? Looking at L.B and Mike-Mike, he had a pretty good idea.

The day after the funeral, Tremaine decided to pay Lisa a visit to do a little investigation of his own. He found out that Los didn't have a will or anything, which wasn't a surprise, because what street nigga did? He did find out from Lisa that Los had fifty thousand dollars at her house. He gave her strict instructions for it to be used only if he ever got locked up, for her to put it towards his bail or for a lawyer, which ever necessary. Also there were another fifty thousand dollars at his mother's house which was to be used for emergency situations. Tremaine tried to mask his frustrations when Lisa told him of the fifty thousand. He knew for a fact that Los had at least ten times that saved up and every single penny now belonged to Lisa and Brittany. He began to contemplate how he would get his hands on Los stash.

20 PLAN INTO PLAY

"Come on Yo, you sure we in the right spot?" Dollar asked Tremaine as they turned off the main road onto a quiet road that was surrounded by woods.

"Hell motherfucking yeah!" Tremaine spoke with a possessed look in his eyes as he caught sight of the exact same house in the woods that Los had taken him to nearly five years ago. There it was, still sitting in the middle of nowhere, surrounded by nothing but woods. After giving it some serious thought, Tremaine figured it would more than likely be the place where Los would stash his money. A nice little house way out in the country that was surrounded by nothing but trees and grass would be any hustlers dream as the perfect stash. When he initially asked Lisa if she knew about the house in the woodsy area, she said no. Tremaine was definitely sure that the money had to be there, there weren't a lot of things that Los didn't tell Lisa. He might not have cared about them other females but he put Lisa on wifey status and she knew damn near everyone that he had business dealings with.

Tremaine put the car in reverse and parked on the side of the main road. He and Dollar walked through the woods towards the back of the house. If someone was inside he didn't want them to be aware that they were on their way up the driveway. After he and Dollar made it through the woods, they snuck around to the side of the house, toward the garage. They peeped in the side window, parked was L.B.'s new 740i but the Benz was nowhere in sight. *Fuck it,* Tremaine thought, he would rather have caught L.B. and Mike-Mike at the same time but one would be sufficient. They slowly crept back around the garage towards the back of the house and looked through the living room window. The curtains were opened slightly and they could see the television on but no one watching it.

After looking around for something to stand on and finding nothing, Tremaine gave Dollar a boost so that he could look through the kitchen window. After seeing no one in the kitchen, Dollar saw that the window was cracked open just a little under a half inch. It looked as if someone had closed it but didn't push it all the way down. Tremaine and Dollar figured that whoever was in the home had to have been upstairs or in the basement, which really didn't matter. All they knew was that they had to move quickly in order to gain access. Tremaine then had Dollar give him a boost up to the open window so that he could slide through quietly. With the boost from Dollar and the window pane that he used as a crutch, he pulled himself up on the ledge going through the window legs first. He then reached down to Dollar who handed him the mac-11. Tremaine jumped down off the counter as quietly as possible while listening to see if he could hear anything but all he could hear was the TV. Without delay, he silently opened the back door for Dollar to come in.

Tremaine tiptoed through the living room, to the steps that lead upstairs while Dollar listened for movement in the basement. Tremaine cuffed his hands behind his ear to see if he could hear anything in the upper rooms, picking up the faint sounds of loud moaning. Upon listening more closely he realized that the sounds he heard were that of someone having sex. He tiptoed back toward the kitchen where he and Dollar simultaneously met back up.

"Shh, they up there fuckin," he whispered to Dollar who simply nodded his head while holding on tightly to the tec-22 in his hand.

They both began to tiptoe through the living room and up the steps, following the sound of the moans. They carefully peeked in each room they passed in search of the moans and any additional people who may have been in the house. After checking all but two rooms, they realized that the sounds were coming from the fourth door at the end of the hall. They peeked in the last existing room before heading towards the fourth door.

"Unhhhh! Unhhh! Right there boo, don't stop! Right there!" The sounds definitely got louder when they approached the door, which was closed. Tremaine tried the door knob and turned it slowly. When he cracked open the door he noticed that the bed was on the other side of the room. He continued to open the door as quietly as possible, careful not to make it squeak and saw that L.B. had a female lying on her stomach with a pillow under her. Her left leg was straight down while her right leg was stretched out across the bed with a sweaty L.B. fucking her violently from the back.

Neither Tremaine or Dollar could fake; the nigga was fucking the shit out of the broad.

"Unhhhh! Shit! Don't! Stop! Please don't Stop!" The girl continued to cry out.

Tremaine and Dollar were standing directly behind them and neither one of them realized it. Tremaine took the Mac-11 and smacked the back of L.B.'s head so hard that blood instantly started dripping, staining the bed sheets. He let out a scream while falling forward on top of the girl. He turned around in a dazed state, holding the back of his head. The female quickly covered up with the sheets, firmly holding them to her chest as if they were bullet proof.

"Fuck what that bitch say, I advise you to stop homie," Tremaine said calmly.

L.B.'s eyes became as big as golf balls. "Tremaine?!?!? Wh-wh-wh what's up cuz?" he asked while blood seeped through his palms, looking back and forth from Tremaine to Dollar.

"Put these on nigga!" Tremaine threw him a pair of handcuffs.

L.B. looked at the handcuffs as if they were some type of foreign object and stuttered, "Co-Co-Come on Yo, what's all this for?"

Dollar then stepped forward and grabbed him by the neck before slamming him down on the bed. "Nigga turn your bitch ass over!" he said.

Before he could get the words out of his mouth, Dollar shoved the Tec-22 into his mouth knocking out two of L.B.'s front teeth. "You sayin' what nigga!" He growled as he glared down into L.B.'s pain filled eyes.

"Ahhhhhh Pleeee Nahhhhhh," L.B. was trying to mumble out words with the Tec in his mouth while blood leaked out of the corners of his lips. There were now tears streaming down his eyes. Dollar forcefully turned him over while he continued to cry and plead. "Please Yo, don't do this, tell me what I did!"

The female, who was a bad little chocolate thing, sat there the entire time with the sheet pulled up to her chest as she silently cried to herself.

"Your turn, put this shit on." Tremaine tossed the second set of handcuffs he carried over to her.

"Hold up, please listen, I ain't got nothing to do with this just let me go and I swear I won't tell nobody," she pleaded.

"Bitch I ain't trying to hear that shit put them muthafuckers on!" Tremaine said as he snatched the covers off of her exposing a very flawless body.

If he had met the girl under different circumstances he was certain that he would have been the one fucking her.

After both of them were handcuffed they were led down the stairs butter ball ass naked and shoved on the couch in the living room. There was no need to put anything over their mouths since the next house was at least a quarter of a mile down the road and noise wasn't an issue.

"Check this out L.B., I'm tired and I'm very impatient right now so I'ma ask you this one time and one time only. I'ma be sure to speak real slow so that I don't have to repeat myself, alright?" Tremaine spoke to a wide eyed L.B., who nodded his head nervously. "Now where the fuck is all that money Los left behind?" Tremaine leaned down to put his face two inches from L.B.'s.

"Wh-wh-what money?" L.B. said stupidly.

"What money, huh?" Tremaine dropped his head as he shook it in frustration. He looked over at Dollar who was sitting on the arm of the couch next to the girl. Without any words being spoken Dollar stood up and put the Tec-22 to the side of the girl's temple.

"NOOOOO...," she screamed out.

BOOM! Her body immediately tensed up as she fell sideways landing in L.B.'s lap with her eyes and mouth wide open. It seemed as if L.B would surely die of shock when his body shook uncontrollably as he looked down at the dead female in his lap, with a hole in the side of her temple. It was impossible for him to speak as he began fighting back the tears that came with the reality of knowing that it was a good chance he would soon be taking his last breath. Tremaine reached out and grabbed the girl by her hair pulling her naked, handcuffed body onto the floor. He then turned his attention back to L.B., who was now crying, and gave him a look that let him know he didn't intend on asking the question again.

L.B. definitely got the picture and began to stumble out his words, "Under the kitchen sink! It's under the kitchen sink!"

Dollar left the room heading towards the kitchen only to return and say, "Man ain't shit up under there."

Tremaine looked back at L.B. who then said, "Nah you gotta pull the refridgerator out and look on the side."

"What?" Tremaine asked frowning his face up. "Nigga get your ass up." He grabbed L.B and led his naked body into the kitchen. "Pull the fridge out," he told Dollar.

Dollar began to slide the refridgerator out of the corner. When he got it out they all looked in the spot and saw nothing but dead roaches and dirt.

"You gotta press on the little door on the side of the cabinent." L.B. instructed.

Dollar and Tremaine both gave him a crazy look not knowing what he was talking about. "On the side, in the lower right hand corner, push it in."

Following the instructions, Dollar got down on one knee to push the wood in, which made a clicking sound and when he let it go, a little compartment opened up. When he looked inside, his eyes caught sight of a small plastic bag of money vacuum sealed together. When he removed that bag there was another one. All together were eight bags. Two was filled with one hundred dollar bills, two held fifties, three held twenties, and the last one was filled with tens and fives. Tremaine found a small gym bag to put the money in and sat it down by the door. He did a last minute assessment to make sure they hadn't left anything behind. There weren't any finger prints because they both wore gloves.

After everything was straight and they were ready to leave, all that was heard was L.B. rambling on, "we cool now, ain't we? You 'bout to let me go ain't you?"

"Yeah, sure you right."

"Please Yo, come on cuz we straight now, ain't we? Huh?"

BOOM! BOOM! BOOM! L.B.'s naked, lifeless body fell to the kitchen floor with three bullets to his head.

"Now we straight," Tremaine said calmly as he and Dollar made their way out of the house.

When they arrived at Dollar's home, they realized his money machine was broke so he and Tremaine were forced to sit there and count the money out by hand. After losing count two or three times they finally got it right, five and a half hours later. The final count was six hundred and seventy six thousand dollars. Tremaine still felt that Los had to have had more money saved up somewhere else, not including the money that L.B. and Mike-Mike had already splurged with. Los's savings had to have totaled well over the one million mark, easily.

Tremaine took one hundred and sixty thousand dollars of the money and split it between him and Dollar. He decided to give six thousand dollars to Black for putting him down about Los. He then obtained through Black, Los' co-defendants' information and sent ten thousand dollars to the boy's mother house. He had Black give the boy a message, telling him that at least he could use the money to get a lawyer to try to give his time back on a post conviction. Lastly, Tremaine placed the remaining half-million dollars inside a bag and paid Lisa a visit.

Lisa was in the process of braiding her daughter's hair when Tremaine arrived at the apartment. When he stepped inside, he calmly walked over to the couch next to her and placed the bag of money down before making his way to the kitchen to get something to drink. Lisa had some nosy ways; she figured that anything that came into her home was her business. Knowing that, Tremaine was willing to bet his life she would look in his bag.

"Tre!" Lisa called out to him from the living room. Tremaine stepped back into the room sipping on a bottle of water. "Boy why in the hell are you walking around with all this money in a bag?" she was standing in the middle of her living room looking at him as if he bumped his head.

"What you want me to carry it all in my hands when I give it to you?" he asked taking another sip of water.

"You ain't gotta carry it in your hands but... Hold up what do you mean give it to me?" Lisa had a confused look on her face.

"Yeah that's your shit," he said nonchalantly.

Lisa looked down at the bag and back at Tremaine again before sucking her teeth. "Boy stop playin'. For real, why are you walking around with all this?" she poked him in the chest with the comb that she was using to do Brittany's hair.

"Come here, let me holla at you for a minute." Tremaine grabbed her hand and walked her over towards the couch. "Look here, you know that fifty thousand you got of Los' money ain't shit compared to what slim really had right?" Lisa looked down at her hands and just nodded her head with a sad look on her face as if Tremaine had just brought up a painful subject. "That money in the bag over there is what yo really had saved up. Now it took me a couple of days to get my hands on it but I did and I brought it over here to its rightful owners, which are you and Brittany." She looked up at Tremaine with a tear falling down the right side of her face. "There's half a million dollars in that bag over there for ya'll, alright?"

"Half a mi…" Lisa was at a loss for words as she peeked over Tremaine's shoulder and looked at the bag sitting on the floor, not believing that much money was sitting in her living room. "That's five hundred thousand dollars in that bag?" she asked in disbelief.

"No bullshit," Tremaine replied with a smile on his face.

"Thank you Tre!" She reached over, giving him a tight hug while kissing him hard on his cheek. They were embracing one another for at least a full minute before either one of them let go. Afterward, Tremaine spent a couple of hours with Lisa while they discussed some of the things she would do with the money. She explained to him her dream of opening a day care center and what college she visioned sending Brittany to. Tremaine put her on to a few tips that he had learned from having his own business thus far. He also shared some of the knowledge that he received at the Black Business Conference.

21 SURPRISES

It was approaching the eight month mark of the eighteen month time line that Tremaine set for himself to give up the streets and go legit. He had already begun to divide certain spots and clientele that he had a strong hold on between Dirty and Dollar. He gave Dollar the apartment complex in Lansdowne, which had expanded to two more complexes, to supply its narcotics needs. He turned Dirty onto lil' L and all the rest of the City strips that he supplied. The "Gold Club" of smokers and the rest of the associates that he supplied in the County were all given to Juice.

Tremaine was actually a little ahead of schedule since his twentieth birthday wasn't for another two weeks. He and Khalilah made plans to go to Atlantic City on that day. She had officially moved in with him. Eventhough it's still only on the weekends, when she came home from school. She could have stayed there throughout the week since it was only an hour and a half drive from Tremaine's house to her school.

Khalilah was attending school on a full academic scholarship that financed her entire education including room and board. She and Tremaine decided that if those white folks were willing to spend their money on her education then she would stay on campus and let them spend away.

Mr. Turner was beginning to act as if everything was cool between him and Tremaine. Especially since "str8 Soul" was jumping off and he was faithful to bring his ass down there at least once a week to receive a free batch of Marie's mother sweet & sour Buffalo wings. The man couldn't get enough of them; actually no one could, because she was definitely putting her foot in the recipe. Getting Mama Nem, the name that Tremaine addresses her by, on his team was like snatching the first pick of the NBA draft. Marie and Jelissa could throw down in the kitchen themselves, but Mama Nem was definitely one of the main reasons that the restaurant was as prosperous and popular as it was. Although he paid Mama Nem well for her services, Tremaine knew that if it need be, she would cook for free since she was a official down South grandmother who enjoyed feeding people and watching them eat.

Tremaine was in the beginning stages of his second business venture which was vending machines. After purchasing twenty used machines, he took the initiative to spread them out at a few different shops that were owned by various acquaintances of his, such as Fat Eric, who owned a popular night club downtown. He also planned to place a few of the machines in Dirty's barbershop/hair salon which was scheduled to open in a few weeks.

To get a few more pointers on the vending business, Tremaine called Mr. Johnson, the brother that he met at the B.B.C in New York. Mr. Johnson explained the art of presentation to Tremaine. He informed Tremaine that the government was required to give a certain amount of opportunities to small minority businesses when it came time to bid on contracts, especially when the business owners were trying to do business within the public school system or government buildings. Overall, the information was very valuable to Tremaine's goals.

Tremaine and Khalilah drove the BMW to Atlantic City on his birthday. Khalilah had taken care of all of the arrangements for that weekend and instructed Tremaine to sit back and let her handle everything. Taking I95, they reached their destination in no time. When they walked inside of the hotel suite that Khalilah reserved, Tremaine was confronted with a room full of enormous sized balloons with 'Happy Birthday' and 'I Love You' messages written all over them. There had to be at least fifty balloons inside of the room as well as a hot bubble bath with candles and rose petals all around the Jacuzzi waiting for him. Tremaine had to admit, his Boo had definitely handled everything. After making love in the bathtub and then on the bed, Khalilah got up and told Tremaine that she had one more gift for him.

"Come on babe, this is more than enough, you ain't gotta give me no more presents."

"Shut up," she said tapping him on his leg as she climbed out of the bed ass naked and walked over to one of her suitcases.

Tremaine didn't care what anyone said, when a female was getting some dick on the regular, their bodies definitely filled out in the right places. Khalilah was already phat when they got back together but it seemed as if her ass was getting juicier by the week, as it held the shape of a perfect apple. When she returned back to the bed, she was carrying a little white box that was the size of a wallet sized picture, a couple inches thick. Tremaine stopped paying any attention to the box, as she sat down and faced him with one leg crossed in front of him and the other hanging off of the bed. Her pussy seemed to be screaming out at him as he felt himself getting an erection all over again.

"Boo umm… I didn't know how to tell you this so I just umm…" Khalilah was nervously shifting her eyes back and forth from Tremaine to the box.

"What are you talking 'bout? What's up?"

"Here just open this," She said nodding at the box in her hand.

Tremaine could see that whatever was on her mind, she wasn't going to reveal it until he opened the box. When he took the top off, there was a baby's bib inside that read, "I Love My Daddy." He was stuck for a moment as he looked at the bib and back at her. Just as he was getting ready to ask her what it was all about the whole thing dawned on him and he looked back at the bib once again. Before he could finish the words, "Boo you pregn..." Khalilah was nodding her head while her eyes began to tear.

Tremaine gazed at her for a full ten seconds with his mouth hanging open and before he could speak she said something that fucked him up.

"You're not mad, are you?"

Tremaine was definitely taken by the question, "Huh? Mad? Why you say that?" he asked sounding hurt by the question.

"Nah, I mean it's just that I know that you've been working real hard lately with the restaurant and trying to get the vending machine business going and..."

"Come here," he said pulling her in close to him and stopping her mid-sentence. "Listen, you just gave me the best gift that anybody's ever given me and no matter what's going on in my life or how busy I am, there ain't no way I can be mad about this, you hear me?"

Khalilah nodded her head while a tear streamed down the side of her face. Tremaine put his hand on the side of her face and wiped the tear away with his thumb.

"Now that you know how I feel about all of this, the question is, how do you feel about it?" He asked with his palm still on her face.

"I don't know," she said shrugging her shoulders with a nervous grin. "I mean at first I was a little nervous when the doctor told me, but then I got excited when I thought about it some more. Then, I got nervous again when I thought about how you were going to take it."

"I'm all for it! I'm still a little shocked, though. I can't believe that we're going to have a baby!" He reached down to touch her stomach.

"Boo you think we ready for this?" Khalilah asked with that nervous grin on her face again.

To tell the truth, Tremaine didn't know. He was an only child and he didn't have a father in his life growing up. But what he did know was that he had to step up to the plate and bring enough confidence with him that he'd be a good father. "As long as I got your back and you got mine, it's whatever with us and you know this babe." He spoke those words while staring straight into her eyes, making sure she felt and understood that he was dead serious. That understanding was sufficient enough for him and Khalilah to calm their worries for the time being.

Immediately after returning from Atlantic City, Tremaine and Khalilah began turning one of the guest rooms into a nursery. They weren't going to buy the baby clothes yet since the sex of the baby was unknown. That first night they were in Atlantic City, Tremaine and Khalilah stayed up the remainder of that night discussing just about everything that concerned the baby, from what his or her name would be, all the way to what college their child would attend. Tremaine asked her if she thought the baby would interfere with her college education and she explained to him that the baby's due date was around the same time that she would be finishing up her final exams for the year. That summer she planned to skip interning to spend time with their newborn baby.

Tremaine was definitely starting to feel the whole baby situation and it had him thinking differently about a lot of things. He began to see getting out of the game more as a need as oppose to a want. He decided to leave the street life before his eighteen months so that he could be a father. He thought about how he was going to be taking his son to football practice, going to P.T.A. meetings at his school and other crazy things like that. He wanted to do all the things his punk ass father never did with him while he was growing up. He was determined to be there for his child no matter what.

In anticipation of the baby, Tremaine had even slowed down on fucking with so many females. Over the last couple of years, he was fucking a different broad at least twice a week, now he would fuck a different broad here and there. The whole thing just didn't appeal to him like that anymore. He knew for a fact that he had fucked at least a hundred females give or take five, he just couldn't enjoy it like he used to.

Things were starting to get too hectic with Aids and other shit going around, once that HIV monkey got on your back there was no shaking it off. All those things were starting to take the fun out of sex for him, so he was beginning to put all of his focus on Khalilah.

It seemed as though since Khalilah had become pregnant, her sexual appetite grew enormously. She stayed horny all day and night. There were a few nights Tremaine was awakened to the sight of her riding his dick or her sucking him off. He didn't mind because it wasn't a bad way to be awakened.

Since he was now serving only his closest homies, Tremaine definitely had more time to focus on "Str8 Soul", while continuing to look for more potential locations for his vending machines. The vending scouting was what occupied the majority of his time since he was still a one man company, for the time being. He was going from location to location to make sure that all of the vending machines were always stacked with sodas, candy bars, chips and things like that.

If he weren't busy with his two business ventures, he would be out shopping because he truly had a strong desire for the malls. There wasn't any need to run the streets anymore because there wasn't shit out there for him.

The thought of him being a father soon, constantly ran through his mind. Tremaine tried to grasp the fact that there would be another life that he would be responsible for. His child's well being would be dependent on him and the decisions that he made in the future.

After taking Khalilah to the doctor and receiving her first sonogram, Tremaine had become even more excited about the pregnancy. Hearing the first heartbeats of their unborn child during the sonogram, Tremaine just knew it was a boy and that thought alone took his mind somewhere else. His shopping habit went into overdrive as he began to buy something for the baby damn near everyday: Clothes, pampers, bottles, car seats and things of the sort. He had even gone to holler at his man, Pierre, to see if he could get a few pairs of Gucci linen shorts for his boy.

One afternoon as Tremaine was out on one of his shopping sprees, he received a call on his cell phone from his mother, and she sounded real worried. She was nervous and talking fast.

"Hold up ma, slow down for a second. What's up?"

"Tremaine have you heard from Juice?" his mother asked him.

"Nah nah, not today why what's up?"

"He's gone Tremaine. Niecey said that somebody came and kidnapped him last night."

Kidnapped?! Juice?! The fuck! Tremaine knew that he had heard correctly but found himself asking his mother again to make sure that he wasn't hearing things. "What? Kidnapped? What you mean?"

"Niecey said that he was in a motel with some girl last night and a few dudes ran in to his room with guns and masks and took him with them."

Tremaine could hear the tears building up in her from the trembling in her voice. "Ma listen, is Niecey in the house now?"

"Yeah, I just got off the phone with her."

"Look, I'ma call you back because I'm 'bout to call her."

"Call me right back Tremaine!" she said.

"Alright I will."

Tremaine quickly dialed the number to his aunt's house, his uncle answered the phone and he could hear his aunt in the background asking her husband who was on the phone and if it was Juice or not. When he told her no and informed her it was Tremaine, she immediately began to instruct him to ask Tremaine if he had heard from Juice. Tremaine knew right then and there, without asking, that the shit was true, somebody had kidnapped Juice. After talking to his uncle for a few minutes he was able to get all of the information on what actually went down. Juice was in a motel, with a girl named Alicia, when three masked gunmen kicked in their door and began pistol whipping and beating on Juice. They dragged him outside to a waiting caravan and pulled off. The kidnappers hadn't put a scratch on Alicia but focused solely on Juice.

Tremaine was familiar with Alicia, since Juice had been fuckin' with her heavily for close to four months. His aunt said that Alicia immediately called the police to tell them what happened. Niecey said that she went to see Alicia that morning and the girl looked as if she was having a nervous breakdown, she was still shaking and crying uncontrollably.

Tremaine listened to all of what his aunt had to say but he wasn't trying to hear none of it. He knew that a lot of females could be scandalous and there was a very strong possibility that Alicia's ass had something to do with the whole demonstration. Without a doubt, Tremaine was about to find out. Even though Tremaine had his mind made up; the streets threw him a sign to let him know that no matter what he did the game was never too far behind him.

As he rushed to leave the mall, Tremaine began to dial Dollar to see if he had heard the news about Juice's kidnapping. And if not, he planned to put him on point. It was because of his dialing while trying to carry a hand full of bags that he failed to notice the two females driving pass him in the parking lot, looking for a parking space. The girl in the passenger seat began pointing in his direction while saying something. Since the windows were rolled up, Tremaine didn't hear what she said. Immediately, the car came to a stop and the passenger jumped out and began walking towards Tremaine calling his name.

"Tremaine," the female yelled while coming up behind him.

Dollar finally answered the phone just as Tremaine was turning around to see who was calling him. It was Latoya, the girl at the cash register, who worked for Jelissa when she managed Burger King. Upon seeing who it was, Tremaine simply gave her the nod and went back to his conversation with Dollar. He thought that was that, until he felt a tap on his shoulder. When he turned around it was her again.

"What's up?" he said with a slight touch of attitude in his voice. Now was not the time to be fucking with some broad, especially one he had already fucked.

"Yo, I gotta tell you something," she responded with her own attitude, reciprocating the same attitude he had just thrown at her.

"Look here, I gotta holla at you later shorty, because right now, I gotta take care of somethin'," he said as he proceeded to walk away in the direction of his car. Tremaine gave her a second glance after noticing that Latoya had put on some weight and was obviously pregnant by the bulge he could see sticking out from the oversized t-shirt she wore. He couldn't believe she was trying to get with him again while she was pregnant.

"Oh you got somethin' to take care of alright, this damn baby you put in me."

Tremaine knew he couldn't have heard what he thought he did.

"Hold on," he said to Dollar as he turned around and saw her standing with one hand on her hip. "What? Girl you done bumped your muthafuckin' head," he said as he brushed her off and began walking away again and going back to his conversation with Dollar.

"I ain't bumped shit nigga," she said as she ran up behind Tremaine and stepped between him and his car. She got dead in his face and said, "I'm eight months pregnant and you were the only nigga I was with at the time."

Tremaine did a quick calculation in his head and thought back to when he had taken her to a hotel out Westview for that one night stand. He knew that it had to be close to seven or eight months ago. That night, he had a feeling that the condom had broke while she was on top of him because there was an increase in the wetness of her pussy. He brushed the thought off, using the new extra sensitive rubbers that he had brought as the reason why it felt as if he were going raw. It wasn't until after he busted his nut inside of Latoya that he saw the condom rolled all the way back to the base of his penis. He never did tell her about it, though.

"Girl that's bullshit! I had a muthafuckin rubber on!" He said stating half the truth.

"Well evidently that shit ain't work," she said pointing to her stomach.

"Yo, we'll talk about this shit later, right now I gotta go." Tremaine attempted to brush pass her and get into his car.

"Later shit," she said side stepping in front of him to block him again.

"Cuz, I'ma call you right back." Tremaine hung up his cell phone and put it in his pocket. "Look you knew my number all this muthafuckin' time but you waited, what was it, eight months to come at me with this bullshit," he said pointing at her stomach.

"Nigga I called the shit out of your ass for the first three months but you acted like you couldn't call nobody back!"

She wasn't lying about that because Tremaine could remember after he fucked her how she kept blowing up his phone, but he never bothered to call her back. He saw no reason to since he had gotten what he wanted from her, and it was bullshit. Tremaine knew arguing with Latoya in the parking lot wasn't going to get him anywhere so he mustered up all of the strength that he could and said in a calm voice, "Look, like I said we can talk about this later on just call me; but right now I got something urgent I need to handle." He then tried to put his keys in the door but Latoya smacked them out of his hands. He began to bite on his bottom lip as he stared at his keys on the ground; it was all he could do to keep from knocking her dumb ass out.

"Look stop fucking playing!" He spoke through clenched teeth with his finger in her face. "I told you that I'm busy right now, I'll talk to your muthafuckin' ass later." He reached down to pick up his keys.

"Later shit, you're going to talk to me right now, nigga!"

Tremaine noticed a black Honda pull up behind his car and a short, fat, wider than all outside, female got out. He paid her no mind as he went to put his key in the car door again. Once again, Latoya side stepped between him and the door. That was it, Tremaine reached out and grabbed both sides of her jaws with his right hand and slammed her back against the car. The fat girl then yelled out, "Get off my sister!" as she stepped towards him and pushed him aside. Immediately, he let go of Latoya and cocked his right arm back with the intentions of stretching that big bitch out. He caught himself when he noticed her closing her eyes and squenching her face up in an ineffective effort to brace herself for the punch.

"Bitch if you ever put your muthafuckin hands on me again I'ma bury your fat ass!" he spit out in rapid fire. Just then, Tremaine noticed a police car pulling up behind the black Honda.

The white officer stepped out of his car, pulled his belt up, and preceded towards him and the girls. *This police got asshole written all over him,* Tremaine thought, as he noticed that the officer had a crew cut and wore a pair of dark sunglasses on his eyes.

"Is there a problem here folks?" he asked as he stepped towards the group, while eyeing Tremaine the entire time.

This shit is getting way out of hand, Tremaine thought before he answered, "Nah, there ain't no problem officer. We were just leaving." He was looking back and forth from Latoya and her sister hoping that they would go along with it.

"Yes there is a problem! This motherfucker just tried to choke me," Latoya said while getting extremely loud.

Tremaine looked at her in disbelief that she was actually about to do some hot ass shit like this. "Man ain't no..." he caught himself before his words were released in a very hostile manner. "You know I didn't choke you, come on don't even do that!"

"Yes you did!" the fat girl yelled out. "And you tried to hit me!"

"Is this true, sir?" the officer asked Tremaine.

"Nah it ain't," he denied.

"You a damn lie, nigga!" Latoya yelled out. "Don't get scared now, tell the man what you do for a living, and all them guns your ass be carrying!"

AIN'T THIS A BITCH!!! Tremaine's inner voice screamed out. He couldn't believe that these two bitches were about to do this shit.

"Guns?!" The officer said in a shocking voice and then reached for his walkie talkie speaking some sort of police talk into the radio extension that was on his shoulder.

Right then and there Tremaine regretted the day that he ever stuck his dick in that bullshit ass bitch.

He definitely regretted letting her see the burner that he carried with him the night they were in the hotel together. He could remember how hard up she was to hold the gun, when she walked in on him putting it under the pillow. She repeatedly asked him if she could hold the gun and cock it back. She begged and he agreed to give her a quick lesson on how to take the bullets out of the clip and how to reload it.

"Sir, do you mind placing your hands on the vehicle?" The officer asked Tremaine.

He knew that he was basically fucked and had no other options at that point. He thought about the Glock 9mm that he carried in his waist and knew that running was not an option with them being in the middle of a large parking lot along with his car and everything

233

still sitting there. There definitely wasn't no talking his way out of a situation with the Baltimore County Police Department.

Tremaine could see two more police cars coming in at the end of the parking lot and surrendered by placing his hands on the car. The officer began to pat him down and by this time, his backup was getting out of their cars. When the officer discovered the gun he shoved Tremaine over the hood of the car and yelled out, "Gun! We Have A Gun!" The other two officers rushed over and they all began to fight Tremaine. Three officers slammed him on the ground. Some put their knees on his neck, while others had their knees in his back, leaving the arresting officer to cuff him.

"Y'all ain't got to treat him like that!" Tremaine could hear that bitch, Latoya, screaming out. That made him even more furious since it was because of her dirty ass, that all of this bullshit was happening in the first place.

22 THIS CAN'T BE LIFE

"All right gentleman, feed up! Feed up!" the correctional officer yelled out over the loud speaker. Tremaine was laying on his bunk when the cell doors opened up for what he perceived to be dinner.

"They got spaghetti; I can smell it, yo." His cell buddy, Ronald, said as he stepped out of the cell door.

Tremaine was laying on his back with his hands folded behind his head staring up at the ceiling. He was thinking about the whole bullshit ass situation he was in. Mainly he thought about Juice, hoping that his mother would hurry up and bring the money for the forty thousand dollar bail that the commissioner had set for him. His mother would only have to pay four thousand, which was ten percent of the bail. Tremaine had already called her and instructed her to get the money from Dollar. It was only a matter of time before she got the money to the bail bondsman.

Tremaine didn't really feel like eating but figured he'd get up just to get a moment out of his cell. His cell buddy was starting to piss him off, talking him to death about a bunch of nothing. The moment Tremaine found out that Ronald was in there for rape, he didn't have any rap for him. But that didn't stop that nigga from constantly babbling and shit, talking cause he got lips.

Tremaine stepped in line like everyone else to receive his tray. He was at the Baltimore County Department of Corrections in Towson. All of the detainees there, which were about one hundred in all, had been arrested within the last forty five days and were waiting to be placed in other housing units, or waiting for their preliminary in court.

After receiving his tray, Tremaine saw that what his cell buddy called spaghetti, was actually cold noodles with tomato sauce poured over top of them. There was a serving of string beans on the side with three slices of bread, along with jello and warm milk. As he looked out at the tables, which were the same tables that cards and dominoes were played on, Tremaine noticed Lil B-Love and Quincy. They were a few dudes that he grew up with a few blocks from Murphy Homes, waving him to come over. He sat down at the table with them and listened to the duo brag about how they were in for shooting the boy, Terrell, another homeboy from the Carey Street area. They were coming from Valentino's and caught the nigga late night coming from a broad house on York Road. They told Tremaine their entire case, as they sat scoffing down their food. They insisted on leaving Tremaine their numbers in hopes of him putting them on, if and when they were released.

When Tremaine got up to dump his untouched tray, the C.O. yelled out that it was rec time. He immediately headed over to the wall which had eight phones lined up on it. Out of the eight, only four of them worked so that definitely was a fight waiting to happen. After waiting for almost half an hour, Tremaine finally got one of the phones and proceeded to call his mother, but got no response. He hoped that it meant she was out paying the bail bondsman. He then called his house and got Khalilah on the line and there was no denying the stress in her voice and the tears in her eyes. He began to assure her that everything was straight and told her not to worry because he didn't want her stressed out while she was pregnant.

He attempted to call Dirty and Dollar's house but got no answers and the jail house phones wouldn't make collect calls to cell phones without T-netix.

Thoughts of Juices' kidnapping rushed back to Tremaine's mind and he began to wonder if he was still alive. Just as he was about to hang the phone up and walk off towards the T.V. area, he heard the words, "Slim you been on that muthafuckin phone too long, your time's up!" Tremaine looked at the source of the words and his first thought was, this nigga got to be a crackhead. The nigga eyes reminded you of a yellow highlighter. They were a permanent yellowish color, just like his teeth, and half of his head was cornrowed while the other half was undone and nappy. Tremaine was about to get off of the phone but since this nigga came at him like that, he wasn't about to get off of shit. This was his first time being locked up but knew better than to let any altercation slide.

All of the detainees on the phones next to him looked over at Tremaine, as well as those waiting for a phone, to see what his reaction would be. All of the frustrations of being locked up, as well as thoughts of Juice and that bitch Latoya, swelled up in him.

"Here you go slim, if you want the phone you can get it." Tremaine spoke with his best game face on. The loud talker began to walk towards him with a mean mug on his face as if he had just won himself a small victory. Tremaine held the phone in his left hand and just as the dude got close enough to reach for the phone, he smacked him in the mouth with it and followed that up with a right hook. When yellow eyes went down, Tremaine immediately began stomping his head into the concrete ground causing blood to rush from his mouth, aswell as the back of his head. He was forced to ball up in a fetal position as Tremaine proceeded to kick him in the back of his head, soccer ball style.

Tremaine was so busy stomping the man's brains out, that he failed to notice everyone locking in as the C.O. hollered out orders for the lock down over the loud speakers. Doors were slamming left and right as the detainees were locked in their individual cells. The next thing Tremaine saw was six, navy blue fake ass police uniform wearing ass, men yelling at him with a German Sheppard leading the way. They yelled orders for him to lay down or they would let the dog loose on him. When he looked up, he was a little confused to see that everyone was gone and that the six muscle bound men were the only ones on the unit. He backed up off the bloody body on the floor and laid down on the ground as he was instructed. The Emergency Response Team (E.R.T), which he later learned that they were also called the goon squad, handcuffed him and escorted him to the lock down unit.

The isolation wing had no T.V. area and only two phones for communication. Tremaine could hear niggas screaming out of their doors talking to one another when he was escorted into the unit. The voices immediately began to curse out the goon squad, calling them all types of "bitch ass niggas" and "dick suckers." After he was placed in a cell and stripped butt ass naked, to make sure he didn't have any weapons on him, Tremaine was given his orange jumpsuit back then was locked inside of the empty cell.

While sitting alone, he began to think back on the incident that had just occurred and without being able to help it, his thoughts led back to Juice. Finally, he laid down on the bare mattress and decided to get some much needed rest.

The next morning, Tremaine was awakened to the voice of a female officer banging on his door, telling him to pack up because he had made bail. *About time*, he thought, as he popped up like toast and informed the C.O. that he didn't have anything to pack up. She escorted him down to the processing area and after getting his clothes and car keys back, he noticed that the $800 he had in his pocket when he got locked up wasn't there. He could care less because after signing a few papers he was a free man.

Dollar was the one waiting on him when he was released from the jail's front door. On the way to get his car from the mall's parking lot, they talked about Juice, who still hadn't been heard from, and what Alicia was saying about the incident. After going home to take a shower and change his clothes, Tremaine hopped in his car, he and Dollar headed down South Baltimore to pay Ms. Alicia a visit to find out exactly what had happened to their cousin.

The entire ride over to Alicia's house, Tremaine and Dollar were trying to figure out who they knew that would be capable enough to kidnap Juice. They didn't know where to begin because they both knew so many cruddy ass niggas in this city. Anyone could have pulled this off, if given the opportunity. It could have been a muthafucka who was watching Juice and saw how he had recently purchased his new SUV, as well as the late model Lexus GS 400, fresh off the show room floor. Either that or what Tremaine's first suspicions were, Alicia setting him up.

When they arrived at Alicia's house on Wilkens Avenue, they walked up the flights of stairs that lead to her apartment. Tremaine leaned his ear to the door to see if he could hear anyone inside. All he heard were the faint sounds of a T.V. When he knocked on the door the sounds of footsteps could be heard approaching the door and the shadow of someone's eye in the peep hole. Finally a female's voice called from the other side of the door, "Who is it?!"

"Is Alicia home?" Tremaine asked through the door.

The door then began to unlock and opened only a few inches since the small thin light skinned lady that opened it kept the chain on. "Who's asking?" she asked looking Tremaine and Dollar up and down suspiciously.

"I'm a friend of Alicia's and I just came by to make sure she was alright," Tremaine said, lying. He could care less about Alicia; his main concern was his cousin.

"Okay Mr. Friend of Alicia's, she's asleep right now so you'll have to talk to her later." The lady said sarcastically and motioned to shut the door.

Tremaine stuck his hand out to stop the door from closing and tried to speak in his calmest voice. The shit was a task because the woman, who he figured to be Alicia's mother, was starting to get on his last nerve. "I mean do you mind waking her up because this is very important." He spoke with a smile that had evil written all over it.

"Excuse you, but can you get your damn hand off my door?!" she said looking a little startled since he was holding her door.

Tremaine was tired of beating around the bush and decided to get straight to the point, also he could hear Dollar behind him sucking his teeth and sighing rather loudly. "Listen, my cousin was with your daughter a couple of days ago when the incident happened and I want her to tell me something about it."

"Oh you're related to Juice?" she asked.

"Yeah," Dollar answered.

"Is he alright? Did he come home yet?" She had what sounded like a genuine concern in her voice.

"Nah, he ain't home yet that's why I'm here trying to talk to Alicia so that I can find out exactly what happened," Tremaine spoke.

"She been back and forth to the police station these last couple of days and when she came home this morning she was still a little shaken up so I gave her two sleeping pills so she could finally get some rest. Now if you give me your number, I'll be sure to have her call you later on today when she wakes up."

Tremaine looked over at Dollar who was looking very irritated since he wasn't trying to leave until he had some answers.

"That's alright, just tell her that we'll stop by later."

"Okay I will and I hope that Juice is alright," were her last words as she closed the door.

That old ass bat had Tremaine heated for real. As he and Dollar headed back to the car, Dollar's feelings were mirroring Tremaine's because the first words out of his mouth was, "I bet if I would've put this mufuckin four-five on that bitch's forehead she would have woke that lil' bitch up!"

Before Tremaine could respond, his cell phone began to vibrate. When he answered, it was his mother and he could hear that she was crying by way she said his name. After getting her calmed down, his mother finally told him the news that he wasn't trying to hear. Niecey decided to drive back over to the new condominium that Juice recently moved into. She used the key that he had given her and opened the door. As soon as she stepped through the door she found Juice lying in the hall, next to the bathroom, with his whole head duct taped and his wrists and ankles taped together in a hog-tied position.

The blow of the news that he had just received caused Tremaine to slam his cell phone down onto the concrete shattering it into tiny pieces. He placed his hands on top of his head and began to walk down the sidewalk. He could hear Dollar behind saying, "Tremaine.. Tremaine... what's up, Yo? What's up, man?"

"Them bitch ass niggas killed him" Tremaine said softly with his hands still on top of his head with his eyes closed. Dollar didn't say a word as he just turned around and got in the passenger seat of the car

241

taking the seat and reclining it all the way back. Tremaine stood on the sidewalk for what it seems like an eternity before he got in the car.

He looked over and saw that Dollar had his arm covering his eyes. He asked Tremaine without moving his arm, "Where they find him at, yo?"

"Niecey found him taped up in his spot."

Dollar took a deep breath and began to clench his jaw muscles.

"Somebody gonna feel this!"

Tremaine looked over at Dollar's still covered face and nodded his head because what Dollar had just said was real talk. Somebody would definitely have to feel their pain.

23 DECEIT?

Over the next two days Tremaine and Dollar made numerous trips to Alicia's house to see her and each time they failed to get a response. Dollar suggested that they climb up her balcony and go through the window to see if anyone was home. Tremaine talked him out of that idea and suggested that they just sit tight until the funeral, which was in another two days. He knew that they could catch Alicia there and get in her ass. And if not, the balcony it was.

As the days went by, more and more details of Juice's killing came to light. Tremaine realized that the last few moments that his cousin was alive had to be hard for him to go through. The coroner described how four of his fingers were broken, as well as his jaw. Juice's right ear drum was busted and there were numerous burn marks all over his body, from what was later determine to be a blow torch. Whoever was responsible for the kidnapping had tortured him and once they were done, they smothered him by wrapping duct tape around his head and face. The only thing that was displaced in his house was the inside of his bedroom closet, where the carpet had been pulled up revealing a small hole in the floor. Tremaine figured that it must have been where Juice kept his stash, and after enduring so much pain he finally told his abductors where the money was. Juice's mother said that she could barely recognize her own son due to the fact that his body had swelled up enormously, as a result of his asphyxiation death.

On the morning of the funeral, Tremaine was up at five o'clock in the morning. The service wasn't scheduled to start until ten but he couldn't sleep because he knew that seeing his cousin lying in that casket was going to fuck with him. He left Khalilah lying in the bed and headed downstairs to the basement to do a couple sets of bench presses. Tremaine had to do something to channel his frustrations, and until he could get his hands on the bitches responsible for his pain, the weights would have to do.

After getting in ten sets of bench presses and a few sets of dumbbell curls, Tremaine headed back upstairs to take a cold shower. The cold water was always like a therapy process for him. It seemed to help him concentrate more and think clearer when something was a little more stressful than normal. Ever since he was eleven or twelve years old, cold showers always had that effect on him.

As Tremaine stood there under the frigid waters, his thoughts focused in on Alicia and whether or not she had actually set Juice up. He was confident that he would be finding out very shortly because her ass was going to tell him something, one way or another, that was damn for sure. Tremaine's thoughts were abruptly interrupted when he felt a small pair of warm hands wrap around his naked waist. He lifted his head from under the streaming water to see Khalilah standing behind him wearing a pair of his boxers and one of his tank tops. She said nothing as she stood there with her hands around his waist and her head buried in his cold wet back.

They both stood under the water in the same position for a few minutes without saying a word. Tremaine would have stood there longer, but he could feel Khalilah's hands and jaws begin to tremble and shiver from the cold water. She was willing to tough it out and stand under the cold water with him to make sure he was alright. He turned the hot water nozzle on so that she could warm up because he didn't want her to catch a cold, especially with her being pregnant. He helped Khalilah out of her wet clothes and they both washed each other up and dried each other off.

As Tremaine proceeded to get dressed, he continued to hear his Aunt Niecey's voice playback in his head over and over, when she ran down the list of injuries that Juice had sustained and how his body was nearly unrecognizable when she found him. In attempts to keep his sanity, he tried to prepare himself as much as possible for what was ahead.

Juice's funeral was held at the church on the corner of W. Lafayette and Fremont Avenue. When Tremaine arrived at the church, he recognized just about everyone he saw. A lot of the older people that he spotted were great-aunts and uncles. The rest of the attendants were either hood rats or homeboys that they had grown up with or had business dealings with. There were a few faces sprinkled in that Tremaine wasn't familiar with and couldn't help but wonder if one of them had anything to do with Juice's death. In the life that he lived, it wasn't unheard of for the person who pulled the trigger to go to their victim's funeral. Some killers did it just to admire their work or to collect some sort of souvenir like an obituary, a flower off the casket or something to remember them by.

There were a number of people in the parking lot, but inside was where the majority of the guests were, since the funeral was about to begin. Upon entering the church, family members then friends were allowed to go down the aisle and view the body at the front of the room. Tremaine noticed his mother and aunts, as well as the rest of his family members, sitting in the first few pews of the church. Every one of them were crying or sitting next to someone who was crying.

Not wanting to go through the whole process, Tremaine chose a spot in the back and decided that he would go up to the casket once they called for the final viewing. Those thoughts quickly changed as he watched the facial expression of the people who chose to view the body before taking their seat. Juice's body had to be fucked up because even though people were trying to hold their facial expressions out of respect, they really couldn't help it. A few of them immediately start crying while others waited until they arrived at their seats to cry or frown their faces as the image of what they just saw replay in their heads. He even witnessed someone, making some crazy hand gesture on their face indicating certain aspects of what they had observed on Juice.

One girl, who Tremaine recognized as one of the girls from Juice's neighborhood, held her daughter, who was no more than two of three years old, in her arms. When the child saw the body in the casket the little girl bust out crying and turned her head while tightly hugging her mother's neck. That was the last draw for Tremaine as he made up his mind that he wasn't going up there to see his cousin all fucked up in that casket. He'd be damned if he let that be his last memory of Juice. He was going to remember him in his truest form and keep those memories with him.

During the funeral, Tremaine caught sight of Dirty and Dollar, who were in the third row. Dollar was looking around the room to see who was in there. He and Tremaine made eye contact for a second and Dollar frowned up his face with a confuse look once he saw where Tremaine was sitting. He quickly subsided that look and nodded his head indicating that he understood him being back there. Before they broke eye contact, Dollar nodded his head and signaled for Tremaine to follow his eyes. Tremaine moved around in his seat to get a better look at what Dollar was trying to show him and could see the back of Alicia's head, six rows ahead of him, leaning on her mother's shoulder.

Khalilah was sitting next to Tremaine and asked him if he had changed his mind about sitting in the back and was ready to sit in the front with the rest of the family. She thought his shifting around was an attempt to find an empty seat. Tremaine informed her that he was just looking to see if he saw someone there that he needed to holler at.

Everyone listened to the preacher talk about Juice as he expounded on all of the good things that he allegedly had been doing in his life. Afterwards, Niecey got up to the podium and thanked everyone for their support and for being there for her and their family in their time of need. She then proceeded to tell a story, reminiscing on a memory of Juice. One of their second cousins' sang a song that was titled "Take Me Back Dear Lord" followed by the preachers' comments on violence and the offering for all attendees to come to the pulpit to rededicate their lives or give their lives to the Lord.

After two hours or so, the funeral service was coming to a close and everybody was given one last chance to view the body before the closing of the casket, before proceeding to the cemetery for burial. Khalilah asked Tremaine if he was ready to go and view the body and he informed her that he didn't want to view something that wasn't really his cousin. She initially gave him a confused look but then wrapped her arm around his waist and they walked out.

Tremaine was one of the first people out of the door. As he and Khalilah waited for everyone else to come out. Lisa was the first to appear in the crowd followed by Dirty, Dollar, and then Alicia. As he began to make his way over towards Alicia, Lisa walked up on him in the process.

"Where were you, Tre? I was looking for you in there," she asked while still wiping away tears.

"I grabbed a seat in the back."

"In the back?" She asked with a confused look.

"I'm sayin' you know...I ain't ...," Tremaine didn't feel like talking about it at that moment.

"I know Tre." Lisa took his hand in hers. "The body in that casket was just that, a body…a shell. That's not the Juice we knew."

While Tremaine listened to Lisa's words, Dirty and Dollar walked up to them. "What's up yo?" Dirty asked.

"Shit." Tremaine turned his attention to Lisa and Khalilah. "Boo here, take my keys and you and Lisa can ride together to the cemetery. I gotta holla at some people right quick. I'ma meet ya'll there alright?" Khalilah took the keys, she and Lisa then walked off.

Tremaine began to look around the parking lot and before he could say anything, Dollar said, "she over there Yo." He nodded in the direction behind him, towards Alicia and her mother as they were opening their car doors to get inside.

"What's up Alicia?" Tremaine said startling her a bit as he walked up from behind.

"What's up Tremaine?" She was holding a handkerchief in her hand. Tremaine couldn't deny that if the girl was faking, she was one of the best actors that he had ever seen. Her eyes were swollen as if she had been crying for days and her voice was nearly shot with its raspy sound.

"How you been doing?" He asked her and then turned to see her mother staring at them with one leg inside the open car door. "How you doing ma'am?" He waved at her.

"Hi. You're Juice's cousin right?"

"Mm hmm." Tremaine nodded his head.

"Alicia this is the boy that I told you was looking for you the other day," her mother said.

"Yeah, I definitely been looking for you!" Tremaine didn't mean for the words to come out to sound the way that he felt. "How you been doing?" He asked again.

"I'm alright," she responded dabbing at her left eye with the handkerchief.

"I'm saying umm... I need to holla at you for a second and since we all going to the same place how 'bout you ride with us," Tremaine proposed.

"Ride with you?" she asked.

"Yeah."

"Hold up." Alicia leaned her head in the car door to speak to her mother, who sat down in the car and was closing her door. "Ma I'ma ride with them to the cemetery."

"You sure baby?" Her mother asked.

"Yes, I'll meet you there."

"Alright," her mother said putting her keys in the ignition.

"Come on, we parked over here." Tremaine lead her over to Dollar's Range Rover.

When they got to the truck, Dollar got behind the wheel, Dirty got in the passenger seat while Tremaine and Alicia got in the back. None of them said a word as they headed out of the parking lot following a long procession of cars. Once they finally got on Fremont Avenue, Tremaine could see Alicia out of the corner of his eye, cutting her eye over at him, while wondering why they wanted her to ride with them, and why were they acting in such an odd way. Tremaine made his move. "Shorty, what the fuck you do to my cousin?" He turned to face her as he spoke through clenched teeth.

"Huh?" Alicia asked with her eyes nearly jumping out of her head.

"Huh, shit! Bitch you heard what the fuck he said," Dirty yelled out while turned around in his seat.

"You had somethin' to do with all this shit! I know your ass did." Tremaine spat.

Tremaine leaned in two inches from Alicia's face. "You know I wouldn't do anything like that. I love Juice." Tears were beginning to form in her already puffy eyes.

"I ain't trying to hear that bullshit. What the fuck happened to my cousin, girl?" Tremaine leaned forward and pulled out the baby nine millimeter that he had hooked to a holster on the back of his slacks, which was covered by his suit jacket. He cocked the pistol so that the sound of the bullet entering the chamber was sufficient enough to let her know that he wasn't bullshitting.

"Look, I swear y'all, I ain't have nothing to do with..."

Dirty reached out and grabbed her by the throat with his right hand, "the fuck you think we playin' wit' you bitch?!"

Alicia immediately began to slobber out of the left side of her mouth while attempting to pry Dirty's grip from her throat. It was then that Tremaine noticed a few things that triggered off some buttons in his head making him realize that Alicia was indeed telling the truth. "Kill all that shit Yo, let her go," he told Dirty.

"Fuck no! This bitch gonna tell us somethin'!" Dirty responded refusing to unlock the grip he had on her neck. He was shaking her like a bobble head doll nearly lifting her off of her seat, causing her to gag.

Finally, Dirty pushed her away from him and let her go from his grasp. Alicia was grasping for air as she coughed and cried at the same time. Tremaine was glad that Dollar had that dark tint on his truck because if not, everyone behind him would have surely saw what was going on inside.

Alicia's crying began to settle to sniffles after a few minutes. "Bitch shut the fuck up!" Orders were yelled from Dollar in the driver's seat.

Tremaine blocked the entire truck scene out of his head as he came to the reality that if Alicia was innocent, then Juice's killer was still out there. As he took another hard look at her, his thoughts were confirmed. The few times he'd seen Alicia with Juice, she was always on point with her looks. She was what some dudes would call a high maintenance type of female, since her shit stayed tight. The girl that Tremaine was looking at in the back seat with him was nowhere near that.

Alicia's hair was jacked up with a rack of dried gel around the edges of her brown shoulder length hair. It looked as if it hadn't been washed in weeks. Tremaine also noticed that while scratching at Dirty's tight grip around her neck, Alicia's fingernails were beat up. She had a white/silver color polish on her nails, or what used to be her fingernails. What was left of her nails were chewed down to the meat and had dirt all in them.

Females who were used to setting niggas up wouldn't go to the extreme of looking this bad to portray such a deceitful act. They would be the main ones crying at the funeral all loud and shit, but their ass did it looking fresh as shit, with the money they received from the setup. Tremaine also noticed that Alicia wasn't wearing any perfume either and to his senses she smelled awfully sweaty. The girl next to him was definitely a far cry from the one he had seen a few weeks before. With that, either Alicia was telling him the truth and was indeed grieving. Either that or fuck Halle Berry, Alicia was the greatest female actor of all time.

When they all arrived at the cemetery, Tremaine was in the front row with the rest of his family to watch them lower his cousin's casket into the ground. He glanced at Alicia a few times and once again she was crying. He couldn't help but wonder if she was crying over Juice again, or the fact that her ass was two minutes away from being placed in the ground her damn self. Tremaine had never experienced such a feeling of uselessness as he had when he sat there in the front row, watching them lower Juice into the ground. He still didn't know who killed his cousin and all he could do was keep his ears to the ground and wait for the streets to start talking.

He was always a firm believer that whenever anyone's homeboy was killed, before they were buried, the muthafucka responsible for their death should already be dead before the day of their homeboy's funeral. He felt that was the only way a soldier could truly rest in peace. After the service, Tremaine explained to Dirty and Dollar his reasons for letting Alicia off the hook and clearing her of any suspicions. They felt what he was saying, but he could see the frustration they were feeling and that no matter what, someone had to feel their pain.

It had now been over two weeks since Juice was laid to rest and Tremaine still hadn't heard shit about his killers. He made it his business to go to all of the different spots that he knew Juice had ties to holler at the fiends and hood rats, all to no benefit. He figured the nigga who snatched Juice up had to have known him from one of those different spots and had been watching him for a minute. Nobody seemed to know shit; it was like the niggas responsible for the whole thing had just disappeared into thin air. With that, Tremaine found himself cutting his eyes sideways at his closest homeboys, thinking that maybe the killing had been an inside job. He hated to think that Dirty, Lil' Chris, or even Dollar would do some shit like that, but he learned a long time ago to expect the unexpected in this game.

All of those things were beginning to interfere with Tremaine's life at home with Khalilah. He still hadn't told her about Latoya. He opted to wait until after the baby was born to see if it was his, before he confessed to the woman he loved about cheating. He hadn't had sex with Khalilah, or anyone for that matter, since hearing the news of Juice's death. Khalilah had gotten all hysterical on him one night when she was trying to fuck and he turned her down. She began to cry and thought his lack of affection was because he no longer found her sexy, with her stomach protruding and all. She couldn't have been any further from the truth, but Tremaine didn't feel like taking the time out to explain to her all the things that were truly bothering him.

If he could have just caught wind of where the niggas who had killed Juice hung out, or what neighborhood they lived in, it would have been enough. With that information alone, Tremaine was willing to go out and shoot up their entire block, not really caring who was individually responsible. Whether he got the right muthafuckas or a few of their homeboys, it didn't really matter as long as he got somebody. He still couldn't believe the streets hadn't started talking yet; usually when shit like that happened, within forty eight hours word would be out about who did what.

24 TROUBLE

As Officer, Matthew Thornhill pulled into the driveway he was deep in thought over the upcoming field trip that he was sponsoring for a group of kids at his local boys and girls club. He was planning to take the kids to the National Aquarium in downtown Baltimore. Officer Thornhill had been participating in the big brother program at Robert C. Marshall's recreation center, to help kids, for a number of years. As he parked his ford bronco and got out, he was thinking about just how he planned to convince his brother, a FBI agent, Zachary Thornhill, to participate in the field trip. He wanted his brother as one of the chaperones for the kids. Matthew knew his brother always complained about how busy he was. Working for the FBI, narcotic division, wasn't an easy task he noted.

Matthew thought about how much his brother had aged since joining the bureau five years ago. Zachary looked as if he could be ten years Matthew's senior instead of the two that he was. He knew his brother had a desire to volunteer his time more but he never seemed to have the opportunity. Matthew came to the conclusion that he wasn't going to leave his brother's home until he had a confirmed yes from him concerning the chaperone favor.

As he made his way up the walkway towards the house in Bolton Hill, Matthew admired the life his brother had acquired. Zachary resided in a nice-sized three bedroom house with a beautiful wife, Michelle, and daughter Ashley. Growing up, everyone thought that Matthew would be the first one to tie the knot since Zachary was a bit of a womanizer in high school. Matthew was always the gentleman. Zachary chose to spend his time running through a number of women and had broken quite a few hearts, but it was Michelle who slowed him down and caused him to focus more on life and the things that he wanted to achieve.

Matthew could recall the exact moment that he knew Michelle was the one for his brother. They were all at a local restaurant and his brother did the simple task of pulling out the chair for her at the table when she sat down. It was the first time that he had ever seen his brother show any type of chivalry towards any female. He knew then, that Michelle would be around for a while. His instincts were correct, two years later she and his brother were married with little Ashley being born a year after. Close to ten years had passed since then, and his brother was still as much in love with Michelle as he was that day in the restaurant, if not more. Matthew still hadn't found the right woman and until he did, he chose to spend his time being a police officer and volunteering to help needy kids.

When Matthew rang the doorbell, he could hear little Ashley yelling out, "I got it!" She then peeked out of the narrow door length glass door to see who it was. Upon seeing her uncle Matty, as she called him, her little face beamed with joy as she rushed to unlock the door to let him in.

"How's my big girl doing?" he said stepping through the door and picking her up in his arms. He noticed that at nine years of age, Ashley was beginning to resemble him and Zachary's mother more and more. Their sandy blond hair and ocean blue eyes were a dead on match.

"I been good, I been good," she said laughing.

"You sure?" he asked.

"Yeah, I been good. Uncle Matty guess what?"

"What is it, baby?"

Ashley leaned over and whispered in Matthew's ear as if she had a big secret. "I got a new bike!"

"Is that right? And who brought you this bike?"

"My daddy," she said smiling.

"Did you ride it yet?" he asked as he kissed her on the cheek and sat down.

"Did you do any wheelies?" He teased.

"No uncle Matty. I can't do no wheelies." She said smacking him on his leg.

"I thought I heard your voice." Zachary emerged through the foyer out to the living room.

They greeted one another with a hand shake that ended with a hug. Matthew and his brother were total opposite in looks. Where Matthew had his mother's blond hair and blue eyes, Zachary mirrored their father with his dark brown hair and brown eyes. The only thing they were in accord with is appearance; both of them were exactly six feet even in height.

"Yeah, I was just in the neighborhood and I thought I'd stop by."

"I thought you worked on Saturdays," Zachary asked.

257

"I did until I changed my schedule about two weeks ago to have Saturdays and Wednesday off."

"Uncle Matty you want to see my bike?" little Ashley asked excitedly.

Matthew kneeled down in front of her and said, "I'd be honored to see your new set of wheels."

"Come on it's in the garage." She grabbed his hand and led him through the kitchen.

"I'll be right back," Matthew said to his brother over his shoulder.

"I'll be in the living room," Zachary responded and walked away from the kitchen.

Ashley showed her uncle everything on her bike from the pink tire spokes, to the pom pom strings that were attached to the grips of the handle bars. Afterward Matthew headed back out to the living room where his brother had ESPN sports center playing on the 42-inch flat screen television. There was a briefcase on the marble coffee table which led Matthew to conclude that, as usual, Zachary had been working before his arrival.

"You want a beer?" he said handing Matthew a cold Budweiser.

"You bet. So where's Michelle?" Matthew asked taking a sip of his beer.

"She went to try to find some seeds for a new flower she's been thinking about planting out front.

"So you're on babysitting duty, huh?"

"Yeah, I've been drafted." Zachary responded letting out a slight chuckle.

"I see that you still haven't learned that all work and no play isn't good for you," Matthew said referring to the briefcase on the table.

"Hey, crime doesn't stop so why should I?"

"Isn't that the truth," Matthew responded.

"So how's everything going on the force?" Zachary asked.

Matthew knew that their conversation would eventually gravitate towards law enforcement talk as it did. They couldn't help it; police work was in their blood. All of their lives, they both knew what they wanted to be. Their father was a retired Kansas City policeman and their grandfather was an ex-military police officer. Even their mother had worked as a secretary for the chief of police in Kansas City for twenty years. Anything short of being cops would have been uncivilized for them.

"Well you know there's never a dull moment that's one thing I can say," Matthew said reaching for the remote control and began surfing through the channels.

"You know the bureau's still hiring, right?" Zachary offered.

Matthew knew it was coming, it never seemed to fail. His brother had been trying to get him to join the FBI for over eight years now, ever since Zachary left the Baltimore City police force and joined the bureau to become a special agent. Matthew always told him that he loved being on the police force, working the beat, because it afforded him the opportunity to make a difference with the community up close and personal. He'd been offered the sergeant position a numerous amount of times, but declined the offer each time. He knew that he wouldn't be out in the field as much if he were a sergeant. Being a part of the bureau was definitely too out of touch with the everyday people that Matthew encountered. "No thank you, I'm quite alright," Matthew said leaning back on the couch after setting the channel on a hunting show.

"Hey, you know I had to let you know, right?"

"Yeah I know. You always do," Matthew said before taking a sip of his beer while watching closely as a man dressed in camouflage gear was getting ready to shoot a deer from up high in a tree.

"Don't you want to make a difference on a broader scale?" Zachary asked.

Matthew turned from the television to look his brother in the eye. "It's not about the quantity but the quality, my brother."

Zachary leaned forward on the couch and said, "I understand that but we've got the same blood flowing through our veins and you were meant for the bureau just like me."

Matthew grabbed a stack of papers out of Zachary's brief case off of the table. "In order for you and your partners to get this info you need me and my men. Without us, you guys wouldn't be able to get these." Matthew sat the stack back in the briefcase. "And besides, taking these pictures," he reached and grabbed a few photos that were next to the papers, "And being so far from the action, just isn't me. I like to be up close at all times and I can't do that with the bureau."

"Why not? We interact with the community," Zachary said.

"Yeah, when you're kicking down someone's door," Matthew said laughing at his own comment.

"Now that's not true." Zachary had taken a little offense to what his brother said.

"Zach it's cool, at least I always know that when it's time for me to make a career move you'll have my back." He patted his brother on the knee trying to avoid an argument which is exactly where the conversation was headed.

Matthew knew his brother loved his job just as much as he loved his, and was willing to go word for word with him on the pros and cons of the bureau.

"Ooh look at him!" he said referring to the hunter who had shot the deer he was stalking.

"So what are you working on anyway?" Matthew reached out to look at the photos that his brother had on the table.

"We're investigating a car salesman who we suspect is selling drugs out of his car dealership," Zachary answered.

"Hmm," Matthew continued to look through the photos.

"Well actually we know he's dealing; now we're just trying to find out who his supplier is."

Matthew was staring at the gentleman in one of the pictures who looked familiar.

"I think I know this fella right here," he said studying the photo more closely.

"Who?" Zachary leaned over to see who his brother was referring to.

"Him right here." He handed him the picture with two gentlemen in it.

"Oh we don't know him right there but this is the one were investigating." He was pointing to the guy who was wearing what appeared to be a very expensive business suit.

"No, this fella right here. I just arrested him a few weeks ago, I believe." Matthew was trying to remember exactly when. Zachary nodded his head in response.

"Yeah he was fighting with his girlfriend in the parking lot and when I went to intervene, the girlfriend informed me that he was carrying a gun."

"His girlfriend told on him?"

"Yeah, if my memory serves me correctly." Matthew knew that it did since he prided himself on his sharp memory.

"Some girlfriend." Zachary let out a light laugh while taking a sip of beer.

"I believe his name was Jer something... Jermaine...No," he said snapping his fingers in remembrance, "Tremaine! That's what it was, Tremaine Jenkins."

"Tremaine Jenkins?" Zachary responded.

"Yeah that's it. What you guys think he has something to do with the car salesman?"

"We don't know yet," Zachary responded. "What did you say you arrested him for again?"

"He had a handgun. A glock, I believe."

"Tremaine Jenkins." Zachary repeated the name while trying to see if it sounded familiar. "I don't know that name but it's definitely worth looking in to." He wrote the name down on the picture, directly over top of Tremaine's head. Zachary figured that if this young man was walking around with loaded handguns, it was definitely for a reason. And with any luck, he was going to find out.

Tremaine thought he was one step closer to finding the dudes who killed Juice, when Khalilah came home one day and asked him if he had read the day's "Baltimore Sun."

"Nah," he answered never lifting his eyes from the Washington Wizards basketball game on cable.

"Ain't that girl, who was with Juice that night, name Alicia?" Khalilah asked.

"Yeah why?" Tremaine was looking directly at her now, the mentioning of Alicia and Juice's name caught his attention.

"Is her last name Pricton?" she asked.

"I don't know. Now why are you asking about Alicia?" Tremaine was getting a little frustrated because she kept shooting out questions, but no answers.

"Read this and tell me if it's her." Khalilah handed him the Maryland section of the paper.

"Read what?" Tremaine asked holding the paper, not knowing which article she was referring to.

Khalilah grabbed the paper back from him and opened it up to the second page, pointing at a little article that was in the lower left hand corner. The title read, "Teenage Female Found Slain." The entire article only consisted of half a paragraph. Before Tremaine could finish reading the article, he was stuck because he knew that it was the same Alicia. The name and age were identical and the victim lived in the same neighborhood as Alicia. The paper said that the body was found about a quarter mile from where Alicia lived.

"Is that her, Boo?" Khalilah said.

"Yeah I think it is her," Tremaine said setting the newspaper down on the coffee table.

"For real?" Khalilah asked putting her hand up to her mouth in shock.

"Yeah." Tremaine's thoughts immediately began racing as he thought about if the same dudes who killed Juice had smashed Alicia. Maybe she did know the dudes responsible for Juice's death and maybe they thought that she would eventually tell on them, so they killed her.

Tremaine began to dismiss that notion because he trusted his gut instinct and honestly believed that Alicia didn't have anything to do with the kidnapping. As his mind continued to run through a few different thoughts, he made it to the kitchen to get a cold Bud Ice to sip on. While in the kitchen, his door bell rang. Tremaine heard Dollar's voice.

"Lilah baby, what's up? Where that nigga at?"

"He's in the kitchen."

"Damn girl what you carryin' twins up in there?" Dollar joked with her.

"Shit boy this one is kickin' my ass, let alone two."

"Ah Ha! Ha! I can dig it."

"What's up shorty?" Tremaine said stepping out of the kitchen.

"You got some more of them up in there?" Dollar asked pointing at Tremaine's beer.

"Yeah they in there," Tremaine said as Dollar stepped off and headed towards the kitchen. "I'ma be downstairs, yo." Tremaine yelled over his shoulder as he headed towards the basement. He sat the newspaper down on the couch beside him and tried to go back to watching the game. The Wizards were losing, as usual, and what made it even worse was the fact that they were losing to the Los Angeles Clippers.

Dollar came downstairs with a half empty bottle in his hand and one unopened one. "What's up my nigga?" He asked as he sat down on the loveseat across from Tremaine.

"Hey yo, you know somebody just smashed Alicia?"

"Yeah I know," Dollar responded breaking eye contact with Tremaine and turned to watch the game.

The way he answered, threw Tremaine off a little because his body language looked as if it was saying 'And? Fuck that bitch!'

Tremaine looked at him for a few more seconds and then it finally hit him. "Yo let me find out," he said.

Dollar looked over at him before taking another sip of his beer.

"You did that shit didn't you?" Tremaine asked.

Dollar said nothing. He finished off his beer and took his car keys out to pry the top off the second one.

"Yo, what the fuck?!" Tremaine asked more so in disbelief.

"That bitch set Juice up! I couldn't let her ass get away wit' that shit!" Dollar was looking down and fiddling with the label on the beer bottle.

"Yo, she ain't have nothin' to do with that shit."

"That's besides the point," he responded.

"What?! How the fuck is that beside the point?"

Tremaine had to catch himself because he was starting to get a little loud and didn't want Khalilah overhearing their conversation.

Dollar sat up on the edge of the couch with his head down, not responding, so Tremaine pressed on. "How is that beside the point, cuz?"

When Dollar looked up, Tremaine could see tears starting to form in his eyes. His face then went into an evil look "You didn't see what I saw in that casket. You ain't see it! I'm telling you Yo, cuz was fucked up!"

"I can dig all that but that girl ain't..."

"Yo!" Dollar spoke with a tear coming down his cheek. "Somebody had to feel that shit, somebody had to feel it."

Tremaine looked into his little cousin's face and could see the hurt and anger written all over it. He really couldn't say anything else. Deep down inside, even though he didn't agree with Dollar, he understood what he was saying. Somebody definitely had to feel their pain and as much as he tried to avoid it, it looked as if Alicia had to be the one.

25 BOSS'S WIFE

Tremaine was finally able to get his head back on straight to take care of his everyday obligations. The situation with Latoya was a done deal, the baby wasn't his. It was much evident when the baby was born and it looked Puerto Rican, which was the ethnicity of her ex-boyfriend. Latoya had the nerve to call and apologize to Tremaine for getting him locked up. She even tried to get him to promise her that he would be the first one to fuck her after her six week check up. Tremaine told her that she was lucky that he hadn't buried her and her unborn child the day that he came home from that county jail. That whole situation was a load off his shoulders. If it would have turned out that Latoya's baby was his, he would have taken care of the baby. Khalilah definitely would have been pissed, but Tremaine didn't have it in him to deny his responsibilities.

Khalilah was back to getting her sexual cravings fulfilled beyond what she could ever dream of. The day after he and Dollar talked about Alicia's killing, Tremaine had dinner and a hot bubble bath waiting for Khalilah when she returned home from her parents' house. His three cheese lasagna, which was one of her favorite, was waiting on the table for her along with a Caesar salad on the side. Tremaine fed her the entire meal not allowing her to lift one finger.

Afterwards, he carried her upstairs and undressed her, while continuously giving her compliments on how beautiful she was, pregnant and all. When he sat her down in the bathtub, Tremaine climbed in behind her and massaged her neck and back before making his way slowly down to her thighs and legs and finishing at her feet. After washing her up, he carried her to their bed and rubbed cocoa butter all over her stomach. He heard that it would keep an expecting mother from acquiring stretch marks.

They made love that night for at least four hours straight, non-stop with Tremaine climaxing four times and Khalilah never giving him a chance to recuperate after each one. Tremaine surely didn't mind because he was determined to show Khalilah that he still found her sexy and desirable in her current state. His Boo was due to have their baby boy in less than three and half months and the closer she got to that date, the closer it seemed like the two of them grew as one. They would stay up late at night and Tremaine would just hold onto Khalilah's stomach and feel his little boy kick and move around. Each moment was always mesmerizing to him.

Most of Tremaine's free time was spent with Khalilah since 'Str8 Soul' was basically running itself. He would stop by for a few hours each day, but everything was everything. Also, with Khalilah doing a monthly assessment on the stores' financial books, everything stayed on track. Tremaine was currently in the process of talking to Gary, one of the crackheads in the "Gold Club," whom he linked back up with since Juice's killing. Gary's brother was in charge of public relations at the M&T stadium that was built downtown as the home for the Ravens. Gary had informed Tremaine that he wanted to set up a business meeting with his brother in reference to Tremaine's vending machines going in the M&T stadium.

Plugging Dirty and Dollar in with Randy directly was what Tremaine wanted to do as soon as possible, instead of waiting until his birthday. He was ready to leave all of that coke shit alone right then and there but Randy wasn't too keen on starting business with dudes he knew nothing about. Tremaine had always respected Randy's wishes of coming alone when he came to do business; Randy would do the same as well. Randy was aware of Tremaine's intentions on leaving the game by his birthday, which was in five months, and he promised he'd be ready for Dirty and Dollar by then, but not a day sooner. Tremaine would have just said fuck all that shit and stopped fucking with Randy, but then he would have been taking food out his homeboys' mouths. He couldn't leave them out there like that so he decided to ride it out for the next five months.

"Alright, what about Shafarea?" Tremaine asked.

"Shafarea?" Khalilah frowned her face up.

"Yeah, that name tight ain't it?"

"Ewww, no sir it is not," she said.

"Tsk!" Tremaine sucked his teeth and looked over at her, "What? That name tight as shit and you know it, stop faking."

"Unh unh, I can't ride with that sweetheart." Khalilah now had her face frowned up as if something stunk.

"It's better than that weak ass name that you said earlier. What was that name......Kel....Kelanty?"

"What Kelvante?" Khalilah said.

"Yeah Kelvante. Now what the hell is that?"

"Shoot, that name alright, I don't know what you're talking about."

Tremaine and Khalilah had been going back and forth, trying to decide on a name for their unborn son, like that for two weeks straight. Tremaine contemplated on making his son a junior but decided against that for the simple fact he wanted his child to have

his own identity in the world. He never did agree with all of that
junior stuff, he figured that as long as a man's son had his last name,
the first name should be one that characterizes that child. As a new
father, he felt that parents should want their child to achieve more in
life than what they did.

"Boo, where are we going?" Khalilah asked.

"I just gotta make a quick stop to holla at my man, Tony, real
quick."

"I wish you would have told me that before I left the house. I
would have bought a bag of chips with me or something. You ain't
got nothing in here? Tic-tacs or something?" Khalilah said searching
into the arm rest for something to snack on.

Tremaine laughed at her greediness, "You are terrible, this is
only gonna take a hot second, after that we going straight to the spot
so you can put something inside that big ass belly of yours."

"But your ass loves this big belly of mine though," Khalilah said
looking at him while making little kissing gestures with her lips.

"I know that's right," Tremaine said.

Khalilah thought that they were going out somewhere to eat.
Technically they were, but Tremaine left out the part that the food
she would be eating would be provided at her surprise baby shower
that they were headed to. He had rented the Lithuanian hall for the
night. His mother, Khalilah's mother, Lisa, and Khalilah's college
roommate, Tonya, took care of the food, guests, decorations and
every other detail of the shower. When they arrived at the hall, there
were only two cars parked in front, just as Tremaine planned.
Everyone else cars were parked in the rear to alleviate any chances of
blowing the surprise. He didn't want Khalilah, observing ass,
recognizing any friends or family cars in the parking lot.

"Hold up, I'll be right back," Tremaine said getting out and walking through the front door. When he got inside, thirty to forty females jumped out and yelled surprise. Tremaine was glad that he didn't park directly in front of the door and that he kept the radio on. If Khalilah was in front of the door, she would have definitely seen all of them jump out when he walked in, and if she didn't see them she would have definitely heard them.

"Nah hold, up she's outside in the car. Y'all get back in position while I bring her in here." Tremaine spoke in general.

"I thought you said you were going to call when you were pulling up?," his mother asked.

"I was, but I couldn't because she was right next to me; that's why I came in by myself first." Tremaine looked around at the faces in the room; a few of them were unknown to him.

Hanging on the entrance wall, was a tailor made scroll that read "Congratulations Khalilah and Tremaine," with a colored sonogram of the baby, matching the décor of the shower. The purpose of it was for the guest to sign. There were flowers, ribbons and balloons everywhere. There were round tables covered with table clothes spreaded evenly around the room. Each table had a centerpiece; the tables were preset for the guests as well. The layout of the tables left an aisle in the middle of the room that led to two decorated chairs with two round tables on each side of them, filled with gifts for the baby. There was a table along the wall that was close to fifteen feet long and covered with a variety of dishes. There was everything from fruit to steak. Tremaine also noticed that they had two cakes; both were three dimensional, resembling baby wood blocks and baby shoes.

He came to the conclusion that they had the shower catered; he knew for a fact that they didn't cook all of the dishes that he was looking at. It was funny how people would go all out to do something when it wasn't their money that was being spent.

Tremaine laughed to himself just thinking about how crazy the bill was going to be for the entire baby shower but it didn't matter because he wanted nothing but the best for Khalilah.

"I'll be back, I'm' bout to go get her right now." He left out of the hall and headed back towards the car thinking what he was going to say to get Khalilah out of the car. "Boo come in here for a minute, I want you to see something," he said as he got into the car and turned off the ignition.

"What? What is it?" she asked.

"I just want to show you somethin', come here."

"Tremaine, I am hungry. So what is it?"

"I want you to see this painting I noticed on my man Tony's wall in here, I think the joint would look nice with our bedroom set." He said knowing that Khalilah would jump at the opportunity to see it. Khalilah had been talking about buying a painting for their bedroom for the last couple of weeks.

"Boy I swear if you don't hurry up and feed me I am going to curse you out something terrible," she said while getting out the car.

When they got to the front door, Tremaine made sure to let her go in first. As soon as they opened the door and stepped inside once again everybody yelled out, "Surprise!" Khalilah stood there with her hand over her mouth in shock. "What is all this?" she asked.

"It's your baby shower," Tremaine said smiling.

She slapped him on his arm and said, "Boy I knew your butt was up to something."

"What's up heffer?" One of Khalilah's girlfriends said walking up to her.

"I know your ass didn't know about this all this time and didn't tell me."

"I don't tell everything, girl. I can keep a secret," the girl said laughing.

"Oh now you can keep a secret. Yeah right I heard that," Khalilah joked.

The girl then led Khalilah into the middle of the crowded room, where everybody was waiting. They all began to pull out the additional boxes and gifts that were sitting next to their seats.

Tremaine just sat back and watched Khalilah enjoy herself. Since she was occupied, he decided to grab him and Khalilah a plate from the buffet table. When he got to the table, there were already a few females there making plates. The ones he didn't know all seemed to ask him the same question, "Are you Khalilah's baby father?"

There were a few of them that Tremaine recognized from the college that Khalilah attended, when he would go and pick her up at times. Everyone else in there was family, his and hers. Just before Tremaine could finish making their plates, one of the broads that he recognized from Khalilah's school approached him. "What's up my nigga?" she said.

Now the only people who would refer to Tremaine as "my nigga" were people from the hood or anyone else he had illegal dealings with. That was why the girl caught him off guard when she called him that. Tremaine gave her a slight facial frown and then acknowledged her with a quick nod of his head.

"You don't remember me, do you?" she asked.

"I seen you up on Khalilah's campus before?," he said.

"Nah, outside of that, you don't remember me?"

"Nah, I mean should I?" he asked.

"Remember that time over lil' Chris house when it was you, Chris and about four other dudes, it was Chris's birthday?"

"Oh yeah, yeah I remember. What? You were one of the girls that was over there?" Tremaine asked.

"I'm the one that you and the other brown skin boy, Dollar, were eating the dessert off of," she replied smiling while sucking on a celery stick that she was sliding in and out of her mouth.

It all came back to Tremaine. Chris had five females over his house that night and the one standing in front of him was the girl lying across the kitchen table, butt naked, with nothing but whip cream and strawberries all over her body. He and Dollar sat at the table for a second, dipping the strawberries while playing with her pussy. She was short, caramel complexioned, with one of those Georgia peach shaped asses that looked extra phatter because of her height. Tremaine would have fucked her that night but her dark skinned friend caught his eye and he fucked with her instead. Dollar ended up fucking the dessert girl that night.

"Oh yeah I remember that," he said looking around to see if Khalilah was watching them. She was paying him no attention, but was in the process of accepting gifts that were being handed to her. Tremaine was trying to get away before Khalilah did notice him with the broad standing in front of him, playing with a celery stick in her mouth.

"You be safe now, shorty. I will holla at you," he said walking off.

"Hold up," she said.

To be honest, she was starting to irritate Tremaine, because she kept calling him as if she knew him or something. He turned around and just looked at the girl.

"I'm saying, once Khalilah have that baby and start taking you through that six week dry spell, and need somebody to make those six weeks more wet for you just holla at me alright?"

Ain't this a bitch? Tremaine thought. Here he was at his girl's baby shower and one of her so-called friends was trying to set up a fuck session with him. Bitches, not woman, but bitches ain't shit but hoes and tricks. Tremaine wasn't even about to disrespect Khalilah by setting up fuck dates after her delivery, on the day of her baby shower at that. He had more than enough drama in his life, concerning that Latoya situation, to go back out and start that creeping shit. Before he start that shit again, he planned to chill out to see how the one female in his life played out. Tremaine kept his game face on with the dessert girl and nodded his head in response before walking off. Tremaine handed Khalilah her plate of food before sitting down beside her. After eating, Tremaine decided to leave after arranging for his mother to drop Khalilah off once the shower was over. He made sure to kiss Khalilah goodbye.

26 ALL FAIR IN WAR

Riiiiing....Riiiinnngg...*Who the fuck is this calling me at two-thirty in the morning?* Tremaine thought as he tried to adjust his eyes while reaching for the telephone receiver on the night stand in the darkness. He fumbled his hand around until he found what he was looking for.

"Who is this?" he said in a deep Barry White voice as he put the phone to his ear.

"Wake up, Yo!" Dirty yelled into the receiver. The sound of loud music in the background made it obvious where he was.

"Yo, what the fuck? What's up?" Tremaine tried to whisper back so that he wouldn't wake Khalilah up.

"Wake up my nigga, I'm on my way over there," Dirty yelled into the receiver even louder.

"What? Holla at me, what's up?" Tremaine was trying to ease up from under Khalilah who had her head lying on his chest.

"The streets is finally talking."

"Hold on for a minute." Tremaine managed to get out of the bed and head into the bathroom, closing the door behind him. "Yeah, now what you mean the streets is finally talking? Talking about what?"

"About Juice cuz, I finally got the scoop on all of that shit."

"What?" Tremaine asked as he was still half asleep and trying to comprehend what Dirty was yelling about.

"Look, here, I'ma be over there in 'bout twenty minutes and I'll holla at you when I get there." With that, Dirty hung up.

Tremaine sat leaning against the sink looking at the cordless phone in his hand trying to replay the broken up conversation he just had with Dirty. He got the scoop on Juice? He hoped Dirty meant what he thought he meant as he headed out of the bathroom and went to pull the cover up on Khalilah. Tremaine then went downstairs to wait for Dirty to come through.

When Dirty arrived he had all of the signs of a man that had just been partying. He reeked of cigarette smoke and he had that sweaty look. They headed down to the basement to talk, Tremaine started to offer him a drink but he could tell that Dirty had his fair share of alcohol for the night from his slurring speech.

Dirty started off by telling Tremaine that he had just come from around Chopper's, a popular little club on Pennsylvania Avenue, and how he had ran into Corey and a few other dudes that Juice used to fuck with over East Baltimore. After they all had a few drinks with each other and blew some haze together, they started reminiscing about Juice.

They all began telling a different story about him and what they remembered most. Dirty explained to Tremaine how one of the dudes with Corey, commented on the Rolex that Dirty had on his wrist. He stated how the gold presidential edition watch with the

278

diamond bezel face looked just like the one a homeboy of theirs named Alonzo owned. Upon first hearing the comment, Dirty thought nothing of it, until he remembered that he and Juice had the same exact watch.

They had bought them a year before Juice's murder, while they were in Philly doing some shopping. The malls up there had similar fashions but they didn't have tax on their clothes, as oppose to Baltimore. While out there, Tremaine, Dirty, Dollar, Juice and Chris came across a jewelry store that had a whole section of the store displaying nothing but Rolex pieces. Tremaine could remember Dirty picking up one of the most expensive watch in the display that read a price tag of twenty-five thousand dollars.

Earlier that day, Juice and Dirty were arguing about some dumb shit. If Tremaine's memory served him correctly, the argument was about how Juice chased females more than he chased dollars. Before arriving at the jewelry store, the dispute had long been over, but after Dirty decided to buy the watch he made a slick comment to Juice. It was along the lines of, "Nigga when you stop chasing those bitches you'll be able to do big boy shit like this, little man." Why would Dirty say something like that, Tremaine never knew, but the minute he did, Dollar began to laugh.

With that, Juice became extra heated and began to curse Dirty out saying, "Nigga you ain't said shit", amongst other things. Juice then decided to purchase the same watch that Dirty had just bought only to prove to all of them that he was far from broke. None of them commented on the fact that the watch was the only thing Juice bought on the whole trip. Dirty was tempted to ride him out about not having any money left with him to buy any clothes and shoes until Tremaine talked him out of it. He knew that Juice would have fucked around and spent his whole stash just to prove to Dirty that he had money too.

As Dirty continued to tell his story, he stated that he pulled Corey to the side and asked him about the kid Alonzo. Corey informed him about how Alonzo was just some lame ass nigga who lived in their neighborhood, but he wasn't out there with the rest of their homeboys that often. As Dirty dug a little deeper, Corey told him that Alonzo had recently purchased two new cars. One was a black Acura RL and the other was a Range Rover, both were a big step up from that rusty ass Buick Regal he was driving before.

Once Dirty began to put two and two together, he explained to Corey why he believed that Alonzo possibly had something to do with Juice's death. Corey was more than willing to give up any info that he knew. He put Dirty down about the house that Alonzo had been chilling in with a chick from New Jersey. No one knew exactly where he lived since he would just pop up a few times a month around the neighborhood. The one good lead that they had to go on was Alonzo's mother and little brother lived on Old York Road. Corey saw Alonzo's brother just about every day as the boy was headed to and from Gilford Middle School.

As Dirty explained his suspicions to Tremaine, he became numb. Tremaine felt neither anger nor sadness. All that he felt was a still coldness in his heart for vengeance.

It was a Saturday night when Dirty told Tremaine of his new findings. Monday afternoon Dirty, Dollar and Tremaine were all sitting outside of Alonzo mother's house in a stolen cargo van that Dollar had stolen that morning. They were waiting for school to let out so they could catch Alonzo's little brother, Lorenzo, coming home from school. Very few words were spoken in that van amongst the fellas as they were all deep in their own thoughts.

Tremaine was well aware that he had to keep the cool head out of the three of them. When he and Dirty first informed Dollar of the situation, his initial reaction was to kill Alonzo's mother and little brother, and when Alonzo came to the funeral for them to kill him and whoever else wanted to die that day. No matter how crazy of an idea that it may have sound, Tremaine knew that if it came down to it, neither Dollar or Dirty would hesitate to follow through with it. Tremaine stood to be the voice of reason. Even though he knew all was fair in war, he wasn't ready to see innocent blood shed just yet. Alicia had already been one innocent victim in the current situation that was caused by these bitch ass niggas. Niggas that Tremaine was determined to get his hands on, but if he couldn't, then and only then, would their loved ones pay the price with their lives.

As they sat in the van, the quietness that their individual thoughts brought forth were broken when Dollar stated, "This might be his lil ass right here," nodding in the direction of three young teenage boys coming down the sidewalk.

As they watched the three get closer to the house they noticed that they were passing what looked to be a cigarillo back and forth. When the kids got to the walkway of the intended house, one of them took two more pulls off of the cigarillo and passed it back to his friends. He then turned up the walkway and headed towards the house while the other two continued walking straight.

"Yeah that's his ass," Dirty said sliding open the side door of the van and getting out to run towards the house.

Dollar, who was driving, with Tremaine in the passenger seat, pulled the van up in front of the house as they both watched Dirty close in on Lorenzo going up the steps. He ran into the house behind the boy and emerged back through the front door wearing a ski mask while holding the boy in a choke hold. Lorenzo was struggling to free his neck from Dirty's strong arm but his putting up a fight was useless. The boy was no match for Dirty's determination as well as his size; he was five inches taller in height and at least fifty pounds heavier than Lorenzo.

Tremaine moved to the rear of the van to open the slide door for Dirty and the boy, while Dollar paid attention to the streets to see who, if anyone, was looking. Lorenzo sounded as if he was trying to scream, but with Dirty's forearm wrapped around his wind pipe tightly, all he could manage were gurgling sounds. Once they had him in the van, Tremaine closed the slide door and Dollar sped off.

"Throw me the duct tape on the front seat," Tremaine yelled out to Dollar as he pulled his ski mask down from over his face. Dollar reached over to the empty passenger seat and grabbed the tape with one hand while driving with the other. Dirty continue to hold Lorenzo in the choke hold with the boy lying face down and his body weight resting on top of him. "Let his ass go, yo," Tremaine told Dirty, who released his hold on the boy. Immediately, Lorenzo began gasping for air and coughing at the same time.

Dirty held Lorenzo's hands behind his back as Tremaine proceeded to heavily tape his wrists together. They then did the same thing with his ankles. Lorenzo began to scream out, "Somebody help me!" and all types of other useless shit. In an attempt to shut him up, Dirty punched him in the mouth, splitting the inside of his top lip. Lorenzo's mouth immediately began to fill with bright red blood. Seeing that they were riding in a van going down the highway, common sense must have kicked in on the boy; he stopped the screaming and just began to cry softly. "Lorenzo!" Tremaine called out to the bloody mouthed boy, smacking him in his face and breaking up his crying mode. "Look here we ain't got time for no crying bullshit you hear me?" Tremaine smacked him again making sure he had the boy's full attention. "Now I want you to look around this van. Sit your ass up and look!" Tremaine yelled out as he sat Lorenzo upright and leaned him against the side of the van. "Now there's a whole lot of shit in here that I could use to make matters worse for your lil ass you hear me?" Tremaine was referring to the saws, blow torches, wire cutters and fire arms they had in the back of the van.

Lorenzo looked around taking in the scene, and began to cry all over again. "What the fuck I tell you, huh? What I tell you?" Before Tremaine was able to smack Lorenzo back into focus again, Dirty hauled off and caught him with a quick right hook to the solar plexus, knocking the wind out of the boy's body and toppling him over to his side in agony.

Before Lorenzo was able to fall completely over, Tremaine caught him and sat him upright again. The boy's head was hanging down with bloody slobber running down his chin. Dirty placed his hand on Lorenzo's forehead and pushed him causing the back of his head to hit the side of the van.

Tremaine wanted to get back to the point. "Your brother Alonzo where do he...," before he was able to get the rest of his question out, he noticed a gold key chain sticking out of Lorenzo's pocket that looked very familiar. When he took it out of his pocket and got a closer look, the whole robbery was confirmed. Lorenzo had Juice's gold picture frame on his key chain, the picture that Juice used to have of himself, Tremaine, Dirty, Dollar and lil Chris had been removed. The picture that they all had taken six months prior at a party had been replaced with a photo of Lorenzo and Alonzo at a swimming pool. Tremaine knew for sure that it was the same picture frame because of the T.R.F. initials that were engraved on the back of it. It stood for "The Royal Family," a name that they had recently started, referring to the group that grew up together.

Tremaine shook his head for a second and handed the key chain to Dirty, who also recognized it. "I knew it! What I tell you? I knew his ass did that shit!" Dirty said getting loud and hyped up.

"What? What did ya'll find?" Dollar yelled from the driver seat.

"Look at this shit!" Dirty crawled to the front of the van and handed Dollar the key chain.

"Oh ya'll bitch ass niggas done fucked up for real! I'm telling you...."

Before Dollar could finish getting his words out, Tremaine had already wrapped both of his hands around Lorenzo's neck and pulled him within one inch of his face.

"Nigga where the fuck did you get this key chain?" he asked him through clenched teeth. If looks could kill Lorenzo's heart would have stop beating on the spot.

"My brother gave me that key chain," he said quickly with his eyes looking as if they were going to pop out of his head.

"Where the fuck is your brother at now?" Tremaine asked, still holding the boy face to face.

"I don't know, he probably at home."

"Where the fuck is home at?" Tremaine asked.

"I don't know, he lives out in the County somewhere," Lorenzo replied.

"Shorty don't start playin' no muthafuckin' games, now where the fuck your brother live at?" Tremaine began tightening his grip around the boy's neck.

"I have only been over there twice. He just moved out there and I don't know how to get there," he said with tears beginning to fall down his face.

I swear I don't know, seems to be a muthafucker's favorite word, Tremaine thought to himself. No problem, he knew he had something that would make anybody remember real quickly. Tremaine reached for the blow torch and immediately Lorenzo began crying hysterically, begging Tremaine not to burn him. Tremaine turned the nozzle of the torch a little, releasing a hissing sound of gas. Dirty produced a lighter and lit the torches' flame. Tremaine began to adjust the nozzle a little more to give the fire that straight narrow edge, along with a roaring sound as if it were a train coming through a tunnel.

Lorenzo tried scooting away from Tremaine and his threatening flame, but went nowhere as Dirty grabbed him by the tape around his ankles and held his feet in front of Tremaine. Tremaine then placed the fire on the front part of the boy's shoes where the laces were and they instantly burned a hole straight through the shoe to the flesh. Lorenzo let out an ear shattering scream as his legs shook to escape the burning of his flesh. His attempts were useless as Dirty held a tight grip holding his legs in place.

After a few rounds of burning various spots on Lorenzo's feet, Tremaine finally stopped and asked him if he could now remember where his brother lived. Lorenzo swore up and down that he didn't know where his brother lived but he did volunteer to call him on the cell phone that was on his hip. They all agreed that if Lorenzo did, in fact, know how to get to his brother's house that the blow torch would have brought the info up out of him. With that, they began orchestrating a plan on what to have Lorenzo say on the cell phone to get them face to face with Alonzo.

It took Tremaine a few minutes to get Lorenzo to calm down to get the stuttering and shakiness out of his voice, despite the tremendous pain that he was in. He then took Lorenzo's cell phone and dialed the number that he gave him to Alonzo's home. As he dialed, Tremaine couldn't help but wonder if the phone had been purchased with some of Juice's money. There was no response at Alonzo's home and when he tried his cell phone the farthest they could get was his voice mail. After leaving three voice messages on his brother's phone, Lorenzo finally got a call back from Alonzo, he went with the conversation as he was coached to do.

Lorenzo lied and told his brother that he was stranded over some girl's house and he needed him to come pick him up. After Lorenzo hit him with 50 questions of who the girl was, how had Lorenzo gotten out there and why did he go over there without a ride back. He finally agreed to come and pick up his little brother.

They chose the apartment complex called Town and Country in Woodlawn, MD as the pickup spot. The sun was beginning to set; the evening hour made their plan sweeter.

As they sat in the parking lot complex, Tremaine was glad that he trusted Dollar's judgment on choosing the spot. The complex was built at the end of a two way street. Particularly, the building they were in front of was the perfect spot; it allowed them the privilege of seeing each and every car approaching and leaving. In addition to this, after pulling into the complex you would have to drive through three different lots to get to the building number Lorenzo had given Alonzo. That was more than enough time to see Alonzo approaching and for them to get out and hide before he reached the building.

The only part of their plan left up to chance, was what kind of car Alonzo would be driving. Would it be his Acura or Range Rover or might he be driving something different? That was the only part the fellas didn't like since they were unsure. It was evident that lady luck was on their side that night when they noticed a dark colored RL coming down the street towards the entrance of the parking lot. Tremaine and Dollar quickly exited the van and went to duck behind two cars that were directly across from each other in the parking lot.

As the Acura approached, it moved slowly through the lot as Alonzo looked at the front building numbers in search of the address that he was looking for. They all watched as he finally made it to their parking lot and stopped almost directly in front of the van, which was parked in front of the 5528 Shaw Court building. Dirty was on the inside of the van with Lorenzo lying down in the back.

There was another occupant in the car with Alonzo. Alonzo began blowing his horn while looking up at the building in search of his little brother. Suddenly Dirty hit the high beams on the van, blinding Alonzo and his passenger with the sudden flash of light.

Their first instinct was to put their hands up to their faces to shield the light. Immediately, Dollar and Tremaine began to run down on the car without Alonzo noticing them. Tremaine snatched open Alonzo's door while Dollar focused on the passenger. With the high beams still affecting their vision, neither one of the niggas saw Tremaine or Dollar until their doors were opened and the dome light inside of the car came on, by then it was already too late.

Before Alonzo could even think about reacting, Tremaine had the Mac-11 pushed up against his temple. The passenger had what looked to be a .357 revolver sitting on his lap resulting in Dollar immediately open-firing on him with the Heckler & Koch .40 that he had. All of the shots rang out and landed repeatedly on the side of the passenger's neck and head. The original plan was to snatch and take him with them. Tremaine stuck to that plan, never firing one shot at the driver. Once Dollar began shooting, Alonzo leaned to his left towards Tremaine in order to avoid the gunfire. In the process, Tremaine was able to grab him by the back of his jacket collar and then began to drag him towards the van.

When he realized where he was being pulled to, Alonzo suddenly caught a case of the "I can't walk," by falling to his knees and acting as if he wasn't going to get up. By that time, Dollar had left the passenger brainless and was making his way towards the van where Tremaine was dragging Alonzo by the collar. Without missing a beat, Dollar reached down and grabbed Alonzo by the back of the waist band of his jeans, he and Tremaine both carried Alonzo to the van. After being smacked in the back of the head numerous times with Tremaine's mac-11, Alonzo was no longer able to offer up any more resistance. Once they got Alonzo to the van and he saw through his dizzy eyes his little brother taped up in the back, he knew he could hang that shit up because that would be his last night as a living man.

The whole kidnapping took less than thirty seconds from the time the first shots were fired, to the moment the van door was being closed and they were heading out of the parking lot. On the way out, Dirty had to ram the front end of the Acura in order to get out of the parking space. Once inside the van, Dollar immediately went to taping Alonzo up while Tremaine followed up with the blow torch. He burned damn near every inch of Alonzo's body including his penis and testicles.

Dirty drove the van around for close to an hour while Tremaine and Dollar worked Alonzo over in the back. Hearing his screams and cries were like music to their ears. Tremaine even took the wheel and drove the van so that Dirty could get some of the action. In between torture sessions Alonzo revealed who was with him the night they kidnapped Juice. One of his accomplices was the passenger that Dollar left brainless. The third one, he said they killed the night after Juice's death, since he was likely to run his mouth and tell if shit got thick.

The fellas were getting bored with torturing Alonzo; they had already cut off most of his toes and fingers. After his body went into shock and he passed out, there wasn't much more they could do to bring any more pain. Finally, Tremaine put four shots in the middle of his forehead. Unfortunately his little brother Lorenzo ended up being one of the innocent bystanders, that Tremaine tried to avoid. When Dirty placed two shots in the back of the boy's skull, they disposed of the bodies in Leakin Park and took the van to Annapolis to set it on fire.

27 DILEMMA

Agent Zachary Thornhill was a little anxious as he sat at his desk with the rest of his co-workers going over last minute details for the upcoming raid that they would be conducting on Randy's car dealership. Due to his hours upon hours of surveillance and investigating, they were finally ready to bring Randy and a number of his associates into federal custody. The raid was scheduled to take place within the next forty-eight hours. Even though they were unable to find out who Randy's supplier was, they had decided to go forth with it anyway.

They were sure they could get someone out of the bunch to turn on the rest and tell them everything else that they needed to know about the operation. Information on who was supplying who and what part each individual played. The FBI agents knew that was basically money in the bank, once they start throwing numbers and life sentence threats, one of them would snitch. When they did, it would more than likely cause a domino effect of loose lips among the rest of the suspects.

One thing that special Agent Thornhill didn't like was the fact that he hadn't been afforded more time to spend investigating that Tremaine Jenkins gentleman. He never really thought nothing on the kid, whom he had only seen once during his surveillance of the dealership until his brother mentioned his arrest for gun possession. Afterwards, he conducted a quick background check on Mr. Jenkins and saw that the gun charge was his only arrest. Agent Thornhill also found out that the kid seemed to be part owner of a very profitable restaurant by the name of "Str8 soul".

Wanting to see the restaurant first hand, the agent took the initiative to pay a little visit to the spot for dinner. The smothered pork chops dinner he ate was delicious and the place was packed. He had even spotted Mr. Jenkins inside mingling with a few customers and placing coconut icing on top of a freshly baked cake. When Agent Thornhill looked up the ownership with Mr. Jenkins and two other women, he was concerned about what he found. What caught the agent's attention was the fact that Mr. Jenkins put up eight thousand dollars for the purchase of the restaurant. It was below the ten thousand mark that a lot folks try to avoid so that the proper paperwork wouldn't have to be filed and sent to the IRS. Another thing that stood out was Mr. Jenkins had a townhouse that wasn't in his name. Looking over the financial records Agent Thornhill had obtained, he saw that "Str8 Soul" was a lucrative enough establishment that he could afford his own town home, so why wasn't it in his name?

He still hadn't brought the young man's file to his supervisor or co-workers attention, since he was basically doing a side investigation to see what he could come up with.

As Tremaine sat in front of the computer screen, he began to rub his temples. He had been sitting with his eyes glued to that screen for well over an hour searching the auction sites for new vending machines. He was able to locate six brand new, late model machines that were being auctioned off for half the price they were worth. Tremaine figured they had to be stolen or something, because it was too good of an offer. Whether they were or were not, he didn't care. He only knew that with those machines being the latest models in vending technology, he wouldn't have to worry too much about them needing any maintenance work any time soon.

As he proceeded to give the auction site his information and place his bid, Tremaine leaned back in his office chair and contemplated on where he would put the new machines. The deal with the executives at the M&T Bank stadium hadn't gone through as of yet, but everything seemed to be falling into place so far. Tremaine also contemplated on who he planned to hire to maintain the current machines that he already owned. The process of keeping them stocked and working was beginning to become too much for him to handle on his own. He currently had twenty machines up and running in everything from hair salons to insurance buildings. He was currently making enough profit with his machines to hire a full-time employee.

Tremaine wasn't thinking too heavily about the pending gun charge that was hanging over his head. His lawyer was telling him that he could postpone the whole ordeal for at least another year, and then he would be able to cop out to no more than two years of probation. Tremaine wasn't really too pressed to postpone the matter; he wanted to get it over and done with so that he could start the bullshit probation. After his bid was processed, Tremaine knew that he had to come back the next day to find out if he had been out bidded. He turned the computer off and headed upstairs to the bedroom where Khalilah sat eating a bowl of peaches as she watched one of those crazy reality shows.

"Boo, come here, look. Watch this," she said pointing at the television where some white man was getting ready to eat something that looked like spit up to Tremaine.

"What the hell is that?" he asked lying down on the bed besides her.

"He's about to drink some grinded up cow balls," she responded.

"Huh?" Tremaine frowned up his face. "Why do you keep watching these wild ass shows?"

"Because they show you that some people would do anything for money." Khalilah fed Tremaine a spoonful of her peaches. "That's exactly why I keep my circle small; I know for the right price, a lot of muthafuckas would kill their own mama."

Tremaine couldn't argue with her on that. He just shook his head as he watched the person on the screen drink cow balls just to win some prize money. After a few more moments, he got up to take a quick shower, then slipped on a pair of basketball shorts and a tank top. He laid down next to Khalilah just as the eleven o'clock news began to come on. The beginning of the news was showing highlights of some of the stories they would be covering that night. One in particular caught Tremaine's attention when the anchorman mentioned something about a drug bust at a car dealership in Southwest, D.C. Once the program went to commercial and came back on, Tremaine turned up the volume on the television and waited for them to report the story.

After reporting a fire at a high-rise building and a family found slain in their home, they finally got to the drug bust. Tremaine's mouth must have damn near hit the floor when the reporter went live to the scene of "Top Notch Motors", the dealership that Randy owned. The reporter was showing how the FBI and DEA were inside of the dealership with the place cornered off, while they continued searching the premises. They explained how the car lot was just one of several raids that the feds had conducted that day. This was just the beginning of a four month investigation that gave lead after lead to various drug distributors in surrounding states, totaling eighteen months of investigating.

Tremaine felt his heart nearly stop beating as he began to contemplate on whether or not he had been a part of that eighteen month investigation. He calmed down once he thought about when the reporter said that they had conducted several raids that day. Obviously, his house wasn't one of them. The news said that a total of nineteen people had been arrested that day. Tremaine immediately began to back track on all of the transactions he had done with Randy. He could count on one hand how many had actually taken place at the car lot.

In the beginning of their business dealings, Randy made sure to meet him and Los somewhere else, like inside of a fast food restaurant's bathroom or a mall bathroom. As time went on, he became more comfortable with Tremaine and would sometimes call him over to a house he had in Greenbelt to make the transactions. It was very rare that they would meet at the dealership. Tremaine always felt more comfortable meeting at a neutral spot that they both agreed on.

Tremaine headed down to his living room and looked out of the window thinking that the feds were getting ready to kick his door in at any moment. He had to get his self together, he was glad that Khalilah was asleep because surely she would have seen the look of worry that he had on his face. Tremaine began to calm down once he began to reason with himself again. He could remember dealing with Randy only, besides Manny, when it came to buying his coke in weight. He never met with anyone else and never drove his legit cars when he went.

Tremaine was adamant about driving one of his throw-away auction cars whenever he was going to make any transactions. He always did that just in case he ever got pulled over by the police during a transaction trip. He could leave whatever it was he had in the car without worrying about them tracing the cheap vehicle back to him. The auction that he always went to allowed him to pay for the cars in cash and complete the paperwork without I.D. The more he thought about it, the more confident Tremaine became. Realizing that if they didn't run down on him with the rest of the raids, then he must have been straight, or so he hoped.

The following morning, Tremaine woke up feeling a whole lot better. His place still hadn't been raided and he was still a free man. As he began to get dressed to head over to 'Str8 Soul,' he wondered how the hell was he going to tell Dirty, Dollar, and lil Chris that the steady flow of coke that they had been so accustomed to for years was suddenly cut off. They never knew exactly where Tremaine was getting the coke once he stopped taking his trips up North. The money was flowing through so abundantly that they could care less who his connect was.

Tremaine knew personally, he was straight, financial wise. He hadn't told anyone, but the night they were celebrating lil' Chris' birthday, he was actually celebrating the fact that he had just hit the one million dollar mark of the paper that he had saved up. The best part about it was that he organized his money to make more money. Not to include his street life, the restaurant and vending machines were doing so well that he could live off of its proceeds comfortably and not have to touch his savings for a while.

Tremaine knew that Dirty had to be doing alright himself. He figured that Dirty had to have one million dollars saved up. If not, he was very close to it considering his coke sales and the three barbershops he now owned. Dollar should have somewhere along the lines of about seven hundred and fifty thousand put away. Lil' Chris shouldn't have no less than four hundred thousand banked, himself. The only downside that fucked with Tremaine was the fact that he was the only one who had dreams of getting out of the drug game. Dirty had profitable businesses but he always said that he would keep hustling to fall back on for life. Dollar and lil' Chris said fuck a legitimate business, they would hustle for the rest of their lives or at least what was left of it.

Dreams of him and his team holding down a legitimate Fortune 500 company had always been Tremaine's desire. He lived by a verse that he heard Master P spit out on Scarface's "My Homies" C.D. when he said, *"They use to seeing CEO's in suits and ties, but we young niggas in tennis shoes and diamonds. Executive street millionaires me and my niggas gonna be 'bout it 'bout it until we grey and in wheel chairs."* That was his vision, spit out in a single verse. Him, Dirty, Dollar, and Chris busting in on Wall Street with their own legitimate corporation, while making billion dollar decisions with a gangsta' hand.

There had been plenty of times that he shared his vision with his homeboys, and they all felt that none of them had the ambition that Tremaine possessed to make it a reality. Dollar had even said something that fucked Tremaine up one time. He told Tremaine, "I'm sayin' yo, that's your thing you know what I'm sayin'? All that corporate America shit, you definitely got the brains to do that. Me personally, that shit ain't for me. I ain't even thinking 'bout that, but you my muthafuckin' man regardless where we go in life. If you ever find yourself needing a nigga to put in some illegal work for you while you doing your legit thing, that's me, that's what I'm here for. 'Cause all I know is the streets and nothing else really matters."

Ever since Dollar spoke those words to Tremaine a few years ago, he had a feeling of guilt on the inside. He always wondered how his little cousin's life would have turned out had he not grown up so fast from being around him and Dirty. Tremaine thought back to when he was eleven or twelve years old, even though he was doing a little hustling it was never to the extent of what Dollar was doing at that age. At the age of twelve, Dollar was already smoking weed, breaking in houses, and stealing cars. By the time he was thirteen, he stayed strapped daily. Tremaine and Dirty didn't start carrying pistols until they were fifteen years old. They had Dollar living the same life as themselves, at a much younger age. Tremaine began to wonder about Manny and if the feds had run down on him as well. If they hadn't then he planned to holler at him to see if he was willing to do business with Dirty and the rest of his homeboys. That way he wouldn't be leaving them assed out without a connect. He was done, he was able to throw in the towel and say that he was one of the select few who had gotten in and been able to get out, on top.

The only issue with that was the fact that he couldn't leave his team out there with nothing. He knew that he had to make sure they were straight before he could truly wash his hands with the streets.

28 LOYALTY?

As Tremaine sat on the bench inside Baltimore's Penn Station waiting on his train to New York, he contemplated on the phone call that he had with Manny. It had been a little over a week since Randy's arrest and Tremaine was down to his last four bricks of cocaine.

Tremaine called Manny earlier that afternoon to see if he was still straight on the coke tip, he knew that he wasn't on no bullshit since he had been the one supplying Randy. Manny told Tremaine that he talked to Randy and come to find out, one of the mechanics that worked at his car dealership was an undercover FBI agent. He had witnessed how Randy would accept straight cash in exchange for cars, without following the proper procedures in regards to the paperwork. On a few occasions, it was observed that Randy had even taken bricks of coke and extensive quantities of weed in exchange for cars. Manny said that the lawyer he had retained for Randy was telling him that so far, things didn't look good for Randy, but he wouldn't know the full extent of the damage until the preliminary hearing. Tremaine stressed to Manny that it was vital that they got together for a face to face meeting. Manny told him to hop on the next train and he would be there to pick him up at the train station.

Tremaine still hadn't told any of his homeboys that their coke connect was no longer available. Dirty did holler at Tremaine about seeing the raid on the news, but Tremaine left it as that. Dirty thought Randy was just some car salesman that Tremaine turned him on to because he had the best car deals. He commented on how he had a feeling that Randy had to be doing some kind of hustling on the side since he would take fifty or sixty thousand dollars in cash for a car and ask no questions. No matter how young or old you were, if a person had the dough, the car was theirs. The entire time Dirty spoke, Tremaine kept his game face on, not revealing the true anxiety he was feeling. He had thought long and hard about just saying fuck it and letting Dirty, Dollar, and lil' Chris know that all the coke supply had come to an end and let them find their own connect but it wasn't in Tremaine to carry it like that. He just couldn't bring himself to just leave the same niggas he had been through so much with out there, high and dry without a real connect. He told himself that he had to at least try to find a new supplier before he gave up. This trip definitely wasn't for him, it was for his team.

Tremaine checked his watch and it read 3:50 p.m. He wasn't scheduled to leave until 4:37, so he stepped into one of the gift shops to kill time. He ended up only buying himself a bottle of water and sitting back down on the bench to wait for the train. He wondered if he should have brought himself a change of clothes but dismissed the idea since he planned to be in and out of the city. His sole purpose was to convince Manny to start doing business with Dirty and Dollar, or at least one of them, so that they could continue to do what they do.

Manny knew of Dirty and Dollar from the few times they had been up New York to go shopping. Whenever they went up there, Tremaine always made it his business to link up with Manny. They might all end up going to a night club that Manny would take them to or just chill out at his house in Harlem to check out a football game or something with some of his homeboys. Even with all of that in his favor, Tremaine knew that Manny still didn't know Dirty and Dollar personally, only as a part of Tremaine's crew. He still didn't know how he planned to finesse the conversation, or exactly what he was going to say to persuade Manny. Tremaine knew that whatever he said it had to convince Manny, otherwise, his homeboys were on their own.

Things didn't go too smooth for Tremaine when he told Khalilah, at the last minute, that he wouldn't be home that night and that he would see her early the next morning. She went off on him even worse once he told her that he was going out of town and couldn't tell her the reason. Tremaine could remember her exact words, "The hell you mean you got to go out of town and you can't tell me why? I deserve to know where you're going and who you're going with," she said. Tremaine told her that he would explain it all to her when he got back and she said that if he was going to carry it like that then he shouldn't bother to bring his black ass back.

Tremaine didn't feel like arguing with her because he had important business that had to be taken care of. He just left out of the house with Khalilah's curses being spat at his back. If he had enough time to explain it to her, he would have. Despite the fact, he felt as though he did owe her that much. When he called the station to make the arrangements, he was told that the next train scheduled to leave for New York was in a couple of hours, forcing him to drop everything that he was doing and head straight to the station.

Tremaine felt guilty about putting Khalilah through so much stress so late in her pregnancy. She was due to have their son in a little over a month. The closer she got to her due date, the more Tremaine began to have feelings of anxiety and fear. Being a parent was going to be a new experience for him and Khalilah, he just hoped that they didn't fail. He constantly reminded himself that after taking that one last trip he wouldn't ever have to look back again, he could go on to live a life that his child could appreciate.

"ALL PASSENGERS FOR TRAIN NUMBER 2306, BALTIMORE TO NEW YORK NOW BOARDING," the voice boomed over the stations intercom. Tremaine snapped out of his daydream and went to board the train.

It was a little after seven when Tremaine stepped off the train in New York. He let out a slight stretch after being seated for such a long period of time. He looked around the station to see if he could spot Manny, who was nowhere in sight. Exiting the station, Tremaine reached for his cell phone. Just as he was in the middle of dialing Manny's number, he stepped through the exit doors of the station and spotted him standing outside. He was standing in front of an all black Ford Excursion that looked to be the size of a boat, compared to the rest of the cars in the lot.

Manny stood there waving Tremaine over. He was wearing a grey, long sleeve Prada linen dress shirt with black linen slacks. Tremaine could tell by the platinum diamond Rolex bracelet that business must have been going pretty good for Manny. It was almost as thick as a cuff and shined as if he had a flash light on his wrist, he also had the Rolex watch to match.

"What's up my nigga?" Manny said grabbing Tremaine's hand and pulling him in for a one arm hug.

"Ain't shit. What's been going on with you, my nigga?"

Manny reached out and pulled at the hair that Tremaine had recently started growing on his chin. "Boy where the hell you get this shit from?" he joked. "You ain't have all this shit the last time I saw you."

"Shit, a nigga gettin' old Yo," Tremaine said smoothing the hair down on his chin with the palm of his hand.

"Man, I hear that." Manny playfully slapped Tremaine on his shoulder. "Come on yo,' let's go." He went and opened the back door of the SUV. When they got in, Tremaine saw that there were five T.V.'s inside, one inside of each head rest and one on the front dash broad, along with two Playstations, as well as DVD players. Accompanying Manny was a large Debo looking bald head, black muthafucka, who drove the truck while Tremaine and Manny sat in the third row of seats.

"I like that watch!" Tremaine said tapping Manny on his arm.

"Oh yeah, this just something that I threw on, he said with a grin. I'm tired as shit forreal, I just came from my man trial at court and I ain't have time to change up yet. The muthafuckin jury was deliberating 'til about six o' clock and still couldn't make up their minds. So they have to go back tomorrow and shit."

"I can dig it." Tremaine was looking at the news, which was playing on the T.V.'s.

"I was just getting ready to get at you when you called me, but I had to get your number out of my other phone. Man, shit been so crazy, I just moved and a lot of my shit is still packed up, a nigga ain't have time to unpack yet."

"Shit has definitely been thick these past few days," Tremaine said. "So when you said you hollered at Randy?"

"I talked to him 'bout three days ago. They got him on no bond status in that bitch," Manny said shaking his head.

"Yeah I figured that," Tremaine said.

I told his ass to hire all fuckin' crackheads as his mechanics but he wanted to be hard headed and hire a muthafucker that he knew nothin' about, now this is the bullshit that happen when you don't listen. Manny contorted his face as if he could remember Randy and his conversation like it was yesterday.

"I'm like alright; you can get a smoker that's professional, you feel me? Just because a muthafucker a fiend don't mean they can't do good work. But nah, he want to go out and get a fuckin' stranger and now look where his ass at. Out of all the mechanics in the world he had to go out and get a damn FBI agent, I swear." Manny continued to shake his head in disgust.

Randy was the main topic of discussion the entire ride to lower Manhattan. The Debo looking nigga, driving the Excursion, pulled up in front of a high rise building and drove into the underground parking garage.

They exited the truck and took the elevator up to the 18th floor where Manny had a nice sized penthouse. Tremaine could see that the place had to be one of many that Manny occupied because the coffee table in the living room had a light coat of dusting on it, looking as if someone hadn't used the place in weeks. The driver stepped off into one of the bedrooms while Manny turned on the television to the Knicks game and passed Tremaine a cold Heineken.

"So what was so important that you had to come up here and holla at me face to face, homie?" Manny asked as he took off his linen shirt revealing the white tank top underneath.

"To get straight to the point, I wanted to holla at you to see how you felt about dealing with my lil cousin?" Tremaine took a sip of his beer while keeping his eyes on Manny.

"What do you mean?," Manny said.

"Let me say this first. Me, I'm done with all of this. I mean I got me a good lil' run in, I'm good on the paper tip, I'm done."

"Damn Yo, so what you sayin' son you not hustlin' no more?" Manny asked, with a confused look on his face.

"Yeah. I'm saying, ain't no need for that no more. You already know about my restaurant and plus I just started fucking with this vending machine business. So I'm straight, you dig? If I keep hustling,' it'll be for nothing you feel me?"

"I feel that Yo," Manny responded with a sincere look on his face.

"Plus I'm 'bout to be a father, something I ever had. Shit, a nigga got somebody else to live for now, you know?"

"Oh yeah, you 'bout to have a kid'?" Manny asked with a smile on his face.

"Yeah Yo, a lil' son," Tremaine responded unable to hold back his smile.

"Big Dogg 'bout to have a lil' puppy," Manny said as they both burst out laughing.

"Damn, this shit is wild, son." Manny had a disappointed look on his face.

"What?" Tremaine asked.

"Peep this. You know that you, Randy and Los were the only niggas I was fuckin' within the Baltimore-D.C. area, right? The only ones I needed to fuck with, for real. Since Los dead and Randy facing an asshole full of time, I was tryin' to get at you to see if you were ready to step your game up two notches." Manny shrugged his shoulders and shook his head.

"What you mean?" Tremaine asked curiously.

"Let me put it to you like this. You think you can move a hundred bricks a month if I give them to you at fifteen a piece?"

"Fifteen?" Tremaine asked feeling light headed all of a sudden.

"Yeah, I just got me a new Columbian connect and that's how I wanted to get down wit' you now. That's why I was tryin' to find your number after Randy got knocked off. The day that he got knocked was the exact day I was able to iron out the details with these new people. He wasn't even getting the numbers that I'm spitting your way. And with these prices you'll be the only one I need to fuck within that area, you feel me?" Manny was rubbing his hands together as if he could feel the money already.

Tremaine did a quick assessment and realized that if he sold the bricks whole for twenty thousand a piece, he would see five thousand off of each one, and that times one hundred totaled a half a million dollars a month. *Damn! That's a lot of muthafuckin' paper,* Tremaine thought. "Yo, you making this hard on a nigga." Tremaine was holding his head in his hands looking down at the floor.

"I'm sayin', I had to let you know the reason I was trying to get in contact with you," Mannt said.

Tremaine sat there thinking about all of the things he could do with five hundred thousand a month. If he got one good year in, he, Khalilah, his children, and his grand children would be set for life. That there was that mansion and yacht money. *NO!!* His inner voice screamed out, *don't be greedy. You got more than enough money right now and with your two businesses eventually expanding, your pockets will continue to grow. Maybe not as fast as it would with those bricks, but nevertheless it will grow.*

Tremaine listened to his voice of reason as it told him all of those things and how he had to think about his son. As the old saying went, "All that glitters isn't gold."

"Hey cuz..." Tremaine stopped for a moment to run his hands over his face, making sure that he was truly ready to stand by his decision, "as tempting as that offer sounds, and believe me it's very tempting, I'ma have to decline."

"Oh yeah?" Manny asked a little caught off guard. "You're dead serious about quitting this shit, huh?" he asked.

Tremaine gave him a fixed expression that said it all.

"You know what, I can respect that lil' homie. Seriously," Mannie said, looking Tremaine up and down as if he was truly seeing him for the first time.

"But hold up!" Tremaine sat up on the edge of the couch. "That goes back to what I wanted to holla at you face to face about."

"What's that?"

"I'm sayin,' you know I got a lot of homeboys that was eatin' off of the shit that I was getting from you and Randy, right?"

Manny nodded his head as he continued to listen.

"Now you remember my niggas, Dirty and Dollar, who I always brought wit' me when I came to holla at you whenever I was up here, right?"

"Yeah I know who you talkin about. One of them your cousin ain't they?" Manny asked.

Tremaine snapped his fingers and said, "Exactly! Now if your offer still stands and you trying to keeps your hands in Baltimore with somebody you can trust, then they're the ones who you need to get with."

"Oh nah, I don't know about that," Manny said shaking his head. "I ain't got time for no fuck ups. I rather deal with niggas who already been tried and true. I done basically watched you come up before my eyes, but I don't know about your mans and 'em."

"I feel that Yo, but I'm sayin' this, them two been with me since we were back in our snotty nose days. Since day one, we all cut from the same tree. Ever since you hit me off wit' them first set of vials back in the day, they been right there wit' a nigga. Wit' the same blood, sweat and tears." Tremaine pounded his fist in his hands for emphasis.

"Hey yo, on some real shit, your word mean a whole lot to me but I just don't know 'bout all that."

Tremaine was determined that he was going to get a yes out of Manny. "I'm sayin' you ain't even got to give them the hundred bricks. You can start them off wit' somethin' smaller until they prove their work to you. 'Cause I'm tellin' you, my niggas gonna make it happen."

Manny just stared at Tremaine for a moment while exhaling a deep breath. He had just begun to fuck with some Colombians directly, instead of the middle man that he used to go through. Baltimore was a spot that he needed now more than ever. Since he was getting so much coke at one time. He knew of the niggas Tremaine was talking about, had them in plenty of pictures with Los, whom he trusted with no discretions. But he wondered if they were anything like Tremaine was boosting them up to be? Manny didn't really want to jump the gun with Dirty and Dollar but with Los dead, Randy locked up, and Tremaine on that retirement shit, there was really no one else he trusted enough to start new business with in Baltimore.

"I'll tell you what," Manny said sliding up to the edge of the couch. "You want me to do you a favor; you gotta do me a favor."

"What's up?" Tremaine asked skeptically.

"I want you to go home and think about this retirement shit for me, alright? I mean seriously think about it," he said poking himself in the temple with his index finger. "I want you to think about how much money you can make in six months. Seriously, that's it, six months and if you still want to retire then maybe. Maybe…" he said emphasizing the word, "we could talk about your homies."

Tremaine knew that there wasn't no thinking about it, his mind was made up and he was done! But to satisfy Manny, he would take a few days and act as if he was actually considering his offer. Tremaine was just glad that Manny had actually left the door open and was considering doing business with the members of his team.

It was five thirty the next morning when Tremaine arrived home. When he went to his bedroom, Khalilah was nowhere in sight, and the bed was still made indicating no one had slept in it. Tremaine went to look out the front window of the townhouse to double check the fact that he had seen her truck parked in the driveway when he pulled up. Once again, it was there. He searched all of the bedrooms and the basement but there was no sign of her.

Tremaine began to worry as he looked around the house for anything out of order. Everything was intact. He tried Khalilah's cell phone and got nothing but her voice mail. He then decided to call Mrs. Turner, hoping that she would know where she was. He was so worried about her whereabouts that Tremaine forgot that it was before six in the morning. The time didn't dawn on him until Mr. Turner answered the phone grudgingly with sleep heavy in his voice.

"Hello?"

Tremaine thought about hanging up but pushed on anyway. "What's up Mr. Turner? Hey umm… is Khalilah over there?"

"Tremaine?" Mr. Turner asked irritably. "Do you know what time it is? It's…" he turned to check his alarm clock. "It's five-fifty two in the morning."

"I know but I just got home from out of town and when I got here, Khalilah wasn't here. That's why I'm tryin' to find out if you've seen her."

"Yes, as a matter of fact, I have seen her. She's in her bedroom asleep right now."

Tremaine let out a much needed sigh of relief since the worry of her whereabouts was a load off his shoulders.

"Now let me give you some much needed advice, Tremaine," Mr. Turner said in his holier than thou tone that he always seemed to convert to whenever talking to Tremaine. "Now, I don't know what it is that you've done to upset my daughter, because she wouldn't divulge it to me. But when the woman in your life is pregnant and is so close to her due date, it's not wise to do ignorant things to upset her."

That's it! Tremaine thought. He was tired of biting his tongue with Khalilah's father. "Ignorant?" he said. "Check this out Mr. Turner, you shouldn't be commenting on somethin' that you don't even know about, alright. So before you decide to give your two cents on it---"

"I don't need to know any facts, Mr. Turner said abruptly cutting Tremaine off. I know that my daughter arrived last night practically in tears and you were nowhere to be found, which led me to believe that you played a part in her distress!"

You bitch ass nigga! Tremaine caught himself getting ready to scream into the phone. Yo, just tell Khalilah that I called. I ain't 'bout to go through this with you early in the muthafuckin' morning!" With that, he hung up on Mr. Turner. I swear this old ass muthafucka don't know that I will bury his ass and then sit with Khalilah and her mother in the front row of his funeral, consoling them, without nobody even having a clue.

After arguing with Mr. Turner and the long train rides he had recently endured, Tremaine decided to take a nice hot bath and let his mind wander. That five hundred thousand a month conversation he had with Manny continued to pop in his head. He thought that he could even sell the bricks in the city for twenty-five thousand and still kill the competition, since powder was of such high grade. Selling them for that price would in turn leave Tremaine making a million dollars a month. He seriously considered on taking Manny up on the six month offer, but told himself no once again.

Tremaine was smart enough to know that six months turned into a year, if he was lucky, and by that time the addiction would be too great for him to back away. Besides, he continued to remind himself that he was straight and did not want for nothing. Get in and get out! That was the name of his game. If he took Manny's offer he would be doing it out of pure greed and sooner or later, it would catch up to him. "Nope, not going to touch it," Tremaine said out loud as he sat in the tub.

The hustler inside of Tremaine wouldn't quit. He began to think of alternative routes he could take to get his hands on that deal and still come out looking clean. Financing the whole operation while letting his homeboys do all of the leg work, was definitely an option. He could orchestrate the pick-ups and drop-offs from a distance and not have to touch any of the drugs itself. Tremaine then came to grips with the fact that he always kept his word with everyone and whenever he said he'd do something for someone he would do it. The same rules applied when he promised himself that he was going to quit hustling when he turned twenty-one, he had to keep his word.

As his mind continued to ponder on different things, Tremaine thought about Khalilah and his unborn son. He decided that when he talked to Khalilah that day, he would tell her everything. He felt that she needed to know. He would tell her about him selling drugs, since she nearly figured it out on her own, and his decision to stop. Also about his connect with Randy getting shut down; leaving him with the responsibility to got out of town and square away a few things for his homeboys before turning over a new leaf. He planned to let her know that within the next seventy-two hours of his life, he would be able to walk away with a clean slate and live the life that he dreamed of for the both of them. Everything was going to be everything, he thought.

At the same time Tremaine was soaking in the bathtub, down in a Virginia federal holding facility, Randy was being escorted out of his cell. The C.O. was taking him downstairs to a conference room that was designed for detainees to have visits with their attorneys. But Randy wasn't going to see his lawyer. In the room sat Agent Thornhill, along with two other FBI agents. They were there in response to Randy's written request to see them about some things he hoped they would like to hear.

29 BONEFIDE HUSTLERS

"Push Ms. Turner! Come on, I need you to push!" The doctor encouraged Khalilah.

"I can't! AAAAAAHH!!" Khalilah yelled out.

"Come on Boo you can do it! Come on just a lil' bit more! Push!" Tremaine encouraged, as he stood beside her bed with one arm around her and holding her hand with the other.

"AAAAAAHHHH! I can't!" Khalilah cried out.

Tremaine continued to coach, "Come on you can do this! You can! Come on push!"

"We're no longer getting a pulse." Tremaine heard the nurse say.

"Ms.Turner I need you to take a deep breath and push okay? I need you to take a deep breath and push as hard as you can." The doctor said in a calm voice as he continued to sit between Khalilah's legs.

They had her sitting on a small bed with her feet propped up in stirrups. There was a sheet covering her legs and the doctor's head was under it as he sat on a stool at the foot of the bed.

"Come on, Boo! I'm wit' you, we can do this! Just come on, push!" Tremaine coached.

"It's been approximately five minutes without a pulse on the fetus doctor," the nurse said.

"AAAAAHHH!!!" Khalilah screamed out as her grip on Tremaine's hand began to loosen up slowly.

He grabbed her hand tighter. "Boo, come on breathe! Push!" Tremaine noticed that Khalilah wasn't frowning her face up anymore and her head began to tilt to the left, as if she was falling asleep. "Khalilah come on don't go to sleep, you gotta push!" Tremaine said.

Suddenly, the nurse jumped up from the little machine she was monitoring, that sat next to the doctor. She rushed around to the other side of Khalilah's bed. "She's losing consciousness!" The nurse yelled out.

The doctor lifted his head abruptly from under the sheet and looked at Khalilah. "Call the O.R. we've got to do an emergency cesarean." He yelled to the nurse, who immediately picked up the room's telephone and began dialing numbers frantically. He then turned his attention to Tremaine, "Mr. Jenkins I'm going to need you to step outside for me."

"What?!" Tremaine responded with a frightened look on his face.

"Boo come on wake up! Push you gotta push!" he said as he held Khalilah's face in his hands.

"Mr. Jenkins I'm going to have to order you to leave sir please," the doctor said.

"What?! What's going on? I ain't going nowhere! Come on Boo you gotta wake up!"

He began smacking Khalilah on her face softly. His vision was beginning to blur as tears started to form in his eyes. "Do something please!" He said to the nurse reaching over Khalilah's body to grab the nurse by the arm. Tremaine was so much in disarray that he failed to noticed the two large orderlies and security guard step into the room behind the doctor who went out of the room to signal them.

"Sir, please let the doctor's do their job. We need you to step out of the room please." One of the tall white orderlies spoke.

Tremaine felt a thousand emotions run through him. He had thoughts to knock one of the orderlies' ass out for trying to take him from Khalilah's side. As the entire scenario changed within seconds, Tremaine found himself sitting in a waiting area chair with his head in his lap, waiting for the doctor to come and see him. After what seemed like hours, he recognized the doctor from Khalilah's room walking down a large hallway towards him. There was no one else in sight but him and the doctor.

Tremaine got up and ran towards the double doors, not waiting for the doctor to reach him. It seemed like the faster Tremaine ran, the slower he moved. After finally getting to the doors and facing the doctor, before Tremaine could speak, the doctor stated, "I'm sorry Mr. Jenkins, Ms. Turner never regained consciousness after passing out and the baby was stillborn. There was nothing we could do to save either one of them."

He felt as though he was floating and everything turned pitch black around him. When he jumped up and opened his eyes he could see nothing but cars and highway.

"What's up Yo, you alright?" Tremaine looked over and saw Dirty driving. When he looked back, Dollar was in the back seat staring at him. He then realized that the whole hospital scene had just been a dream. "What's up, yo?" Dirty asked him again, looking back and forth from him to the highway.

"Ain't shit." Tremaine mumbled, looking at the highway and then placing his hand on his chest and felt his heart beating as if he had just run a marathon. As he looked around, it was all coming back to him. They were on their way to meet Manny. After three days of constantly considering to take Manny up on his offer, Tremaine finally called him to let him know that he was sticking to his guns and getting out of the game. After Manny's last minute tactics of trying to persuade him didn't work, he finally told Tremaine to come back up New York and bring Dirty and Dollar with him.

What the fuck is up with that dream? Tremaine thought. He grabbed his cell phone and called his house to make sure that Khalilah was alright after having that wild ass dream.

"Hello," Khalilah picked up the phone on the second ring.

"What's up Boo?" he asked feeling a little better after hearing her voice.

"What's up? What's wrong?" she asked nervously.

"Oh nah, everything cool I was just calling to make sure you was alright," Tremaine assured her trying to calm her nerves a little. After the long conversation he had with her the night she returned from her parents' house, she became very understanding of his situation. But it also made her worry about him more than ever. He basically told her about everything that occurred in his life starting from the time he was fourteen to the present. He informed her all about the drug dealings, the robberies, burglaries and everything except for the murders. He didn't feel as though she needed to know about that.

Tremaine talked to her about Randy and where he rushed off to on his last-minute train trip. Khalilah was aware that the purpose of this last trip was solely to insure that his team was straight before he could get started with a new phase in his life.

She cried a lot and then told Tremaine that she already knew about his street life. Khalilah said she could never prove it, but she knew he was doing something illegal just by the lifestyle that he live and the money she witnessed he and his friends throw away.

Khalilah and Tremaine stayed up until sunrise discussing their future, and that of their son. They also talked about the new house that they wanted to move into and where it would be located. Tremaine felt a huge burden being lifted off his chest as he and Khalilah talked that night. Basically, she took the whole situation like a trooper. She understood his feelings about not leaving his family stranded and assed out, and that he had to see them through before he could truly step back away from everything.

"I'm straight, I was just in here taking the dishes out of the dishwasher," Khalilah said.

"Alright. Well I say umm… I'ma call you when I'm on my way back. I should be done in a couple of hours."

"Boo make sure you be careful," Khalilah spoke with sincerity and worry filling her voice.

"Already," he said.

"I love you," she said.

"I love you, too."

When Tremaine looked over at Dirty after hanging up and glanced back at Dollar through the rear view mirror, they both had the same expressionless, yet determined looks on their face. It reminded Tremaine of how he felt the first time Los took him out of state to do business. He was in the mind frame of being ready for whatever, hoping for the best but prepared for the worst. Their demeanor had been the same ever since earlier that afternoon when Tremaine told them to gas up the car because they were taking a little trip to New York.

Initially, Dirty and Dollar thought they were going on one of their usual shopping trips. But when Tremaine informed them that they were leaving within a half an hour to go up top, they could sense the urgency in his voice over the phone and knew it wasn't going to be a casual trip. Once they all piled up in Dollar's Range Rover and headed out, Tremaine broke everything down to them about Randy's situation. When he relayed to Dirty and Dollar that their coke supply had been eliminated, the look of fear and helplessness that they gave him made Tremaine that much more glad that he had taken the initiative to holler at Manny for them.

Tremaine had to admit that he had a soft spot in his heart when it came to his team. Had he not been able to convince Manny to work with Dollar and Dirty, he wondered if he would have actually been able to walk away without leaving them a steady connect. He probably would have taken the route of staying in the game for at least another six months just to show Manny that fucking with his team would be just as good as fucking with him but he to consider the promise that he made to himself.

When a person reaches a certain level in the game they definitely know who is who in their city; they would know who are the six and seven figure niggas, such as themselves. Tremaine was just relieved that Manny was coming through for him in regards to fucking with his niggas, so he could finally bow out from the game gracefully.

When they arrived in New York, Tremaine couldn't bring himself to remember exactly where Manny's building was located, on the lower eastside. New York City was nowhere near as small as Baltimore, where it didn't take long before a person would be able to navigate their way through the whole city. No matter how many times Tremaine had been up top, he could never remember how to get to the same place twice. They decided to jump off the Westside Highway at the 96th street exit. Tremaine called Manny to let him know that they were in town, and they needed the address to his place. When Tremaine found the address that Manny had given to him, he noticed that it was to a bakery on Riverside.

When they approached the door, the sound of a few loud voices could be heard coming from the inside. Tremaine rang the door bell and the same Debo look alike, who was driving the Excursion on his last trip up there, answered the door. He looked at Tremaine and began trying to remember his name. "Uhh...Tremaine, right?" He said in his deep voice.

"Yeah. Is Manny here?" Tremaine asked.

"Yeah, he's in the back room. Do y'all want something to eat or drink?" he asked after opening the door wider and placing a large .50 caliber Desert Eagle back into the shoulder holster that he had draped over his large body.

"Nah, we cool," Tremaine said.

At that point, Tremaine was a little alarmed that he, Dirty and Dollar had not decided to bring their pistols with them. But usually when they would head up New York or any spot out of state to do a little shopping, they would leave their guns behind. Their Maryland license plates were like magnets to get pulled over by the police, especially since they were all black males in the car. Even though Tremaine didn't feel as though he needed to be strapped to visit Manny, he just couldn't stand to be around someone who was armed and he wasn't. It just didn't feel right to him.

When they stepped through the door, they headed straight to the back room. Manny was sitting there with two other gentlemen. One looked to be a Puerto Rican while the second man was black.

Manny and the black dude were playing the Playstation on the flat screen T.V. They were obviously gambling as they both had a few hundred dollar bills laying before them on the coffee table.

"What's up my nigga?" Manny said as he paused the game and got up to embrace Tremaine. "Dirty and Dollar, what's going on?" he said turning his attention to them and pulling them both in for one arm hugs. "This my man, Nico," Manny pointed to the Puerto Rican, "and my man, Stuff," he said, pointing to the black man.

"What up son?" They both said in unison.

"Go 'head and make ya'll selves comfortable while I finish whooping this nigga ass and takin' his dough," Manny said.

"Shit nigga, I'm up fo'teen zip, that shit ain't happenin'," Stuff responded.

After Manny got his ass whooped, twenty-eight to zero in Madden, they all sat around and blazed up a few Cigarillo's and sipped on Corona's. Manny informed Tremaine that he had floor seats to the New York Knicks game against the Lakers at Madison Square Garden that night. Tremaine was a little hesitant about going because he didn't want to turn the occasion into a social visit. He focused on coming to an agreement on the business proposition and rolling out, but he went along with the program since he had never been to Madison Square Gardens, or the Garden, as the locals called it.

Before heading out with the rest of the group, Tremaine stepped into the bathroom and called Khalilah to let her know that he would be a little later than he thought. He told her that he would be returning sometime early that next morning. Tremaine didn't like stringing her stress along the way that he was. It would have been different if she did not know why he was up there, because she wouldn't have a reason to be worried. But being as though he was out there to make his last coke deal, he knew that was what worried Khalilah the most.

Everyone piled up in the Excursion to head out to the game. They were all a little high from the haze and Corona's as they sat watching "The king of New York" on the truck's television screens. Once they arrived at the game, the parking was crazy. Manny let Tremaine know that if his homeboys were strapped they could leave their guns in the truck. Tremaine informed Manny that they were alright. Manny had a secret compartment that he had built in the hatch back of his SUV that he used to stash his guns.

When they all entered the arena, it was evident that there were more Lakers fans than there were Knicks fans. After watching the Knicks lose 104-89, the fellas all headed back to Manny's bakery.

Once inside, Manny called Tremaine, Dirty, and Dollar upstairs into one of the rooms that appeared to be an office. He asked them all to have a seat while he leaned against the desk.

"I'm sayin' this off the top, just to let ya'll know, this day has been real. Now we're ready to get to the real reason y'all are here."

None of them said anything as they looked at him.

"Now I'm pretty sure your man already hollered at the both of you about me fucking with y'all on the weight tip. Let me be real with the both of you. I'm still skeptical about doing direct business with either one of you," Manny said looking back and forth at Dirty and Dollar. "I mean don't get me wrong, both of y'all are cool people, but this here would be taking shit to a whole 'nother level? Now the only reason why I'm even considering this is because I fucks wit' this nigga." Manny was pointing at Tremaine with his eyes glued on Dirty and Dollar. "It wasn't too long ago that he came to me a lil' young buck sitting in Los' shadow. But it definitely didn't take long before he was able to step up from under Los and take care of his own business.

Now from my understanding, y'all were wit' him since day one, when he stepped out on his own. Now with slim, it took me some time to truly trust him and his loyalty. But as time went on, I saw that neither one of them were to be questioned. But the point is, it definitely took some time to get to that level. With y'all two, I don't have a lot of time."

"My man right here sayin' that he's done with all of this shit and I need to know right here, tonight, right at this moment, if I can trust you two?" Manny kept his attention fixed on Dirty and Dollar for a moment before he continued. "That motherfucking Nico down there, I just got some disturbing news about his ass the other day. I found out he was a fuckin' rat, an informant to the Feds. Now to get straight to the point, Tremaine I got a train ticket for you to get home."

Manny pulled out a white envelope from one of the desk drawers behind him.

"It'll be leaving in a little over an hour and I already called a cab for you. It should be pulling up any minute now. Dirty and Dollar, Nico is getting ready to go handle something for me and I want one of y'all to accompany him, while the other one inconspicuously follow that nigga to his destination. Once he get there, I don't expect him to make it back, if you know what I mean."

As they sat there in that office, Tremaine, Dirty, and Dollar knew exactly what Manny meant. He wanted Dirty and Dollar to prove their loyalty by killing Nico's snitching ass. Tremaine was the first to speak up, "hold up Manny, I'm sayin' this right…" he said as he stood up out of the chair.

Dirty jumped up along with him, placed his hands on Tremaine's shoulder and said, "Nah, don't even trip, its cool baby."

"I feel that, but I'm just sayin'…"

Tremaine was cut off again by Dollar when he said, "He right cuz, everything is everything." Dollar stood up also. "Go 'head and take that ticket and go home to your son and wife, we got this. You know for a fact this ain't nothin' heavy," Dollar spoke with a grin.

"You already took care of your part of the deal, it's up to me and cuz to close the muthafucka, you feel me?" Dirty said.

Tremaine looked back and forth from Dirty to Dollar and realized that they were right. He had indeed done what he set out to do by getting them in tight with a new connect. With the deals that Manny was talking about, they were definitely going to see more paper than ever before. Tremaine just couldn't shake the feeling that he was walking out on his family for that one last mission. He was willing to go with them and leave Nico's brains all over his dash board to insure that his team were squared away with Manny. Tremaine finally took the train ticket from Manny and embraced him whole heartedly. He told Dirty and Dollar to call him the minute they were on the turnpike heading home.

As they all walked out of that room, back downstairs, and into the back room, Tremaine could hear the taxi out front blowing its horn. Nico was playing Stuff in NBA Live on the playstation and just smiling up a storm.

That nigga just don't know that Manny done turned a pair of pit bulls loose on him and they're gonna take a vicious bite out of his ass, Tremaine thought as he headed out the front door.

The soft sway of the train with the quiet humming of the tracks was like aromatherapy to his soul. However, the ride from New York had been filled with mixed emotions. He had feelings of gaiety, gloom, dismay, apprehension, and perplexity. All of those emotions fed Tremaine's different thoughts.

Overcoming a fear that few warriors had been able or wanted to accomplish is what went through Tremaine's mind. He had beaten a lifestyle that few lived to tell about. To be able to emerge out of it all without a scratch on his body was even more unbelievable. A load of uncertainties rushed Tremaine as the reality of him being done with drug dealing and killing settled in.

What would he do now? Could he honestly live a life without illegal substance? Would he still hang around the same people? Would a conflict of interest hinder his relationship with the team that he had grown up with? Would his team still see him as being their true family? Would he continue to stay strapped with a burner everyday or would there be no need to? Was he really ready to be a father and what kind of father would he be?

Did his own father have the same feelings of anxiousness that he was feeling when his mother was pregnant with him? And if so, would those feelings wear off as time passed causing him to abandon Khalilah and his son, just as his father had done to him? Could he see himself being with Khalilah for the rest of his life, waking up to the same woman day after day, week after week, month after month and year after year? Was that even possible? If his businesses suddenly took a turn for the worst, would he go back to hustling?

All of those questions and a million more ran through Tremaine's mind as he returned home on that train. Dirty and Dollar called him after an hour into the ride, informing him that everything had went straight and they were heading back home themselves. Tremaine could hear the joy in their voices when Dirty told him that Manny would be giving them the sweat shirts for seventeen a piece. Meaning, he would be selling them whole kilograms of powder cocaine for seventeen thousand, with the promise that if things went well, he would eventually give them up for fifteen thousand a piece. Dirty and Dollar asked him to accompany them to Las Vegas that night to celebrate but Tremaine had to decline. He felt like a man just home from prison and all he wanted to do was take a nice quiet week and chill in the house while trying to get his bearings together. As the train entered into Penn Station in the early morning hours,

Tremaine began his exit from the train feeling like an entirely different person with a new identify.

The sun was beginning to lift above the edge of darkness when Tremaine arrived home. He made his way up the stairs towards the bedroom where he had expected to see the two things that made his life worth living, Khalilah and his unborn son. When he entered the room he could see Khalilah lying on her side with her back towards the door. She was sleep with nothing on. *Yeah I can see myself doing this for a while*, Tremaine thought as he sat down quietly on the side of the bed and began to rub on her stomach.

Tremaine leaned over to kiss her stomach then sat for nearly twenty minutes with his hands still on her stomach while staring at Khalilah's closed eyes. He then decided to get up and prepare breakfast for the both of them. The bed stirred a little when he got up causing Khalilah to roll over on her back. "Tremaine?" she asked squenching her eyes.

"Oh my bad Boo, I ain't mean to wake you," he said as he headed back towards the bed to lay down beside her.

"You alright?" she asked sitting up on one elbow.

"Yeah everything straight." He assured her while laying down on his back next to her.

Khalilah said nothing as she reached out to place her palm on his cheek and rubbed it with her thumb. Tremaine put his arm around her shoulder and pulled her in for a soft, yet sensual, kiss. She pulled the covers up over them both and laid her head on his chest. Tremaine could feel the wetness of her tears as they landed on his shirt. He wrapped both arms around her in a firm hug and was glad knowing that her tears were of joy and not hurt.

30 THE FINALE

"Alright let me ask you this, how do I know you're hungry enough for this job? I mean, I want to know if you're willing to put in hard work? Also, how do I know you ain't no thief, huh? Do you steal?" Tremaine asked the young man who sat in front of him at his office in 'Str8 Soul'.

It had been little over a week since he had returned from New York on what he considered his retirement trip. He was currently in the process of interviewing an eighteen year old black male who he was considering to hire as his first employee at his vending company. The young man was a freshman at Baltimore City Community College. The boy was originally applying for the vacant position of bus boy at his restaurant until Tremaine informed him of the vending position and that the job paid two dollars more an hour. Hard up for money since he was in college, the young man agreed to the vending position.

Tremaine had already made up his mind that he would hire the young brother just on the fact that he was going to college. Tremaine knew how costly it was to go to college and the young man needed all of the financial help he could get. He was just giving the boy a hard time to see what type of reactions he could get out of him, with his unorthodox interviewing style. The whole scene was a little crazy with Tremaine being only a few years older than the teenage boy.

"No sir I don't steal. I've never stolen anything in my life," he answered nervously.

"Oh I doubt that. But look here; let's say that I was to ask one of your closest friends to describe your characteristics to me, what do you think they would say?" Tremaine leaned back in his office chair waiting on the boy's response.

With no hesitation he responded, "They would say that I'm hard working, dependable, trust worthy, consistent, ambitious and...," the young man looked up in the air while contemplating more characteristics to throw out.

Before he could finish thinking Tremaine blurted out, "You know what? I think you're lying. Call one of your homeboys right now so I could holla at them." He picked up his desk phone and sat it in the front of the boy.

He searched Tremaine's face to see if he was serious or not before reaching slowly for the phone.

"Nah, I'm just fuckin' with you," Tremaine said grabbing the phone out of his hand and sitting it back in the cradle. "Look here I'ma give you a shot, alright?"

"Thank you and I appreciate this opportunity." He smiled and shook Tremaine's hand.

"Don't appreciate it, just make the most of it," he said getting up and opening his office door to let the young man out.

Once he was done with the interview, Tremaine called to confirm the delivery of his new vending machine that he had brought off of E-Bay. He then headed out to the kitchen area of the restaurant where Mama Nem was putting together one of her delicious creations. Mama Nem was truly a genius when it came to the culinary trade. She told him anybody could cook, but it took a certain type of person to season the food correctly. She always said the real flavor was in the seasoning, it was all about the seasoning.

"What's up Mama Nem?" Tremaine said as he headed over to her at the sink. She was in the process of cleaning a batch of collard greens.

"Hey baby?" She said in her southern grandmother voice.

"So what's the lesson for today in cooking 101?"

"Oh I'm just cleaning these dawgone greens," she said placing some of the greens in a large pot.

"So I guess you're gonna season it with the usual fat back, huh?" Tremaine asked.

"Fat back?!" she squenched her face up as if something stunk. "That thing ain't got no mo' flavor than a ice cube." She rolled her eyes. "This what you use baby." Mama Nem reached over to the counter behind her and grabbed a tray of smoked turkey necks. "See you boil the smoked turkey necks, baby, for a few hours. Then you add the greens. You make sure you add a pinch of sugar to cut the gas, along with my secret ingredients and let it all simmer together, that'll add the flava. That's how you give 'em dat strong smoke flava', now you see if a nasty ol' piece of fat back can do that."

Tremaine had to laugh at the feisty old woman who was five feet tall in height but carried herself like a giant. "I hear you Mama Nem." Tremaine reached for the vibrating cell phone in his pocket.

"Yeah"

"Tremaine!...Tremaine!" he could hear Khalilah's mother yelling into his phone.

"Mrs. Turner?" He asked, not sure if it was her.

"Tremaine it's time! Khalilah's water just broke," she said frantically.

"Huh? What, her water just broke? Where y'all at?" Tremaine felt his whole body begin to break out in goose bumps.

"I just took her to the emergency room. We were at the mall when her water broke."

"Which hospital are y'all at?"

"We are at University."

"Ok I'm on my way, right now!" Tremaine said as he rushed off the phone.

"Lord have mercy and bless this child. You betta get on over to that hospital then."

"Look, tell Marie I said that... that's alright I'll tell her myself." Tremaine headed out of the kitchen area into his office to grab his keys. He passed Marie, who was in the dining area chatting with a customer, and said, "It's that time, Marie, It's that time. I'm 'bout to be a daddy," as he headed out the door.

"Congraaaats!" She responded with a smile on her face. "You make sure you call me tonight to let me know how everything goes," she yelled after him.

"Alright," Tremaine answered already halfway out the door.

As he sped through the city streets, Tremaine felt as though he was going to flip his new GMC Denali as he hit a few corners at such a high speed. He was cutting through gas stations and other parking lots whenever he came to a red light. He couldn't believe that the time had actually come. It seemed as if the fact of him being a father never fully registered until he had gotten that phone call a few minutes ago.

Tremaine had to take a deep breath to calm down when he nearly ran into the back of a lady in the car with her daughter, as he was taking one of his short cuts through a side parking lot. He was doing well over seventy miles an hour through the city but it seemed as if he was only doing thirty-five. My Boo about to have my lil' son, he screamed on the inside.

When he finally pulled up into the hospital's parking garage, he waited in line in order for the gate to rise so he could gain entry into the parking area. After finding a parking space and whipping the Denali into the space, Tremaine was parked crooked but didn't seemed to care. That's not the only thing he failed to see. As he placed the SUV in park and began to remove his keys, he hadn't noticed that ever since he left his restaurant, there had been two all black Chevy Suburbans cutting corners and tailing his every move. Both trucks came to a screeching halt behind him as he began to exit his truck. Tremaine hit the power lock button and when he turned around to head towards the hospital, the occupants of the Suburbans, which were eight in all, jumped out with guns drawn and began to yell, "FBI! Freeze, don't move!! Get on the ground, now!!!"

Tremaine looked behind him in shock, as uncertainty flowed like a chill through his body, wondering and hoping the fatigue wearing men were talking to someone else. But they wasn't; he was the man they were looking for and had finally gotten.

EPILOGUE

(SIX YEARS LATER)

As Tremaine made his way back in from the yard, he felt sore and fatigued in his entire upper body. It was a good feeling of pain though; the kind that let him know that he had went to the extreme with his workout routine. "If it didn't hurt, then it wasn't right," was his motto when it came to his physical regimen. He planned to stop by his man 'L's' building. He was sent to the same federal penitentiary, two years after Tremaine. 'L' worked in the kitchen and would always have some sort of food platter, sandwich, or sub waiting for Tremaine daily.

After retrieving the roast beef and cheese sub that 'L' had for him and chilling for a minute, Tremaine decided to head for the shower before going back to his cell to eat his food.

"It don't look good for your homeboy." His cell buddy, Gray-el, said to Tremaine as he sat reading the Maryland section of the Baltimore Sun. Gray-el is an older cat who was in the Moorish Science temple.

Even though Tremaine was locked up all the way in Louisiana, he was able to get a subscription of the newspaper from his hometown. Gray-el handed him the front page section of the paper and Tremaine saw the headlines, "Notorious Leader of Murderous Drug Ring Found Guilty on All Charges." "Damn," was all that Tremaine could mumble as he sat down at the pull out stoop that was connected to the desk in his cell. As he read on, he saw that the jury had found Dirty guilty of eleven different murders, along with distribution charges as well as running a criminal enterprise.

The article went on to talk about how Dirty was the known leader of what was dubbed as the "The Pennsylvania Avenue Boys." Various members of The Avenue Boys were also convicted along with Dirty. The paper talked about how the group was known for making sure that each of its victims received closed caskets at their funeral by repeatedly shooting the person in the head and face. Tremaine knew that Dirty was already expecting to be found guilty of the charges since so many lame ass niggas, who were petrified to even come outside when Dirty and his crew were at their prime, had started coming from everywhere to testify against him. They wanted to make sure that neither Dirty, or any of the niggas he had up under him would ever see the streets again.

Tremaine and Dirty would send their messages to one another through Khalilah since Dirty's incarceration. The verdict was still a blow to the chest. Everyone's hopes began to rise, as a result of the jury taking over three weeks to reach a decision. The trial itself had lasted four months, Tremaine kept constant updates on it through the papers or through Mr. Matin, the lawyer that he and Dirty both retained. Tremaine could do nothing but shake his head as he laid

the paper down on his bunk and left out of the cell with his
bag slung over his shoulder.

Over the last six years that he had been locked up, shit
definitely changed in Tremaine's life. As he stood under the warm
water of the shower, Tremaine looked down at the tombstones of
Juice and Dollar that he had tattooed on his forearm. It had been
almost two months since Dollar's death and Tremaine still felt the
sting as if it had happened yesterday. His little cousin always said that
he would never return to another jail cell and he held true to his
word.

The day that federal agents conducted various raids to bring
down members of The Avenue Boys, they wasn't been prepared for
the raid they conducted on Dollar. When they tried to knock down
the door of Dollar's condominium on St. Paul Street, they ran into a
few problems. For starters, he had the front door to his
condominium specially built, being nothing but metal on the inside
with a thin wood covering on the exterior. As the agents pounced on
the door, they finally got it open after about thirty minutes. They
were confronted by an AK-47 wielding Dollar, what followed next
was self explanatory. Dollar was able to critically wound two of the
agents and killing four, before he was shot and killed.

To be honest, Tremaine saw his little cousin as being lucky, by
not having to go through the daily mental strains that he, and so
many other black males were subject to while incarcerated. Tremaine
let out a heavy sigh each time he thought about the remainder of his
time in prison. He had at least four more years to go on his twelve
year sentence, since the Feds wanted over eighty-five percent of their
time served. He ended up copping out to twelve years instead of
taking his chances at trial and receiving the life sentence that he was
facing.

Randy's bitch ass put a spin on his confession and told the Feds
that it was Tremaine that he was getting his coke from, when in fact

was the other way around. With Randy's willingness to testify and take down so many other people, and he did, Tremaine and Khalilah decided that going to trial wasn't worth the risk. Everyone that Randy testified against, the Feds were handing out basketball score sentences. Even the dudes who were on some small time, hand to hand corner dealings had received sixty to seventy-five years going to trial, thanks to Randy's snitching ass. It fucked Tremaine up to know that the Feds were giving out those types of sentences, strictly off of hearsay. Shooting a dice game with his life was not something that he was willing to do, which was why Tremaine opted for the plea bargain.

At least Randy had gotten what was coming to him. After he did the three years that he was sentenced to, Randy headed back to New York thinking that Manny, who was still doing his thing, would receive him with open arms since he only told on Baltimore niggas. Manny kept the game face on with him the entire time that Randy was locked up. A week after his release, they found Randy in a parked car in Harlem with so many gunshot wounds to the head that they had to identify him through his fingerprints.

Khalilah had turned out to be more than what Tremaine ever expected as she continued to ride his sentence out with him. She had taken over his restaurant and took it upon herself to expand the establishment into two more restaurants. She also took the initiative to seal the deal on his vending proposition with the M&T Bank Stadium. She also managed to get a contract with the Baltimore City and County Public school system, to place his vending machines in their schools.

For the first time, Tremaine almost broke down and cried in front of a female. Khalilah proposed to him on a visit, immediately after they sentenced him. She brought the ring with her and everything just to let him know how serious she was. They were married in a quick ceremony inside of the penitentiary with plans to have a real wedding once they released him.

One of the biggest regrets that Tremaine had was not being there to see little Tristan born, being able to see his first steps, or hear his first words. There was definitely no denying that the boy was his, since he looked as if Tremaine had spit him out. Lisa, who now had two daycare centers, joked about how the six year old's feet and toes even looked like Tremaine's feet and toes when he was younger.

Khalilah was faithful to make the trip twice a month to Louisiana with Tristan to see Tremaine. He was currently waiting for his transfer to come through so that he could move to another prison to be closer to home.

Tremaine went back to his cell and began to eat his food. He thought if someone had told all of them, at the age of 14 that their lives would have turned out the way that it had, they would not have believed them. Juice and Dollar was dead, Dirty was facing multiple life sentences, and he was incarcerated with twelve years. The only one out of their immediate crew who was still out in the streets was Lil Chris. He moved to Las Vegas to try his hands in the porno business. Tremaine had seen Chris' name a few times in some of the freak magazines that he got his hands on, as being the director of certain movies.

All in All, Tremaine couldn't say that he had many regrets since he did make out with all of the money he had accumulated in the game over the years. In addition to the business moves that Kalilah was making for them while he was locked up, they were definitely set for life. At the end of the day, he could sit back and laugh because he was able to play a game that kept him on his toes simply because he remembered what an old head told him a long time ago, "Every game has there own set of rules and once you know the rules to the game then you know how to go about playing the game. This game was called *Get In and Get Out*."

To the average person 12 years is considered a lost of life but to Tremaine it was a new beginning.

ABOUT THE AUTHOR

Dante Hammond is a gutsy, gifted, courageous new voice to the urban book community. He was born and raised in Baltimore City. Although he made a few mistakes throughout his life, he was determined to do something better. He decided to write books and build a publishing company. He is driven by his passion to write stories he envision. He is currently working on his next full length book. Dante believes that in life, you go through trials and tribulations but it is up to you to right your wrongs. Everybody has a chance to turn their life around, but it is up them to decide that time. Visit the author at Facebook.com/DHammondpublishing.com or write to him at DHammond Publishing P.O. Box 18669 Baltimore, Maryland 21216.

ORDER FORM print, fill out, mail with money order or check to:

DHammond Publishing

P.O. Box 18669

Baltimore, MD 21216

1. **Mailing Address**

_____

Name

_____

Address

_____

City   State   Zipcode

2. **Book Order Information**

Book Price $14.99

Quantity (Multiply $14.99 X Quantity)   _____

Sales Tax (.06 or 6%)   _____

Shipping & Handling (Via U.S. Mail)
$3.95 1-2 Books, $5.95 3-4 Books
add $1.95 for ea. additional book   _____

Total   _____

Forms of Accepted Payments:

Institutional checks and Money Orders

Note: All mail in orders take 5-7 business days to be delivered

ORDER FORM print, fill out, mail with money order or check to:

DHammond Publishing

P.O. Box 18669

Baltimore, MD 21216

1. **Mailing Address**

_____

Name

_____

Address

_____

City   State   Zipcode

2. **Book Order Information**

Book Price $14.99

Quantity   (Multiply $14.99 X Quantity)   _____

Sales Tax   (.06 or 6%)   _____

Shipping & Handling (Via U.S. Mail)
$3.95 1-2 Books, $5.95 3-4 Books
add $1.95 for ea. additional book   _____

Total   _____

Forms of Accepted Payments:

Institutional checks and Money Orders

Note: All mail in orders take 5-7 business days to be delivered

ORDER FORM print, fill out, mail with money order or check to:

DHammond Publishing

P.O. Box 18669

Baltimore, MD 21216

1. **Mailing Address**

_____

Name

_____

Address

_____

City   State   Zipcode

2. **Book Order Information**

Book Price $14.99

Quantity (Multiply $14.99 X Quantity)   _____

Sales Tax   (.06 or 6%)   _____

Shipping & Handling (Via U.S. Mail)
$3.95 1-2 Books, $5.95 3-4 Books
add $1.95 for ea. additional book   _____

Total   _____

Forms of Accepted Payments:

Institutional checks and Money Orders

Note: All mail in orders take 5-7 business days to be delivered

ORDER FORM print, fill out, mail with money order or check to:

DHammond Publishing

P.O. Box 18669

Baltimore, MD 21216

1. **Mailing Address**

_____

Name

_____

Address

_____

City   State   Zipcode

2. **Book Order Information**

Book Price	$14.99
Quantity (Multiply $14.99 X Quantity)	_____
Sales Tax (.06 or 6%)	_____
Shipping & Handling (Via U.S. Mail) $3.95 1-2 Books, $5.95 3-4 Books add $1.95 for ea. additional book	_____
Total	_____

Forms of Accepted Payments:

Institutional checks and Money Orders

Note: All mail in orders take 5-7 business days to be delivered